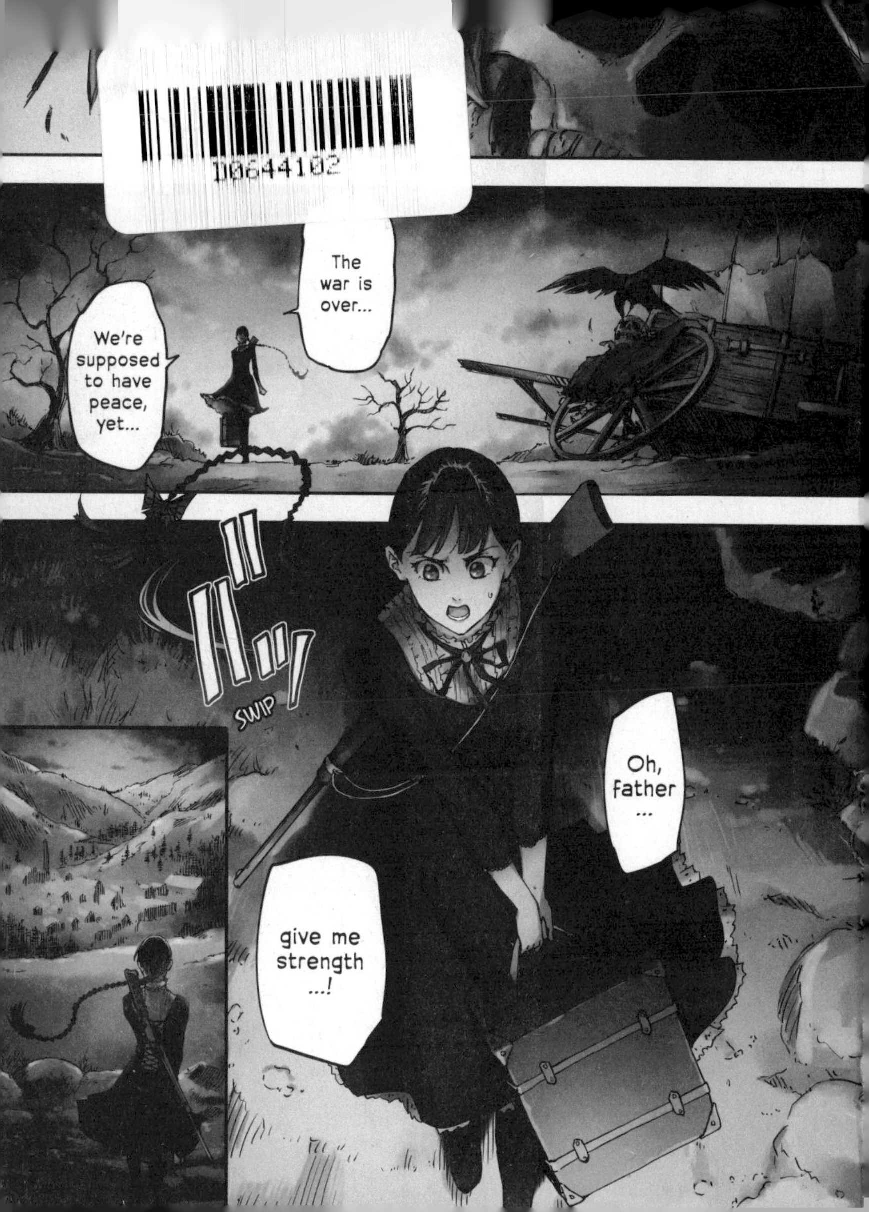
The war is over...
We're supposed to have peace, yet...
SWIP
Oh, father...
give me strength...!

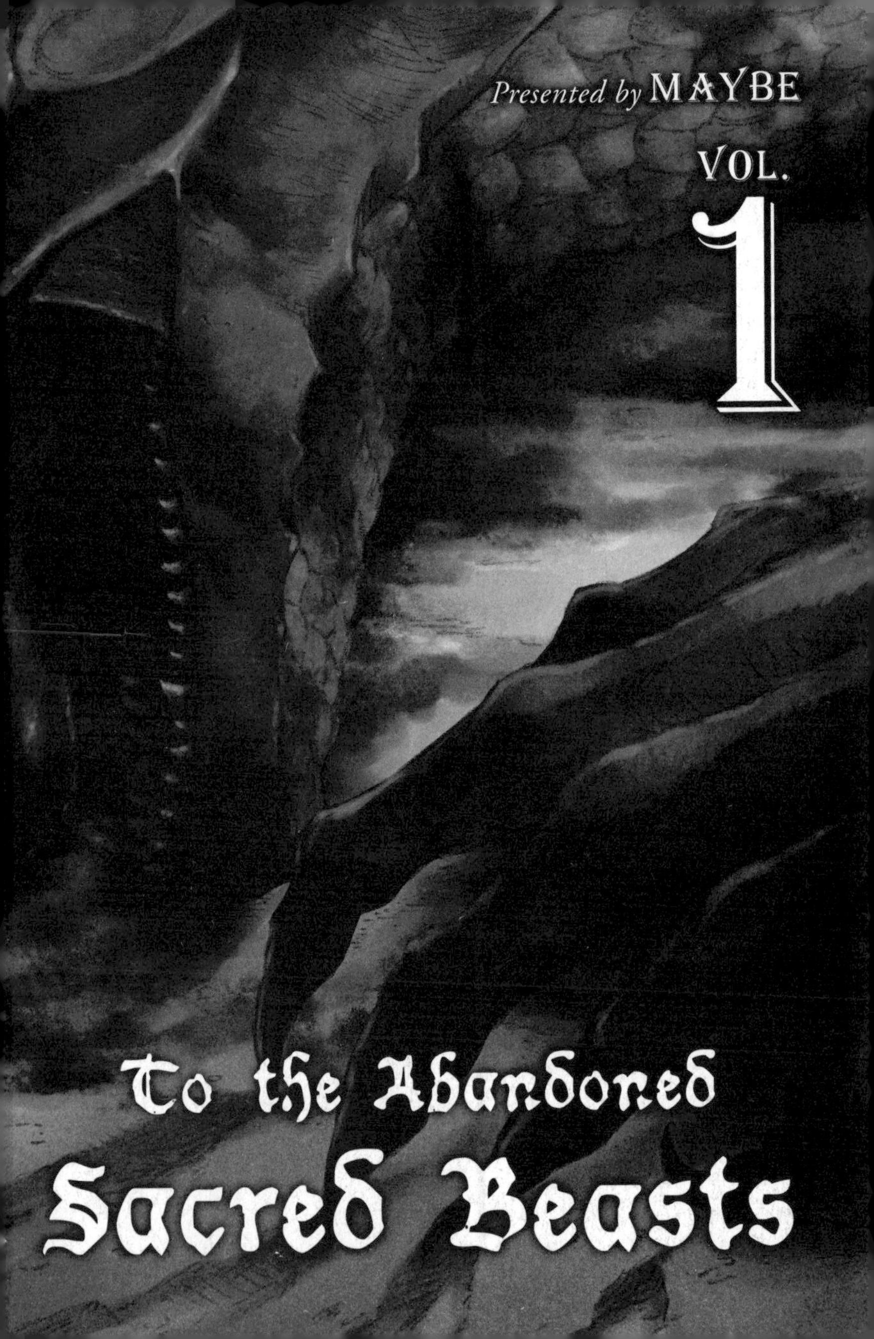
Presented by MAYBE
VOL. 1
To the Abandoned
Sacred Beasts

Chapter 1: Beast Hunter

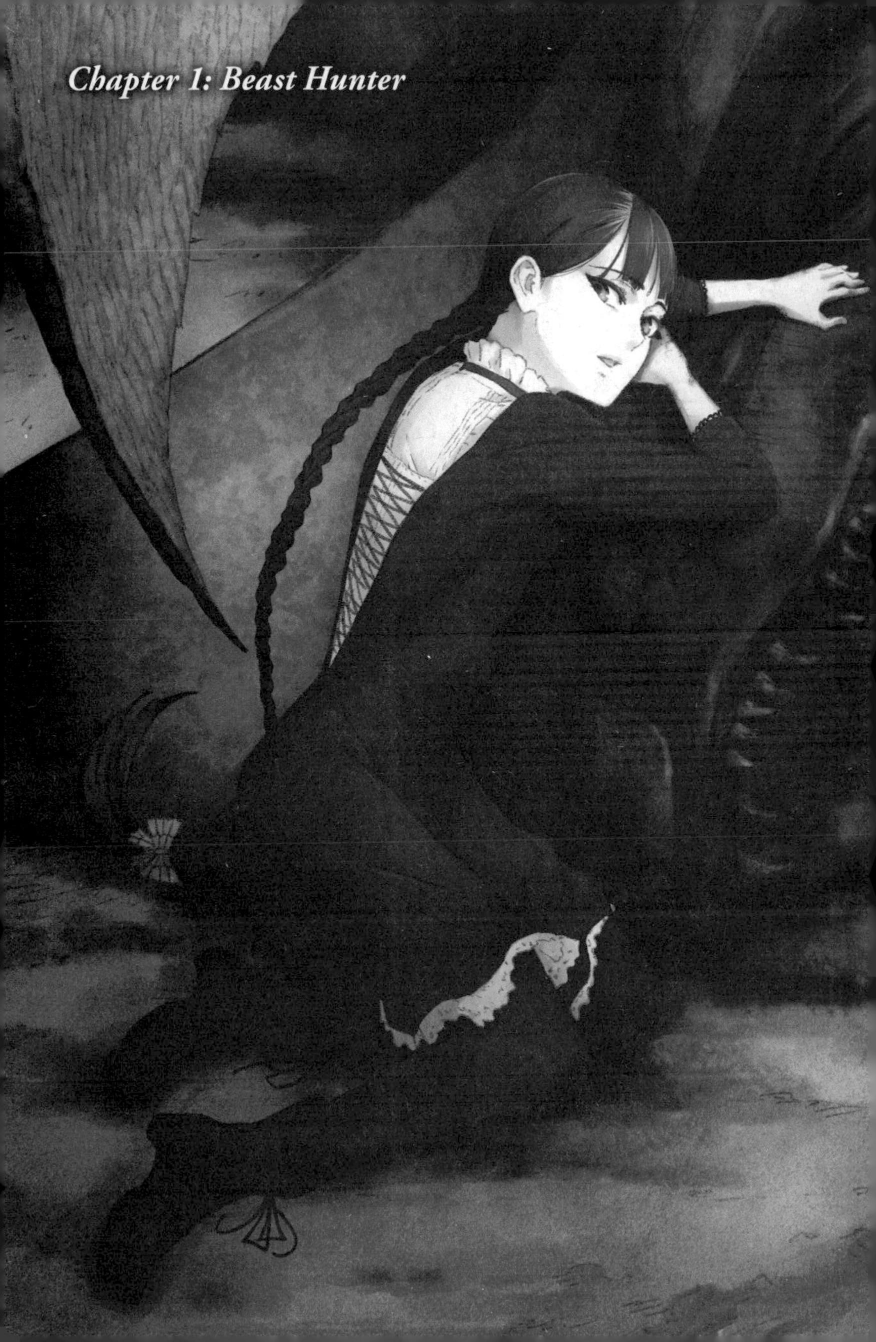

CONTENTS

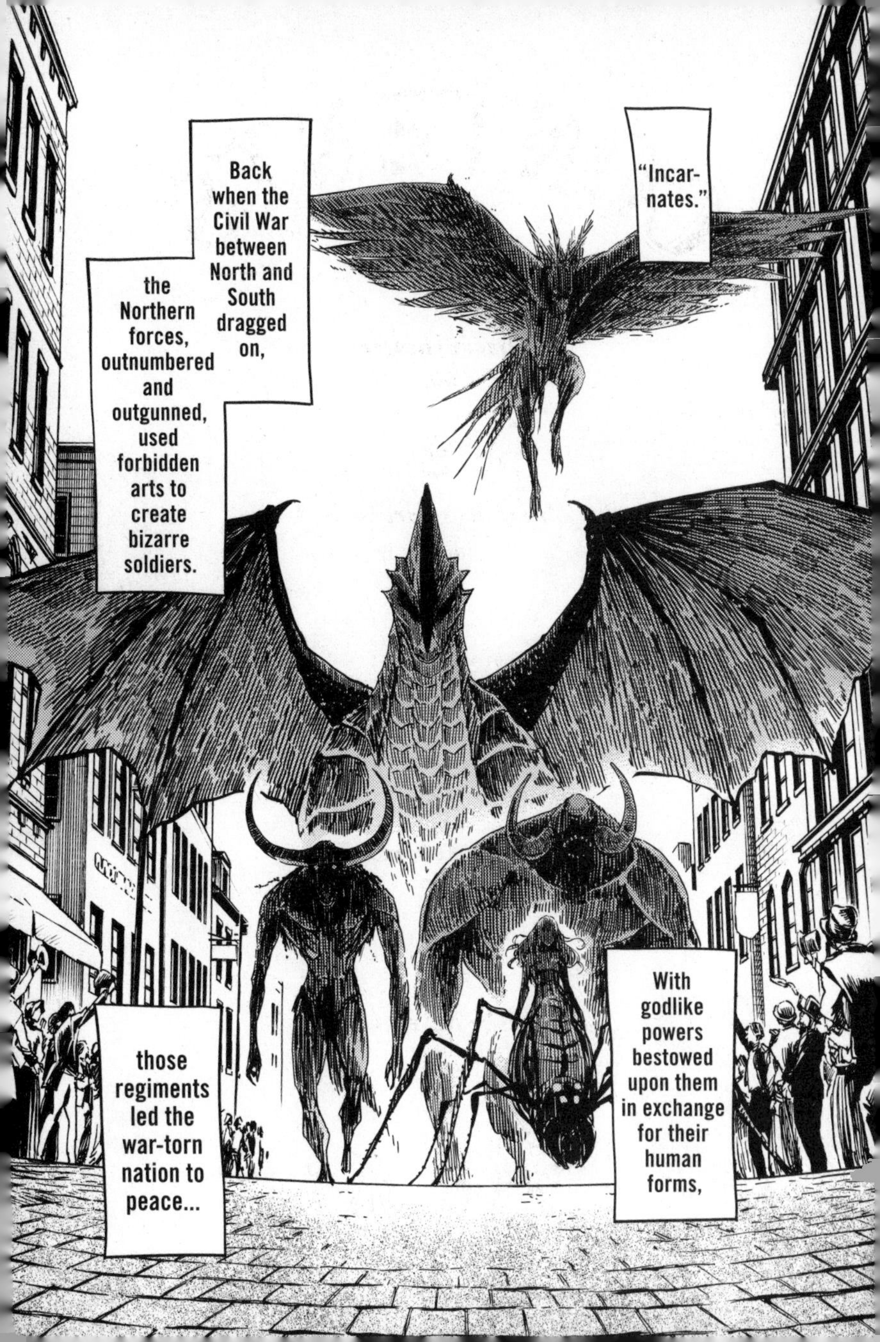
Back when the Civil War between North and South dragged on,
the Northern forces, outnumbered and outgunned, used forbidden arts to create bizarre soldiers.
"Incarnates."
With godlike powers bestowed upon them in exchange for their human forms,
those regiments led the war-torn nation to peace...

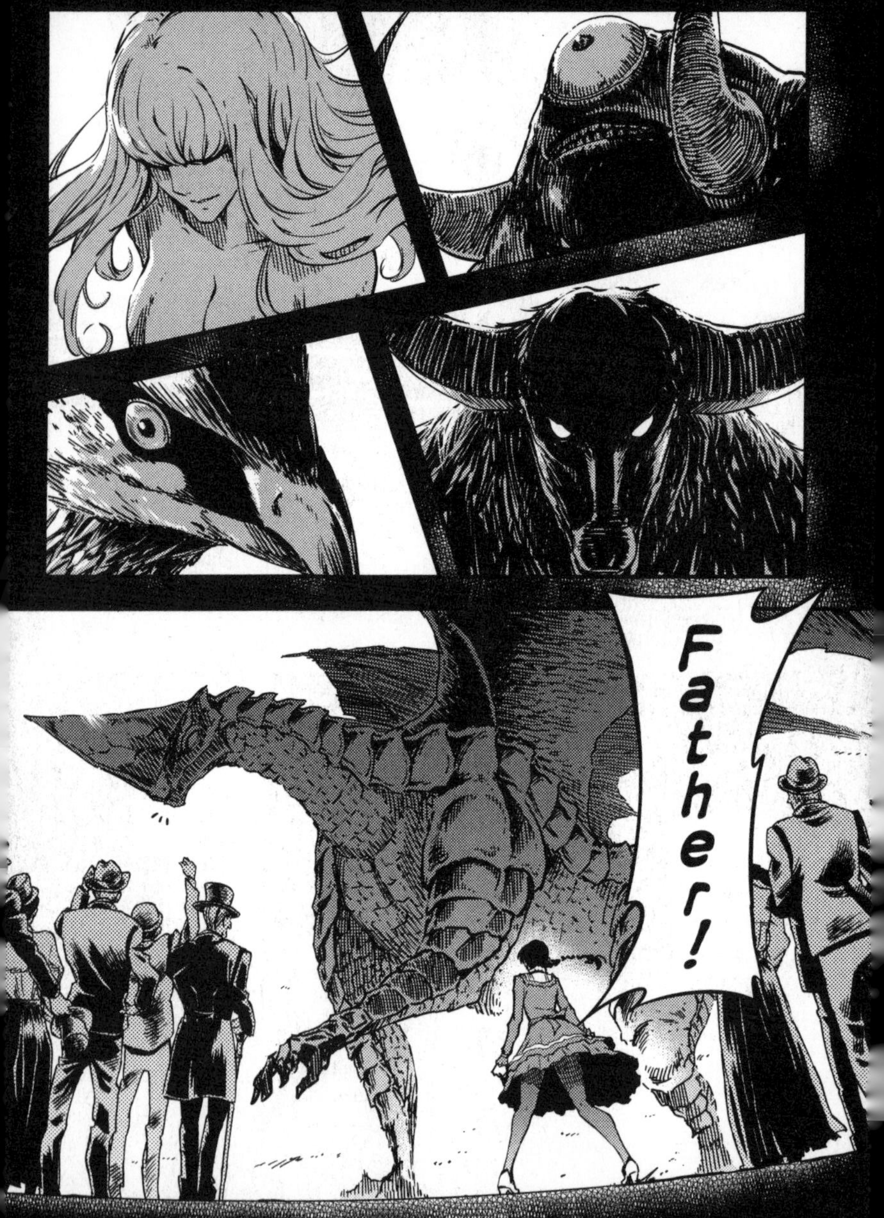
Father!

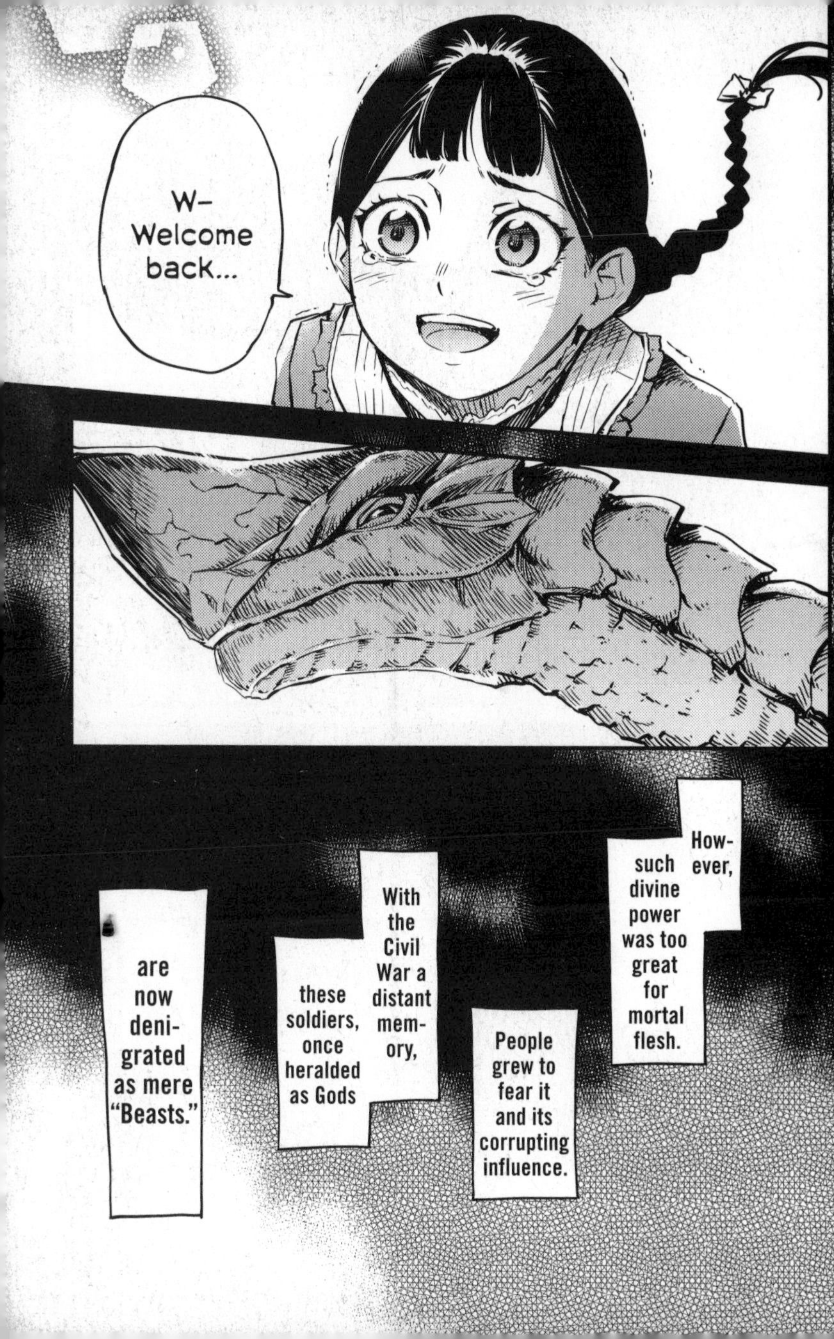
W- Welcome back...
However, such divine power was too great for mortal flesh.
People grew to fear it and its corrupting influence.
With the Civil War a distant memory,
these soldiers, once heralded as Gods
are now denigrated as mere "Beasts."

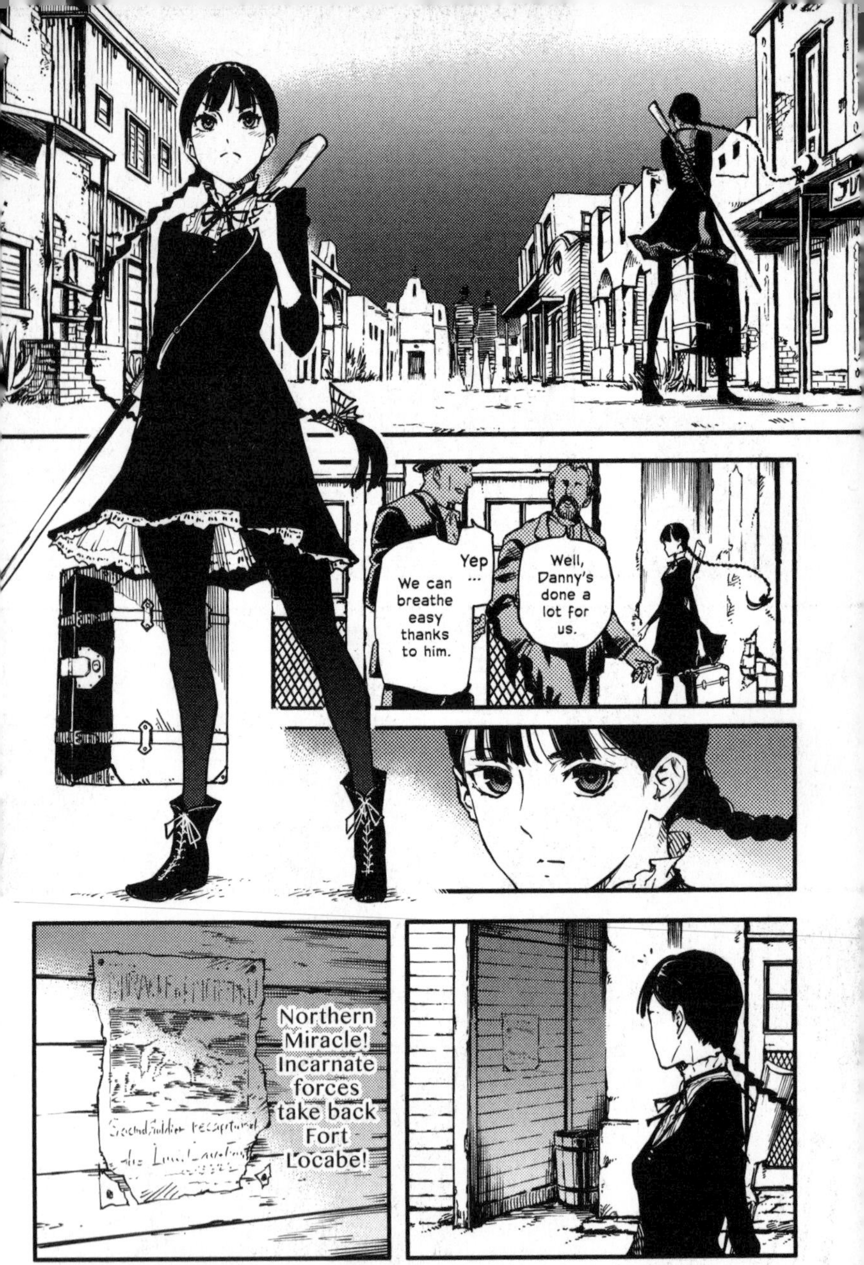
Well, Danny's done a lot for us.
Yep ... We can breathe easy thanks to him.
Northern Miracle! Incarnate forces take back Fort Locabe!

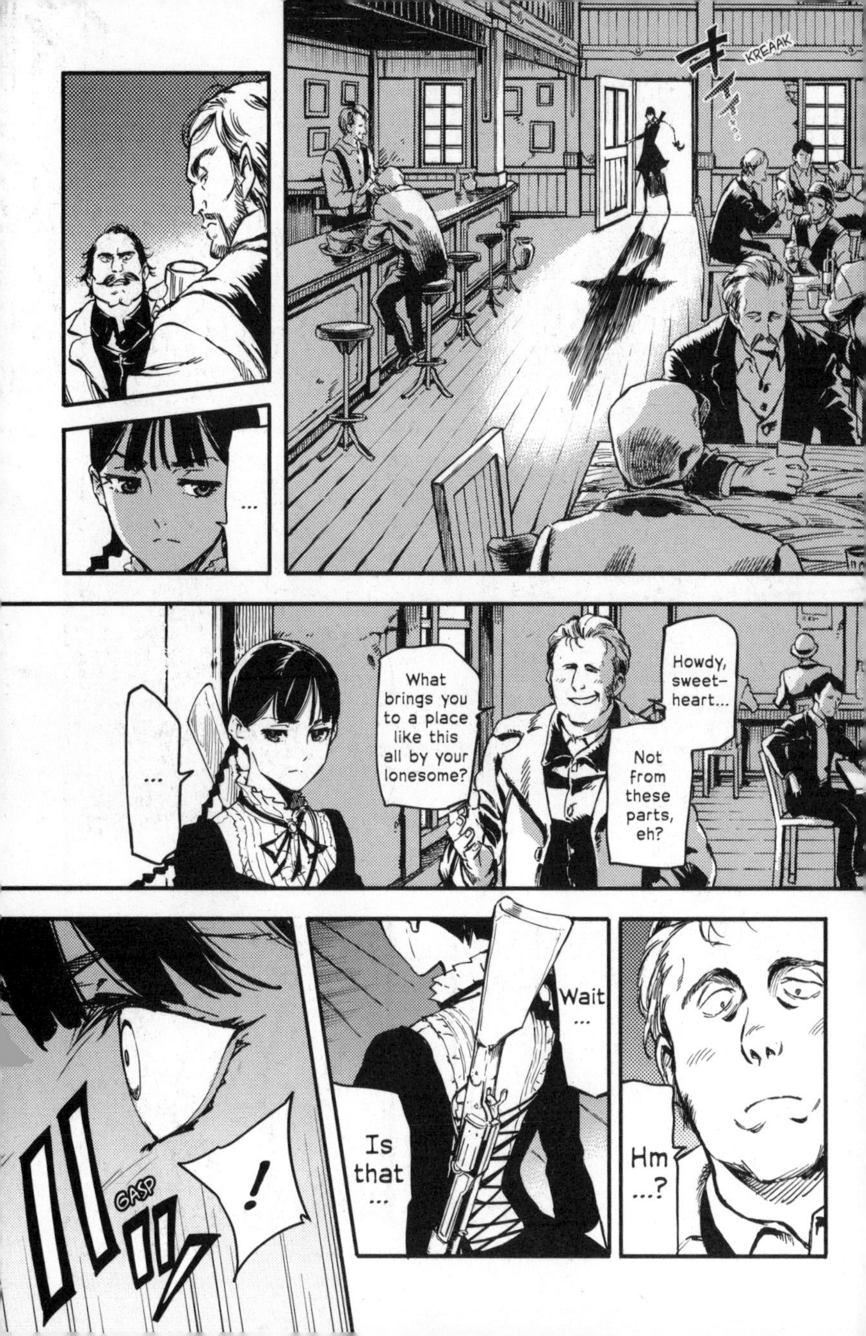
KREAAK
...
Howdy, sweetheart...
Not from these parts, eh?
What brings you to a place like this all by your lonesome?
...
Hm ...?
Wait ...
Is that ...
GASP
!

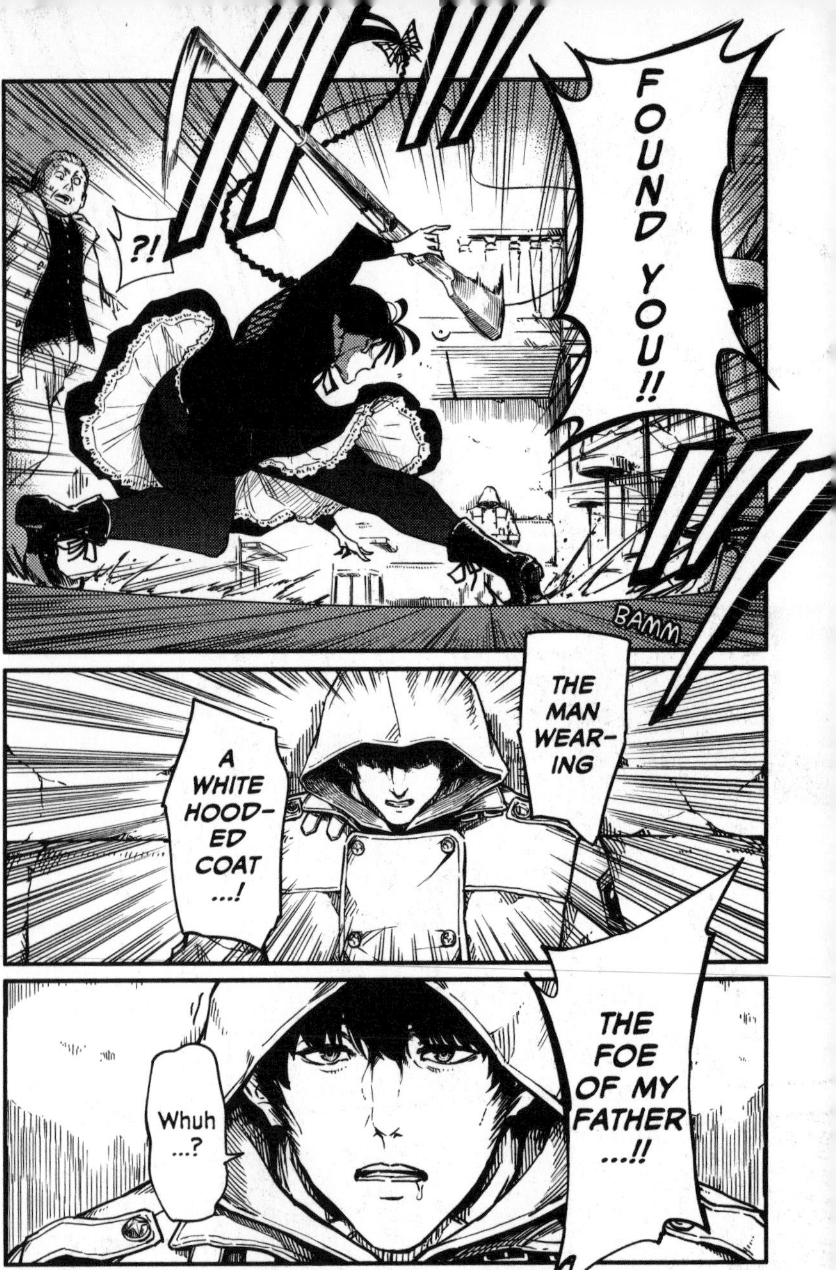
FOUND YOU!!
?!
BAMM
THE MAN WEAR-ING
A WHITE HOOD-ED COAT ...!
THE FOE OF MY FATHER ...!!
Whuh ...?

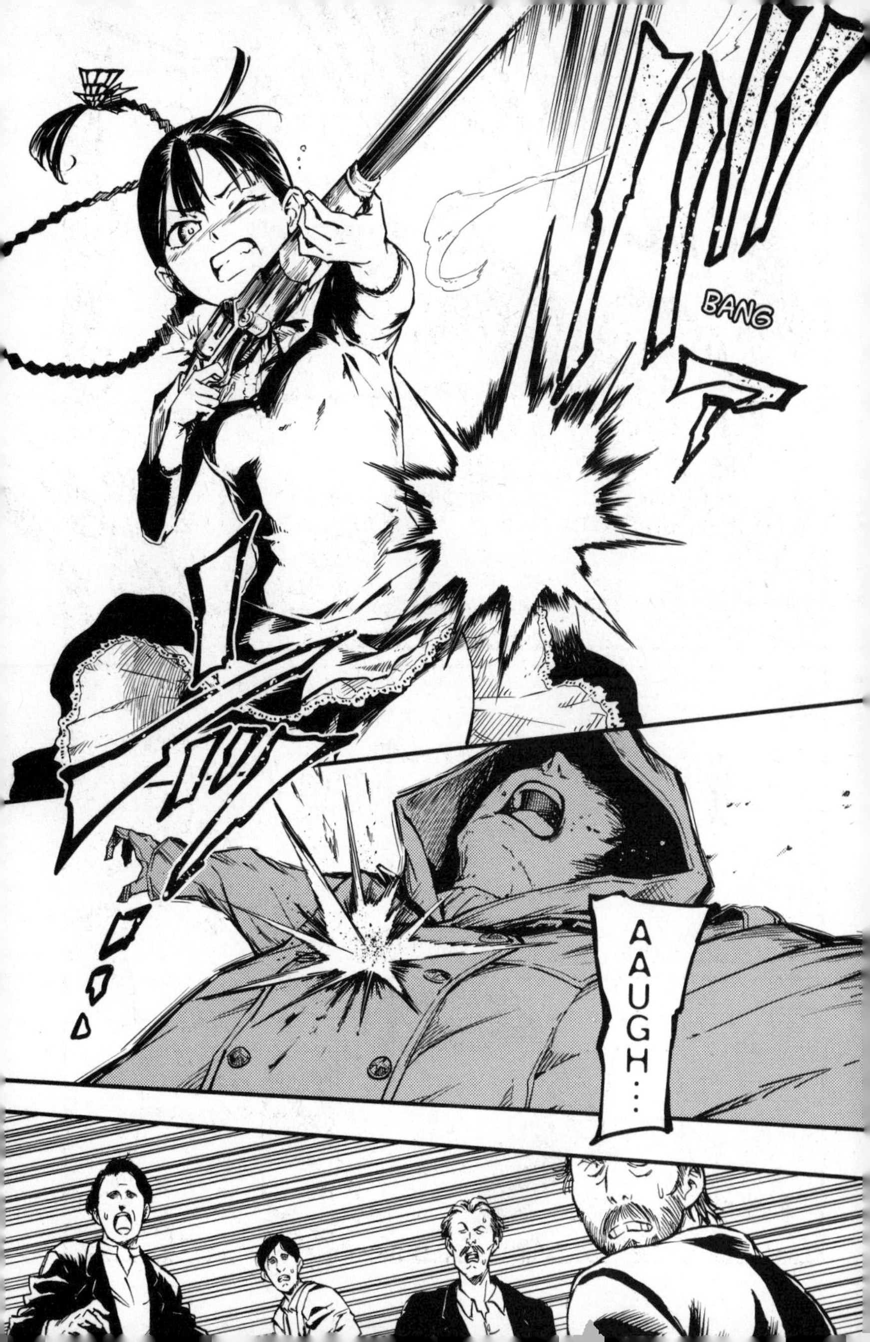
BANG
AAUGH...

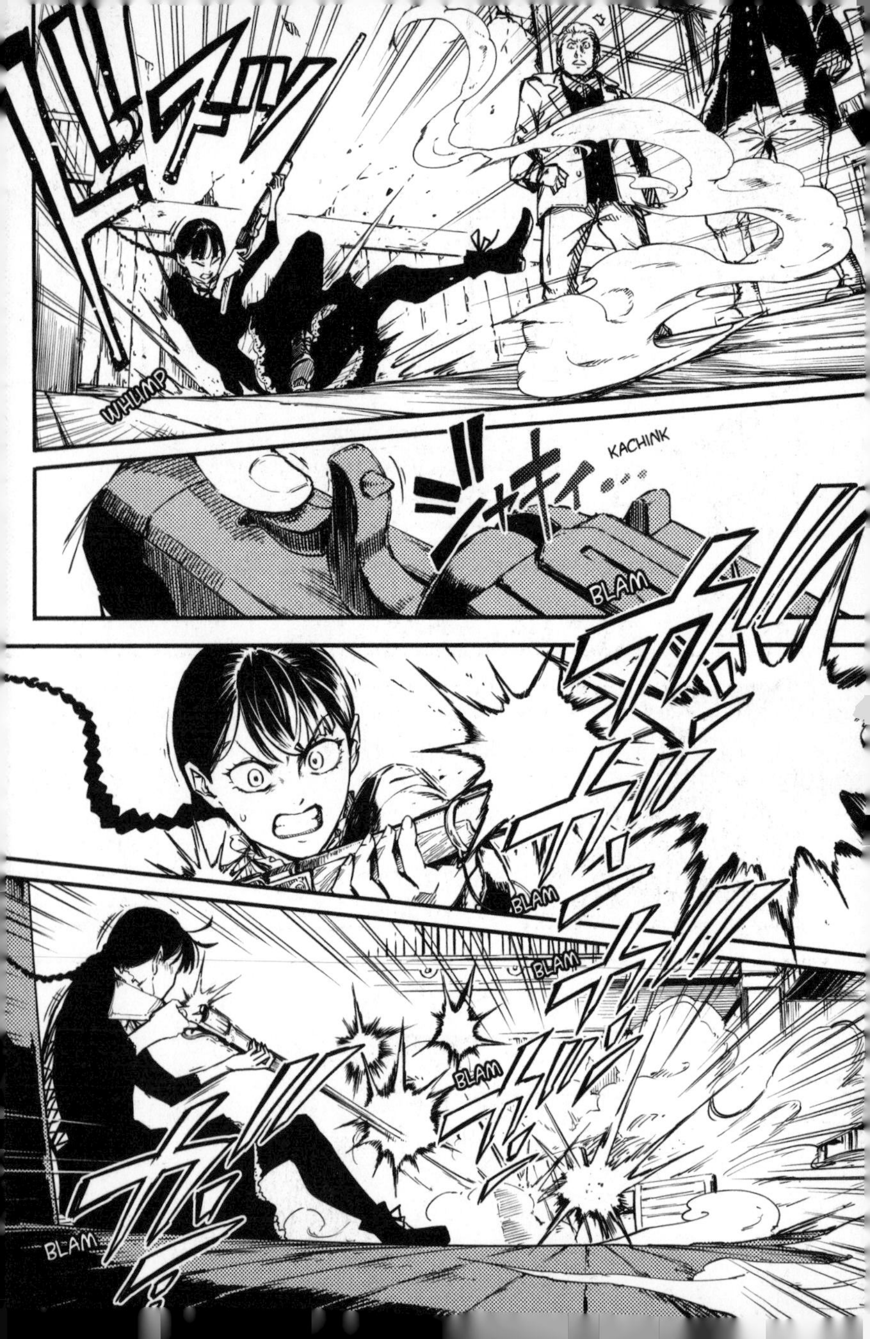
WHUMP
KACHINK
BLAM
BLAM
BLAM
BLAM
BLAM

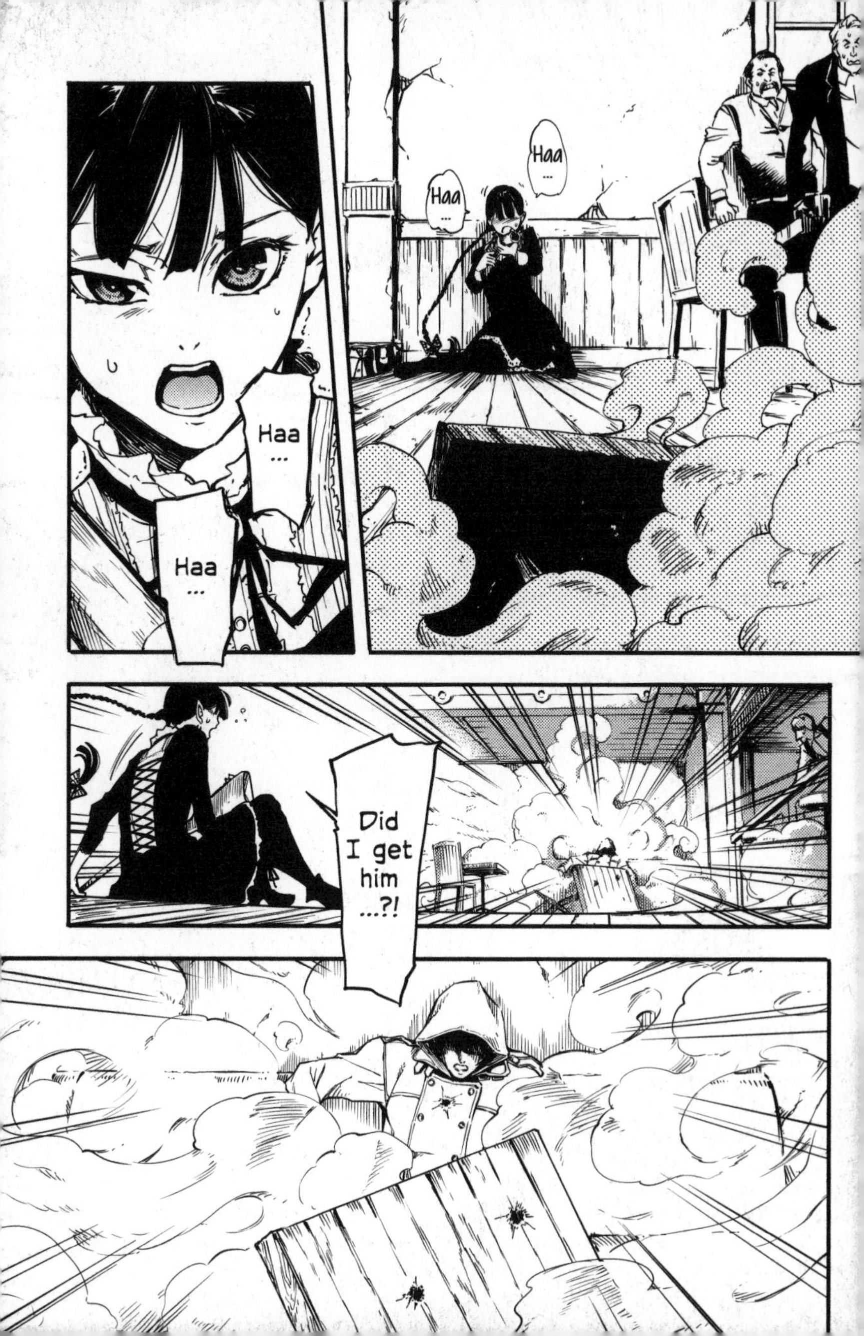

Haa ...
Haa ...
Haa ...
Haa ...
Did I get him ...?!

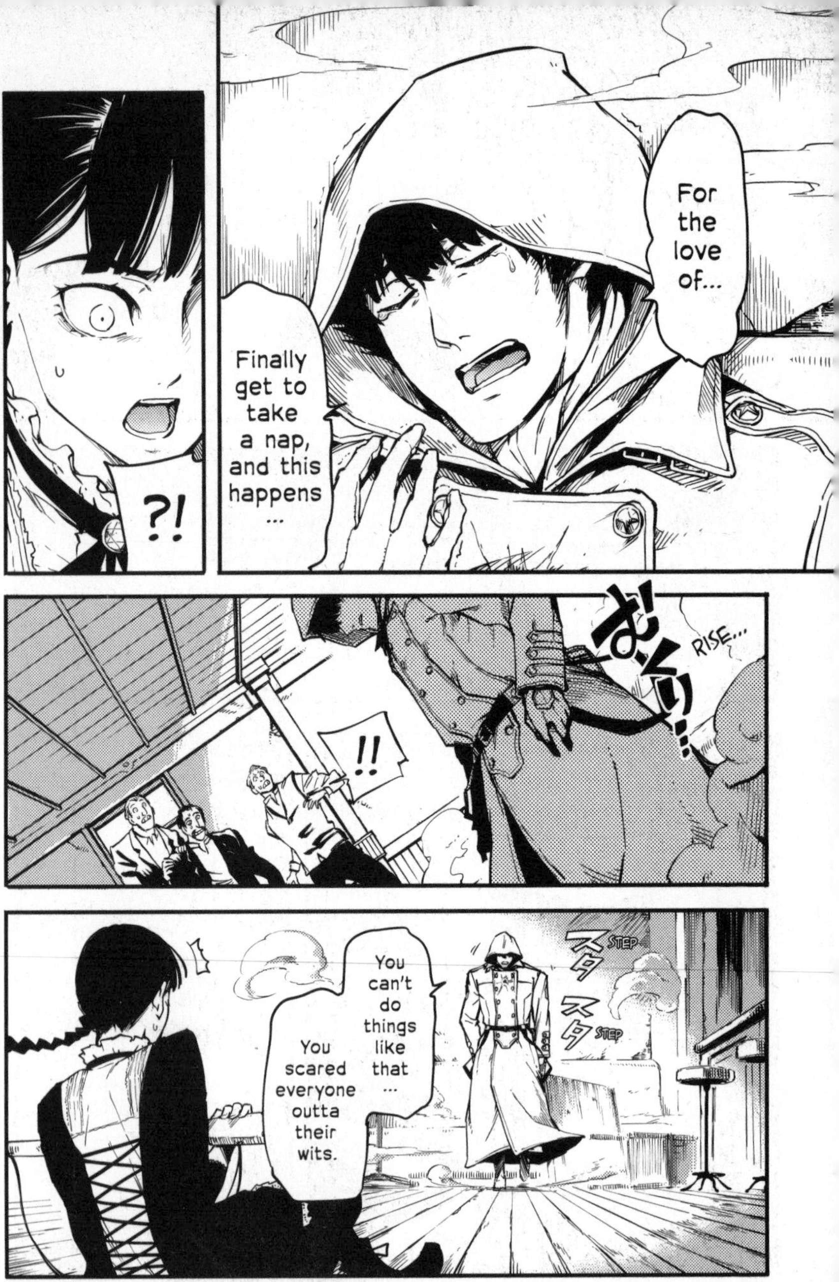
For the love of...
Finally get to take a nap, and this happens ...
?!
RISE...
!!
スタ
STEP
スタ
STEP
You can't do things like that ...
You scared everyone outta their wits.

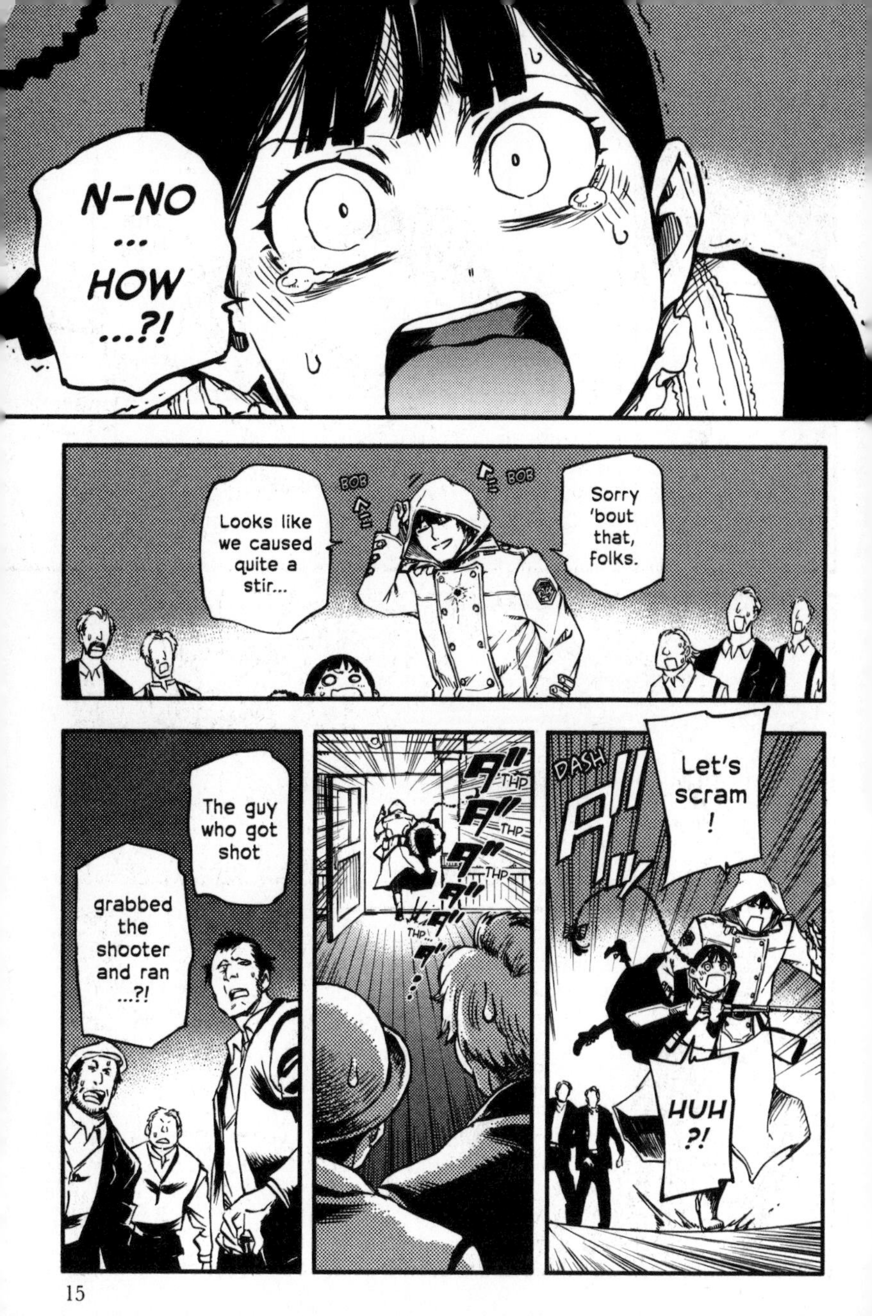
N-NO ... HOW ...?!
BOB
BOB
Sorry 'bout that, folks.
Looks like we caused quite a stir...
DASH
Let's scram!
HUH?!
THP
THP
THP
THP
The guy who got shot
grabbed the shooter and ran ...?!

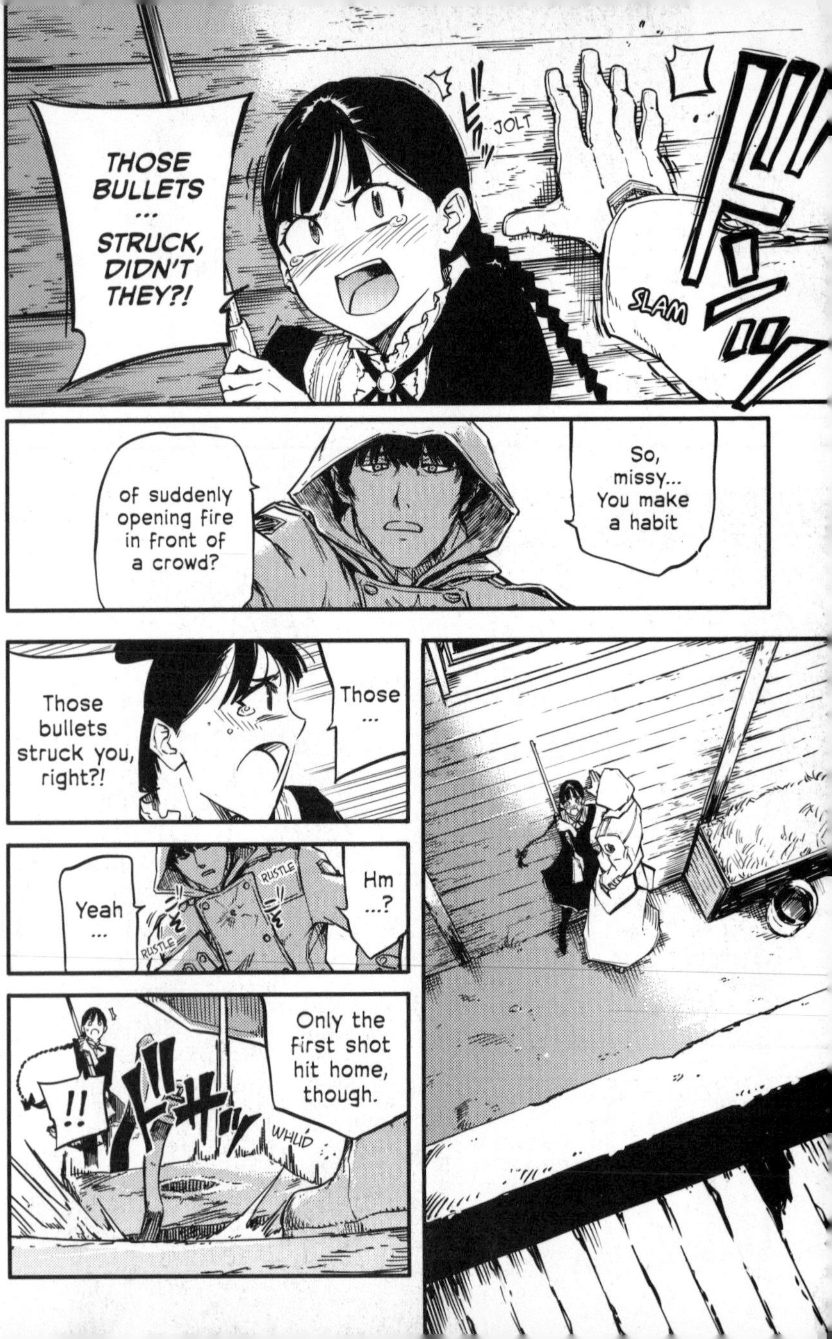
JOLT
SLAM
THOSE BULLETS ... STRUCK, DIDN'T THEY?!
So, missy... You make a habit
of suddenly opening fire in front of a crowd?
Those ...
Those bullets struck you, right?!
Hm ...?
RUSTLE
RUSTLE
Yeah ...
Only the first shot hit home, though.
WHUD
!!

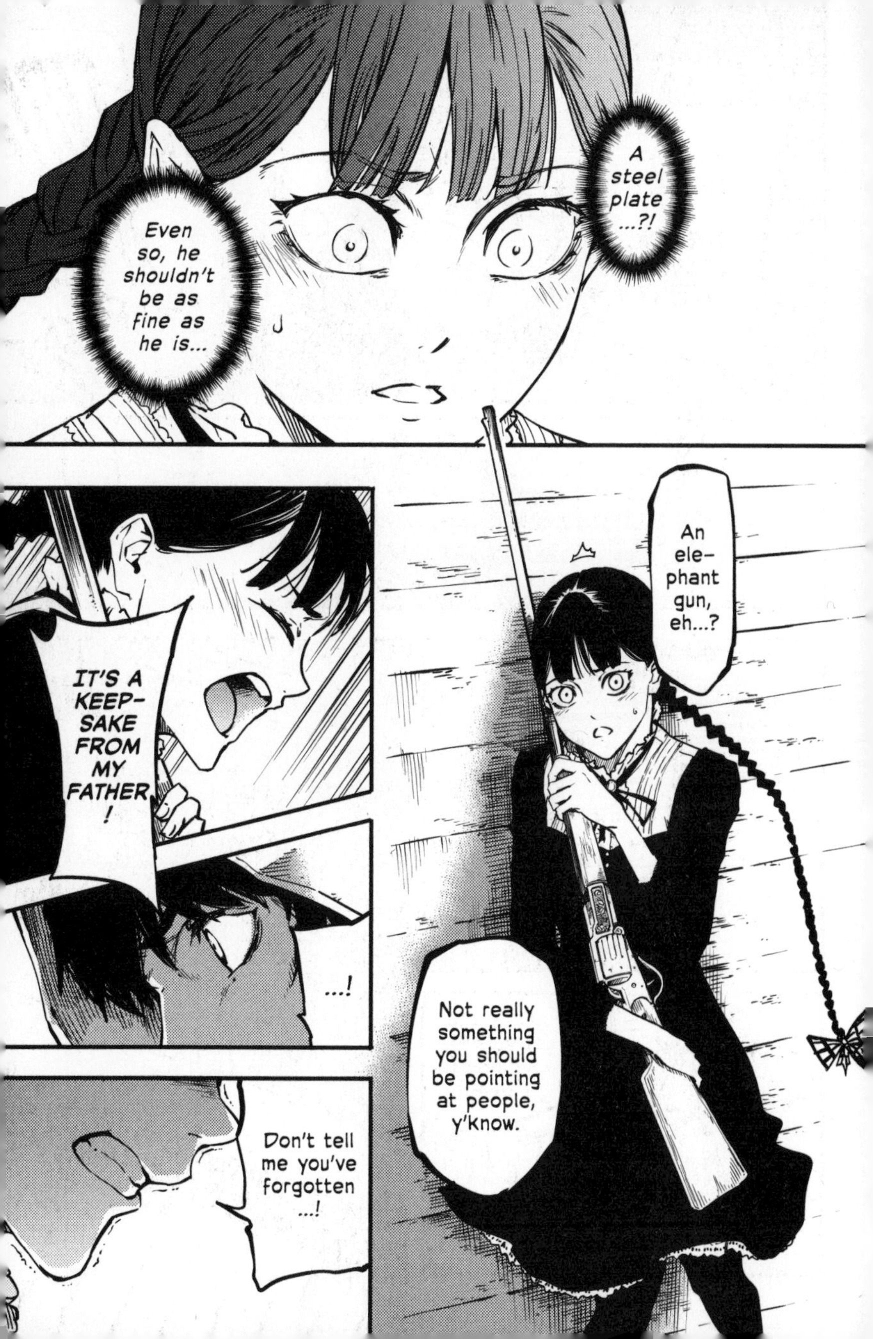
A steel plate ...?!
Even so, he shouldn't be as fine as he is...
An ele-phant gun, eh...?
Not really something you should be pointing at people, y'know.
IT'S A KEEP-SAKE FROM MY FATHER!
...!
Don't tell me you've forgotten ...!

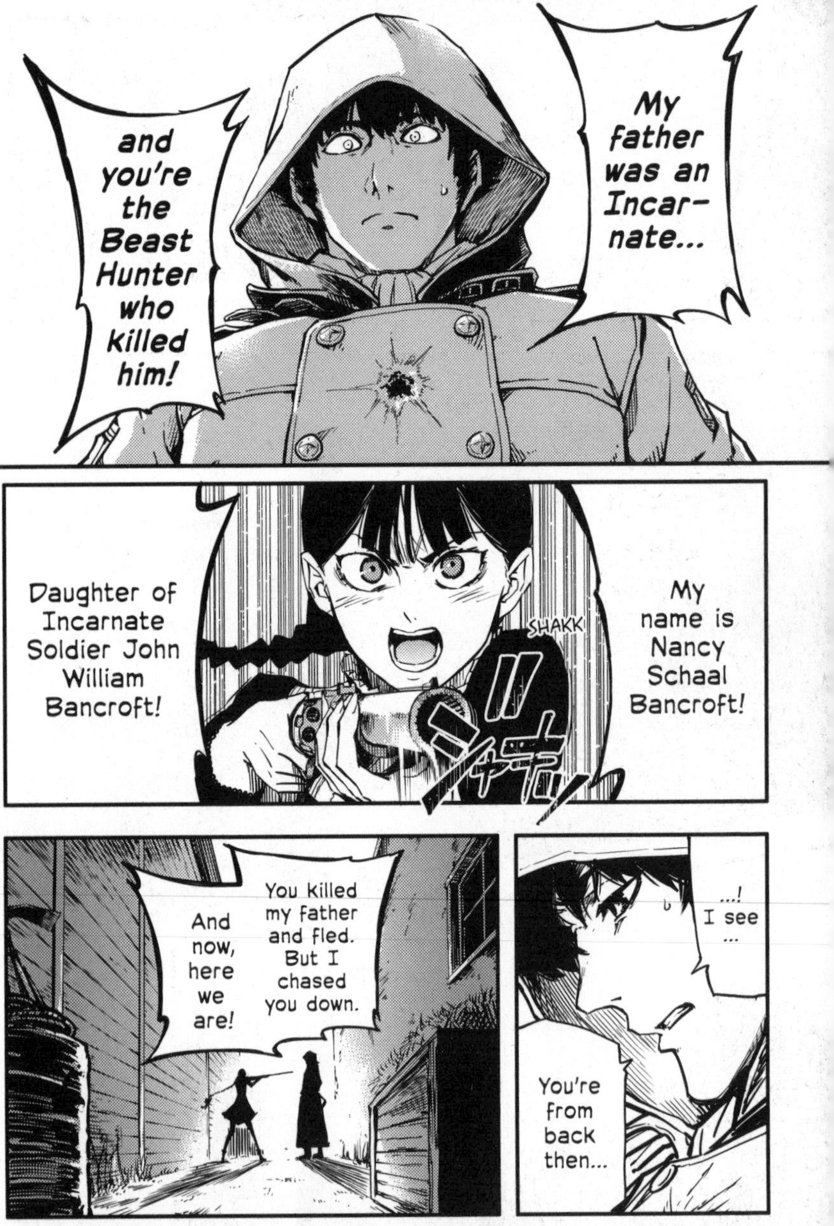
My father was an Incarnate...
and you're the Beast Hunter who killed him!
My name is Nancy Schaal Bancroft!
SHAKK
Daughter of Incarnate Soldier John William Bancroft!
...! I see ...
You're from back then...
You killed my father and fled. But I chased you down.
And now, here we are!

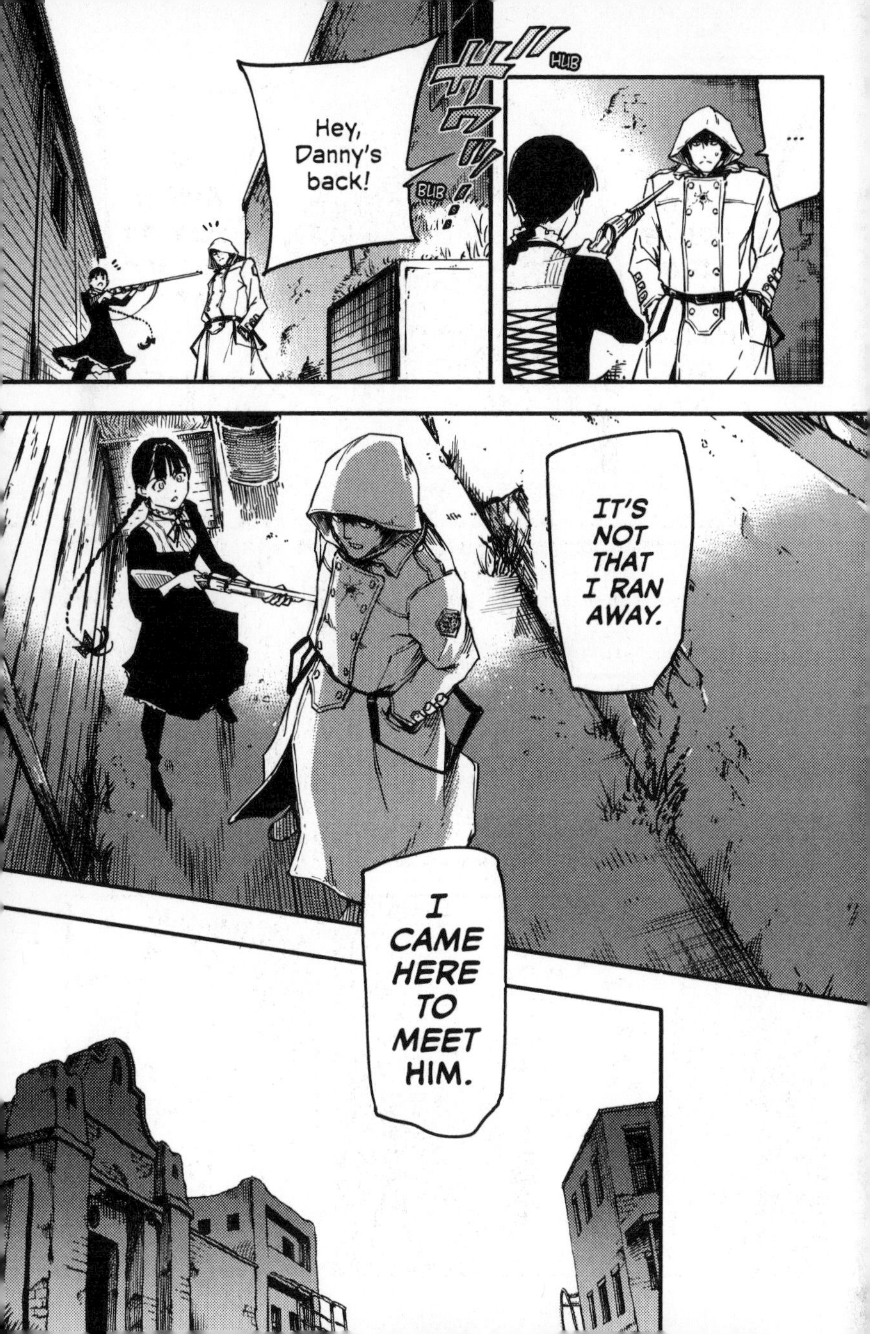
...
HUB
BUB
Hey, Danny's back!
IT'S NOT THAT I RAN AWAY.
I CAME HERE TO MEET HIM.

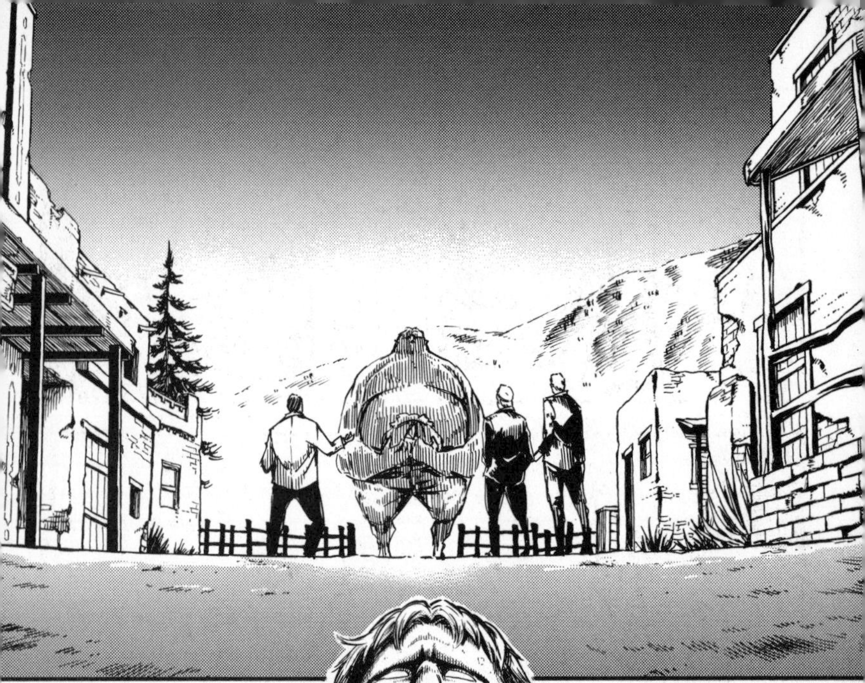

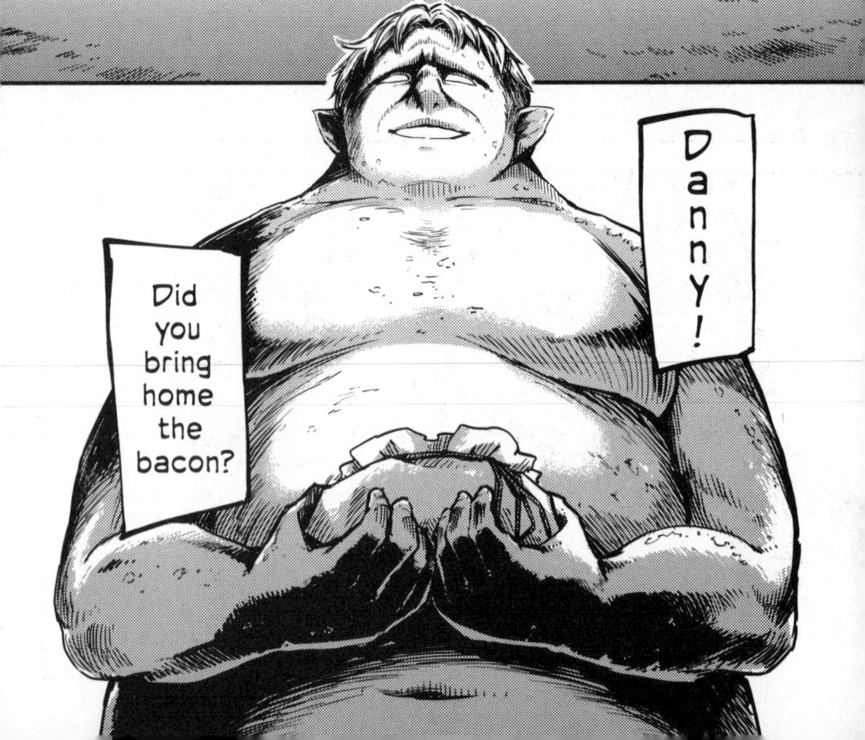
Danny!
Did you bring home the bacon?

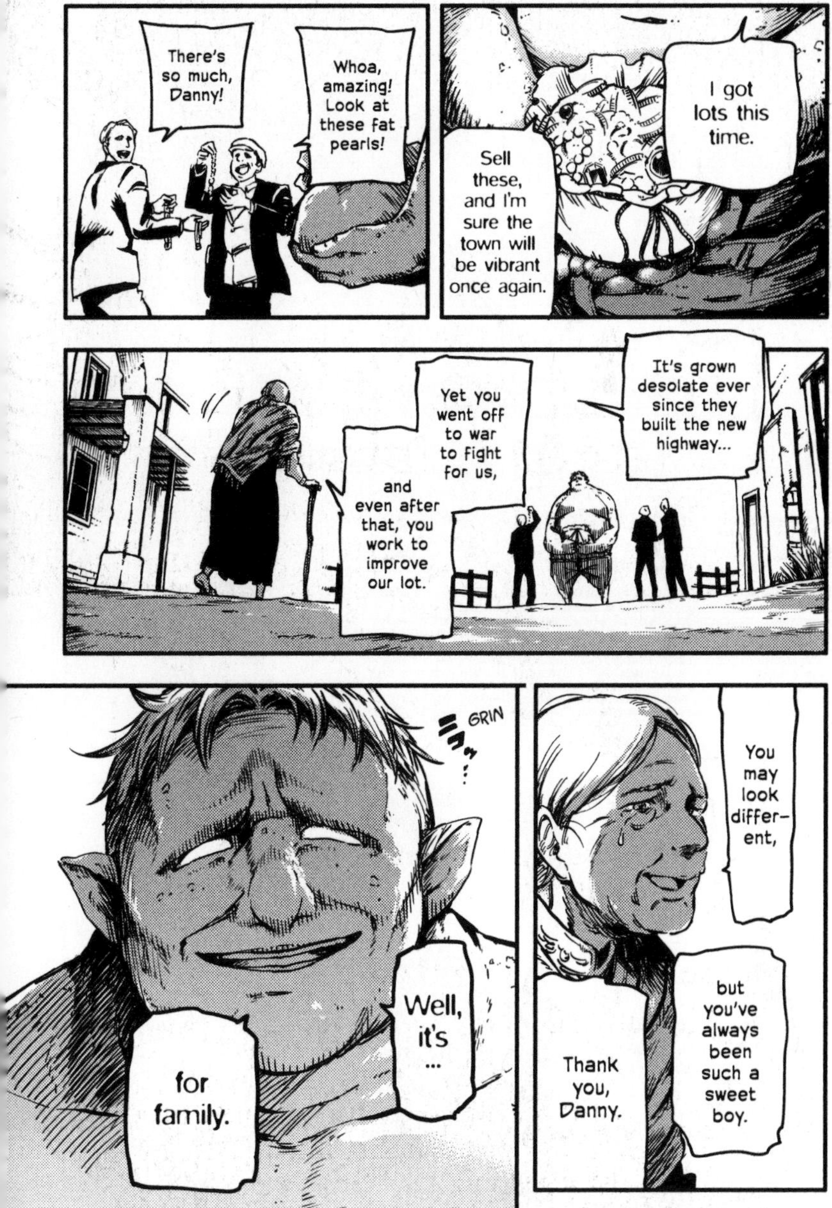
I got lots this time.
Sell these, and I'm sure the town will be vibrant once again.
Whoa, amazing! Look at these fat pearls!
There's so much, Danny!
It's grown desolate ever since they built the new highway...
Yet you went off to war to fight for us,
and even after that, you work to improve our lot.
You may look differ-ent,
but you've always been such a sweet boy.
Thank you, Danny.
GRIN
Well, it's ...
for family.

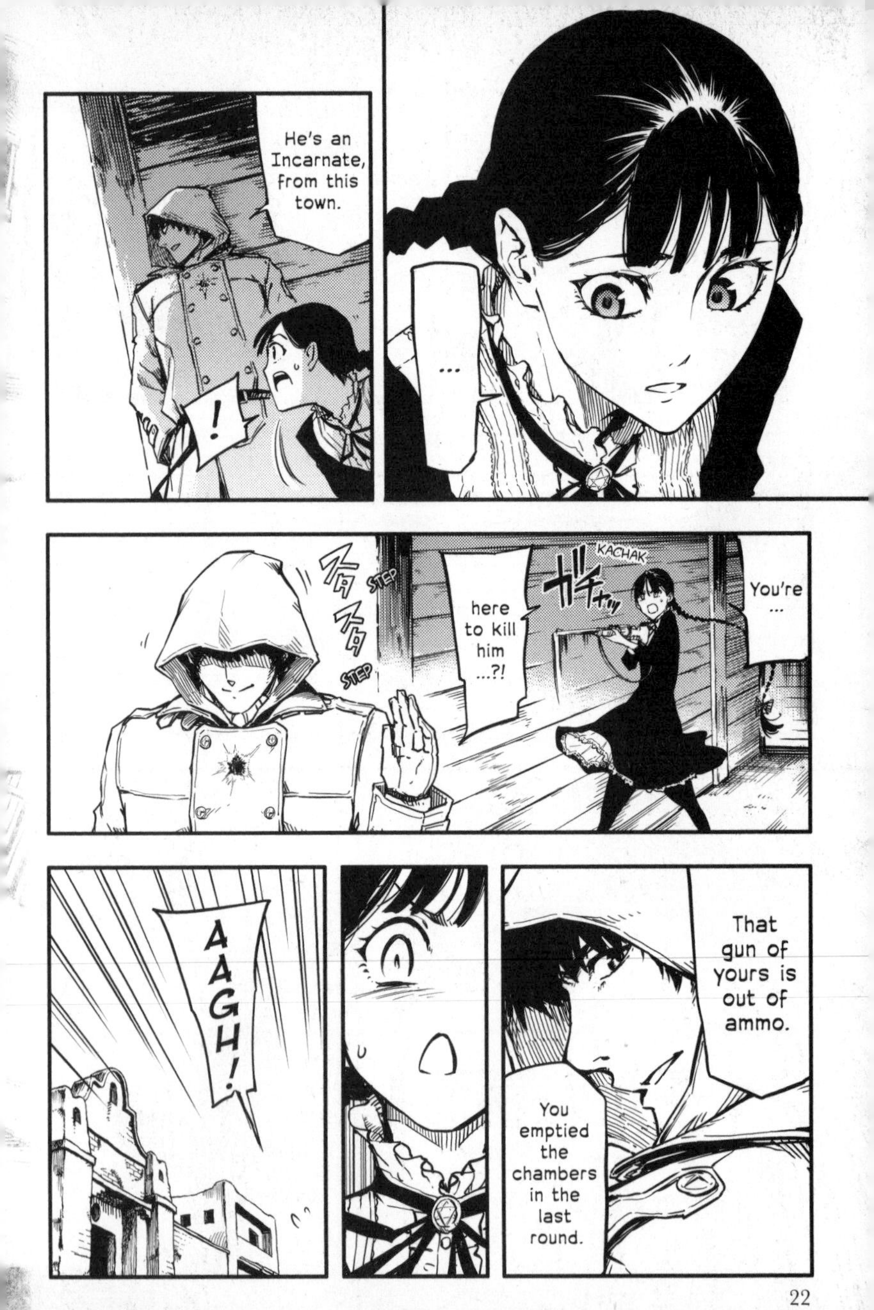
...
He's an Incarnate, from this town.
!
You're ...
KACHAK
ガチャッ
here to kill him ...?!
スタ STEP
スタ STEP
That gun of yours is out of ammo.
You emptied the chambers in the last round.
AAGH!

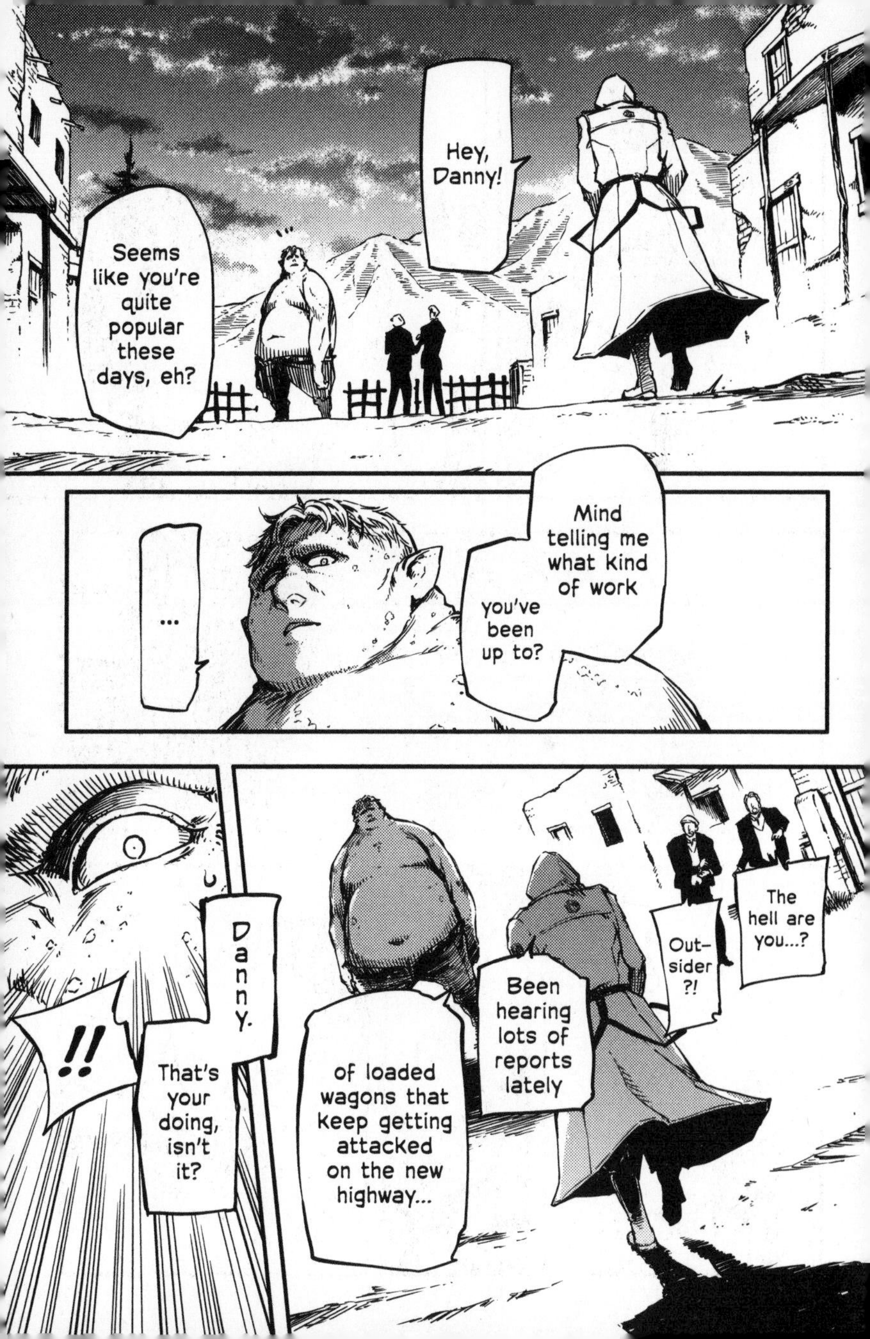
Hey, Danny!
Seems like you're quite popular these days, eh?
Mind telling me what kind of work you've been up to?
...
The hell are you...?
Out-sider?!
Been hearing lots of reports lately
of loaded wagons that keep getting attacked on the new highway...
Danny.
That's your doing, isn't it?
!!

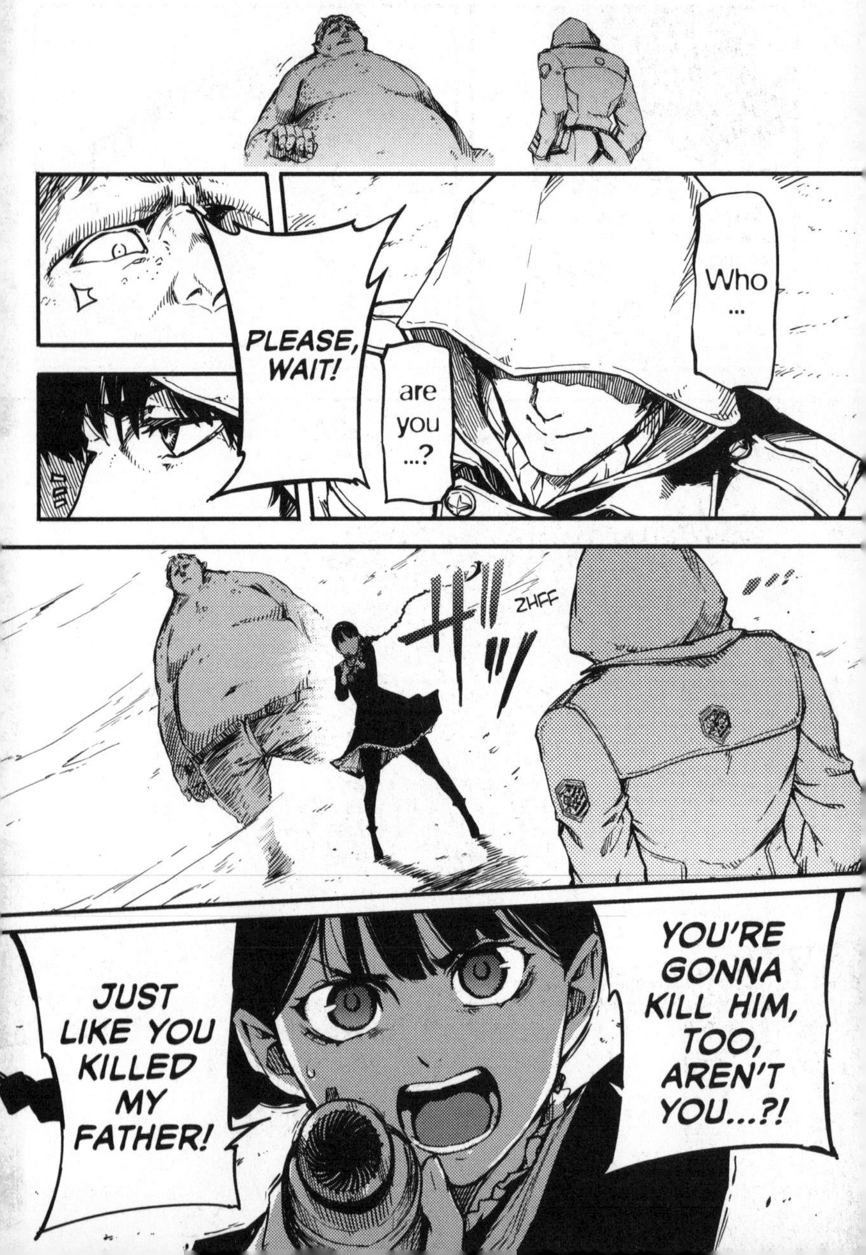
Who ...
are you ...?
PLEASE, WAIT!
ザッ
ZHFF
YOU'RE GONNA KILL HIM, TOO, AREN'T YOU...?!
JUST LIKE YOU KILLED MY FATHER!

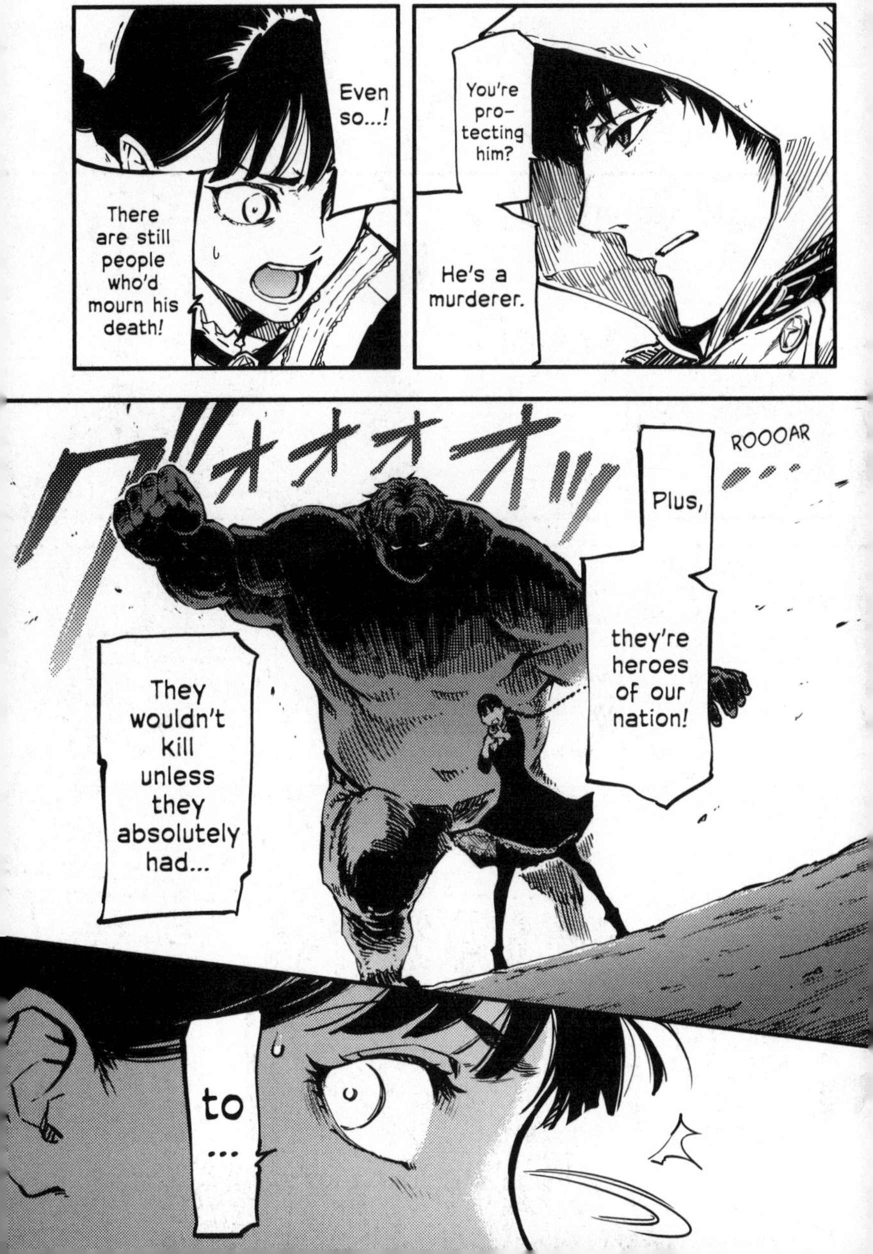
You're pro- tecting him?
He's a murderer.
Even so...!
There are still people who'd mourn his death!
ROOOAR
Plus,
they're heroes of our nation!
They wouldn't kill unless they absolutely had...
to ...

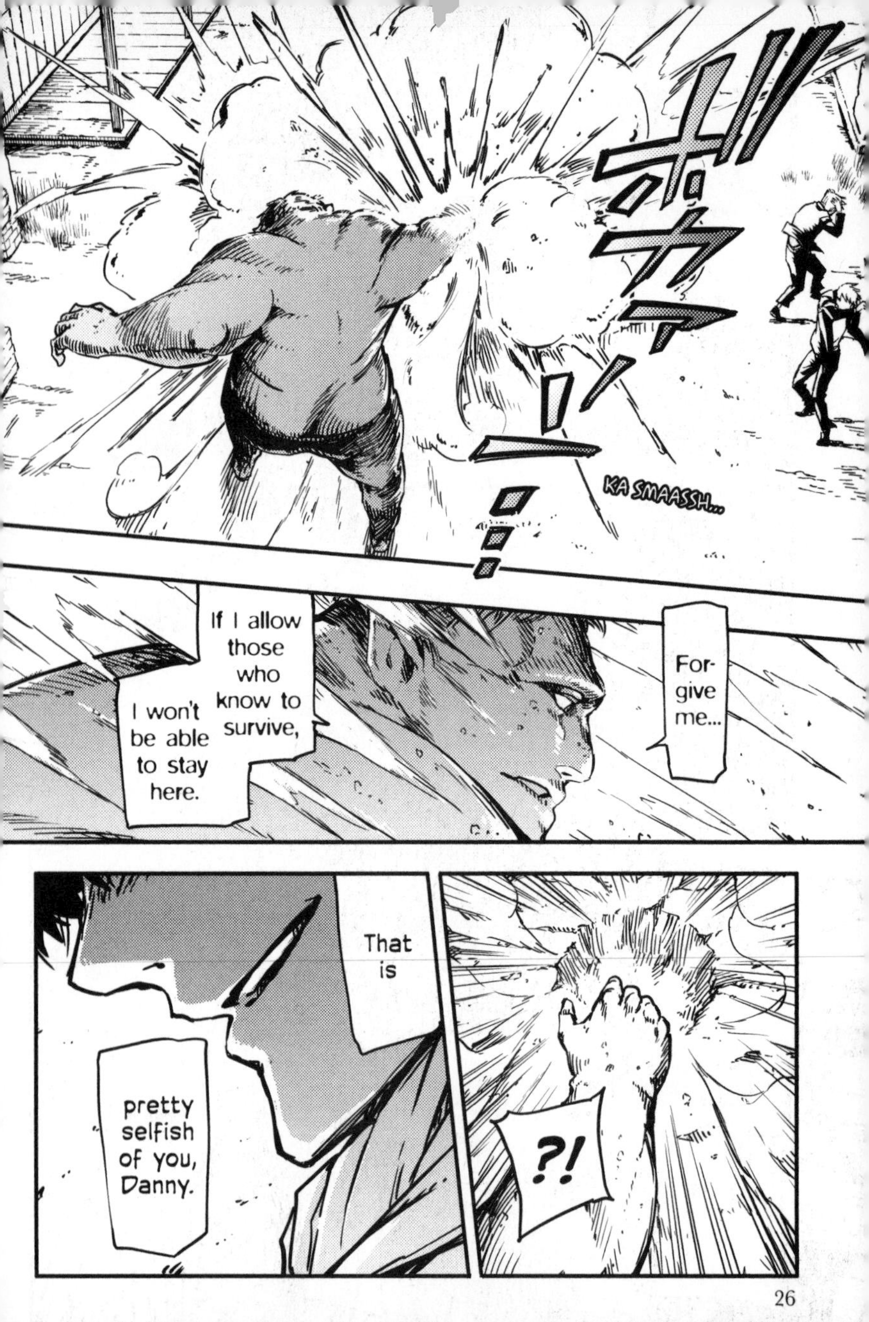
KA SMAASSH...
Forgive me...
If I allow those who know to survive,
I won't be able to stay here.
?!
That is
pretty selfish of you, Danny.

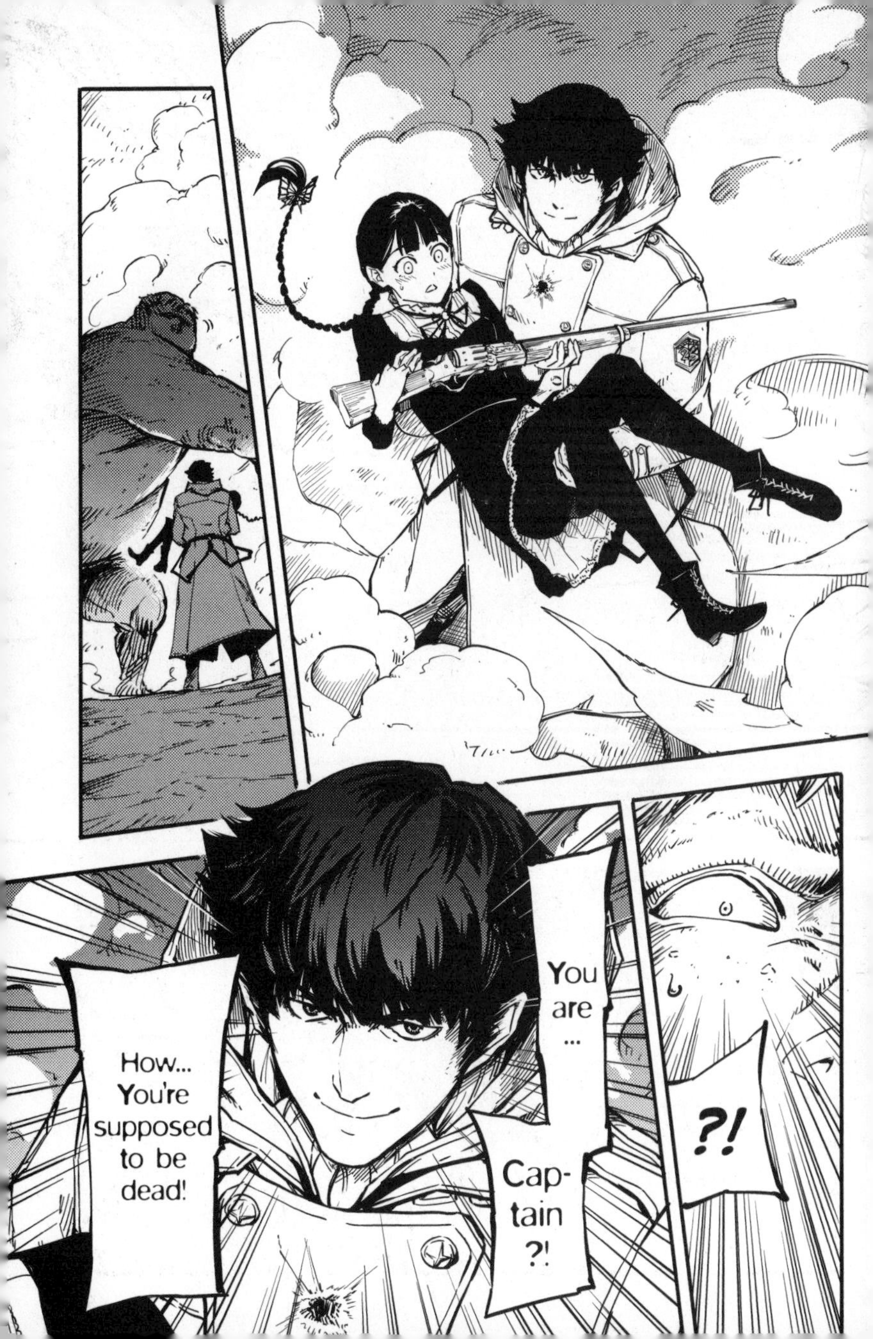
?!
You are ... Captain ?!
How... You're supposed to be dead!

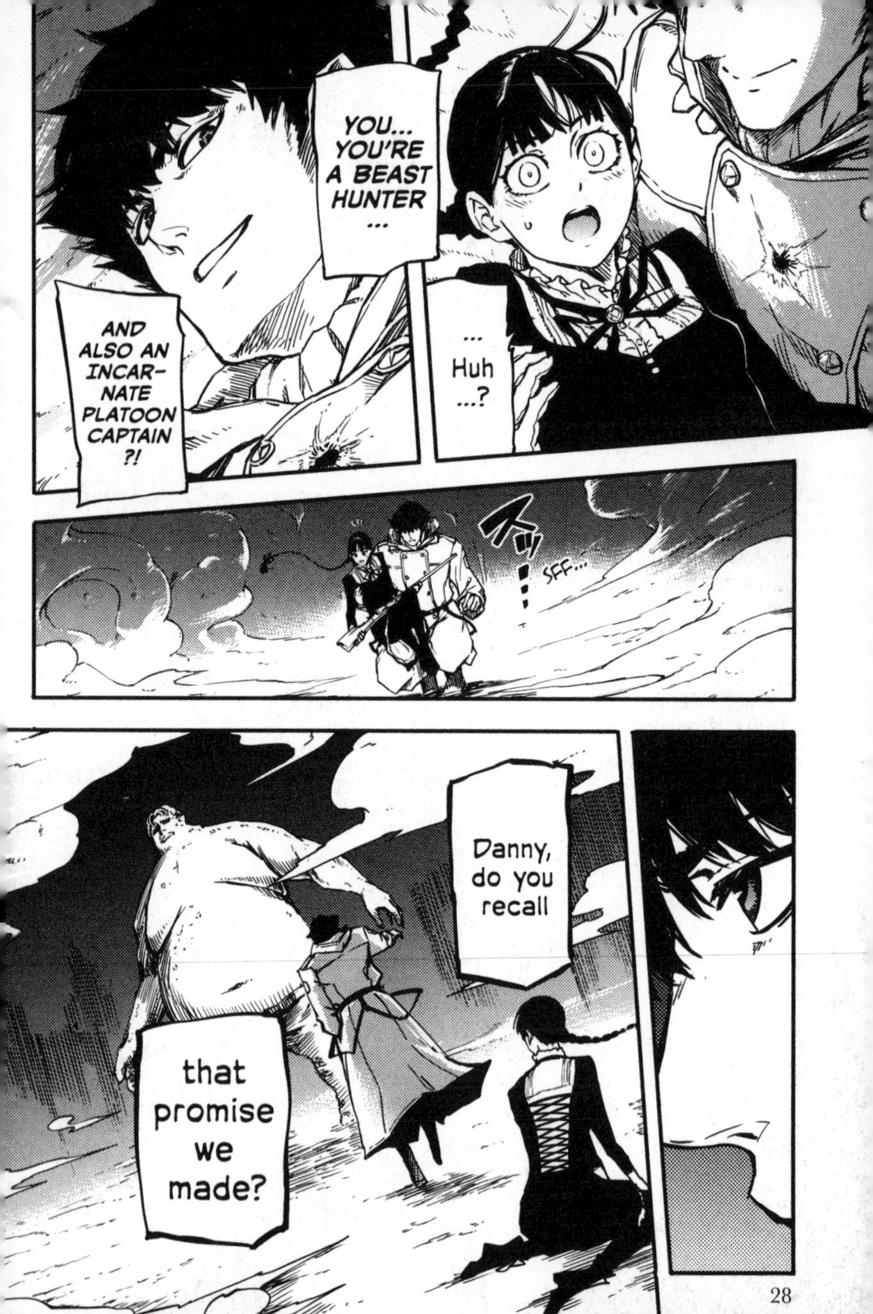
YOU... YOU'RE A BEAST HUNTER ...
... Huh ...?
AND ALSO AN INCAR-NATE PLATOON CAPTAIN ?!
スッ
SFF...
Danny, do you recall
that promise we made?

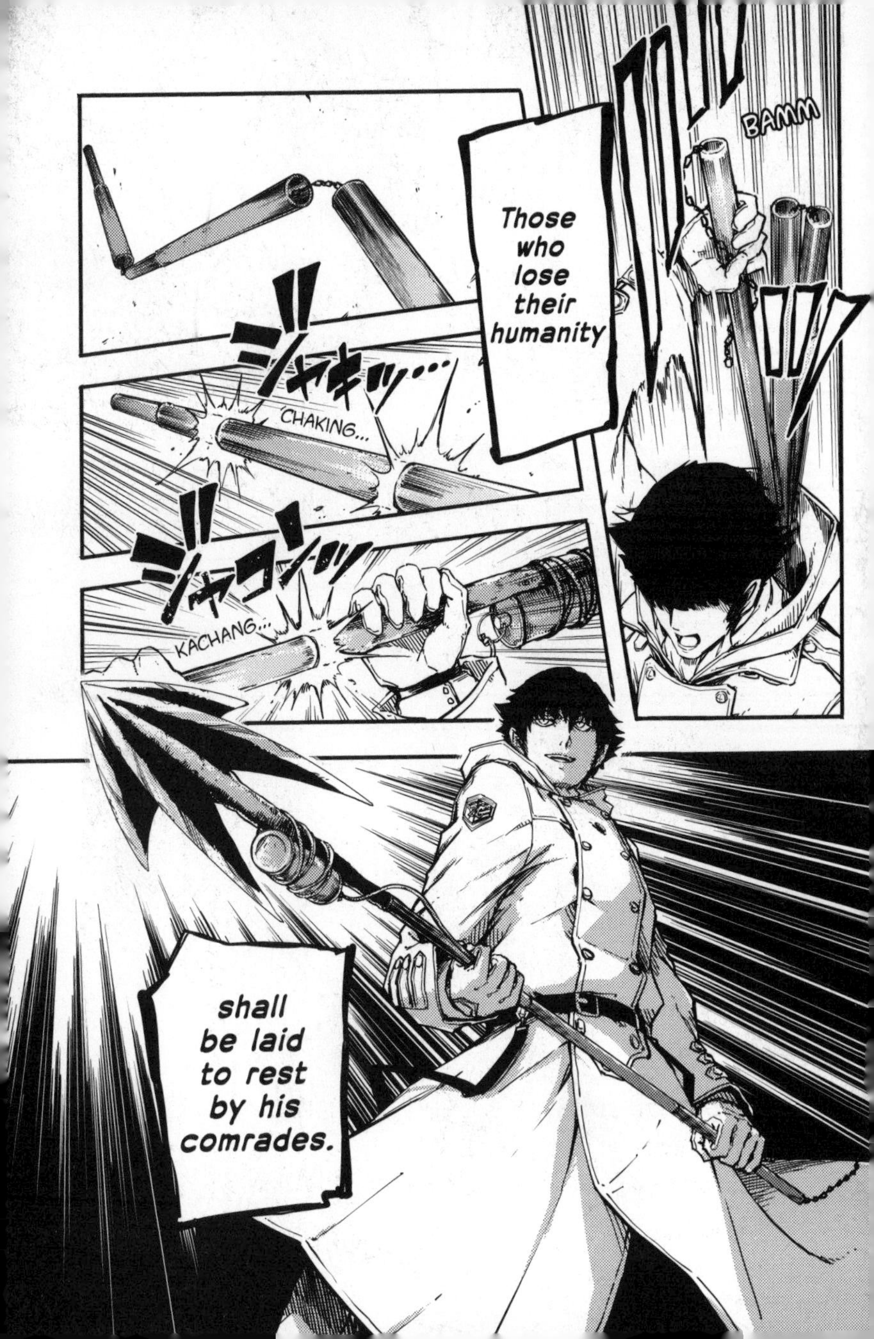
BAMM
Those who lose their humanity
ジャキッ…
CHAKING...
KACHANG...
shall be laid to rest by his comrades.

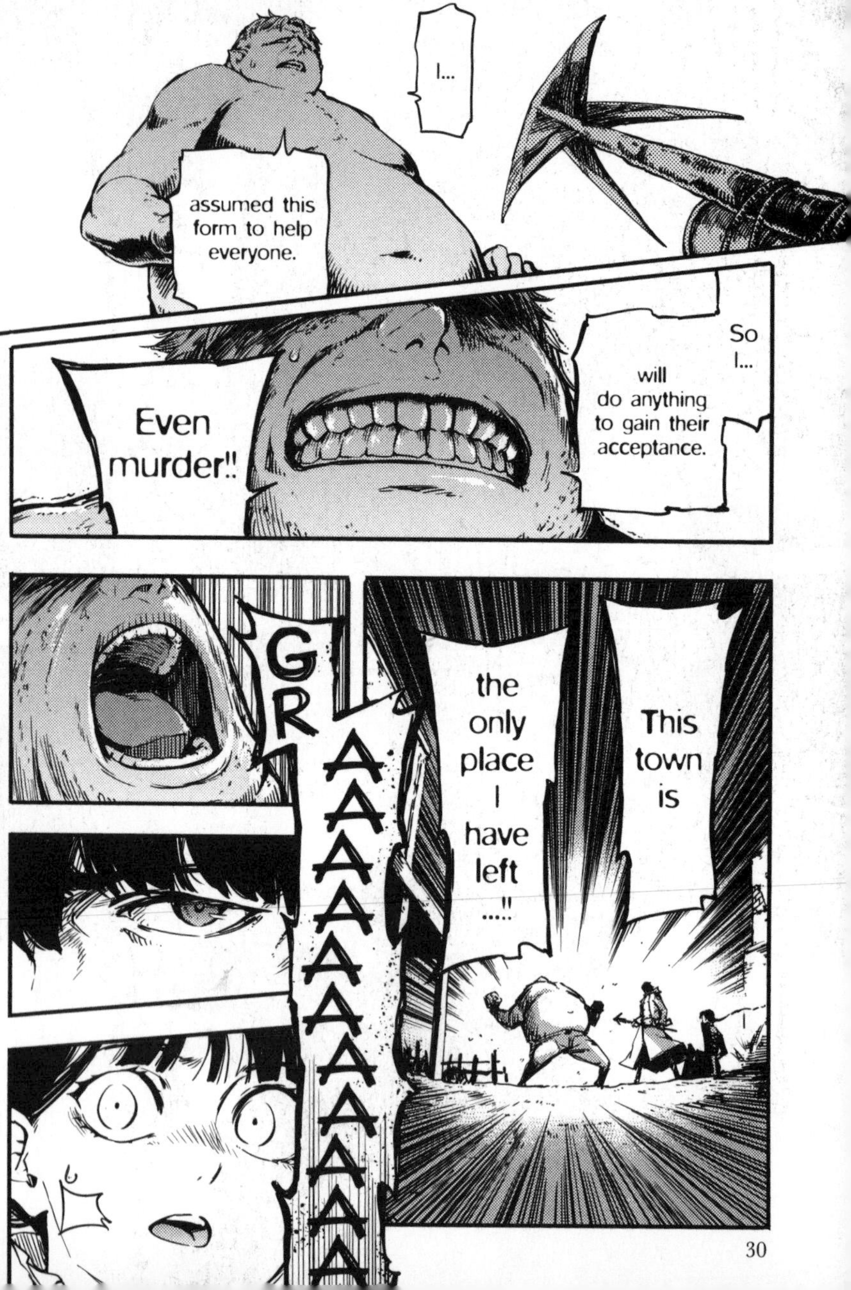

I...
assumed this form to help everyone.
So I...
will do anything to gain their acceptance.
Even murder!!
This town is
the only place I have left ...!!
GRAAAAAAAAAAAAA

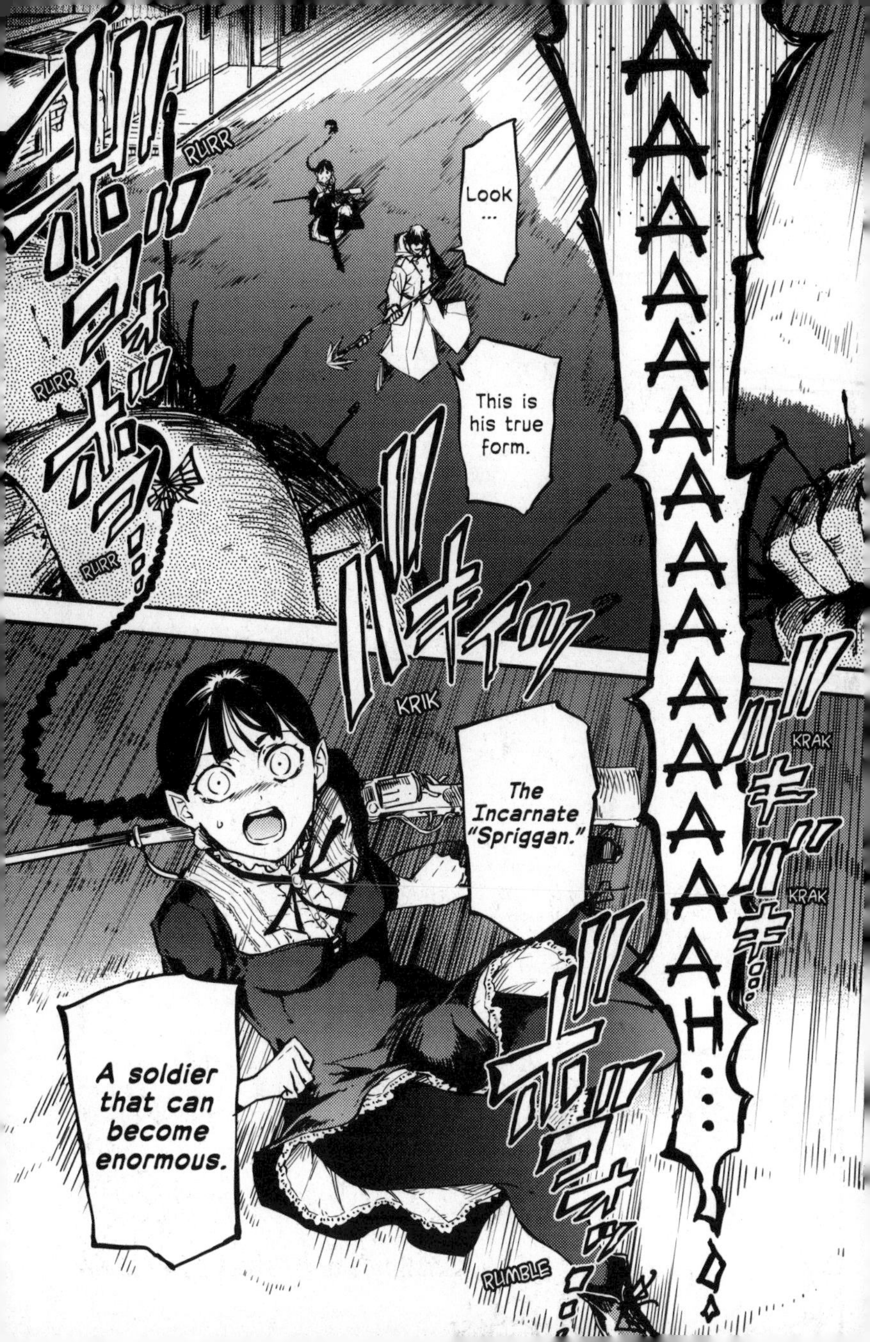

AAAAAAAAAAAAAAAAH...
Look ...
This is his true form.
RURR
RURR
RURR
KRAK
KRAK
The Incarnate "Spriggan."
KRIK
A soldier that can become enormous.
RUMBLE

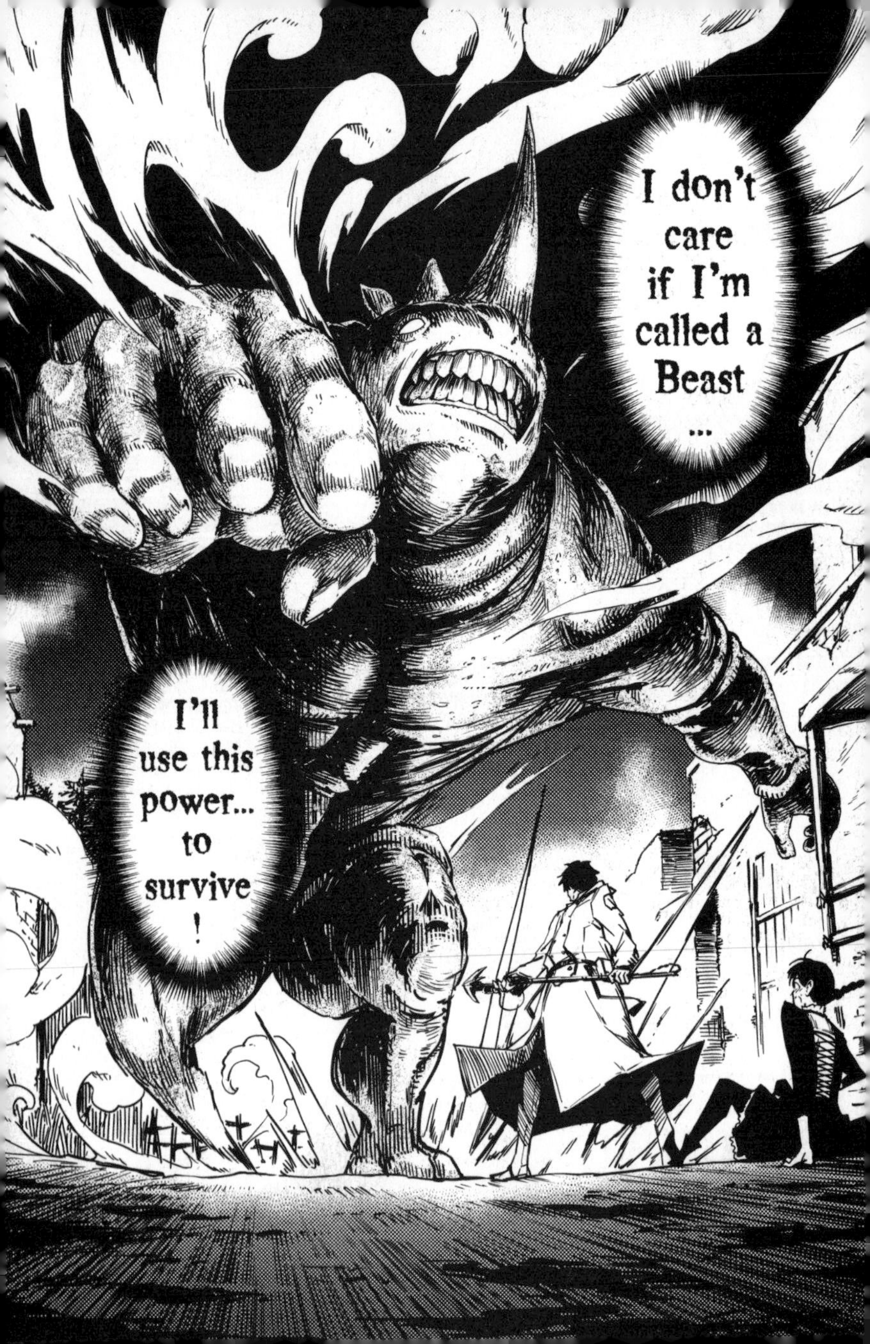
I don't care if I'm called a Beast...
I'll use this power... to survive!

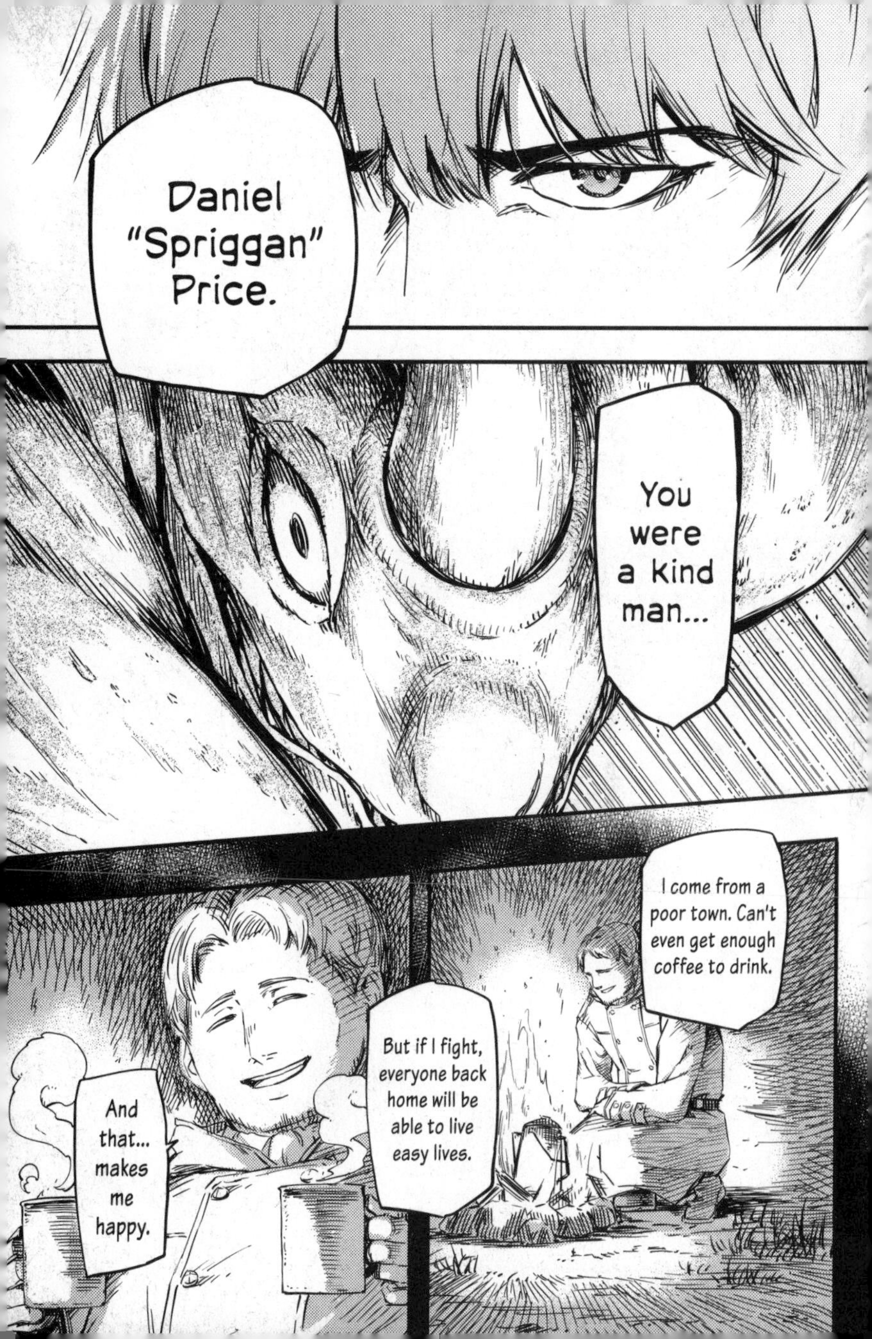
Daniel "Spriggan" Price.
You were a kind man...
I come from a poor town. Can't even get enough coffee to drink.
But if I fight, everyone back home will be able to live easy lives.
And that... makes me happy.

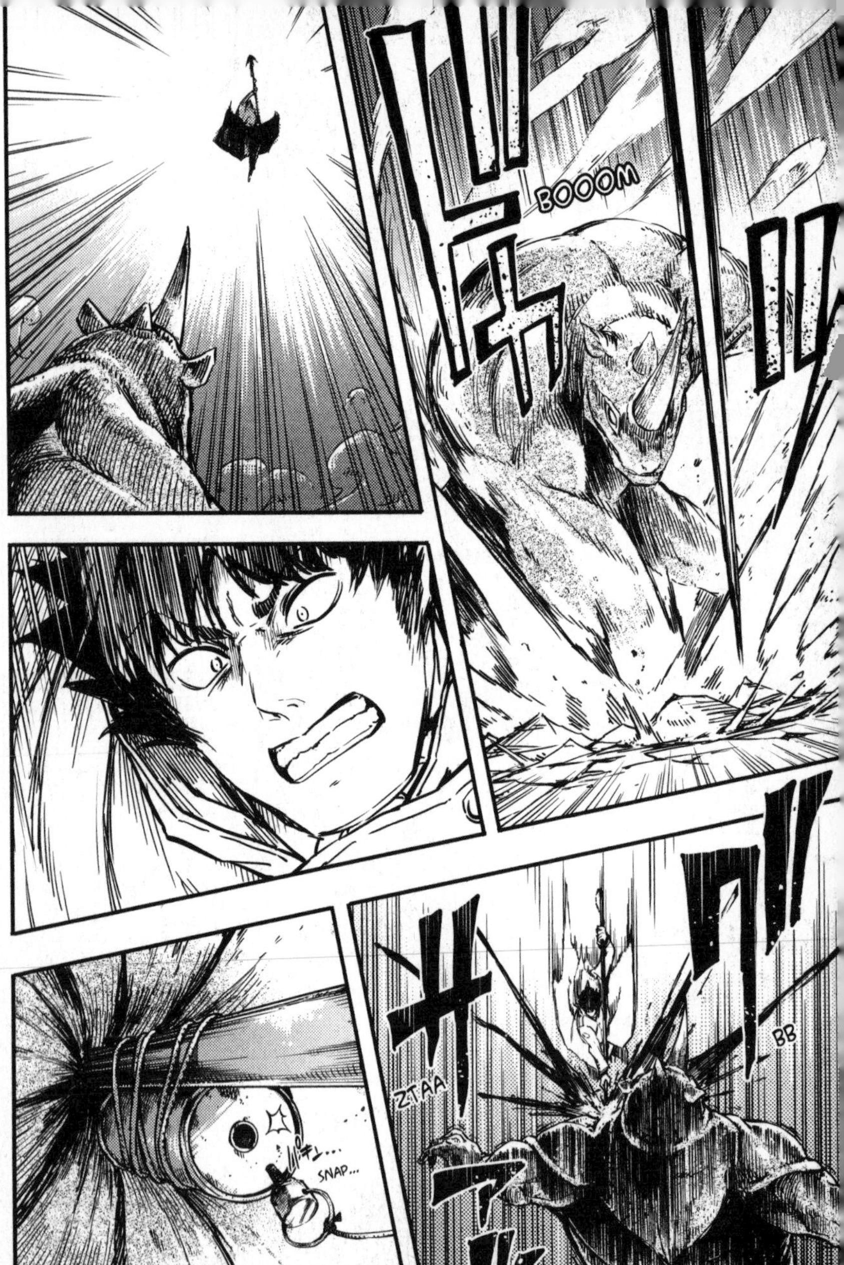
BOOOM
BB
ZTAA
SNAP...

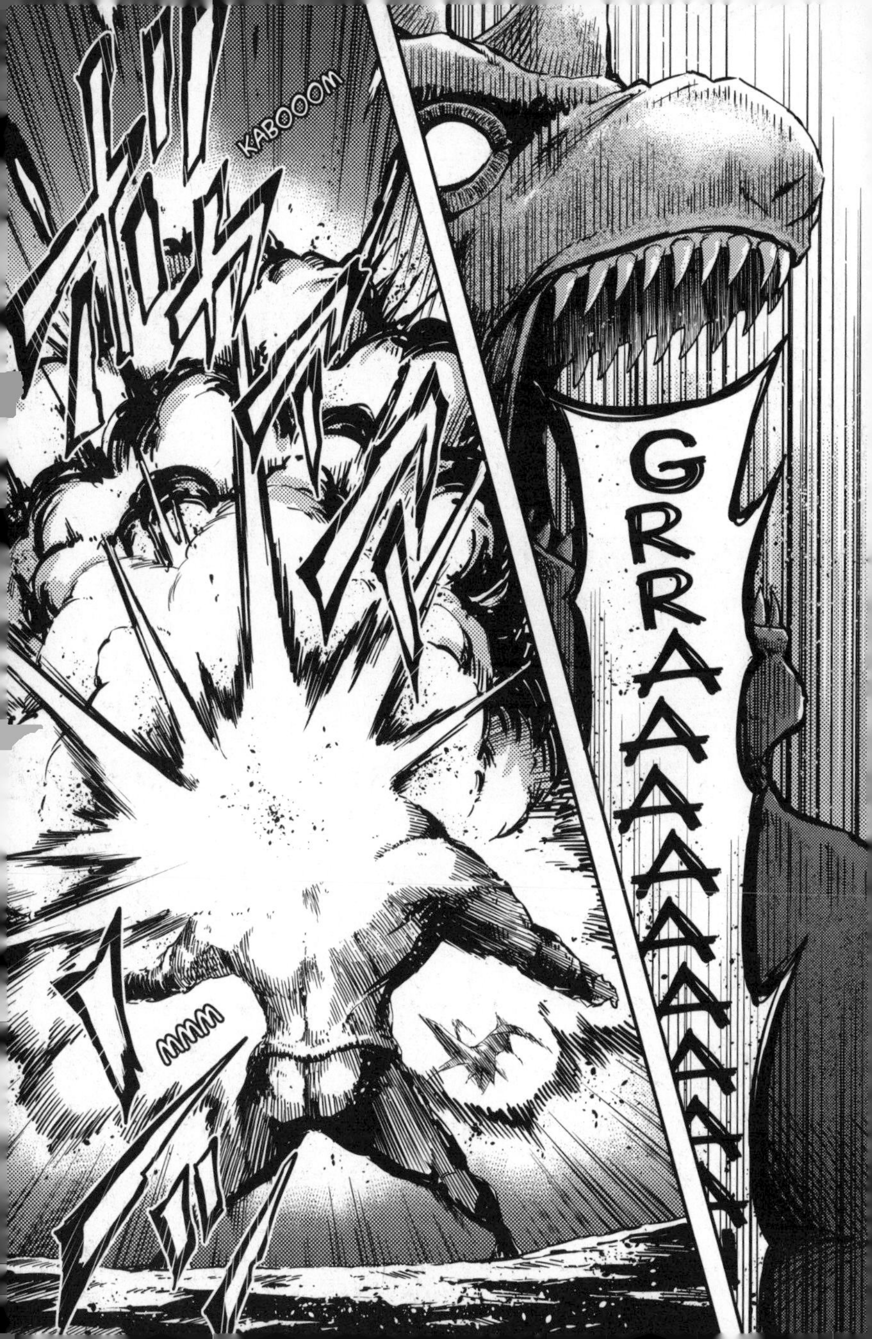
GRRAAAAAAAAA
KABOOOM
MMM

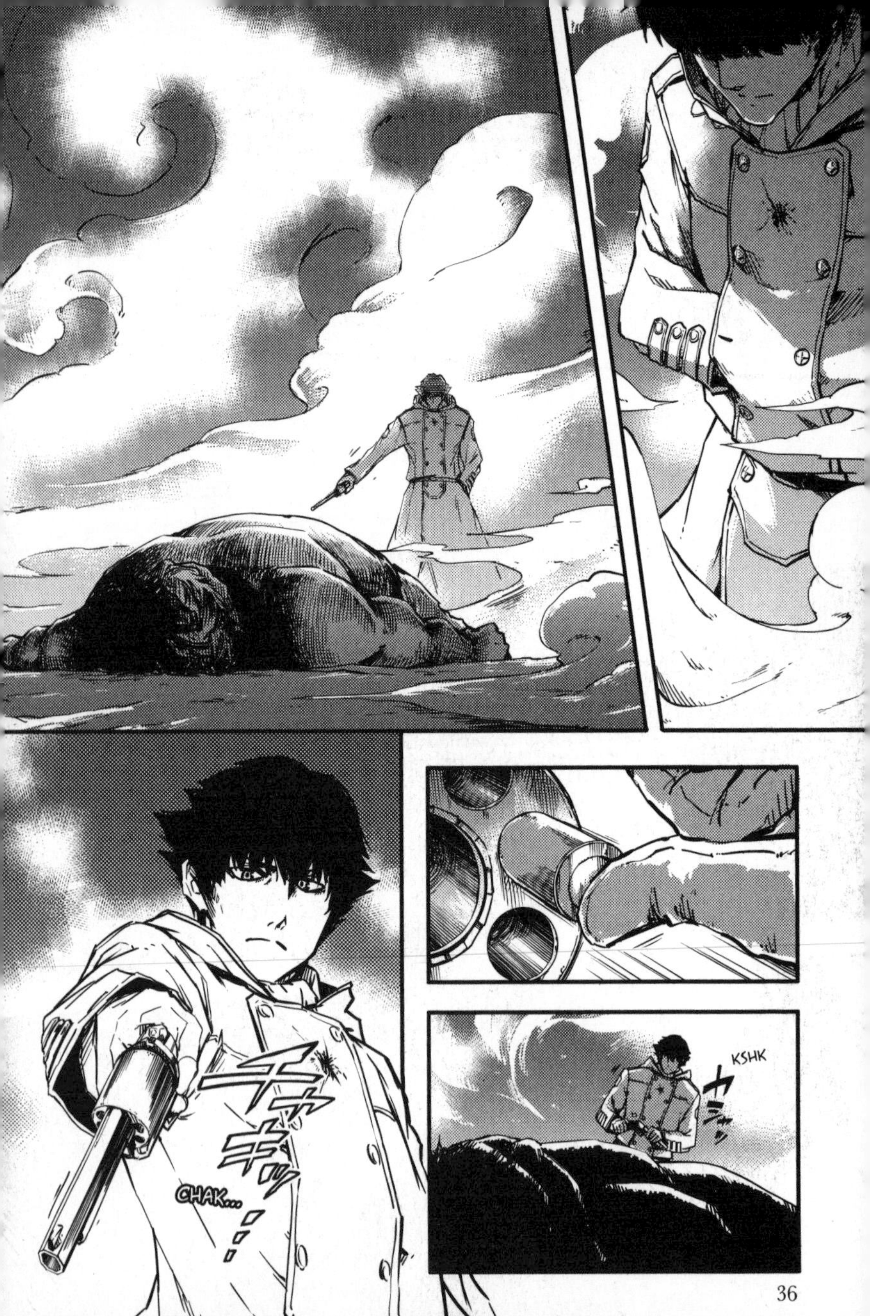
KSHK
カシャッ
CHAK...
チャキッ

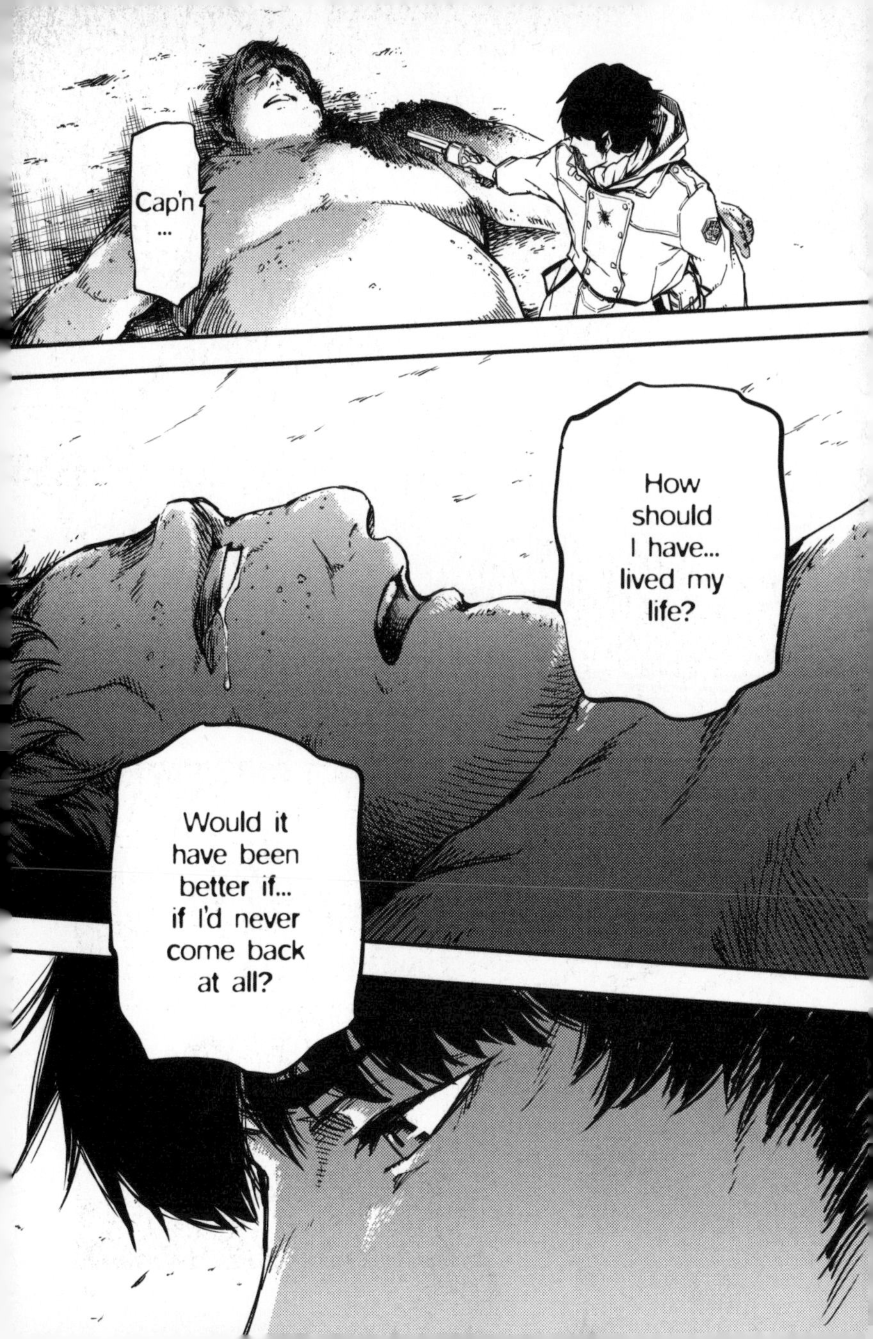
Cap'n
...
How should I have... lived my life?
Would it have been better if... if I'd never come back at all?

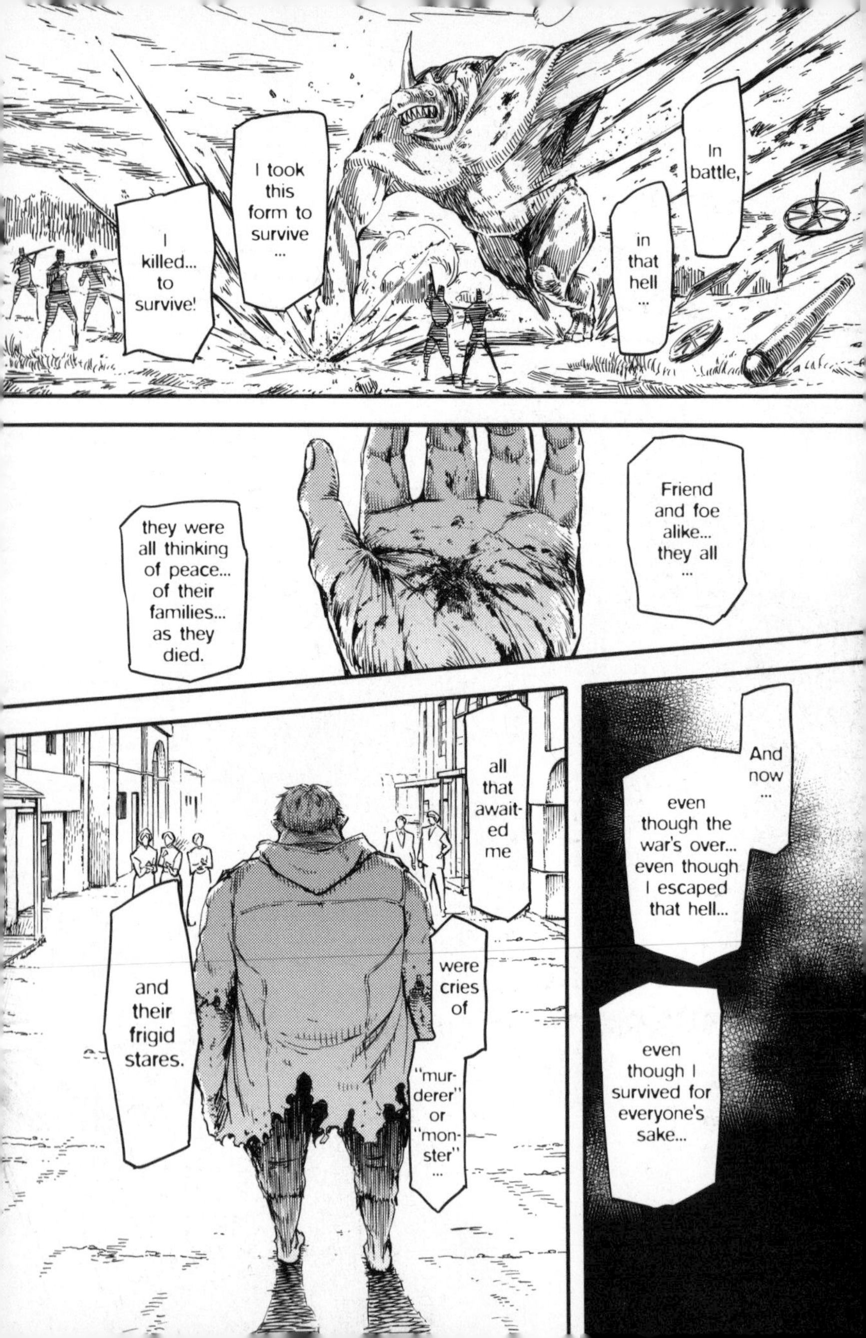
In battle,
in that hell ...
I took this form to survive ...
I killed... to survive!
Friend and foe alike... they all ...
they were all thinking of peace... of their families... as they died.
And now ...
even though the war's over... even though I escaped that hell...
even though I survived for everyone's sake...
all that await-ed me
were cries of
"mur-derer" or "mon-ster" ...
and their frigid stares.

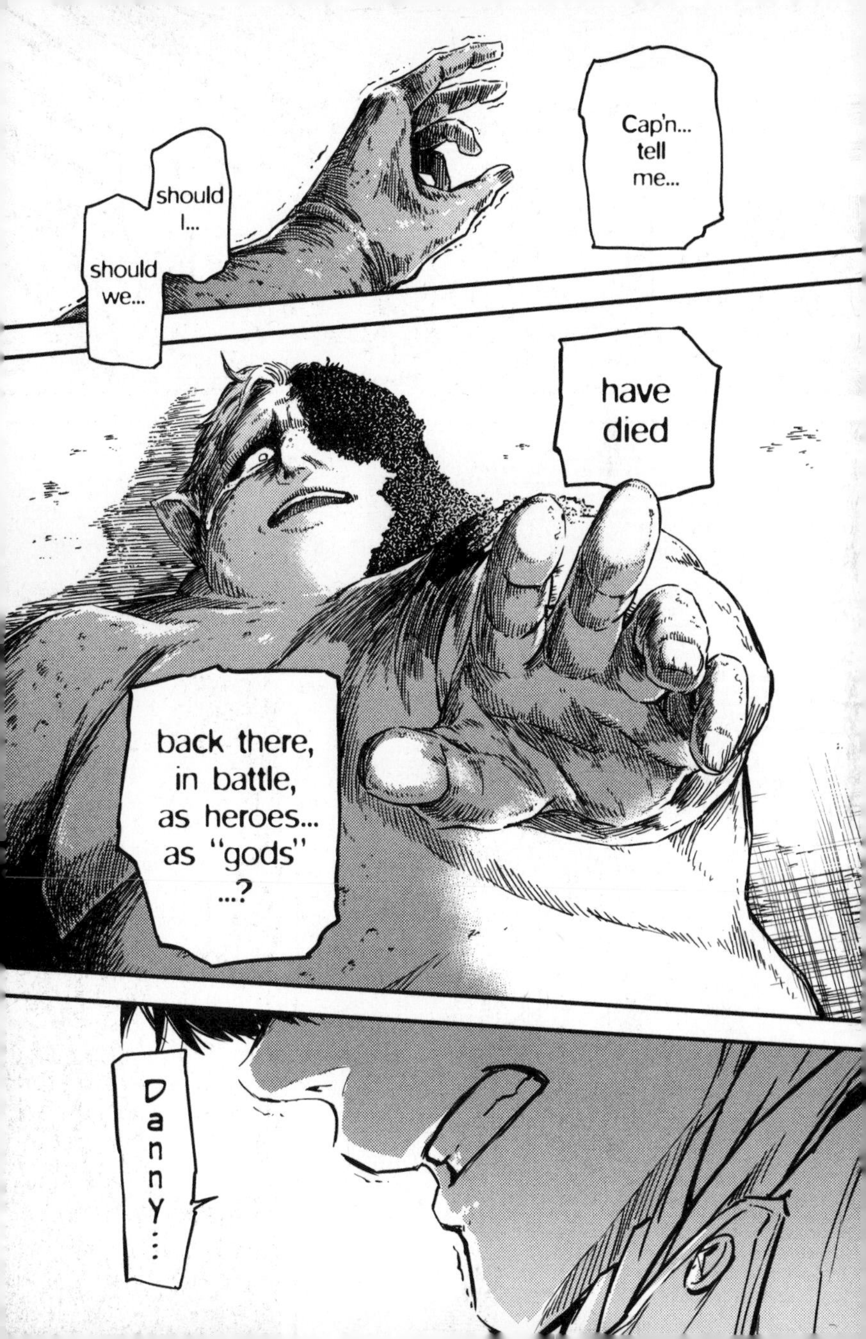
Cap'n... tell me...
should I...
should we...
have died
back there, in battle, as heroes... as "gods" ...?
Danny...

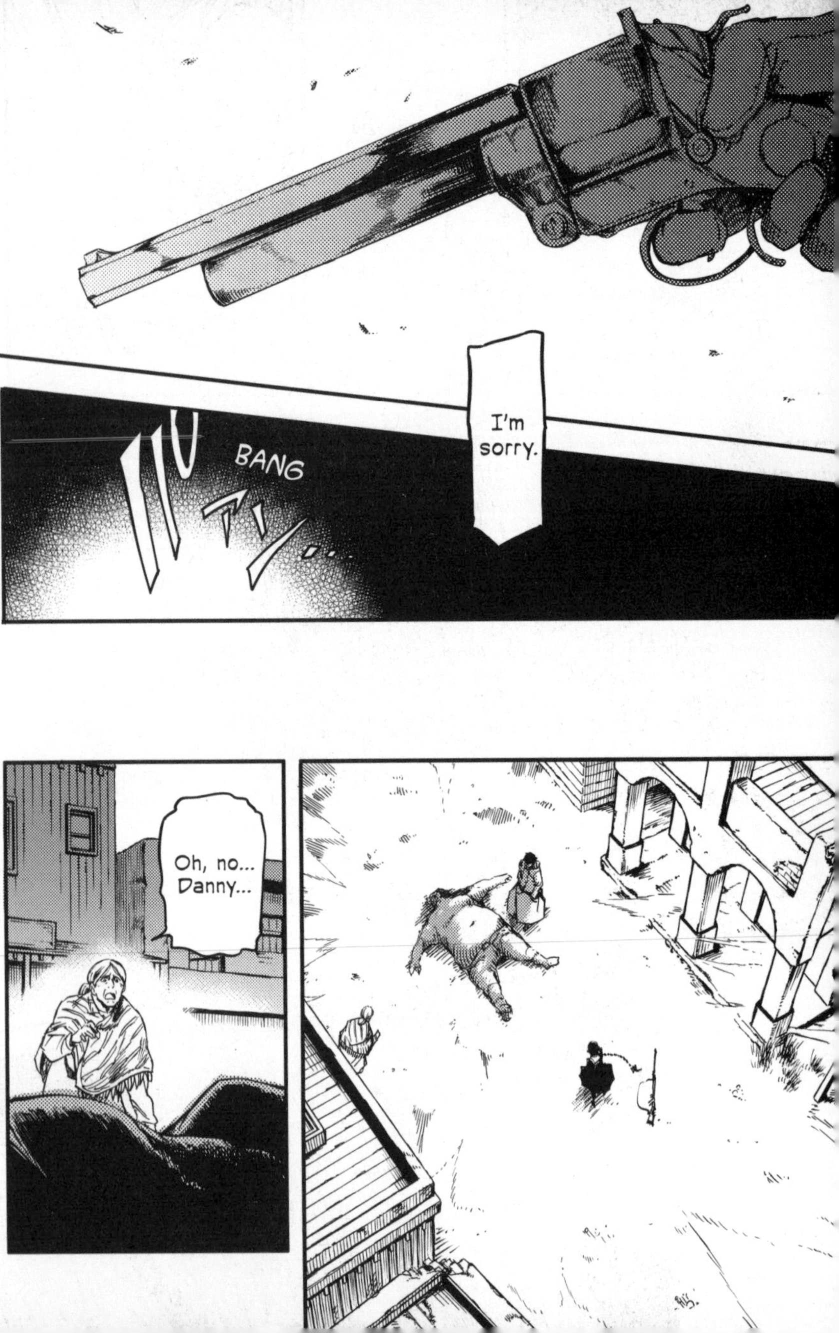
I'm sorry.
BANG
Oh, no... Danny...

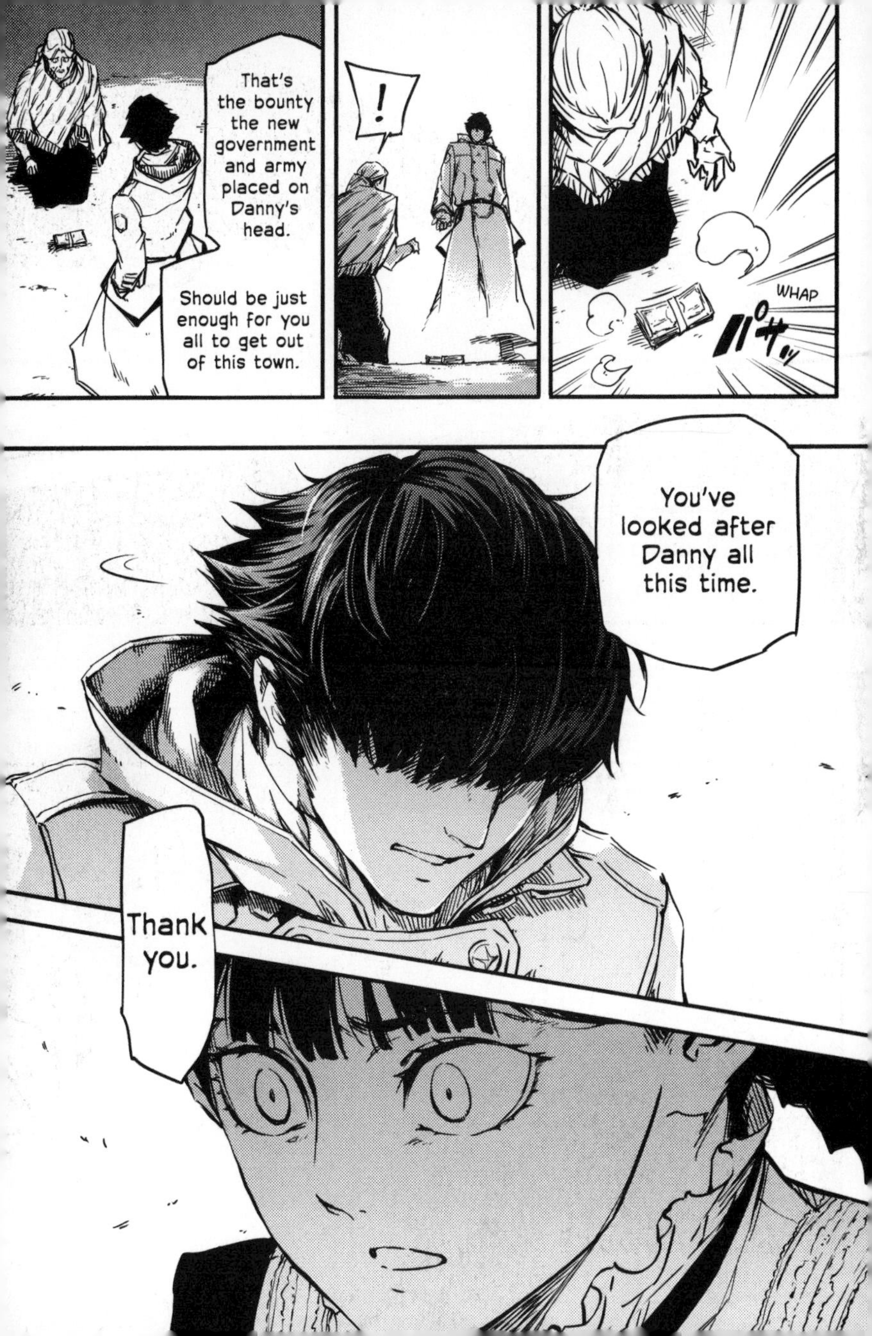
WHAP
パサッ
!
That's the bounty the new government and army placed on Danny's head.
Should be just enough for you all to get out of this town.
You've looked after Danny all this time.
Thank you.

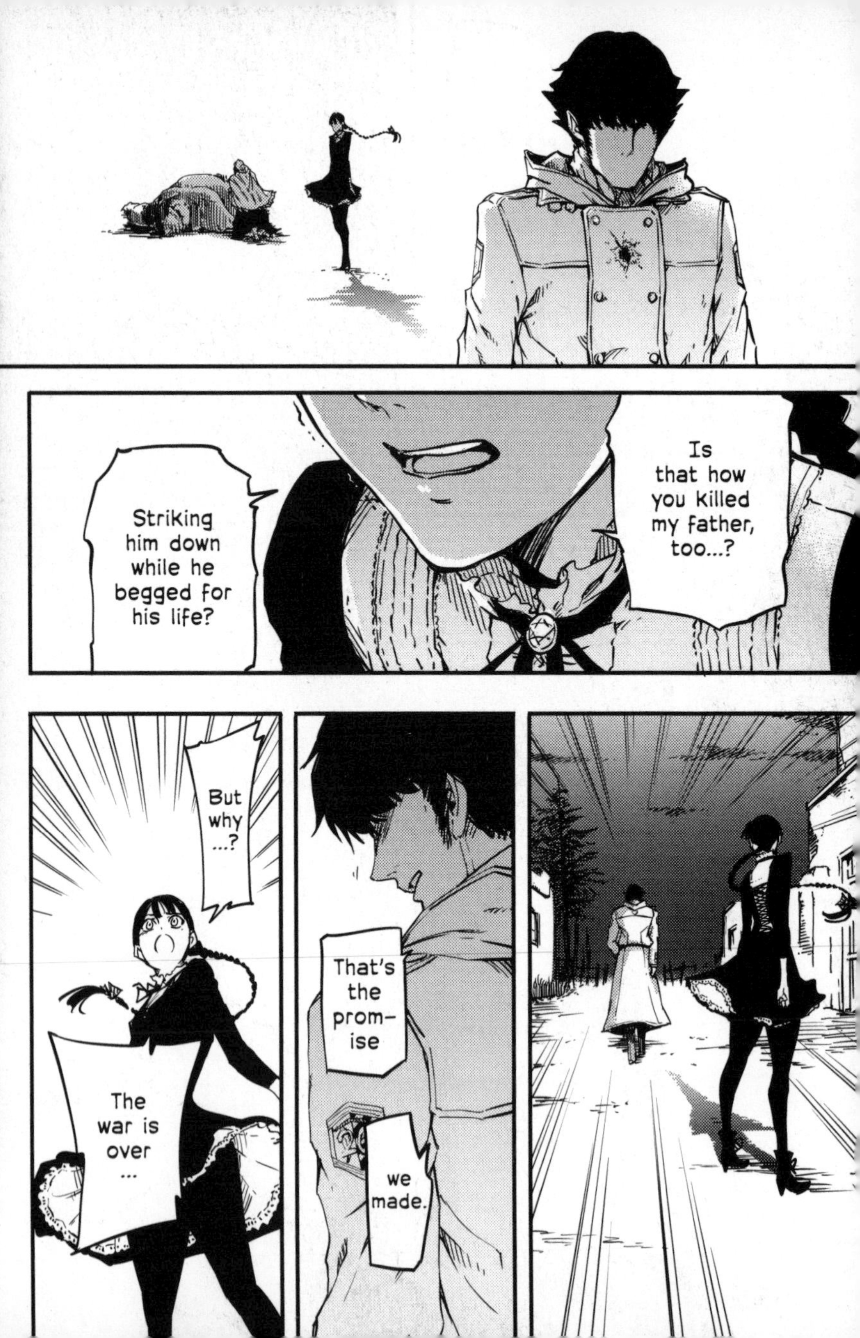
Is that how you killed my father, too...?
Striking him down while he begged for his life?
That's the prom-ise
we made.
But why ...?
The war is over ...

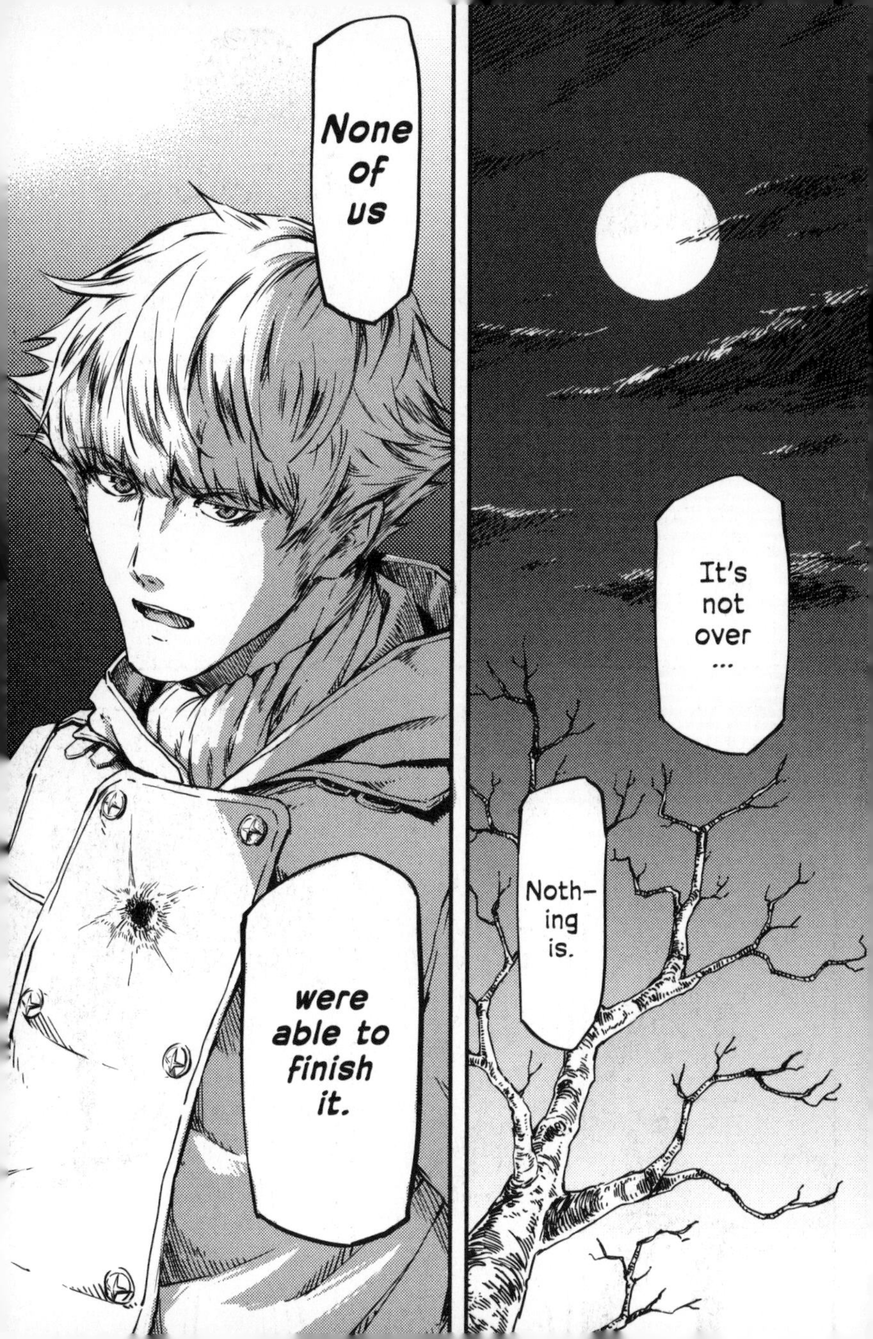
It's not over ...
Noth-ing is.
None of us
were able to finish it.

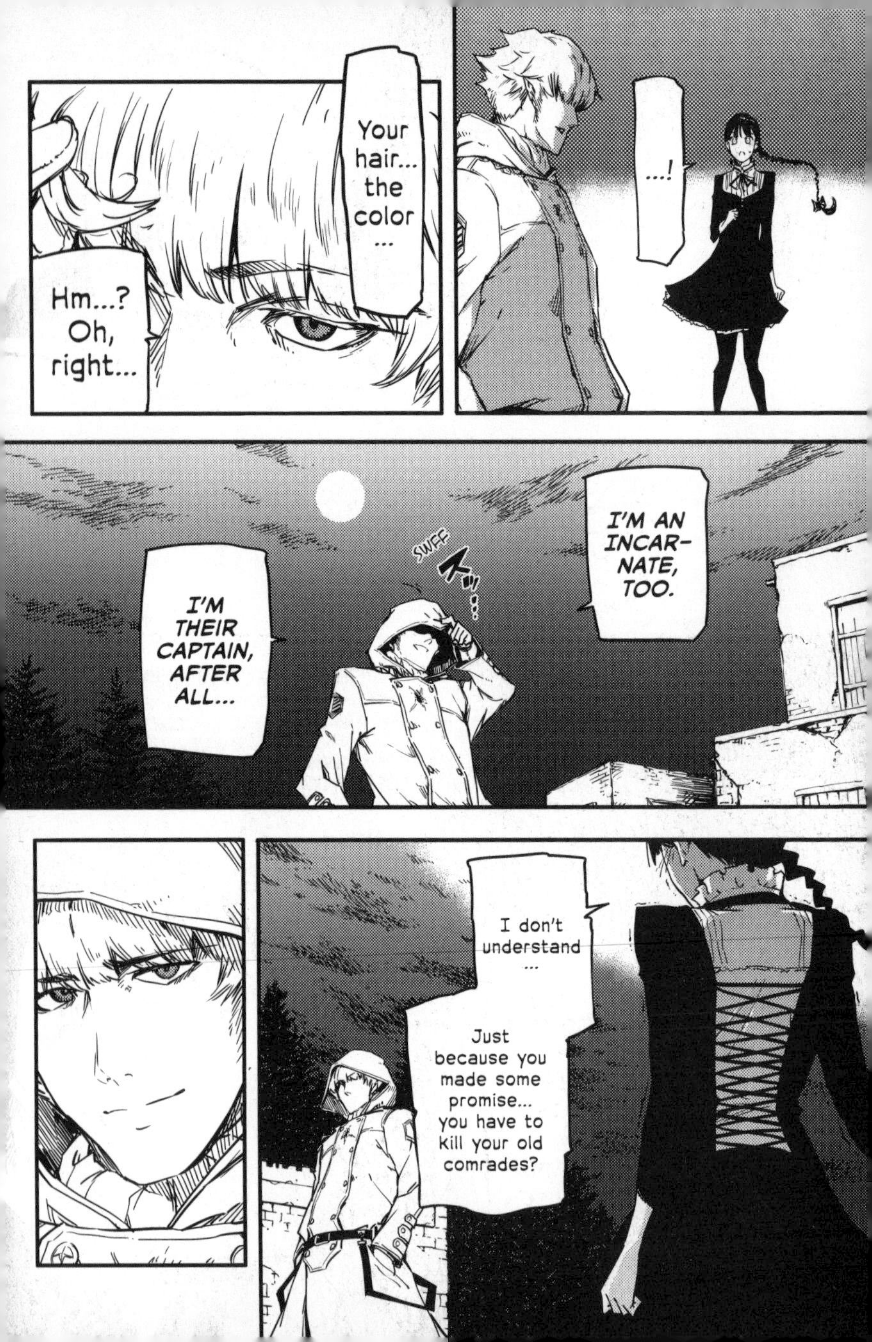
...!
Your hair... the color ...
Hm...? Oh, right...
I'M AN INCARNATE, TOO.
SWFF
I'M THEIR CAPTAIN, AFTER ALL...
I don't understand ...
Just because you made some promise... you have to kill your old comrades?

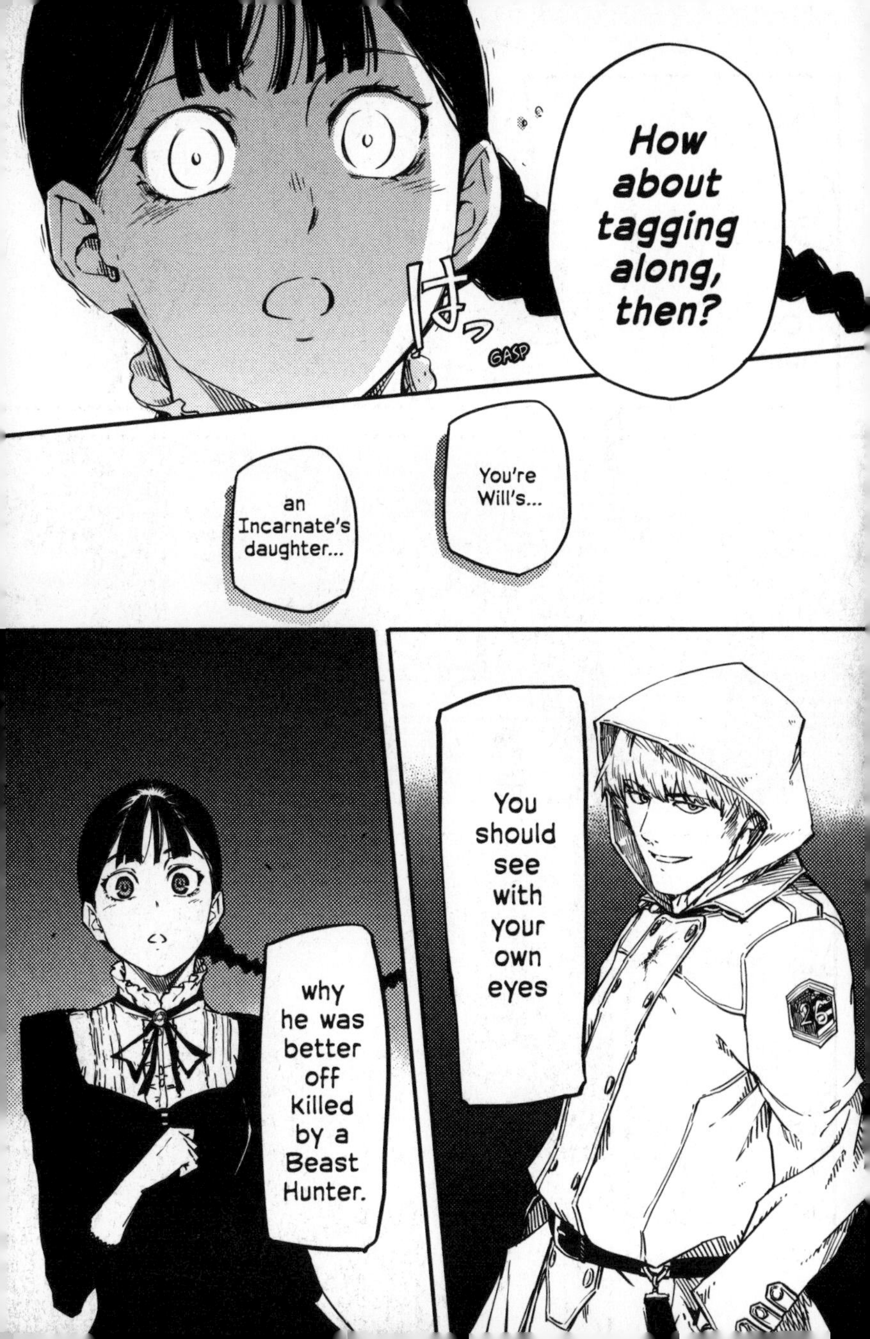
How about tagging along, then?
はっ
GASP
You're Will's...
an Incarnate's daughter...
You should see with your own eyes
why he was better off killed by a Beast Hunter.

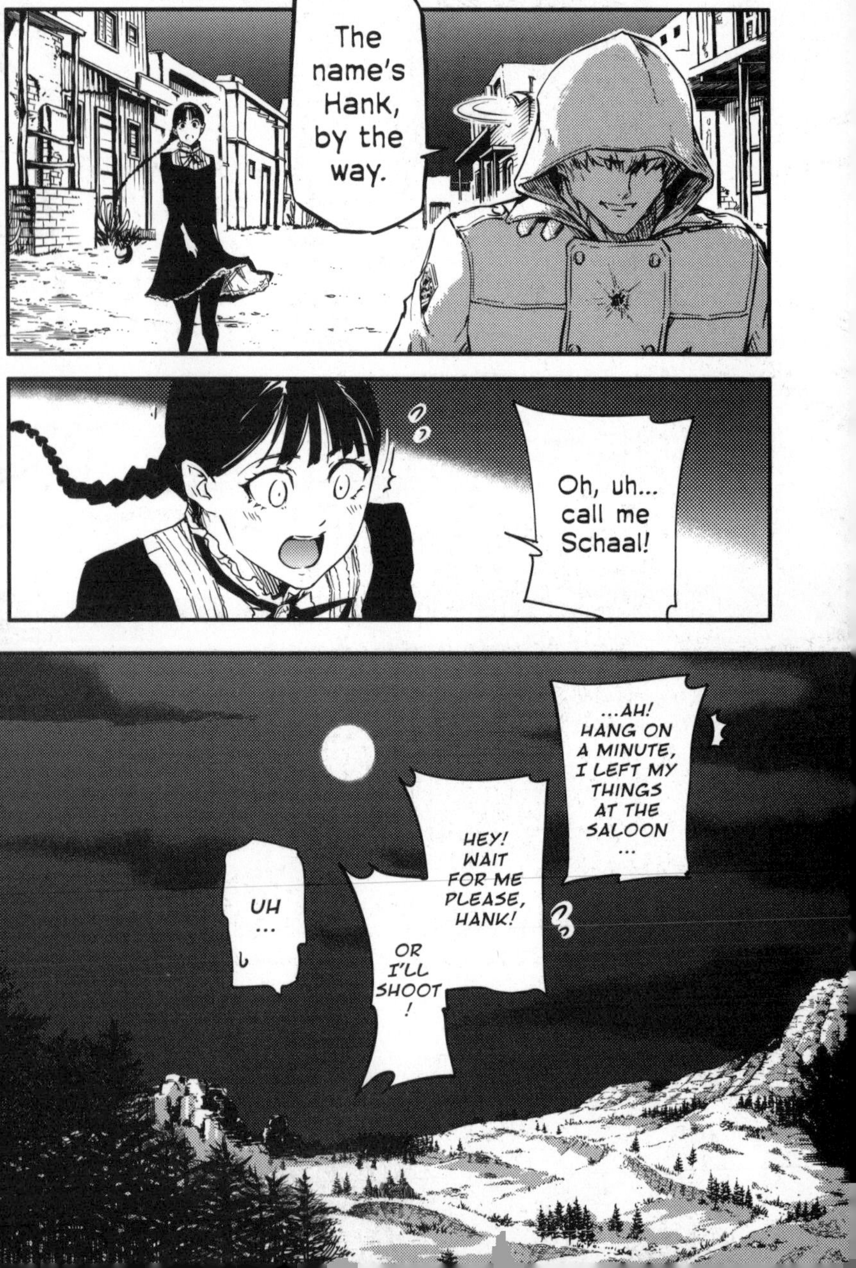
The name's Hank, by the way.
Oh, uh... call me Schaal!
...AH! HANG ON A MINUTE, I LEFT MY THINGS AT THE SALOON ...
HEY! WAIT FOR ME PLEASE, HANK!
OR I'LL SHOOT!
UH ...

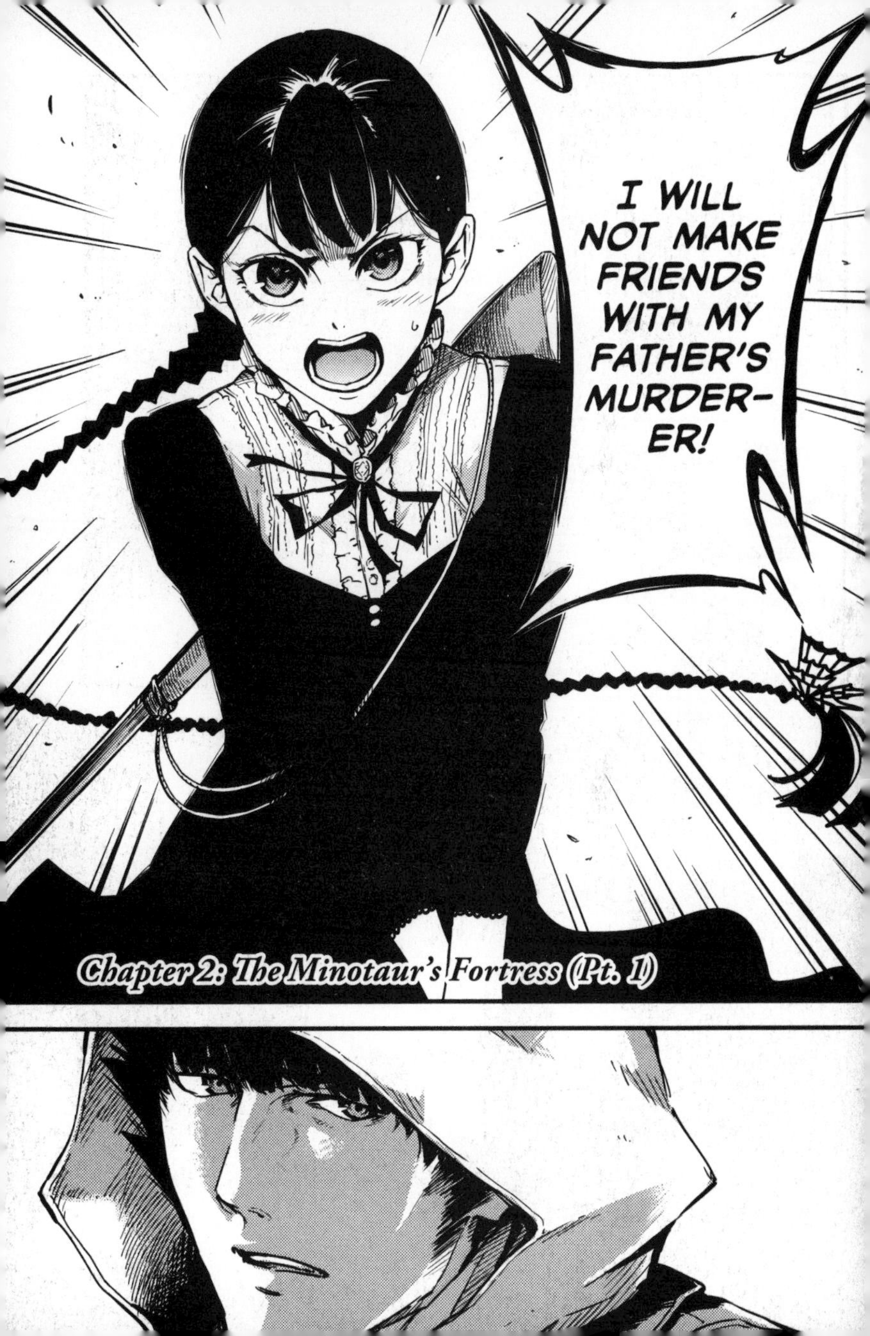
I WILL NOT MAKE FRIENDS WITH MY FATHER'S MURDER-ER!
Chapter 2: The Minotaur's Fortress (Pt. 1)

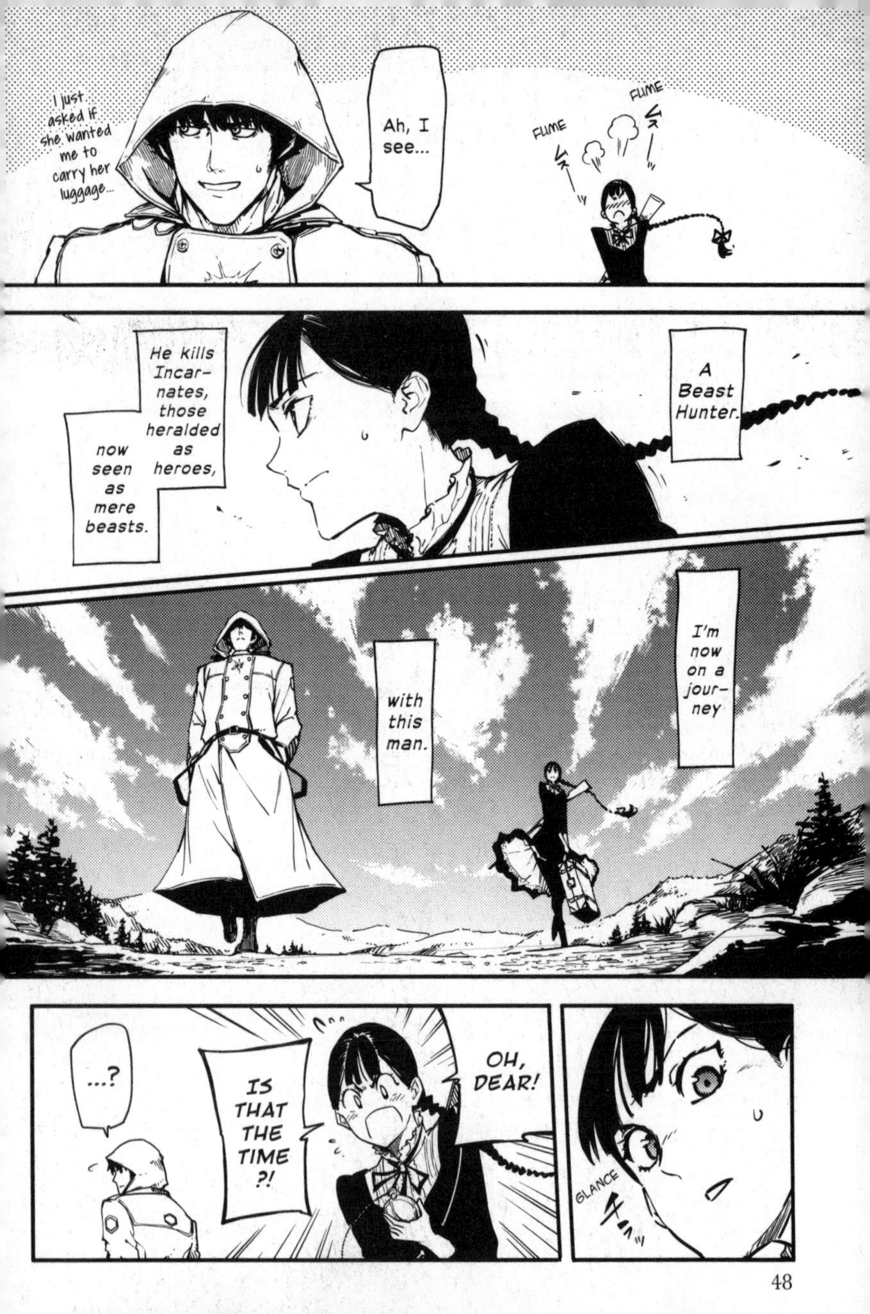
FUME
FUME
Ah, I see...
I just asked if she wanted me to carry her luggage...
A Beast Hunter.
He kills Incarnates, those heralded as heroes,
now seen as mere beasts.
I'm now on a journey
with this man.
GLANCE
OH, DEAR!
IS THAT THE TIME?!
...?

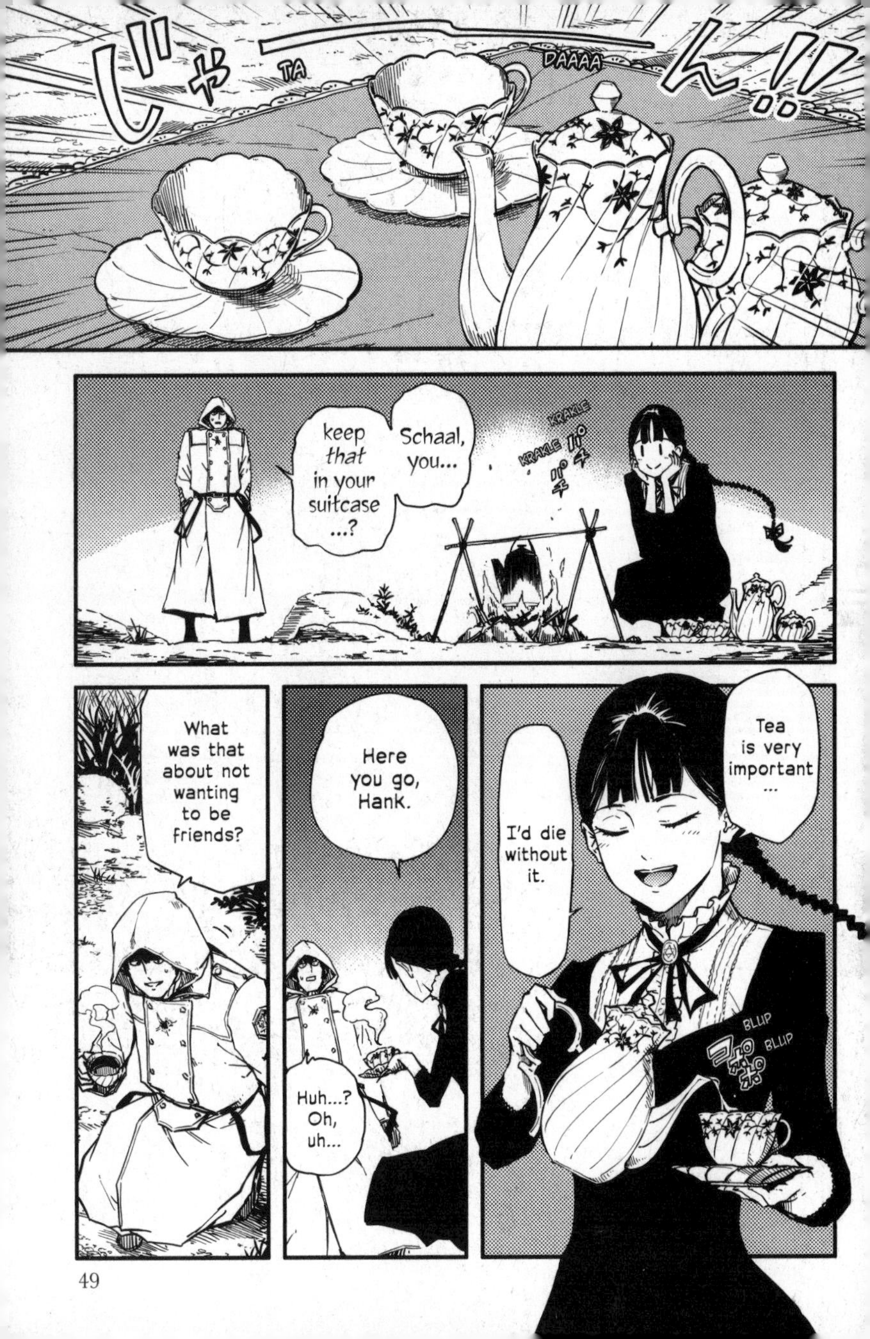

じゃーん!!
TA DAAAA
KRAKLE
KRAKLE
パキ
パキ
Schaal, you...
keep *that* in your suitcase ...?
Tea is very important ...
I'd die without it.
BLUP BLUP
コポポ
Here you go, Hank.
Huh...? Oh, uh...
What was that about not wanting to be friends?

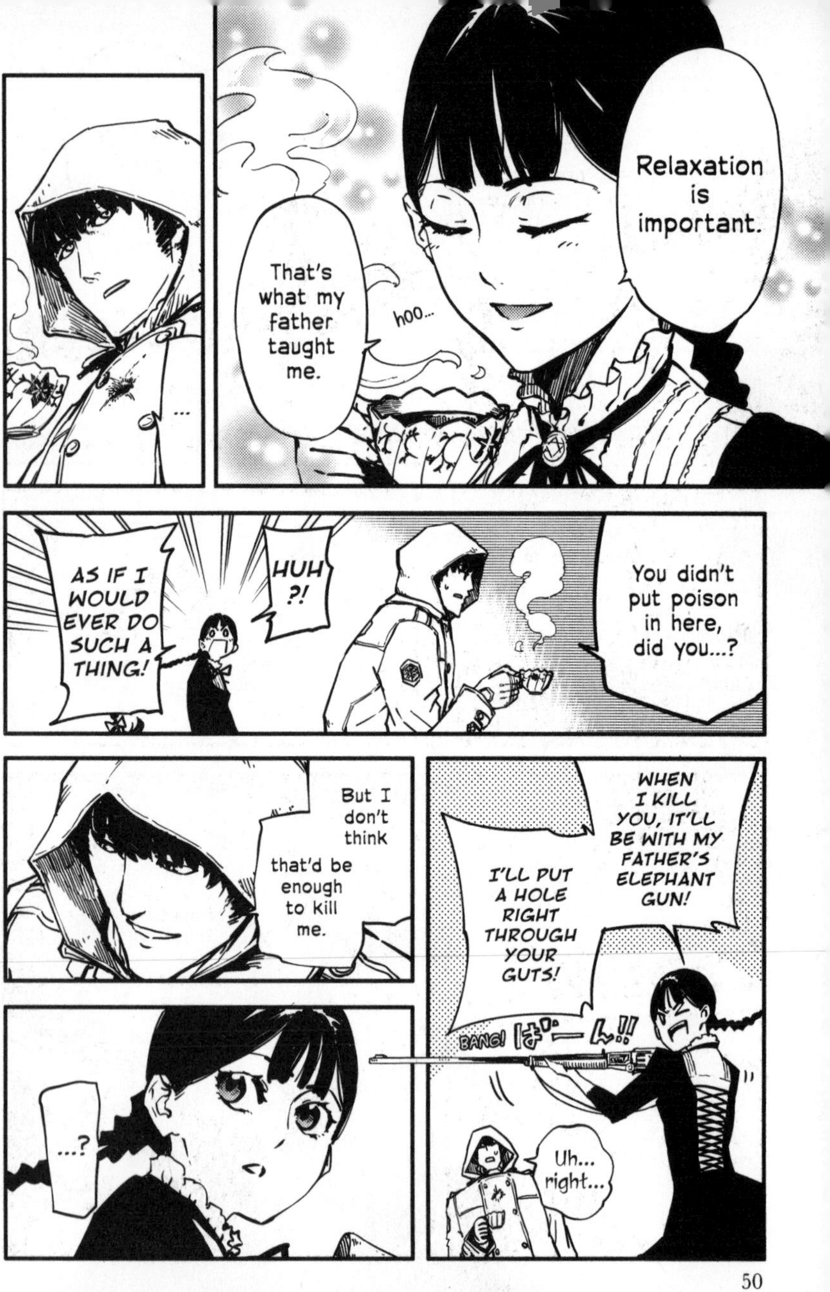
Relaxation is important.
That's what my father taught me.
hoo...
...
You didn't put poison in here, did you...?
HUH?!
AS IF I WOULD EVER DO SUCH A THING!
WHEN I KILL YOU, IT'LL BE WITH MY FATHER'S ELEPHANT GUN!
I'LL PUT A HOLE RIGHT THROUGH YOUR GUTS!
BANG! はどーん!!
Uh... right...
But I don't think that'd be enough to kill me.
...?

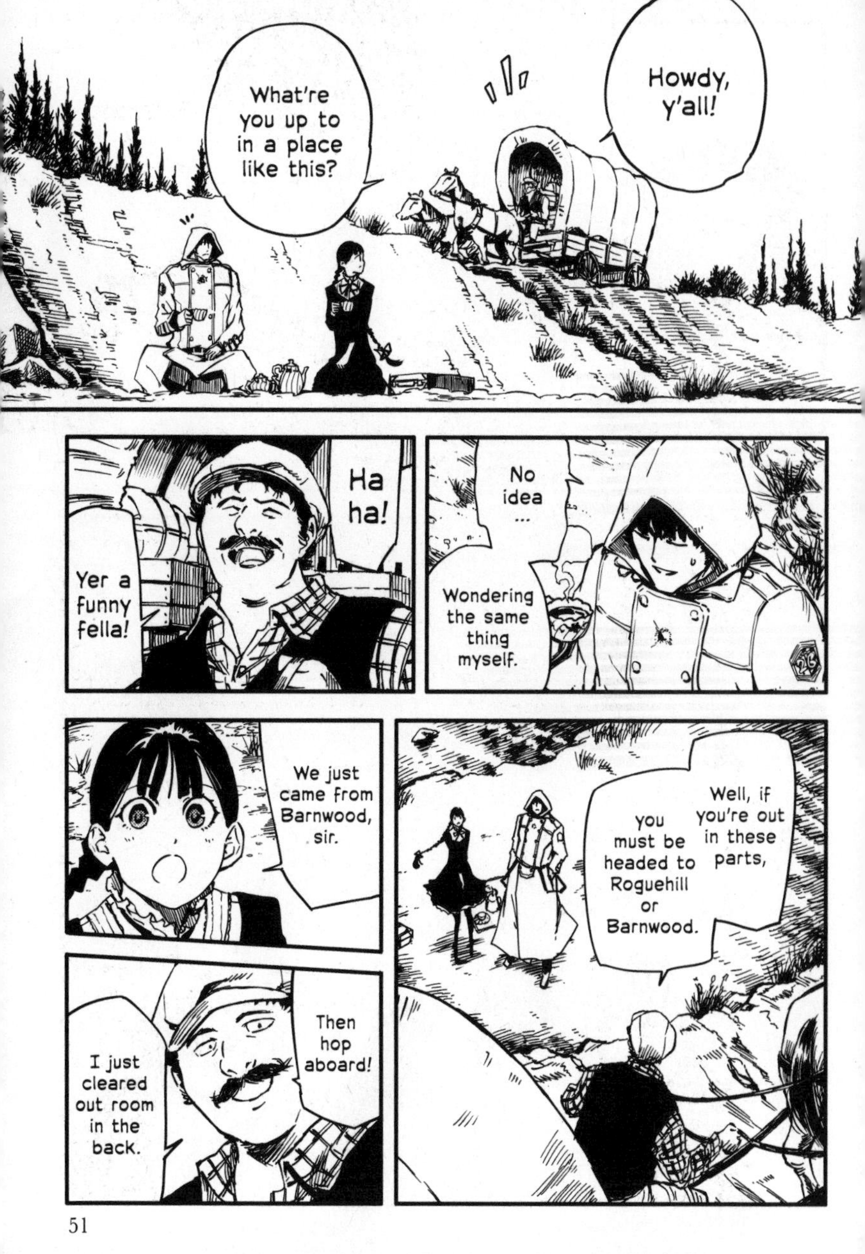
Howdy, y'all!
What're you up to in a place like this?
No idea...
Wondering the same thing myself.
Ha ha!
Yer a funny fella!
Well, if you're out in these parts, you must be headed to Roguehill or Barnwood.
We just came from Barnwood, sir.
Then hop aboard!
I just cleared out room in the back.

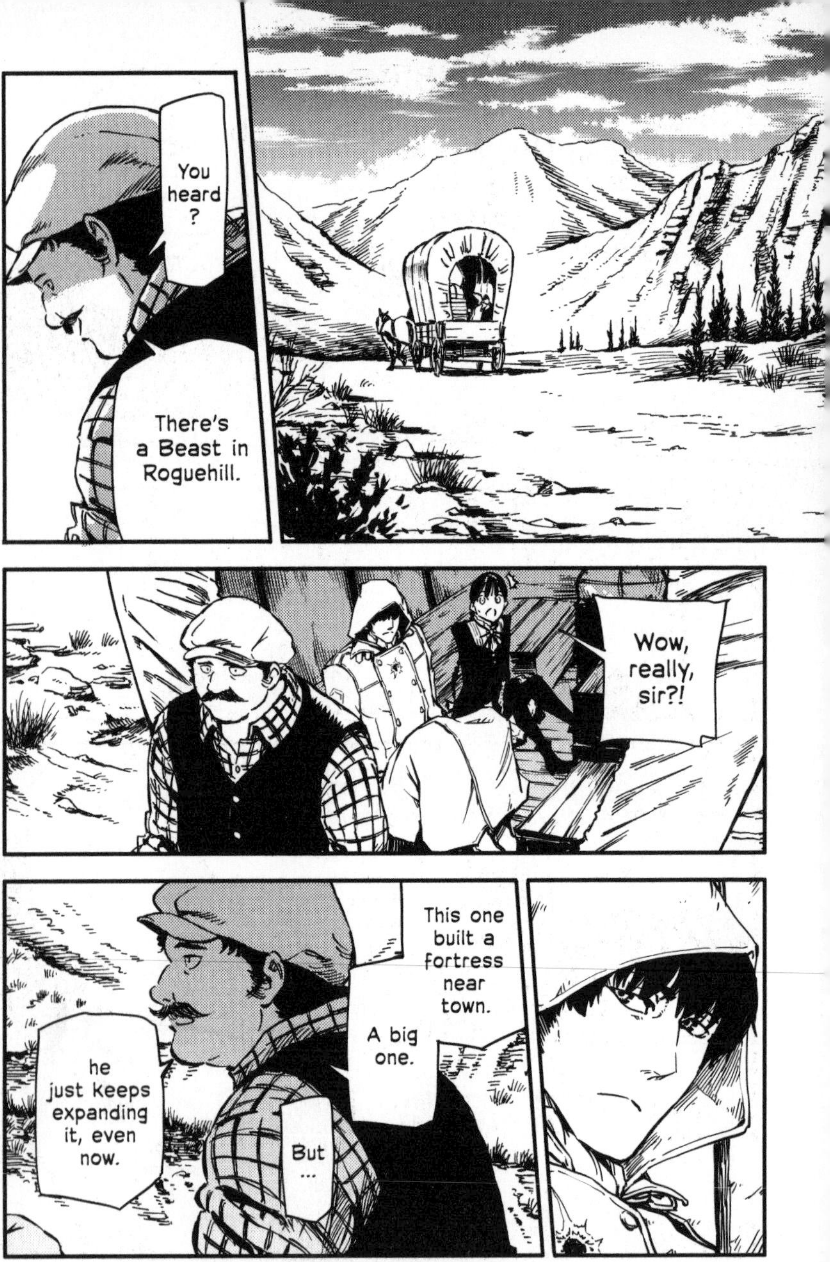
You heard?
There's a Beast in Roguehill.
Wow, really, sir?!
This one built a fortress near town.
A big one.
But...
he just keeps expanding it, even now.

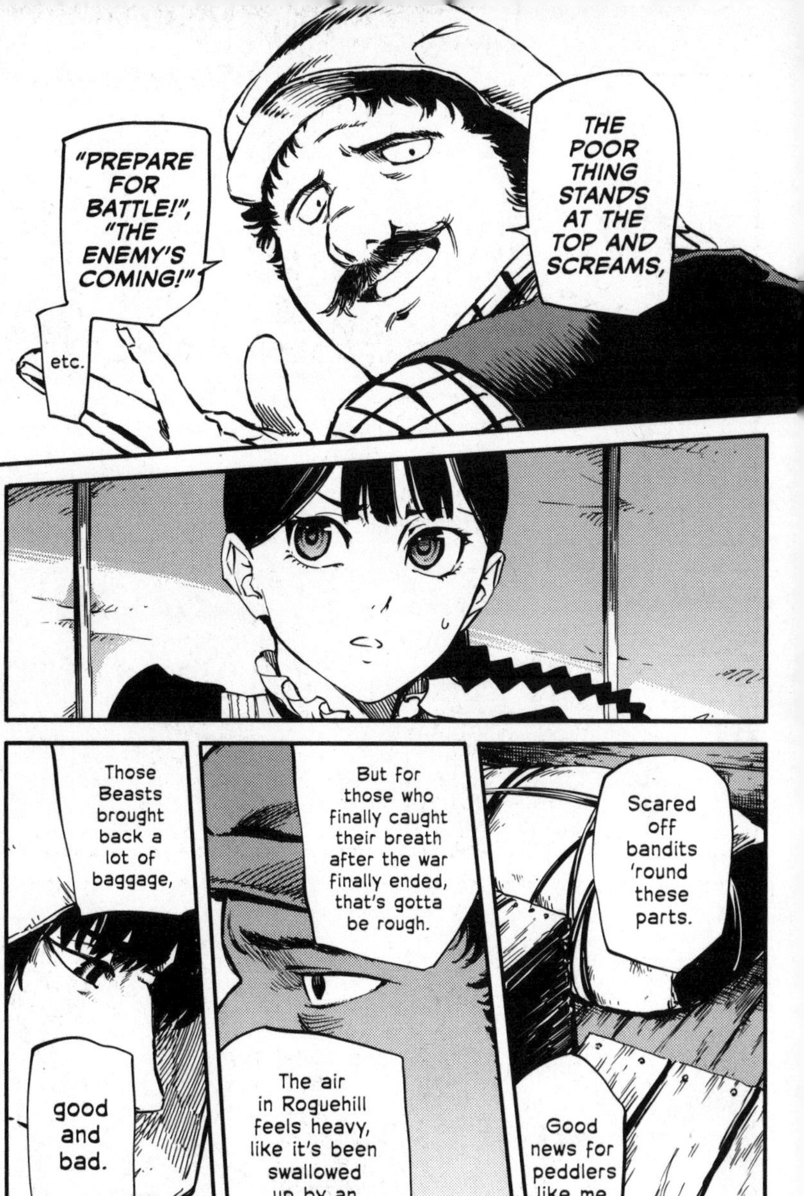
THE POOR THING STANDS AT THE TOP AND SCREAMS,
"PREPARE FOR BATTLE!", "THE ENEMY'S COMING!"
etc.
Scared off bandits 'round these parts.
Good news for peddlers like me.
But for those who finally caught their breath after the war finally ended, that's gotta be rough.
The air in Roguehill feels heavy, like it's been swallowed up by an endless war.
Those Beasts brought back a lot of baggage,
good and bad.

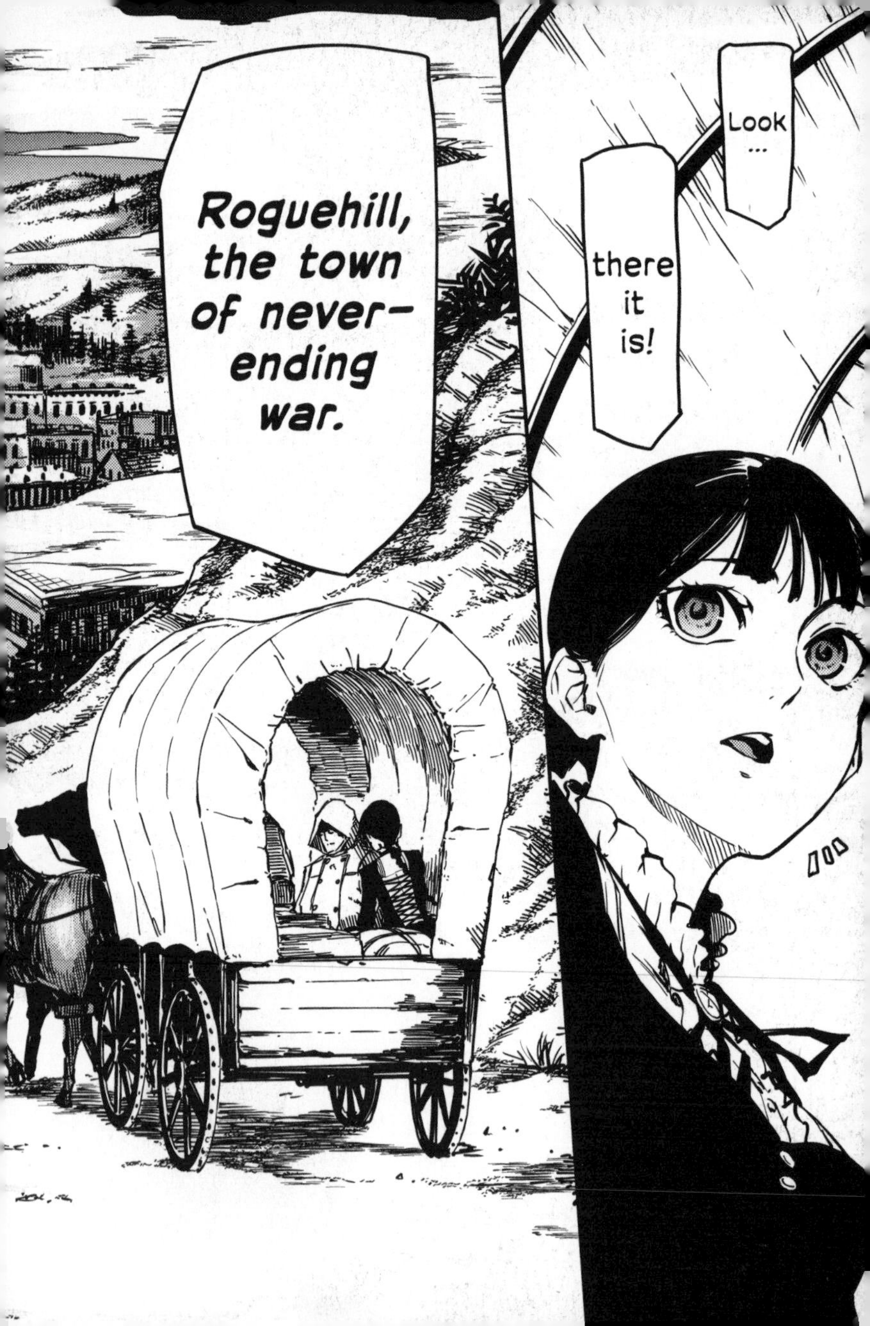
Look ...
there it is!
Roguehill, the town of never-ending war.

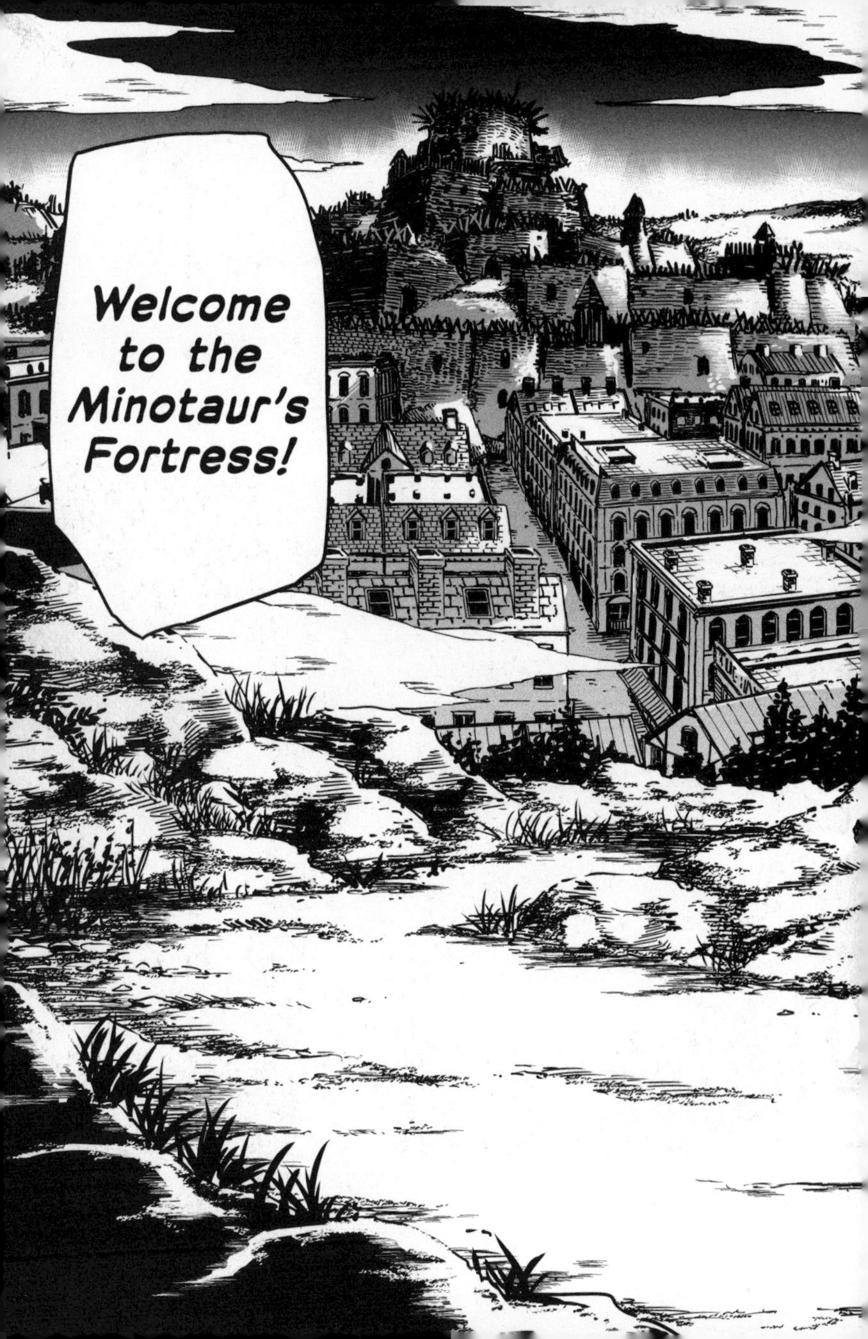
Welcome to the Minotaur's Fortress!

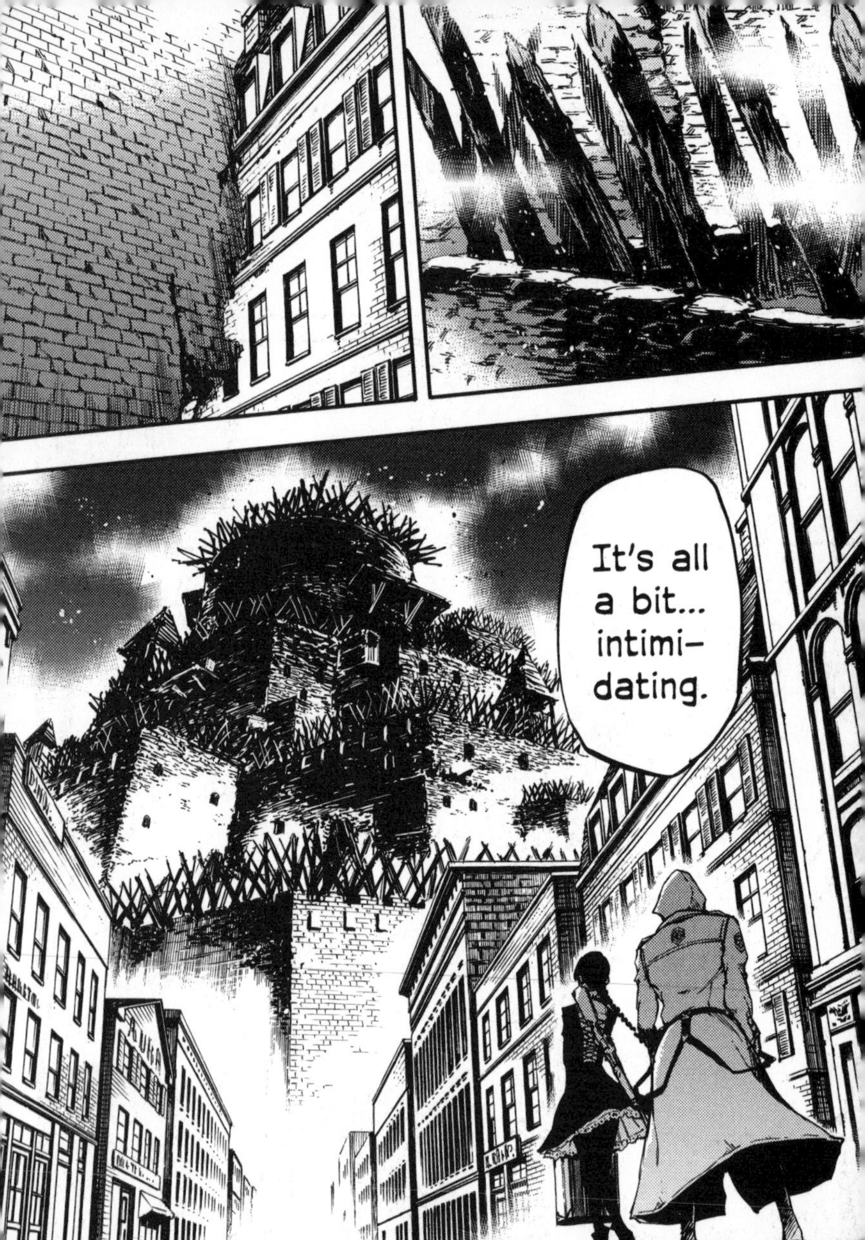
It's all a bit... intimi-dating.

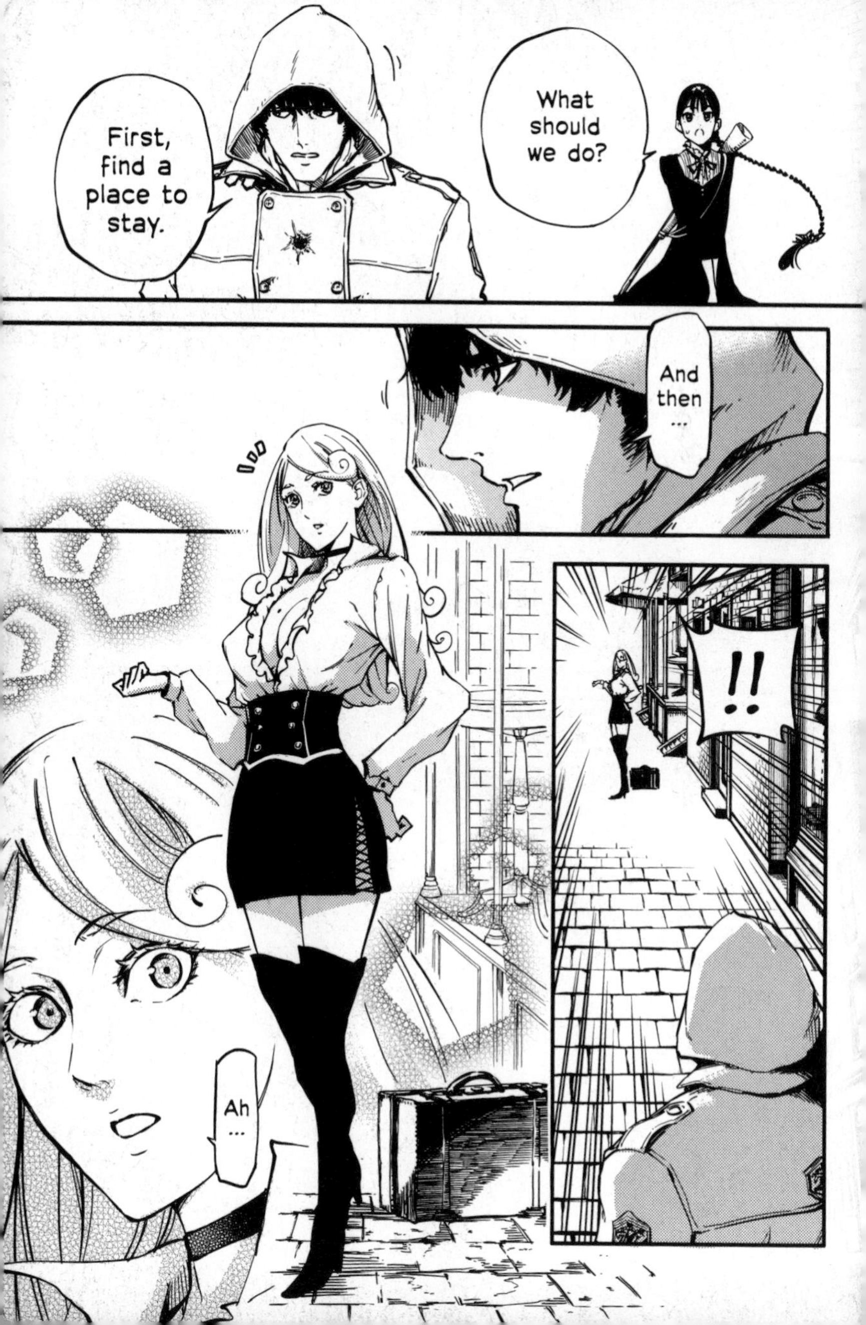
What should we do?
First, find a place to stay.
And then ...
!!
Ah ...

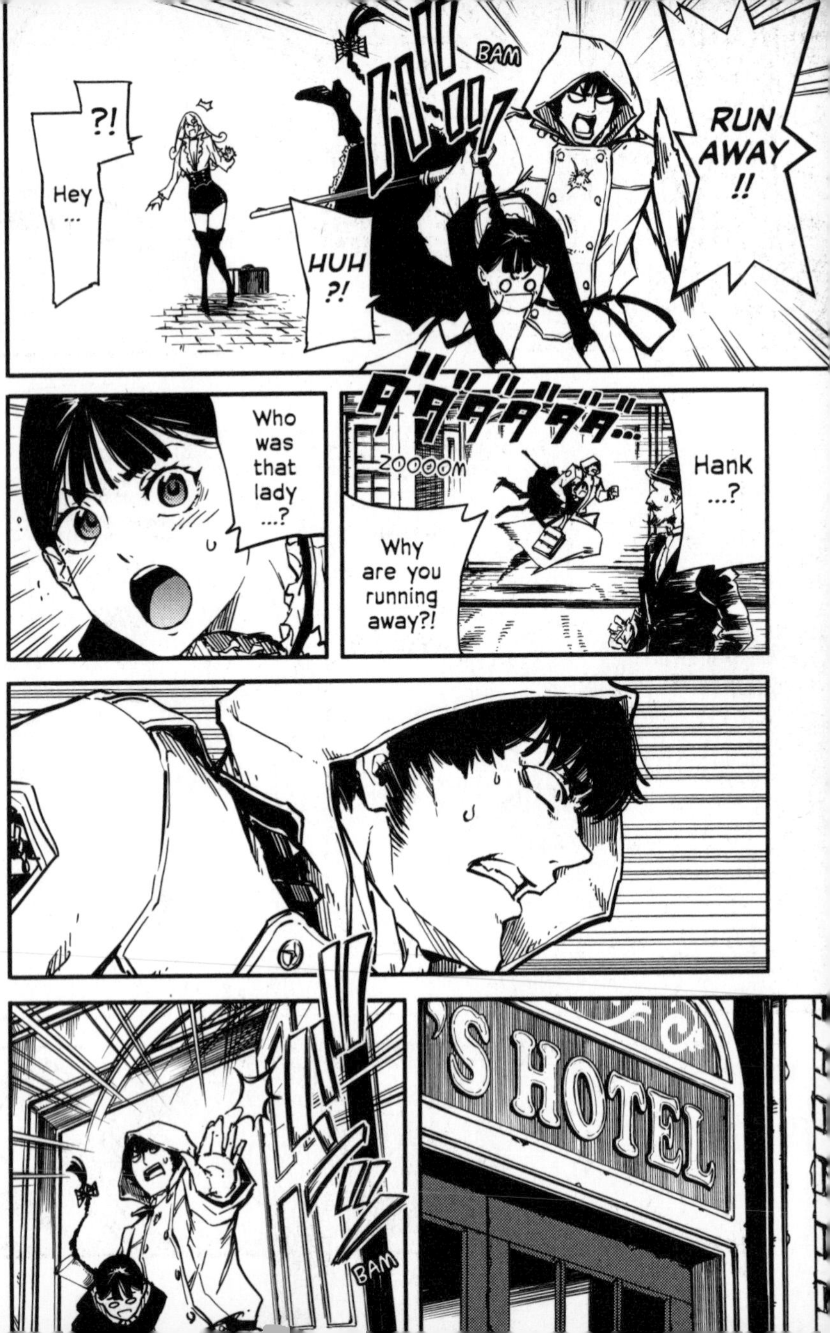
RUN AWAY!!
BAM
HUH?!
?!
Hey...
ダダダダダダ...
Hank...?
ZOOOOM
Why are you running away?!
Who was that lady...?
'S HOTEL
BAM

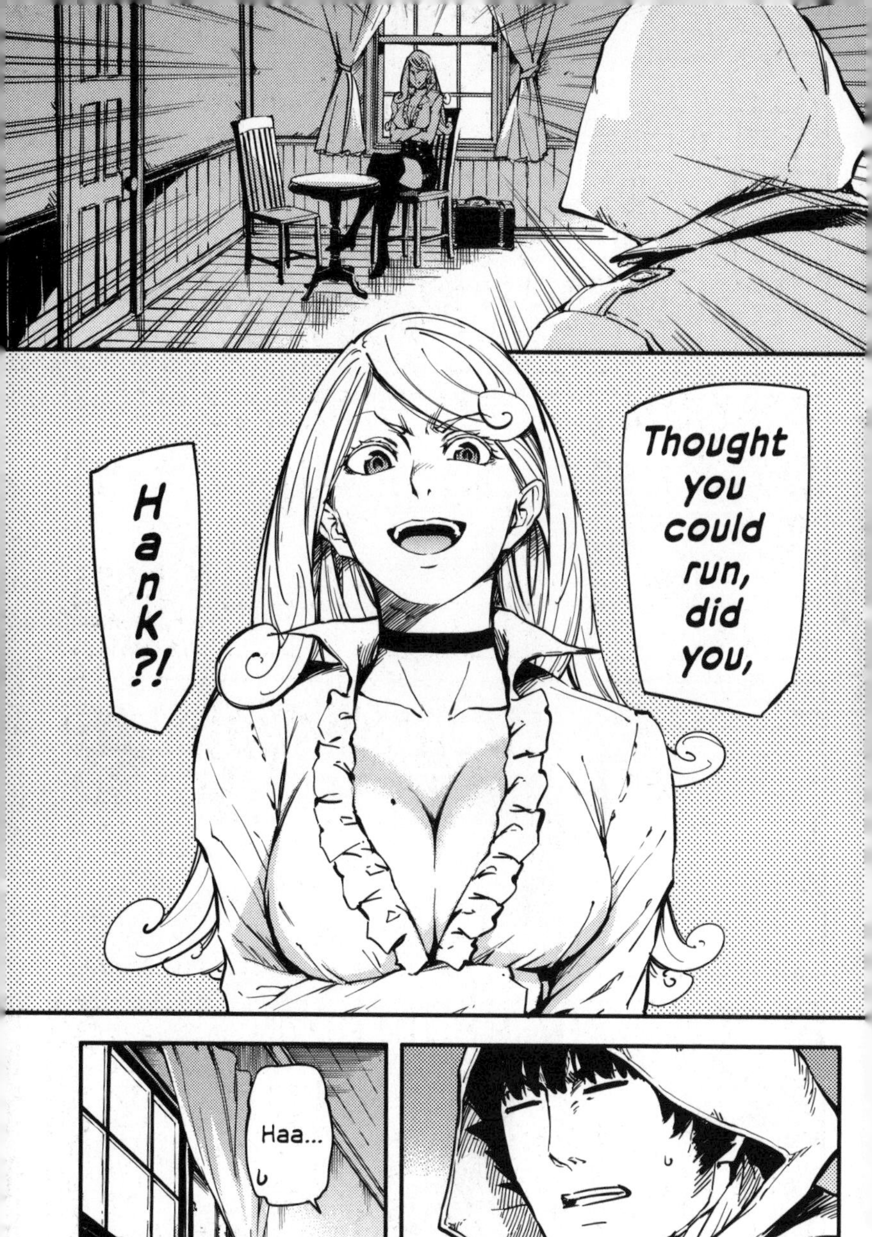
Thought you could run, did you,
Hank?!
Haa...

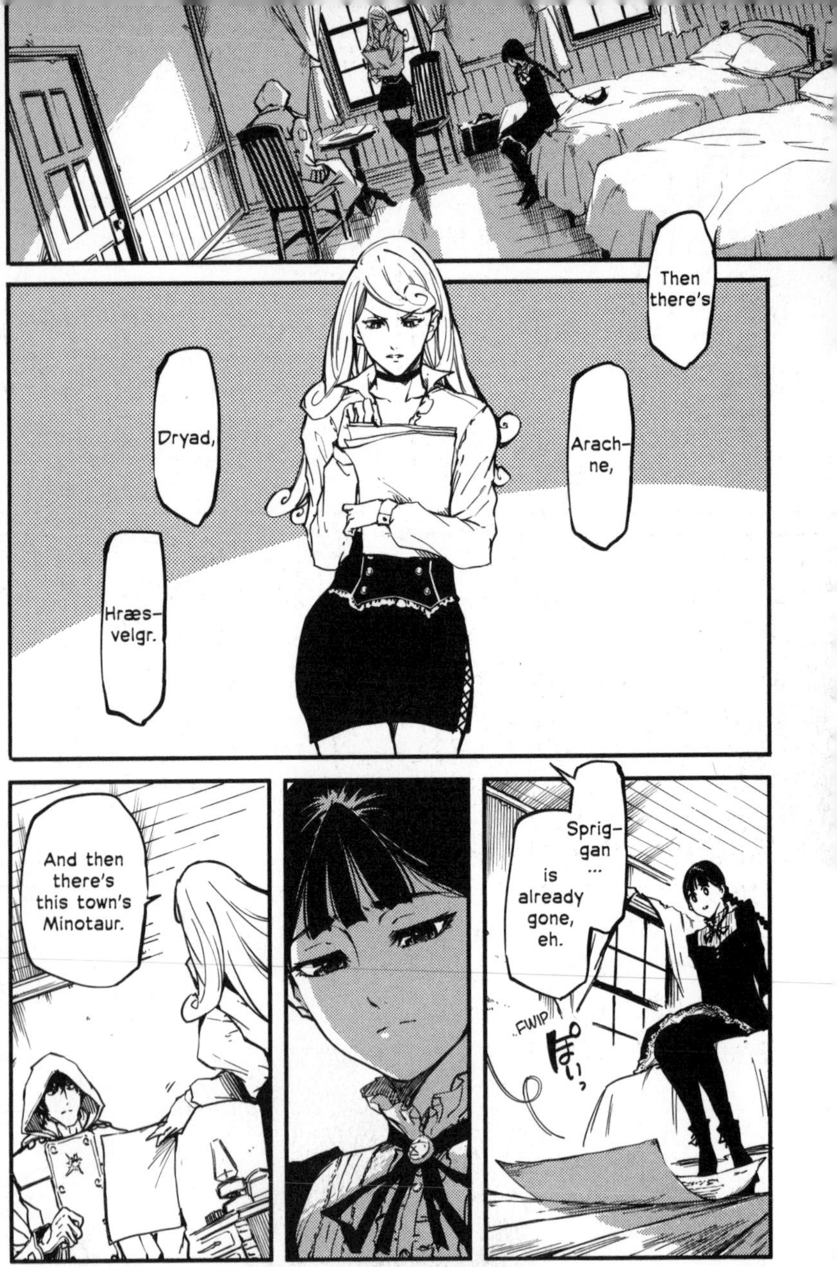
Then there's
Arach-ne,
Dryad,
Hræs-velgr.
Sprig-gan ... is already gone, eh.
..FWIP
ぽいっ
And then there's this town's Minotaur.

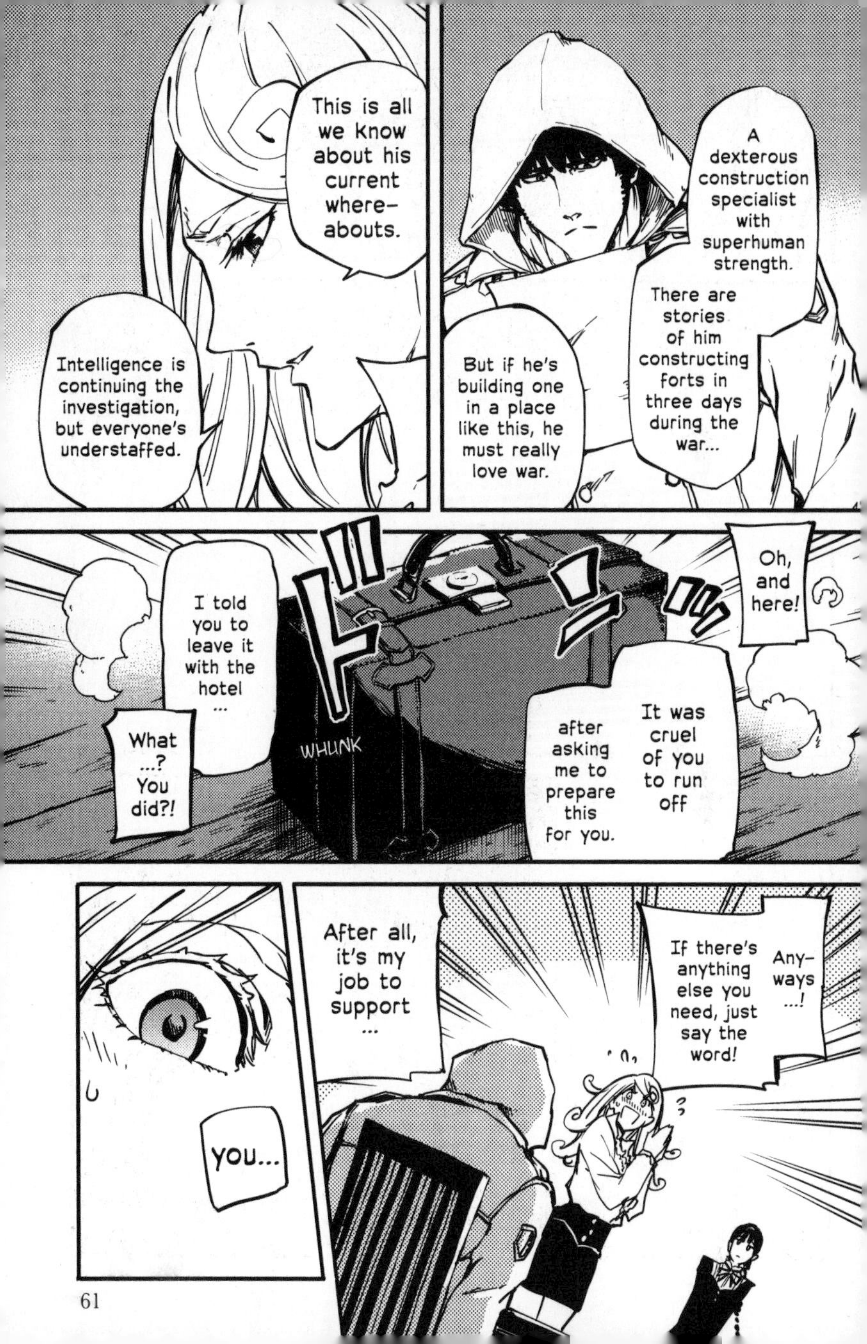
A dexterous construction specialist with superhuman strength.
There are stories of him constructing forts in three days during the war...
But if he's building one in a place like this, he must really love war.
This is all we know about his current where-abouts.
Intelligence is continuing the investigation, but everyone's understaffed.
Oh, and here!
ドン
It was cruel of you to run off
after asking me to prepare this for you.
WHUNK
I told you to leave it with the hotel ...
What ...? You did?!
Any-ways ...!
If there's anything else you need, just say the word!
After all, it's my job to support ...
YOU...

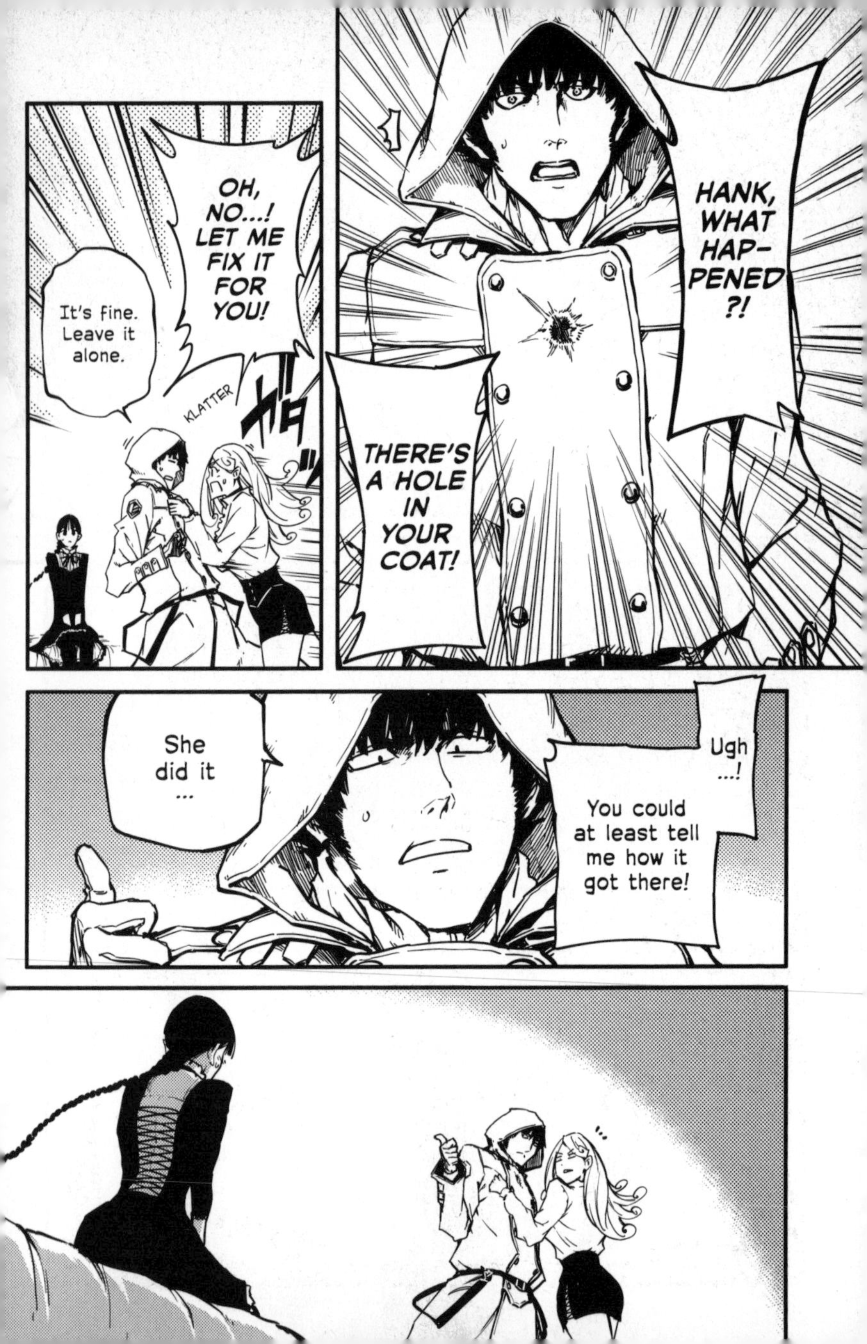
HANK, WHAT HAP-PENED ?!
THERE'S A HOLE IN YOUR COAT!
OH, NO...! LET ME FIX IT FOR YOU!
KLATTER
It's fine. Leave it alone.
Ugh ...!
You could at least tell me how it got there!
She did it ...

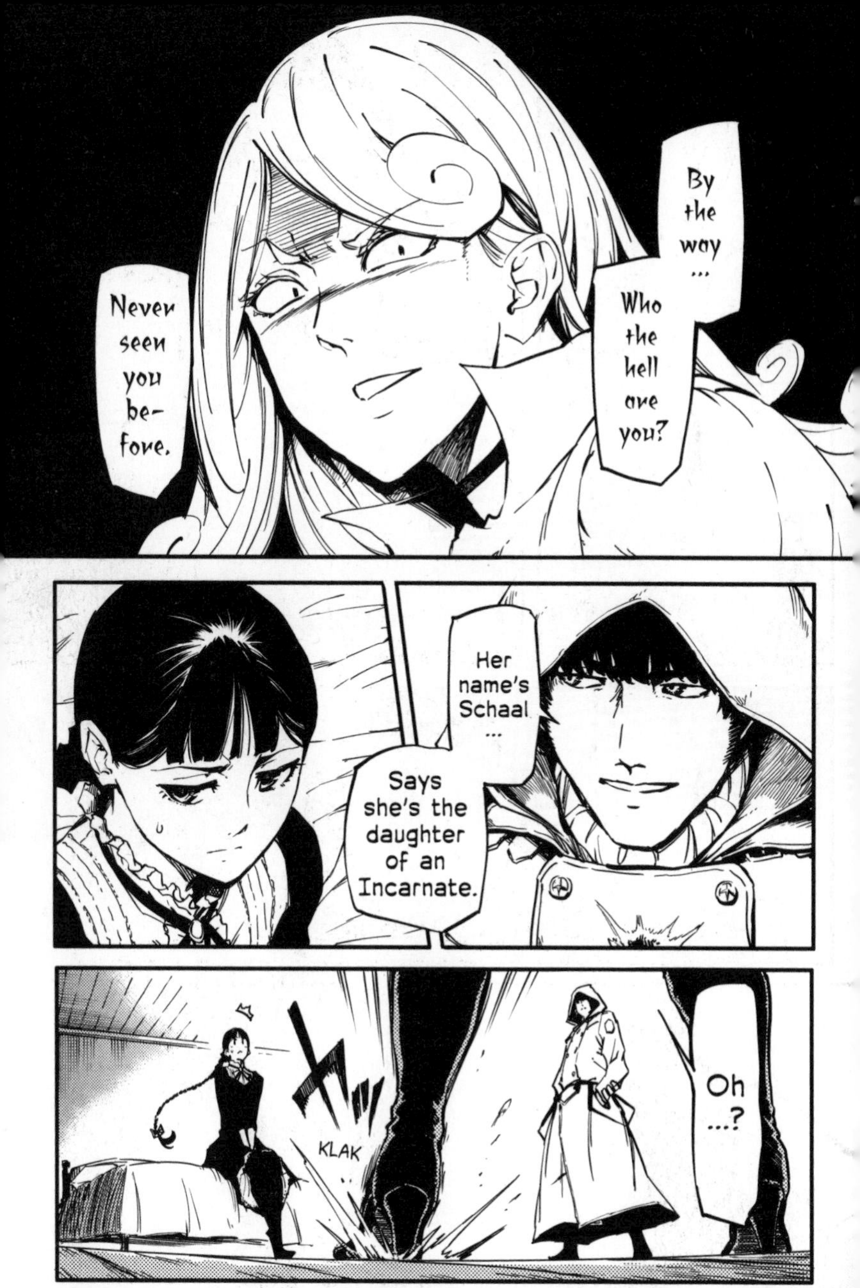
By the way...
Who the hell are you?
Never seen you be-fore.
Her name's Schaal...
Says she's the daughter of an Incarnate.
Oh...?
KLAK

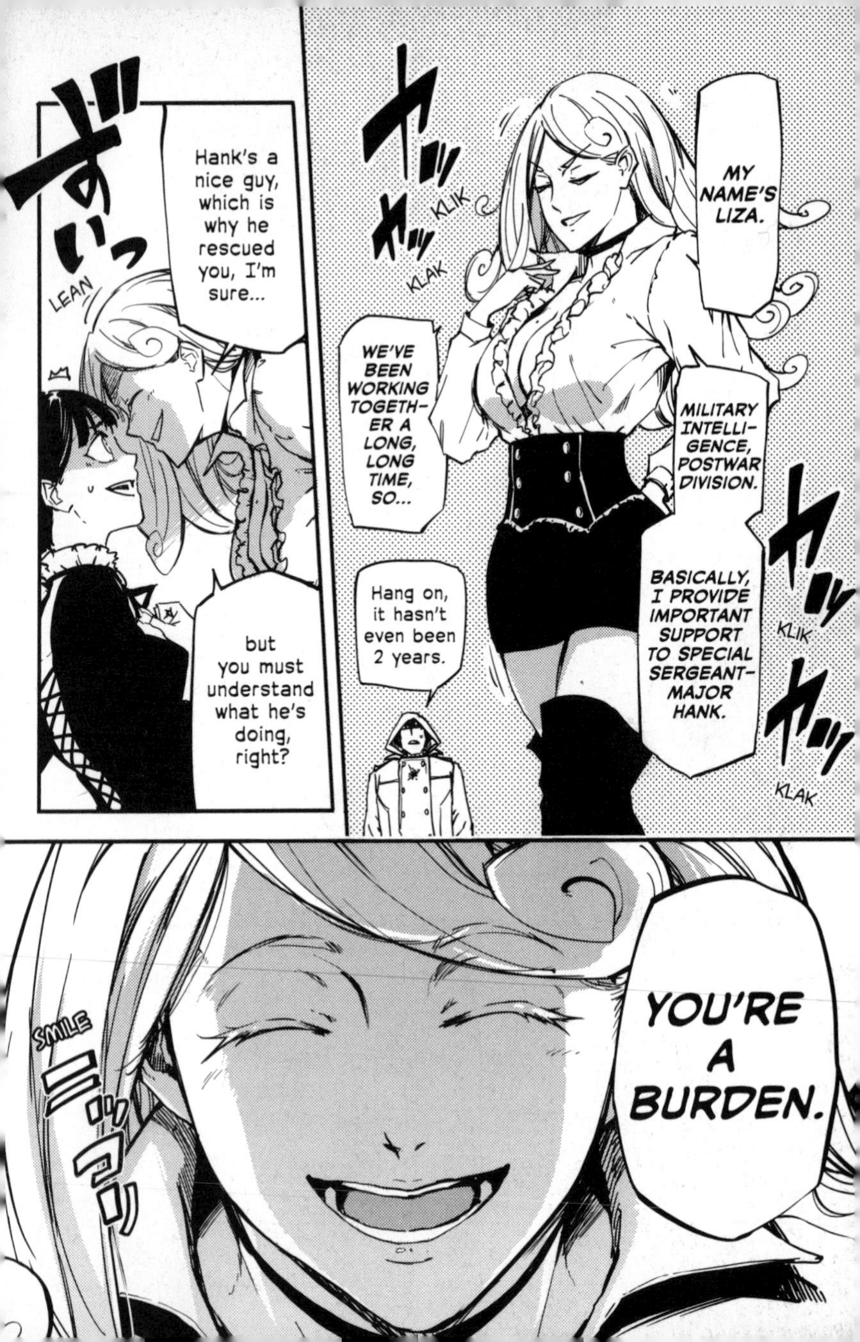
MY NAME'S LIZA.
MILITARY INTELLI-GENCE, POSTWAR DIVISION.
BASICALLY, I PROVIDE IMPORTANT SUPPORT TO SPECIAL SERGEANT-MAJOR HANK.
KLIK
KLAK
KLIK
KLAK
WE'VE BEEN WORKING TOGETH-ER A LONG, LONG TIME, SO...
Hang on, it hasn't even been 2 years.
LEAN
Hank's a nice guy, which is why he rescued you, I'm sure...
but you must understand what he's doing, right?
YOU'RE A BURDEN.
SMILE

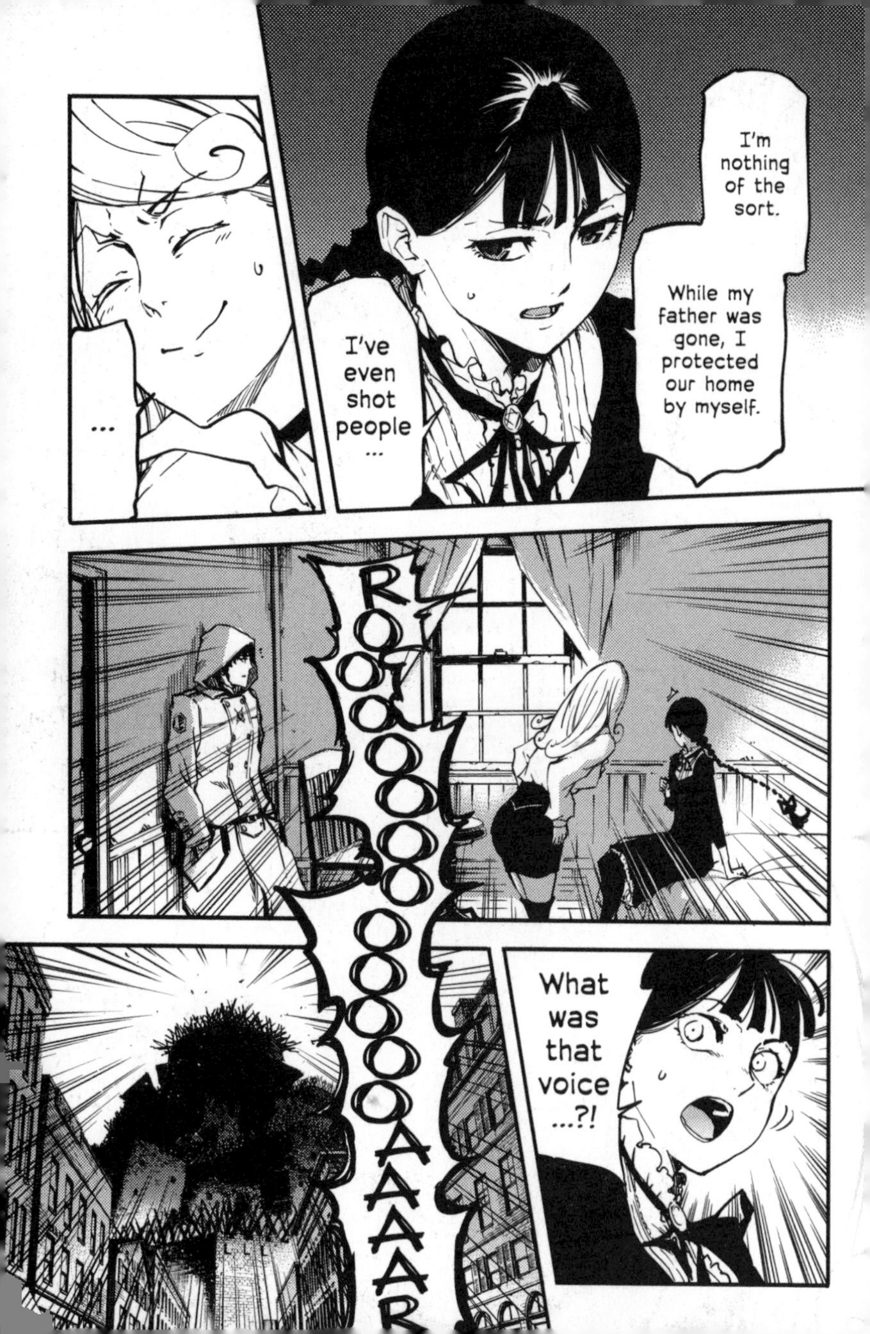

I'm nothing of the sort.
While my father was gone, I protected our home by myself.
I've even shot people ...
...
ROOOOOOOOOOOOOOOOAAAAR
What was that voice ...?!

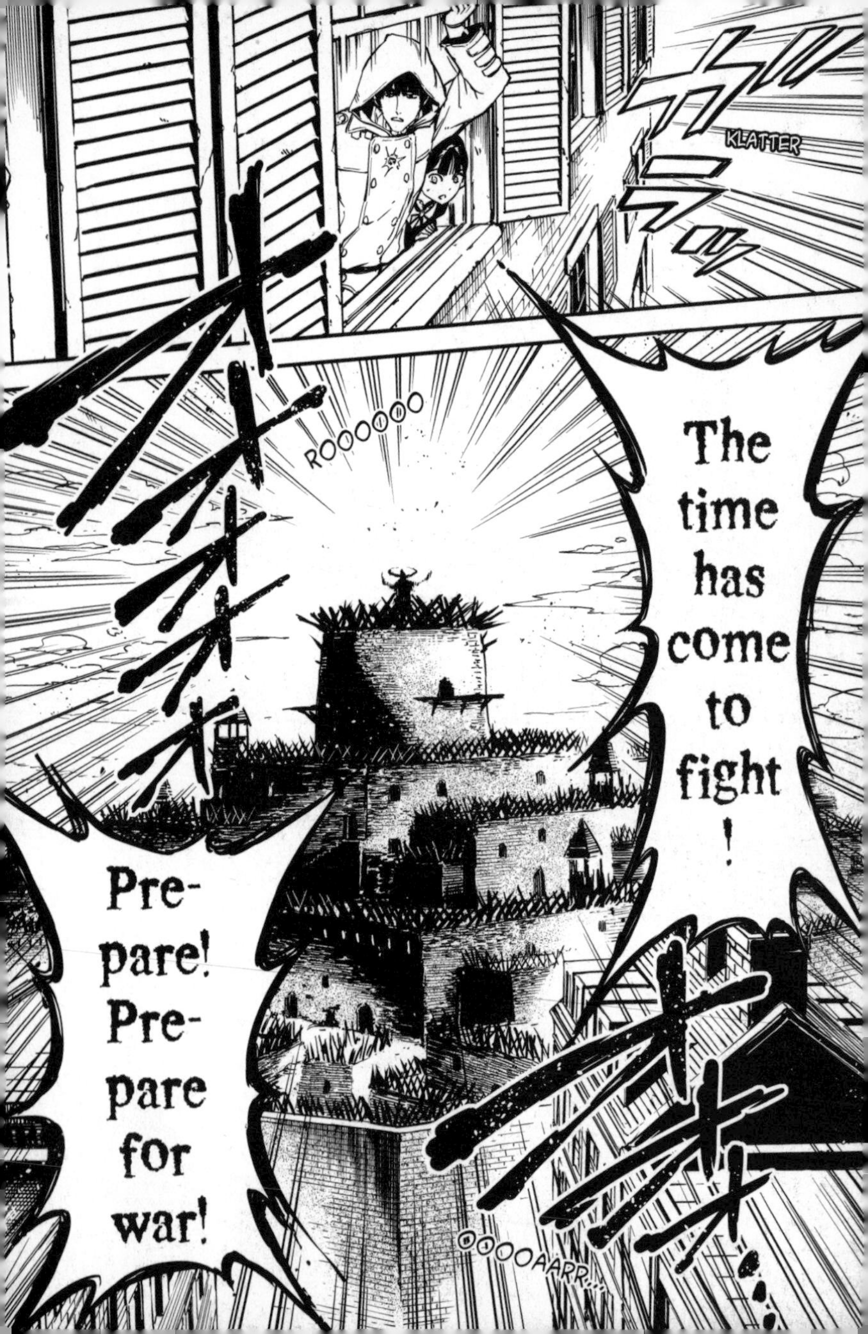
KLATTER
The time has come to fight!
ROOOOOO
Pre-pare! Pre-pare for war!
OOOOAARR...

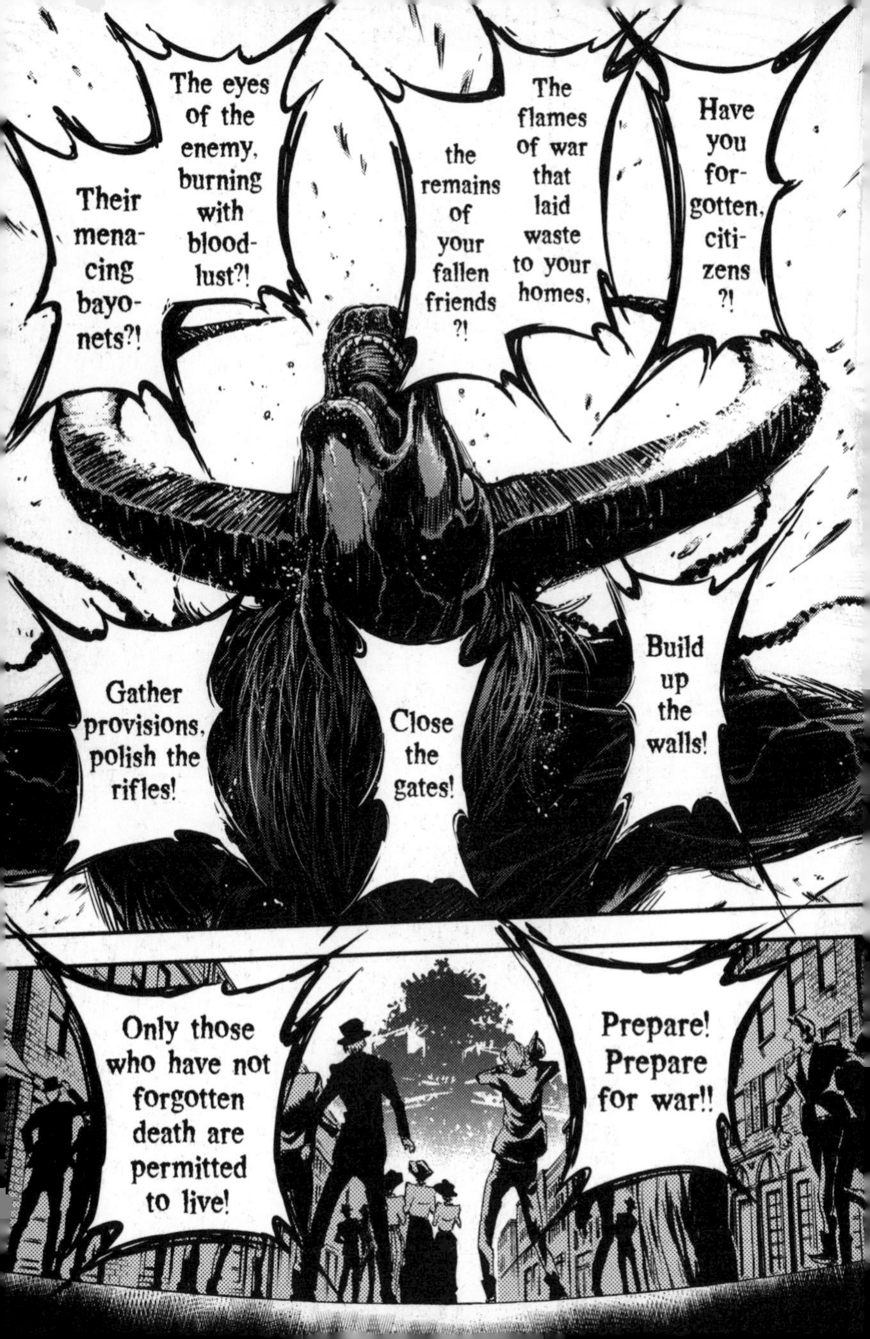
Have you forgotten, citizens?!
The flames of war that laid waste to your homes,
the remains of your fallen friends?!
The eyes of the enemy, burning with bloodlust?!
Their menacing bayonets?!
Build up the walls!
Close the gates!
Gather provisions, polish the rifles!
Prepare! Prepare for war!!
Only those who have not forgotten death are permitted to live!

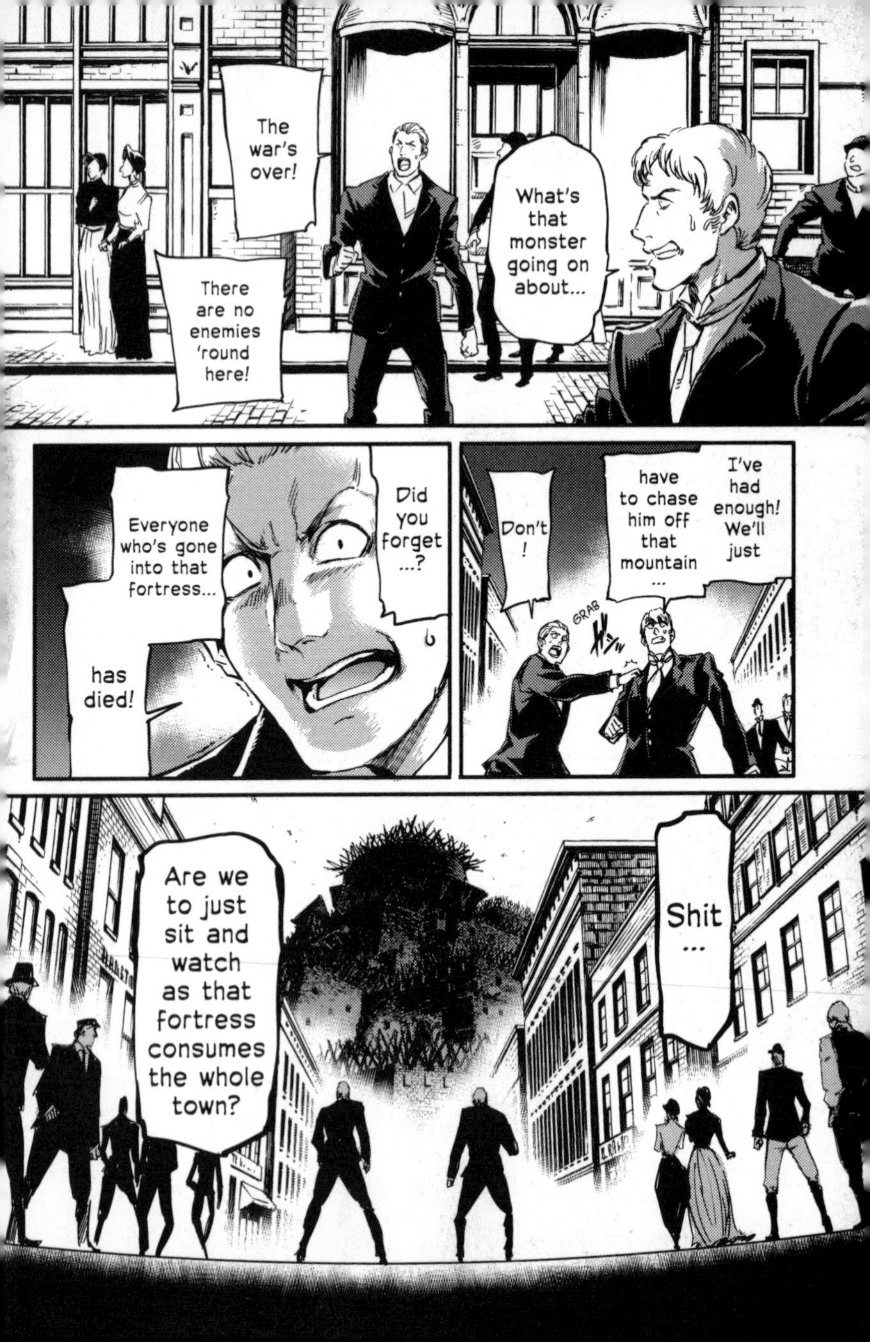

The war's over!
There are no enemies 'round here!
What's that monster going on about...
I've had enough! We'll just have to chase him off that mountain...
GRAB
Don't!
Did you forget...?
Everyone who's gone into that fortress...
has died!
Shit...
Are we to just sit and watch as that fortress consumes the whole town?

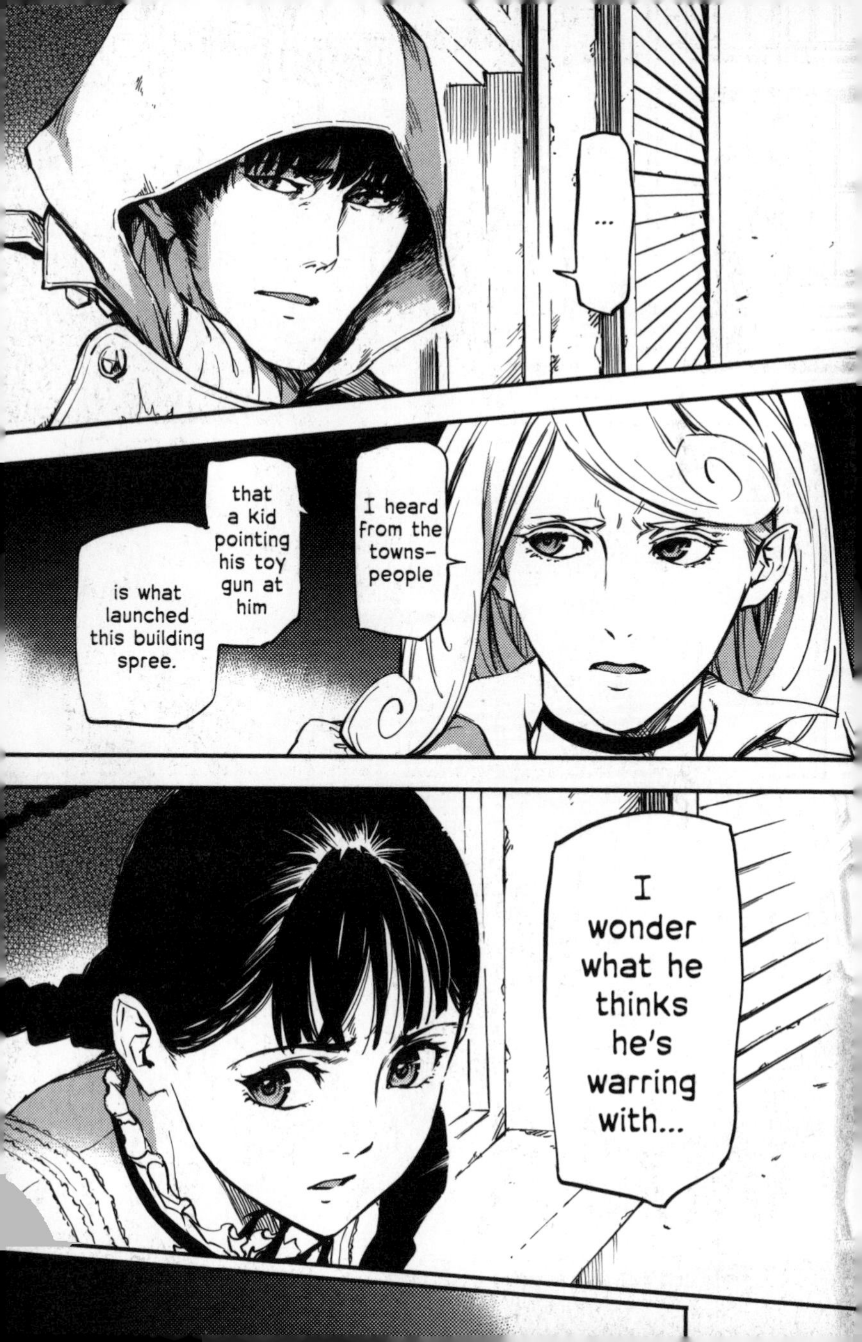
...
I heard from the towns-people
that a kid pointing his toy gun at him
is what launched this building spree.
I wonder what he thinks he's warring with...

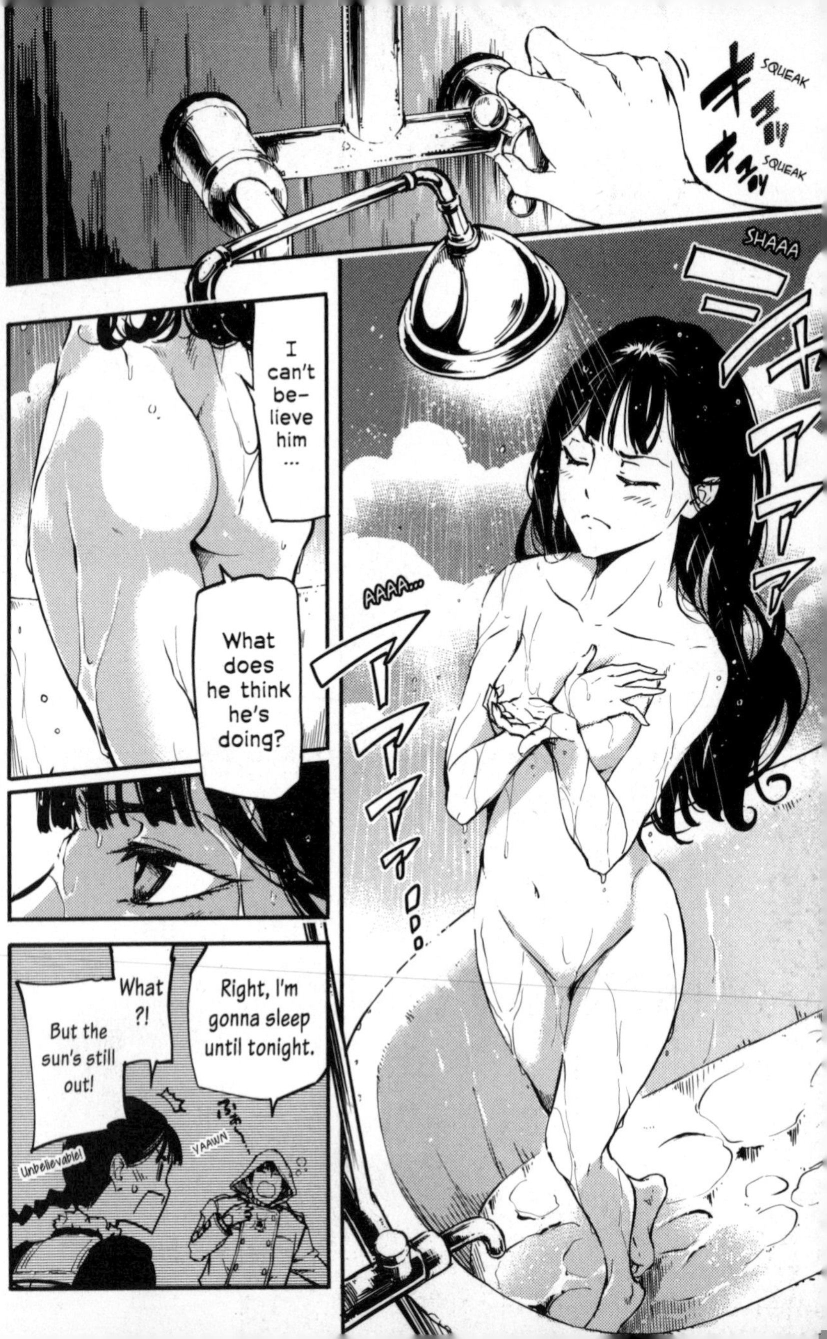
SQUEAK
SQUEAK
SHAAA
AAAA...
I can't be-lieve him ...
What does he think he's doing?
Right, I'm gonna sleep until tonight.
What ?!
But the sun's still out!
YAAWN
Unbelievable!

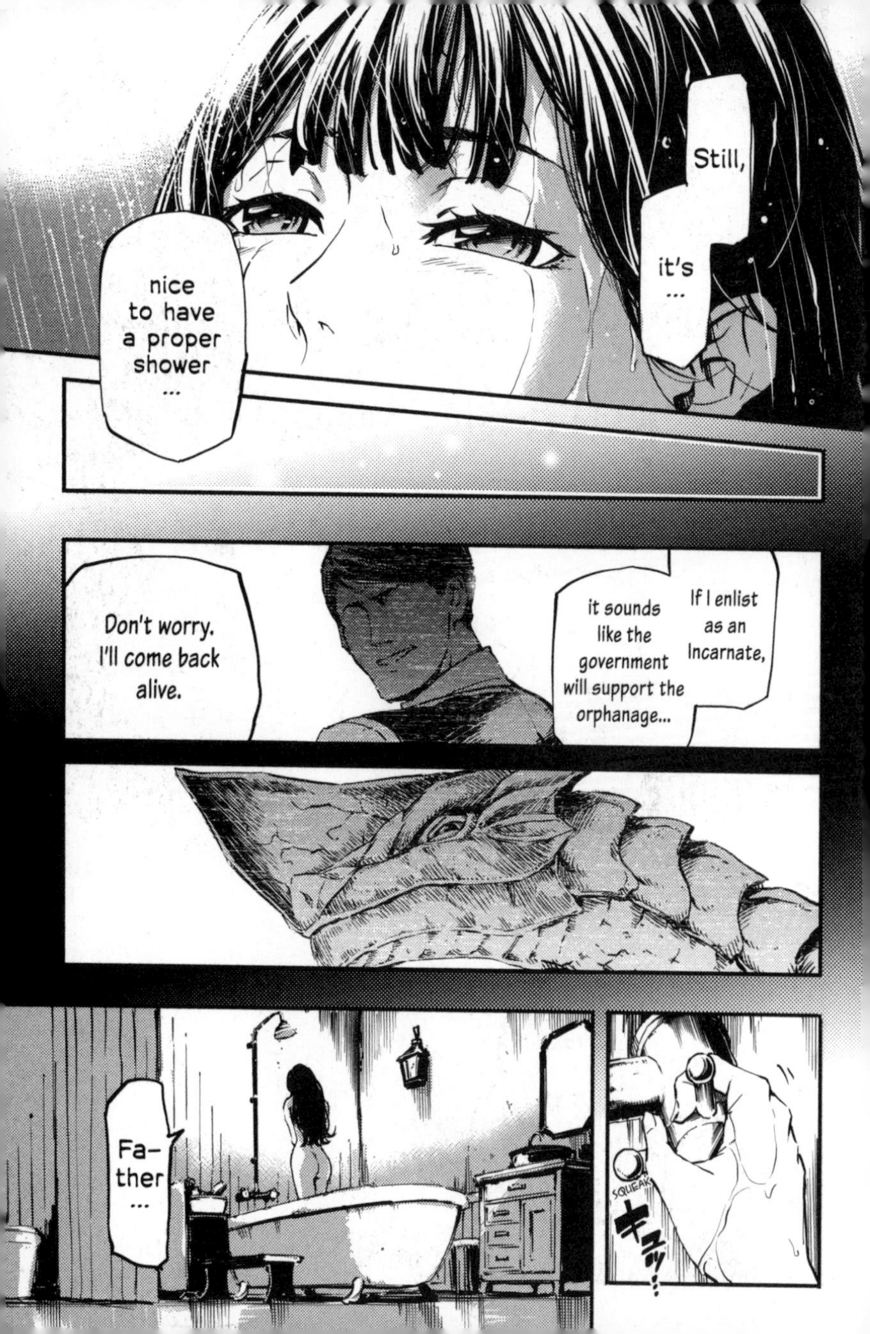
Still, it's ...
nice to have a proper shower ...
If I enlist as an Incarnate, it sounds like the government will support the orphanage...
Don't worry. I'll come back alive.
SQUEAK
キュッ!!
Fa- ther ...

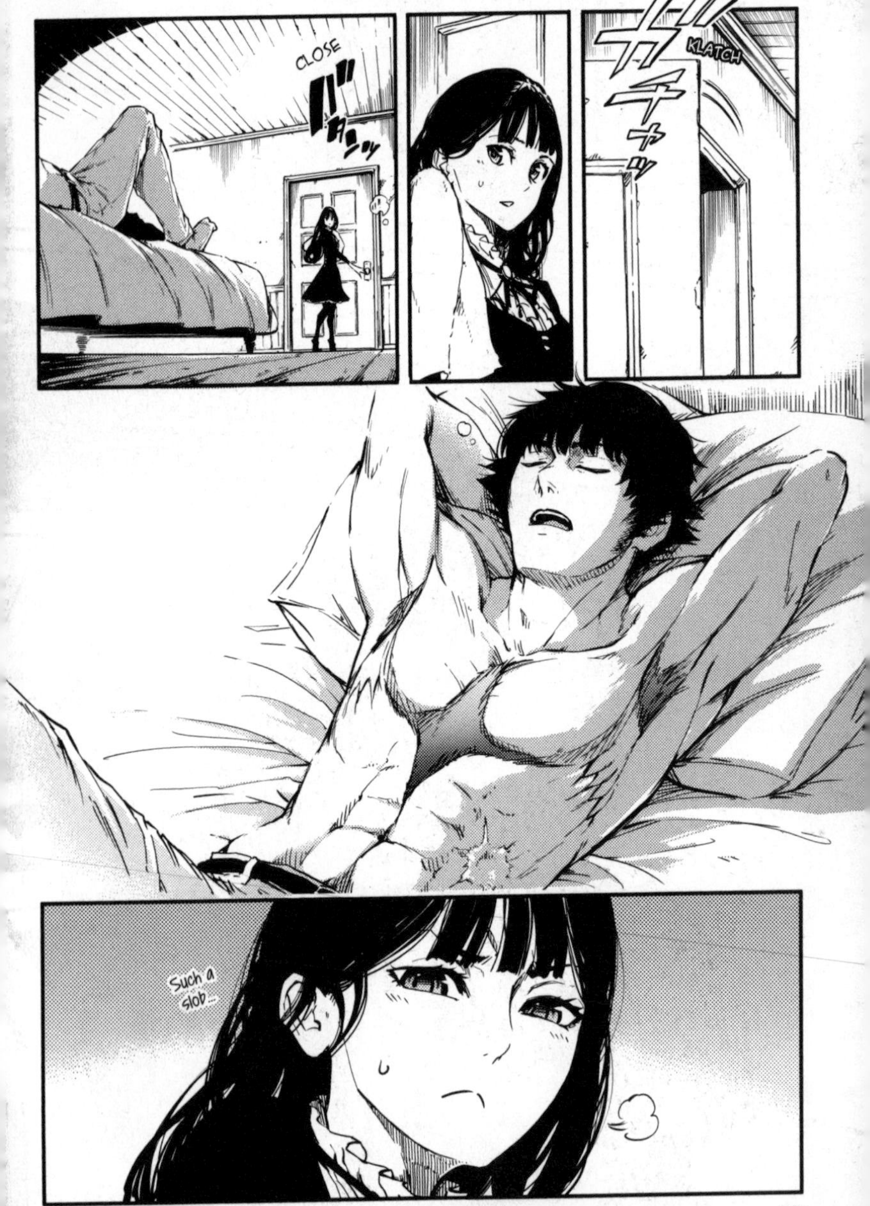
ガチャッ
KLATCH
CLOSE
バタンッ
Such a slob...

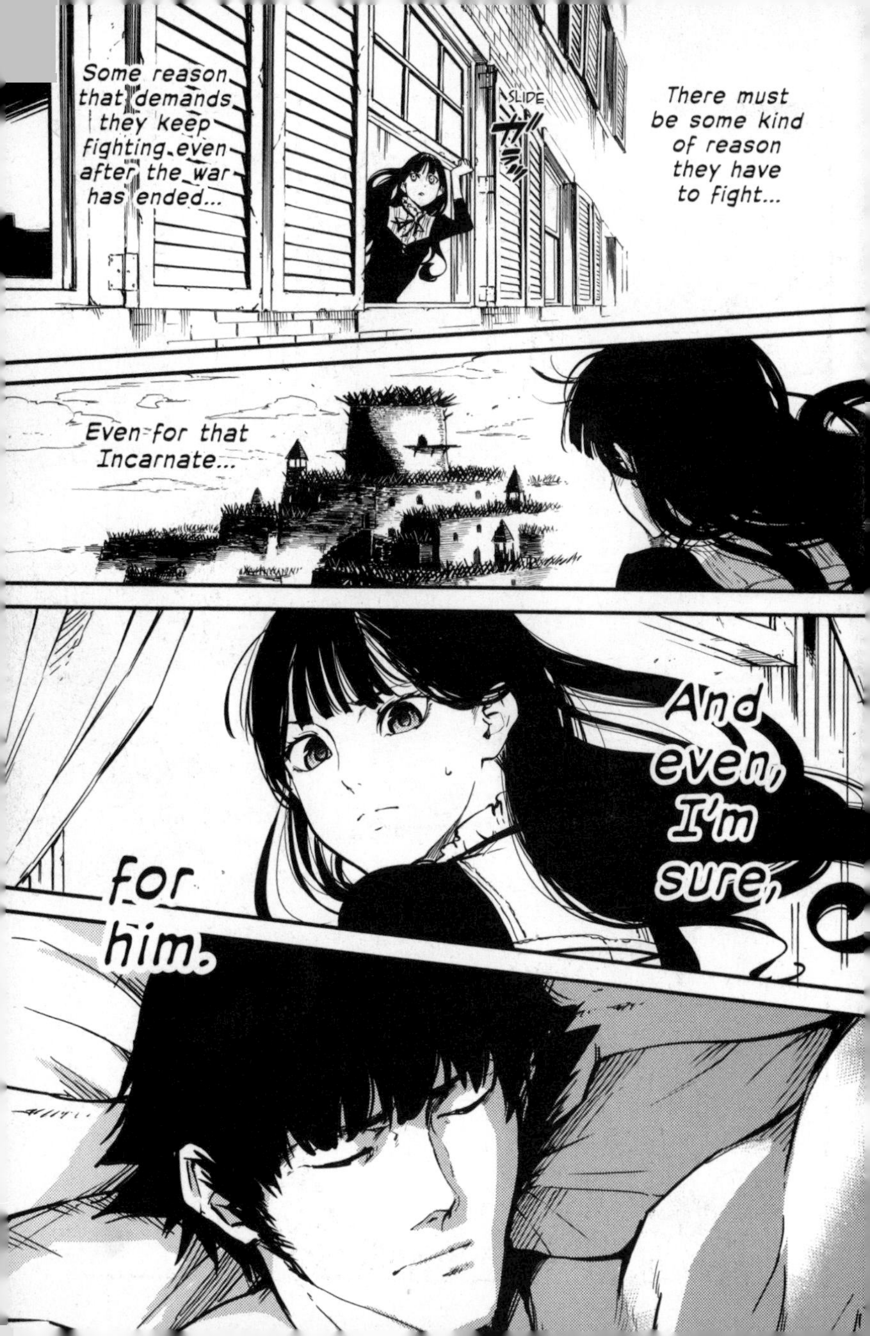

There must be some kind of reason they have to fight...
SLIDE
Some reason that demands they keep fighting even after the war has ended...
Even for that Incarnate...
And even, I'm sure,
for him.

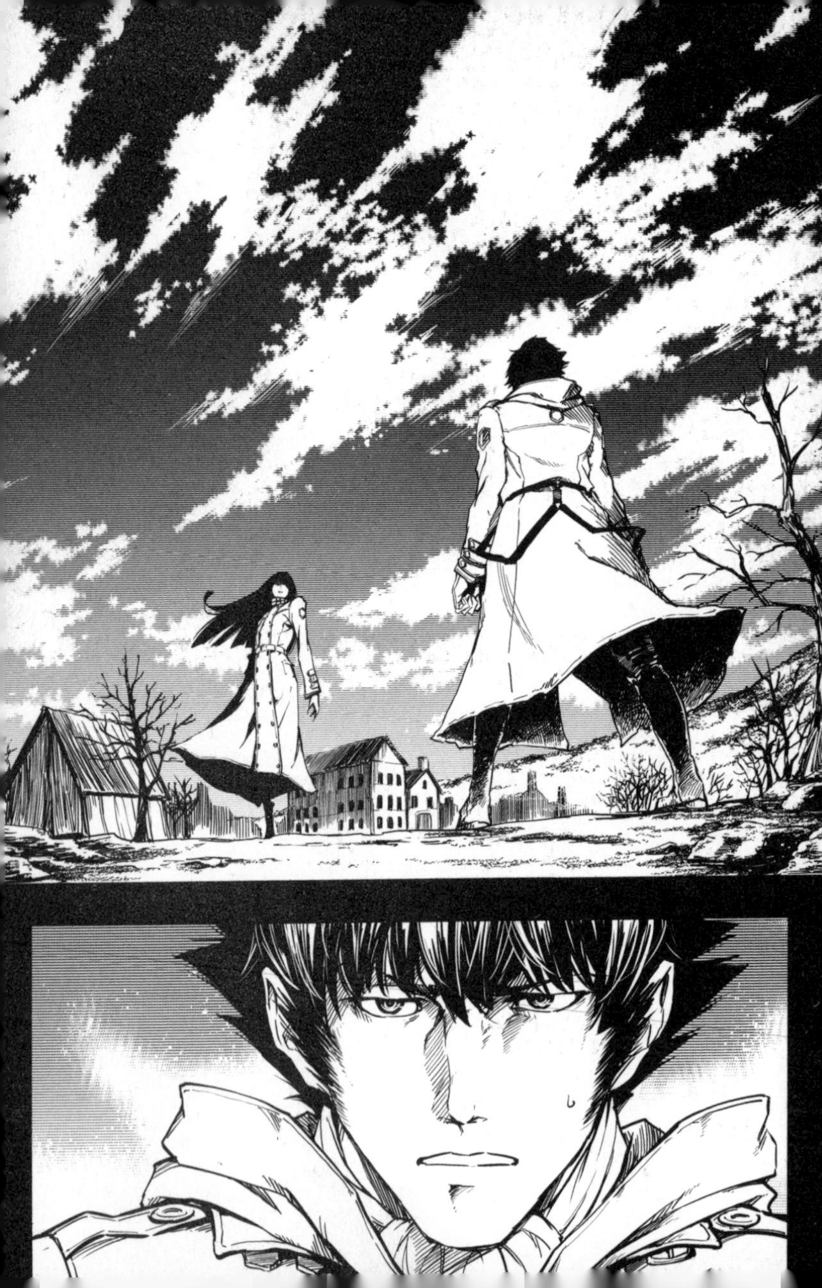

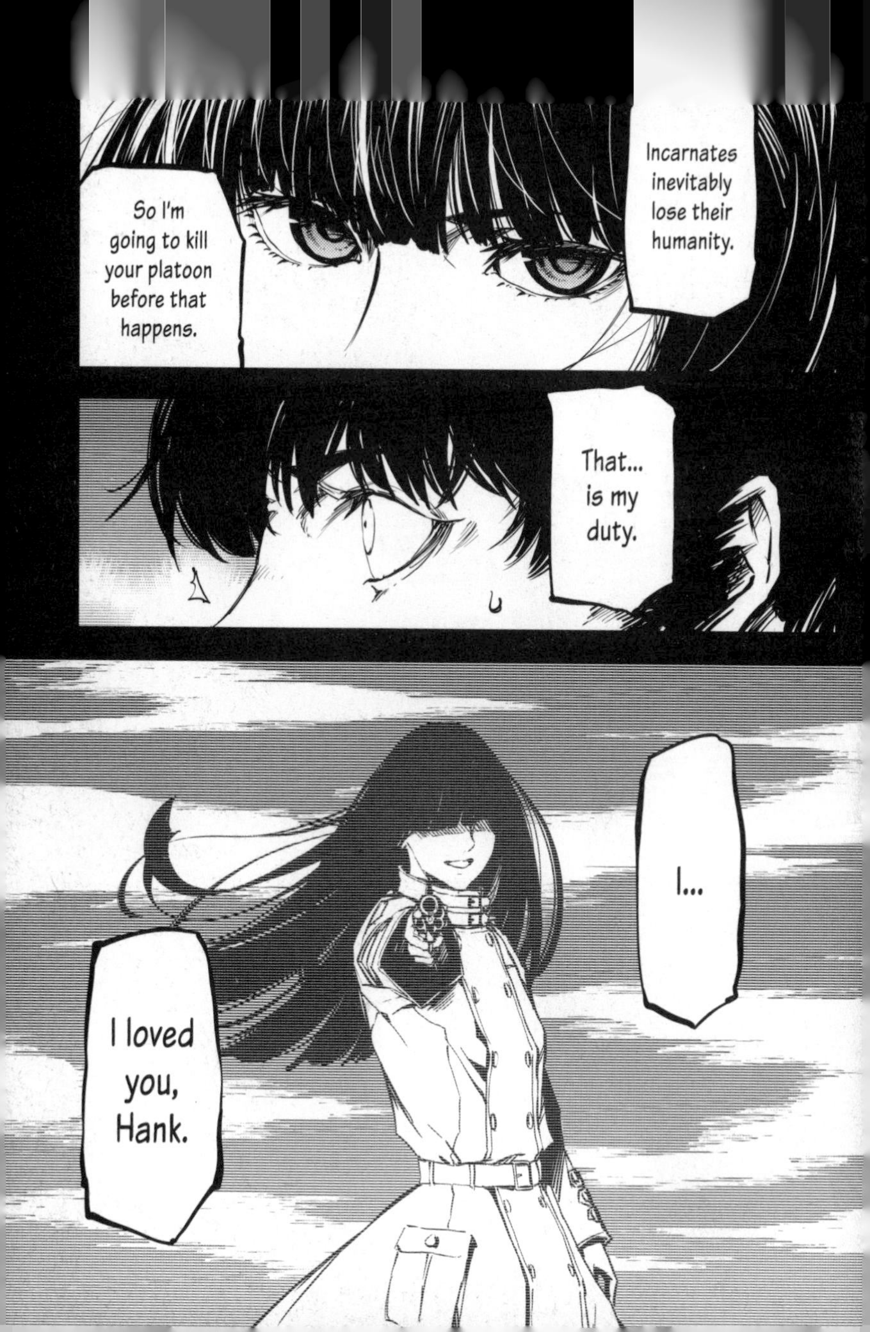

Incarnates inevitably lose their humanity.
So I'm going to kill your platoon before that happens.
That... is my duty.
I...
I loved you, Hank.

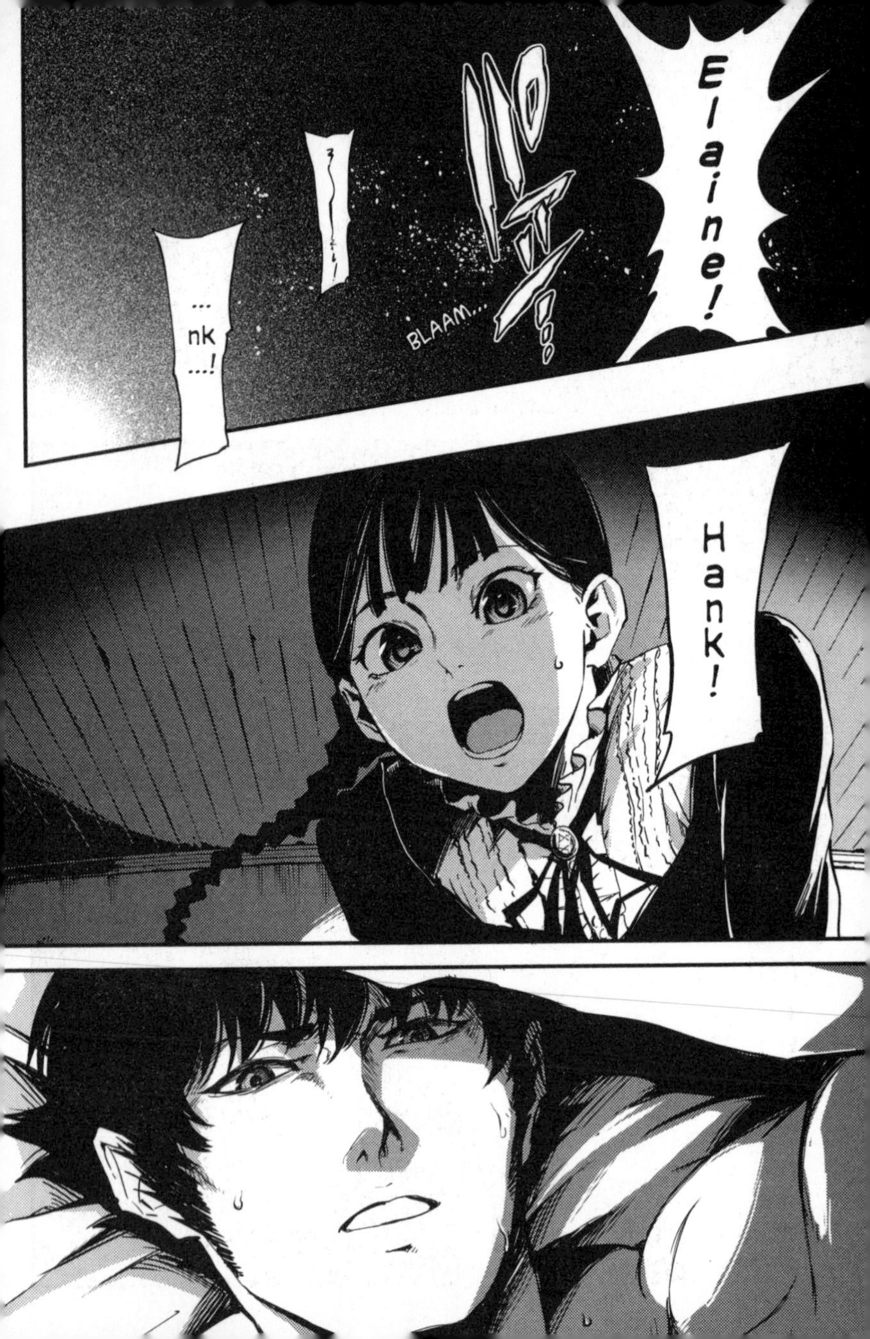
Elaine!!
BLAAM...
...nk...!
Hank!

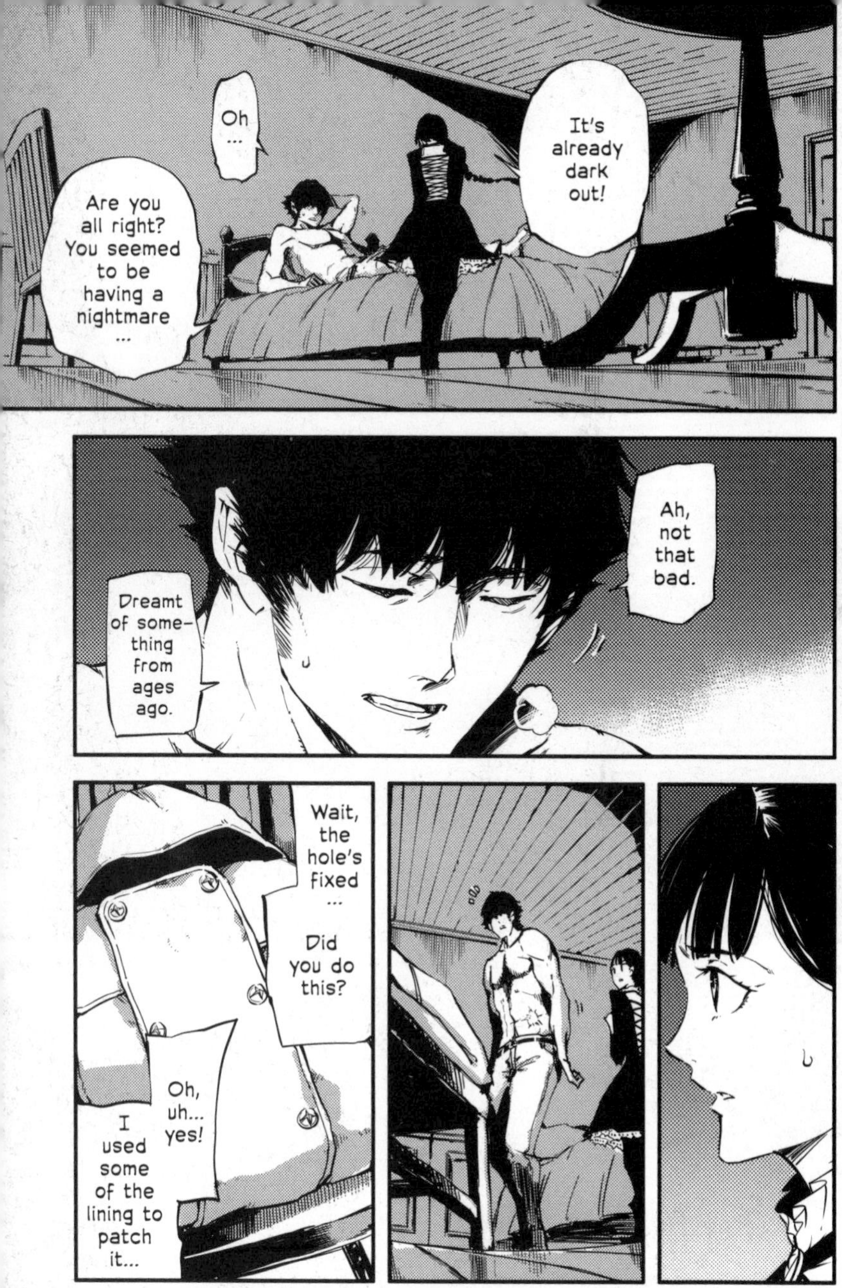
It's already dark out!
Oh ...
Are you all right? You seemed to be having a nightmare ...
Ah, not that bad.
Dreamt of some-thing from ages ago.
Wait, the hole's fixed ...
Did you do this?
Oh, uh... yes!
I used some of the lining to patch it...

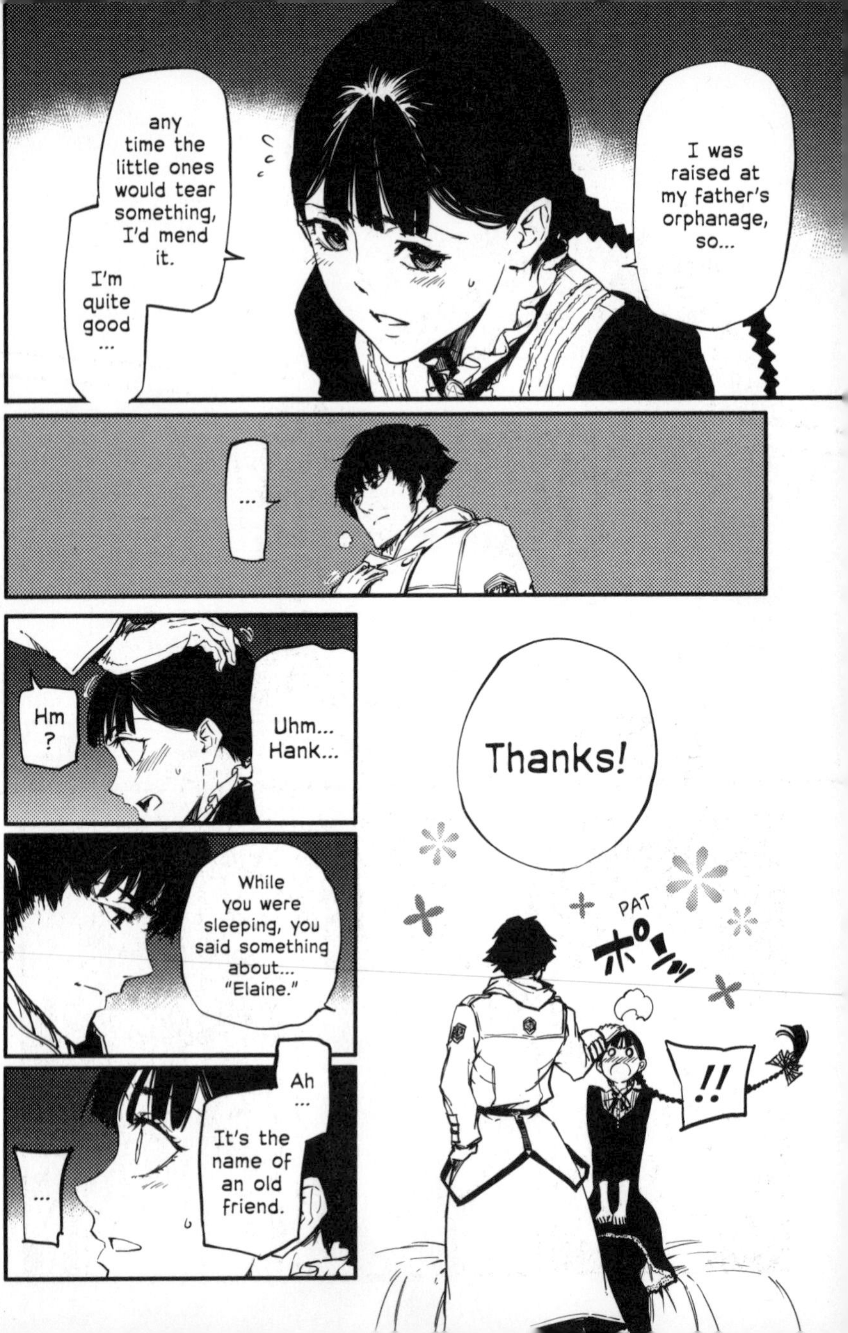
I was raised at my father's orphanage, so...
any time the little ones would tear something, I'd mend it.
I'm quite good ...
...
Thanks!
PAT
ポンッ
!!
Uhm... Hank...
Hm?
While you were sleeping, you said something about... "Elaine."
Ah ...
It's the name of an old friend.
...

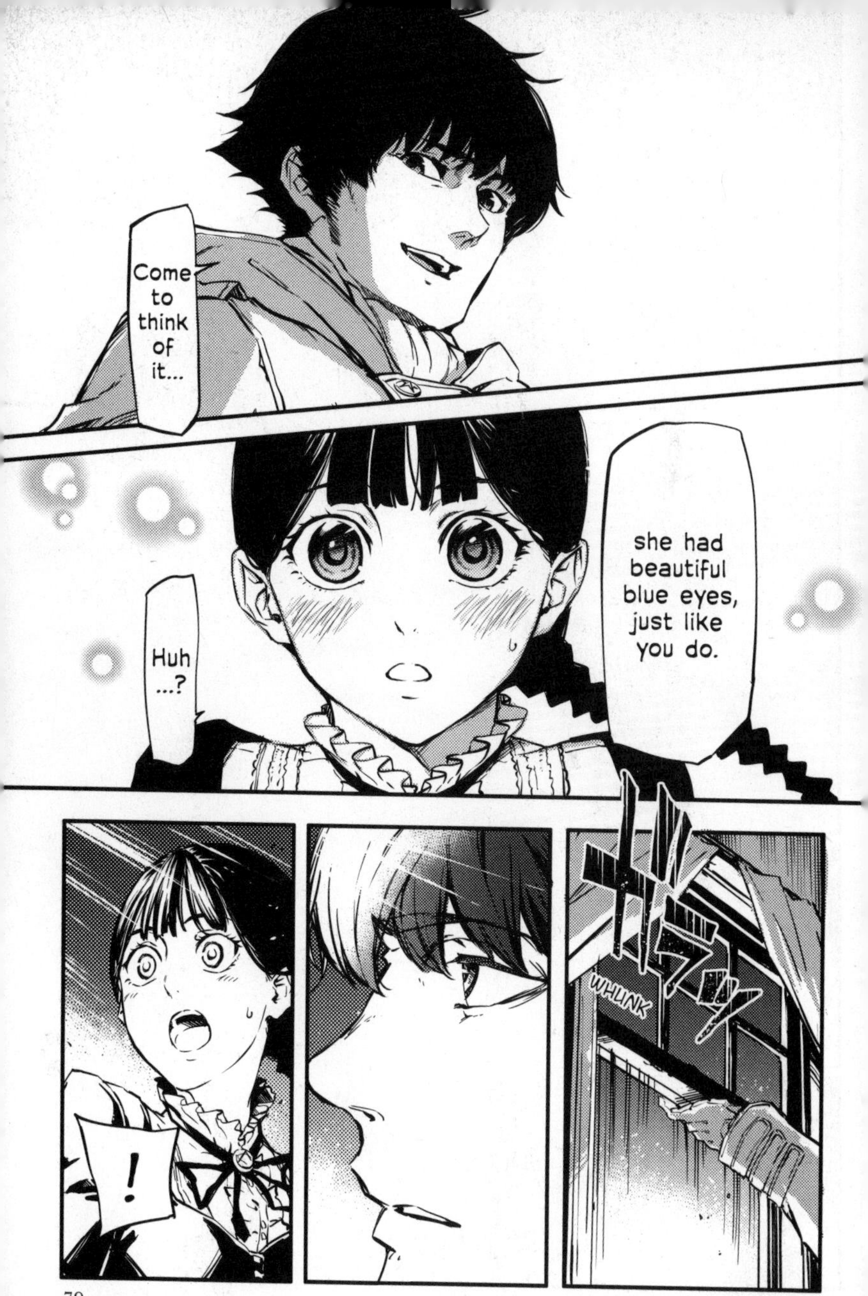
Come to think of it...
she had beautiful blue eyes, just like you do.
Huh ...?
WHLINK
!

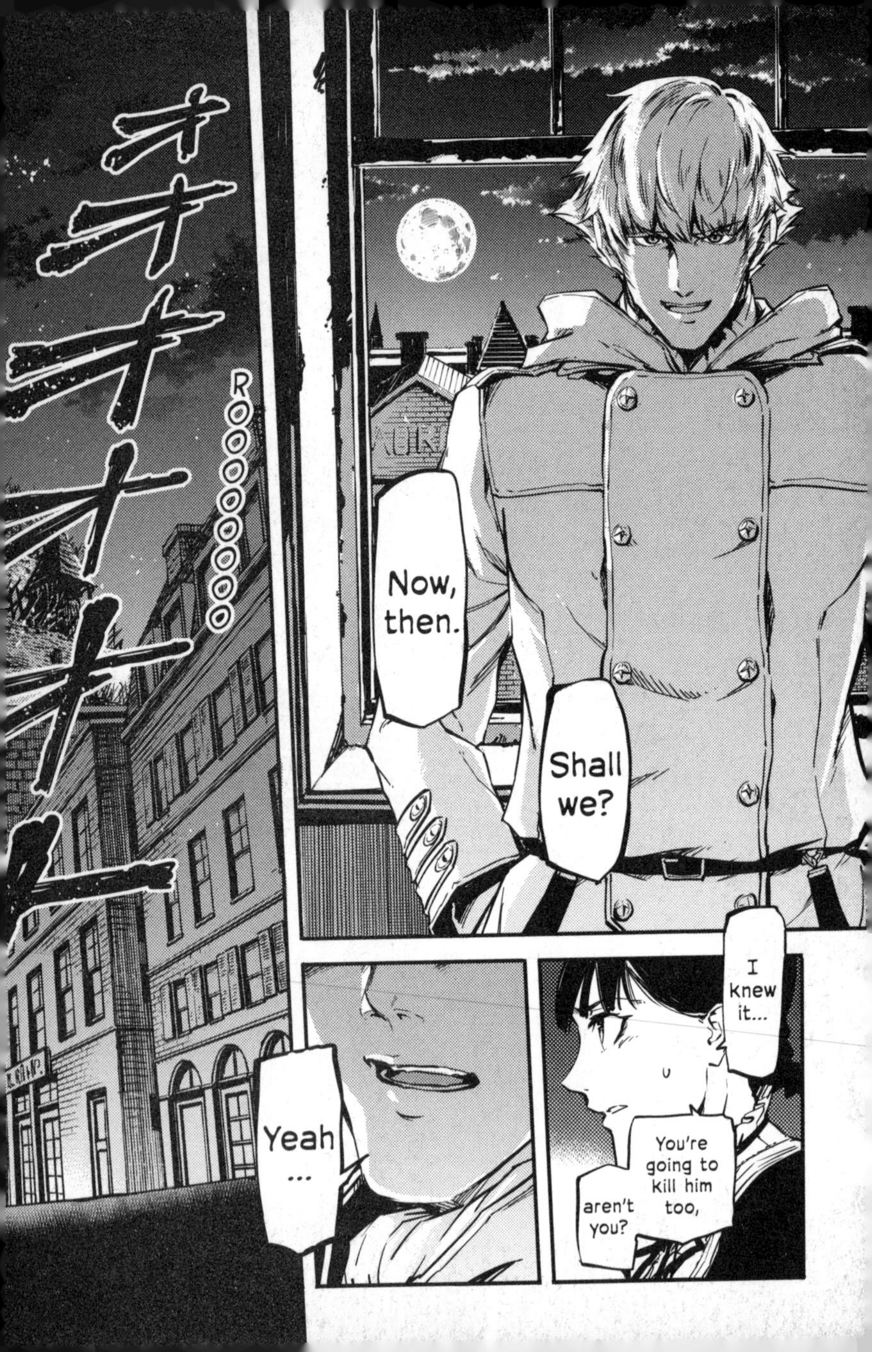
Now, then.
Shall we?
I knew it...
You're going to kill him too,
aren't you?
Yeah ...
ROOOOOOOOOO

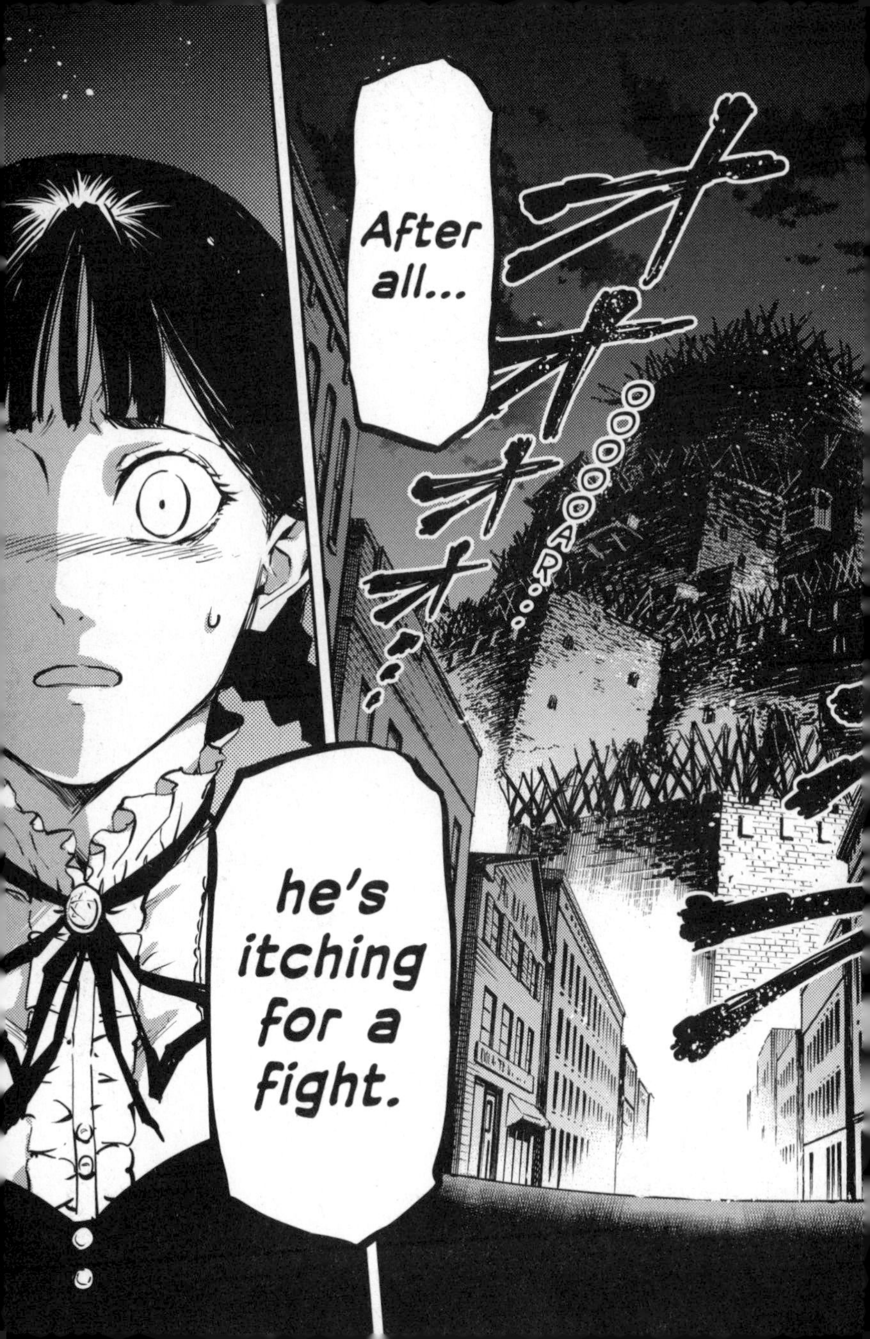
After all...
OOOOOOAR...
he's itching for a fight.

To the Abandoned
Sacred Beasts

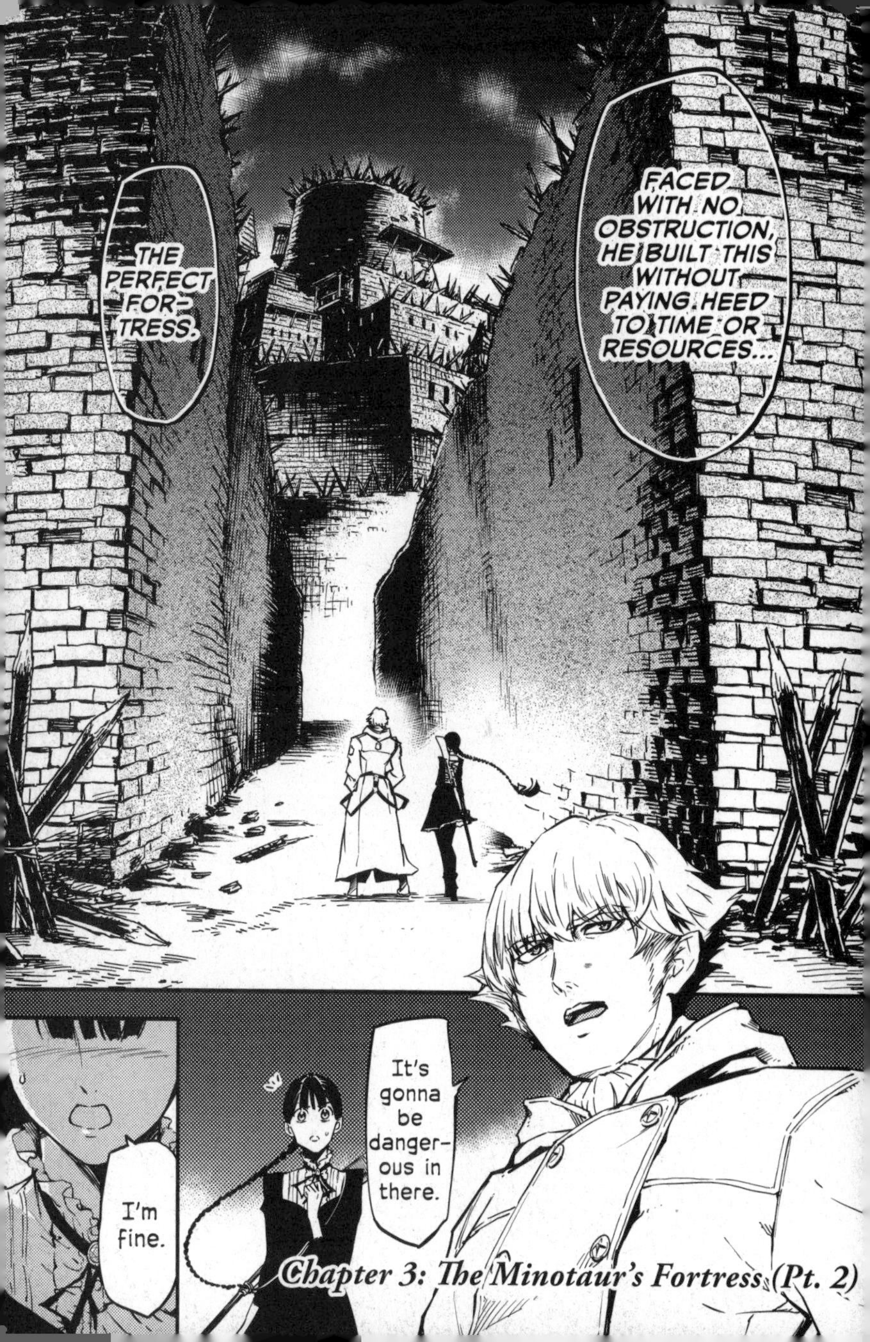
FACED WITH NO OBSTRUCTION, HE BUILT THIS WITHOUT PAYING HEED TO TIME OR RESOURCES...
THE PERFECT FOR-TRESS.
It's gonna be danger-ous in there.
I'm fine.
Chapter 3: The Minotaur's Fortress (Pt. 2)

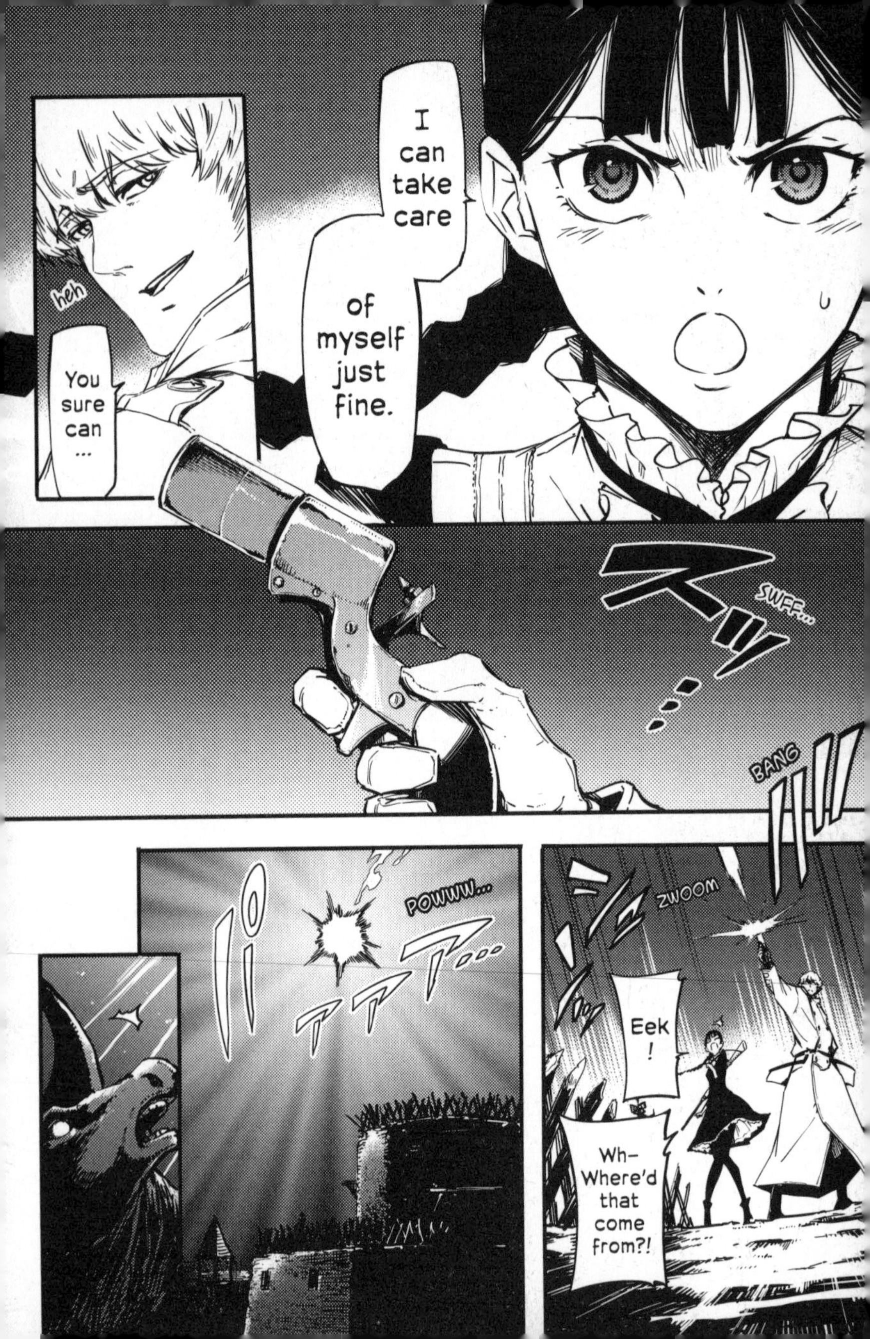
I can take care of myself just fine.
heh
You sure can ...
SWFF...
BANG
ZWOOM
Eek!
Wh- Where'd that come from?!
POWWW...

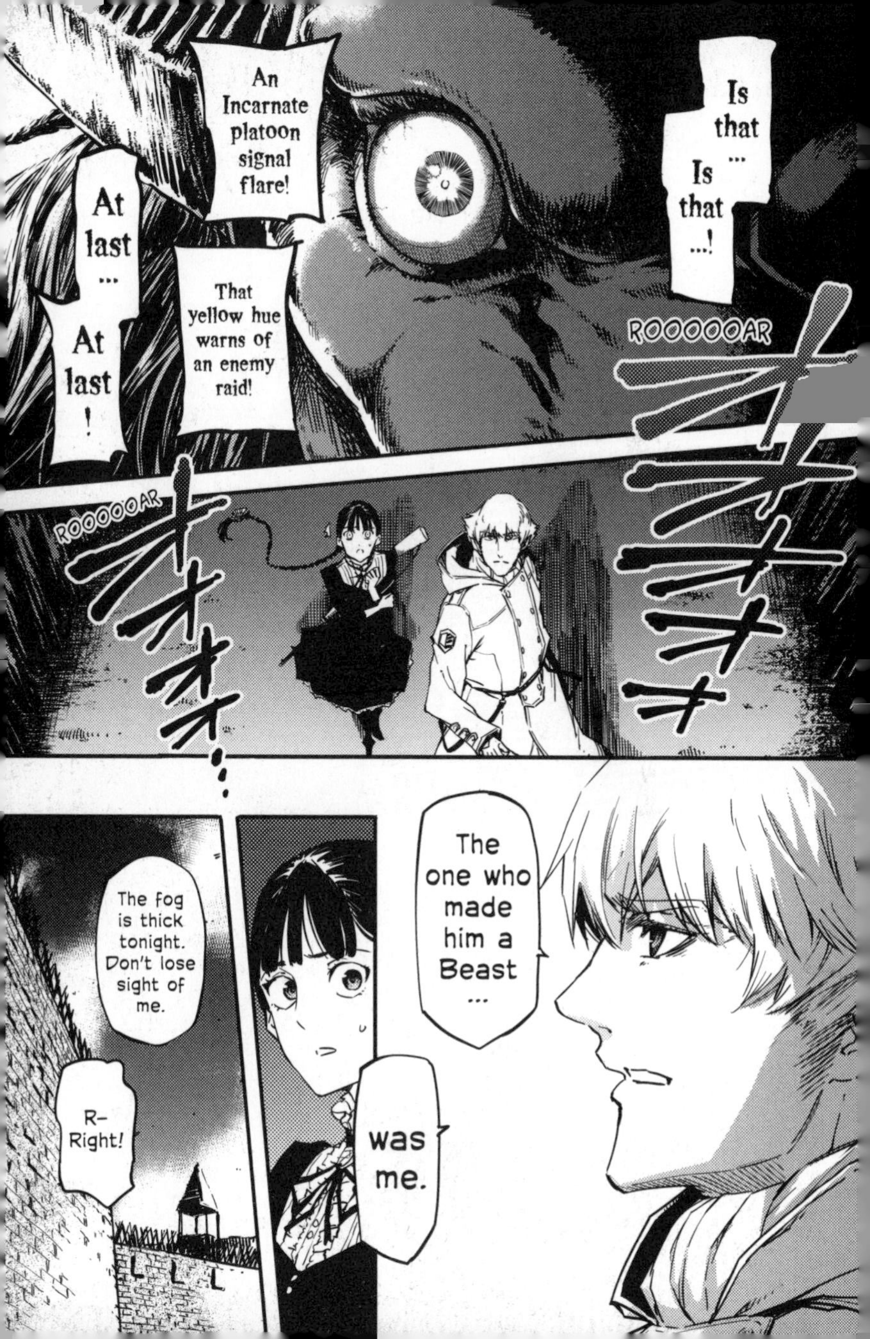
Is that ... Is that ...!
ROOOOOAR
An Incarnate platoon signal flare!
That yellow hue warns of an enemy raid!
At last ... At last!
ROOOOOAR
The one who made him a Beast ...
was me.
The fog is thick tonight. Don't lose sight of me.
R– Right!

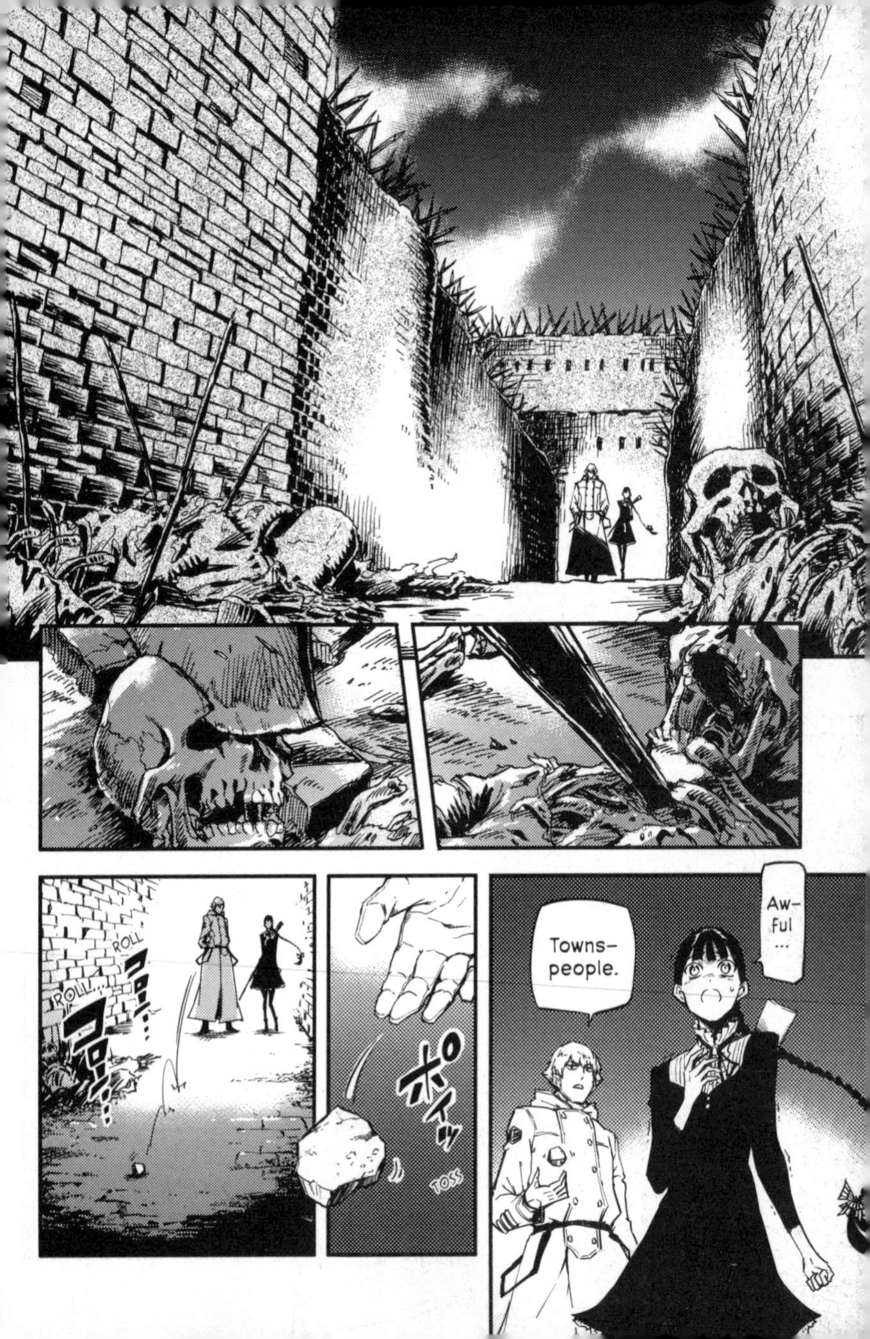
Aw—ful...
Towns—people.
ポイッ
TOSS
ROLL
ROLL...

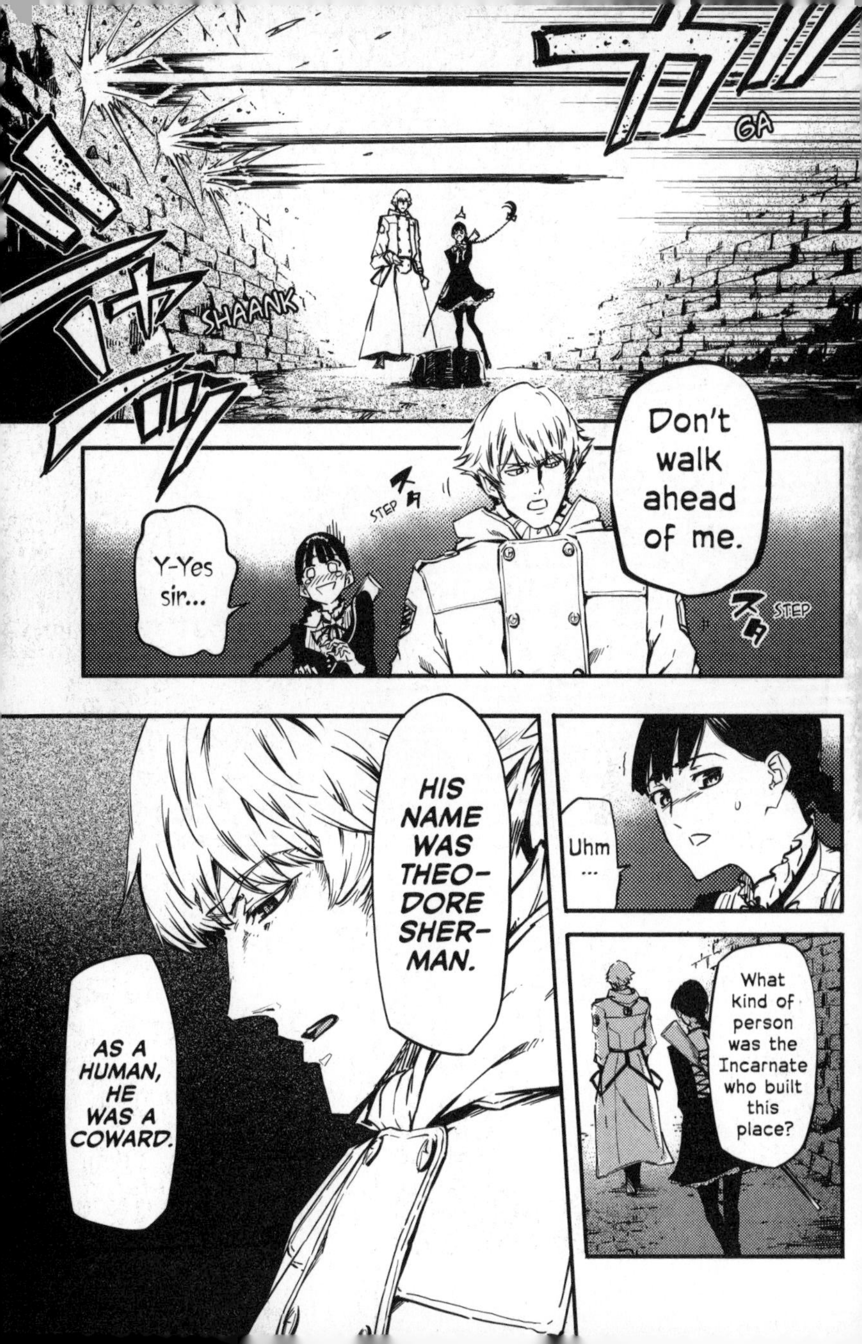
GA
SHAANK
Don't walk ahead of me.
STEP
STEP
Y-Yes sir...
Uhm ...
What kind of person was the Incarnate who built this place?
HIS NAME WAS THEODORE SHERMAN.
AS A HUMAN, HE WAS A COWARD.

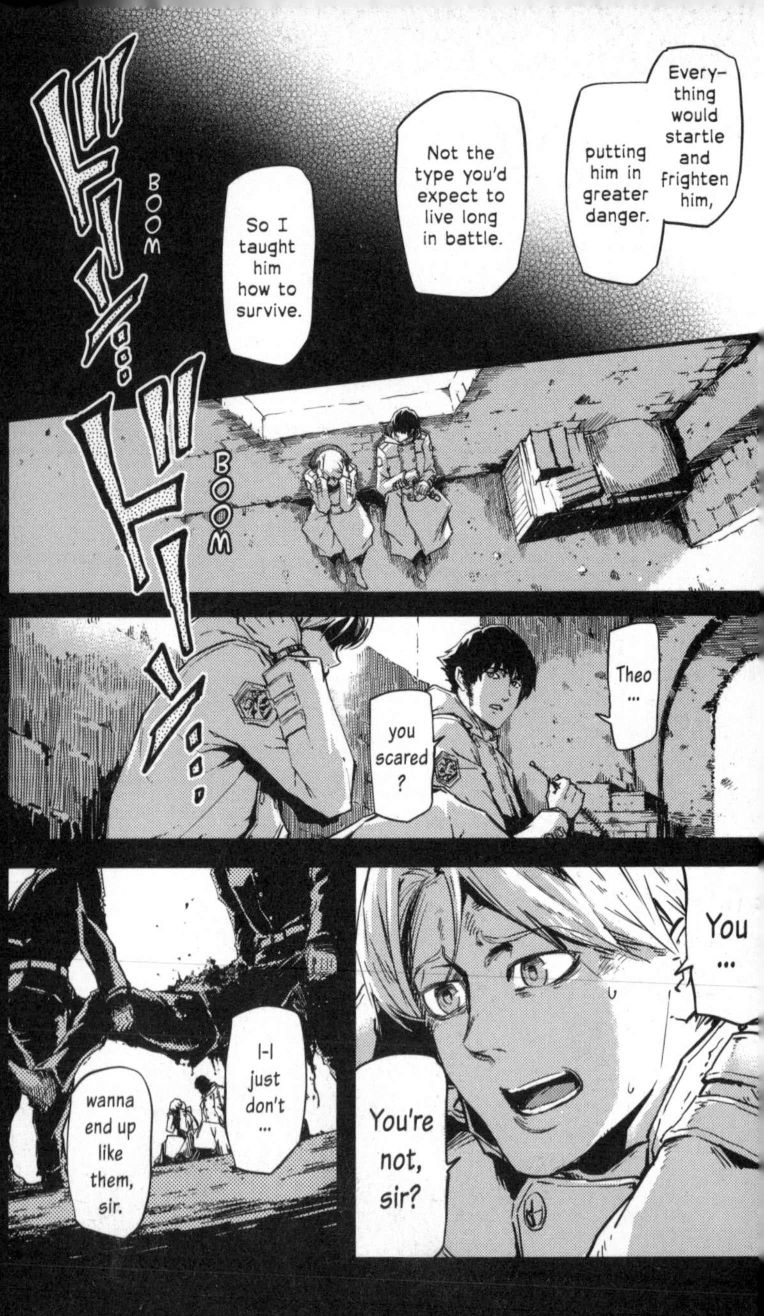

Every-thing would startle and frighten him,
putting him in greater danger.
Not the type you'd expect to live long in battle.
So I taught him how to survive.
BOOM
BOOM
Theo ...
you scared?
You ...
You're not, sir?
I-I just don't ...
wanna end up like them, sir.

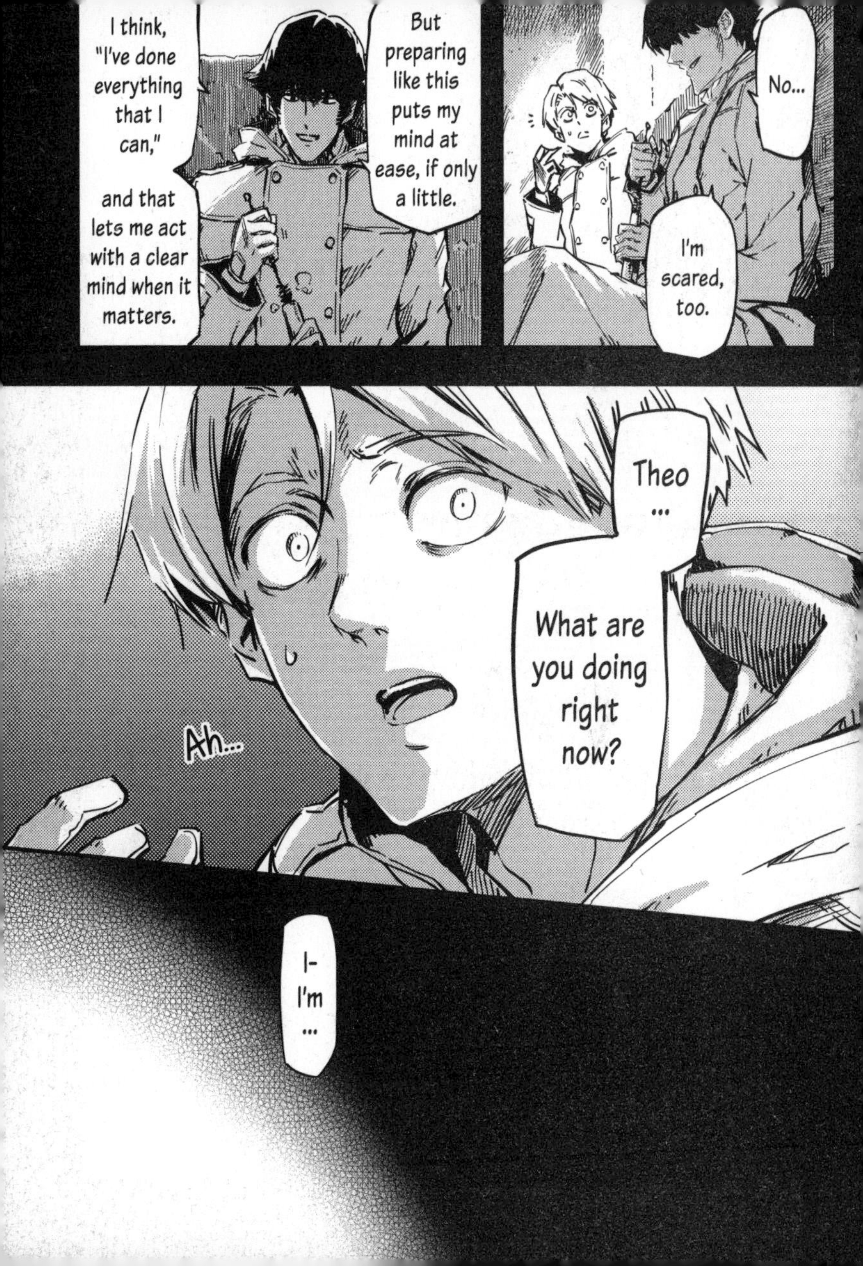
No...
I'm scared, too.
But preparing like this puts my mind at ease, if only a little.
I think, "I've done everything that I can,"
and that lets me act with a clear mind when it matters.
Theo ...
What are you doing right now?
Ah...
I- I'm ...

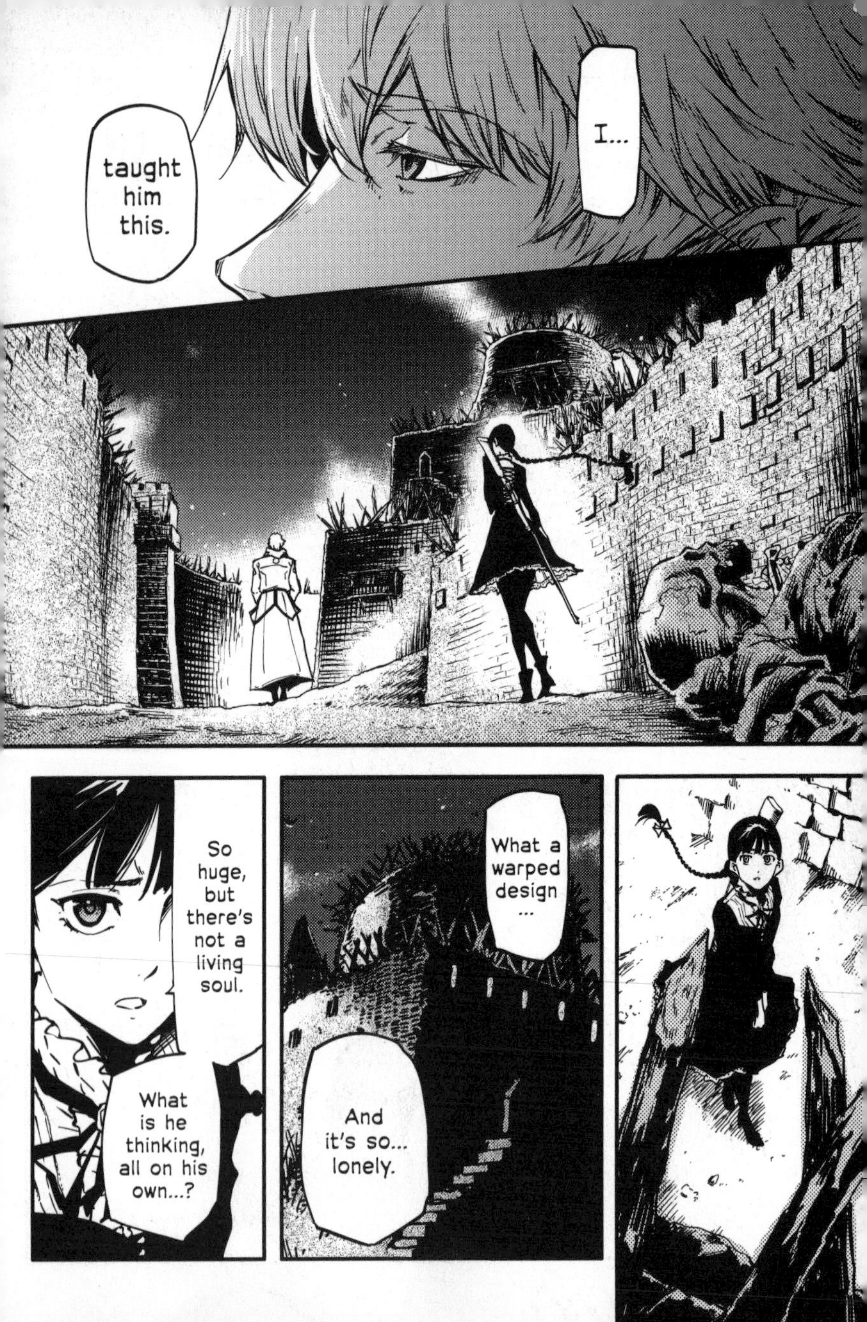
I...
taught him this.
What a warped design...
And it's so... lonely.
So huge, but there's not a living soul.
What is he thinking, all on his own...?

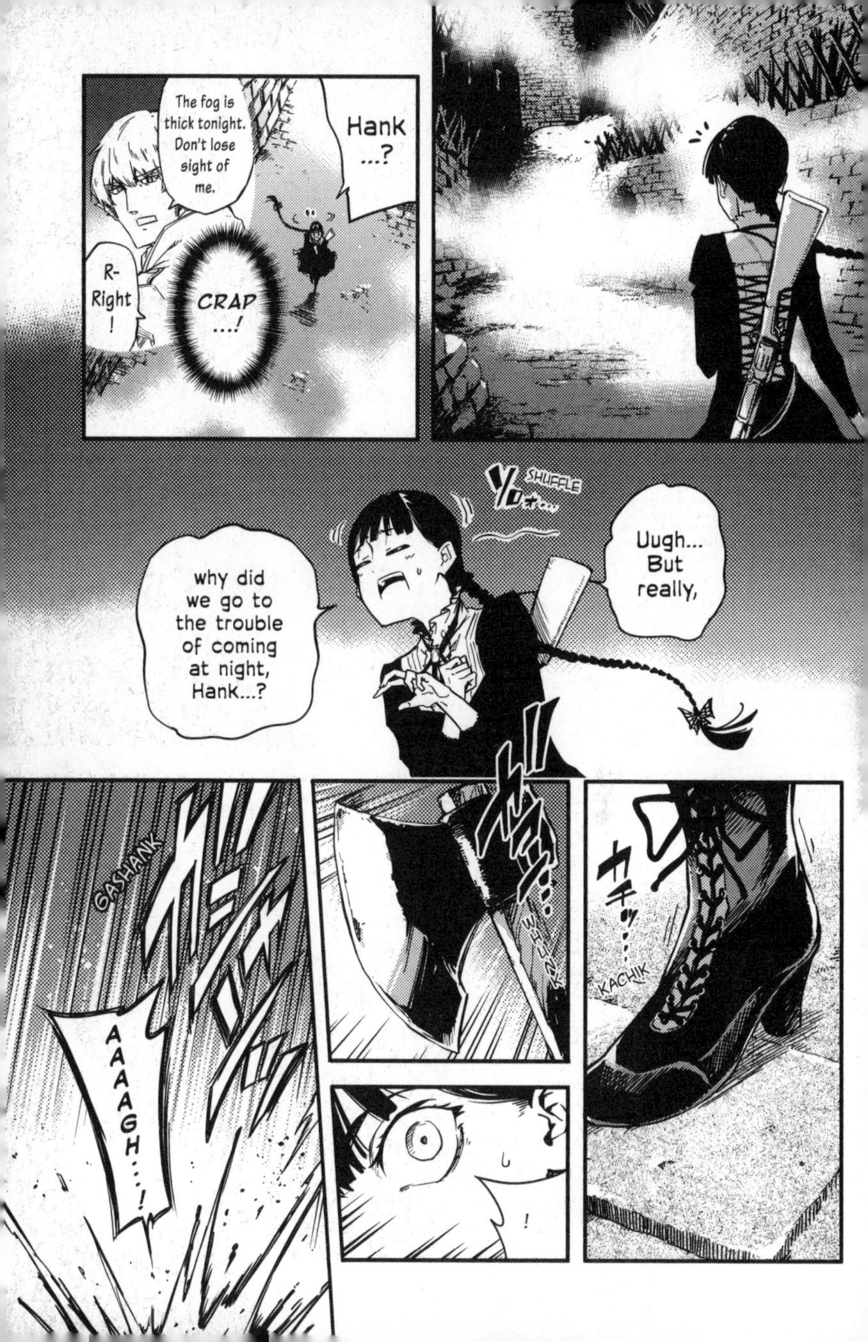
Hank ...?
The fog is thick tonight. Don't lose sight of me.
CRAP ...!
R-Right!
SHUFFLE
Uugh... But really,
why did we go to the trouble of coming at night, Hank...?
KACHIK
WHUNK
!
GASHANK
AAAAGH...!

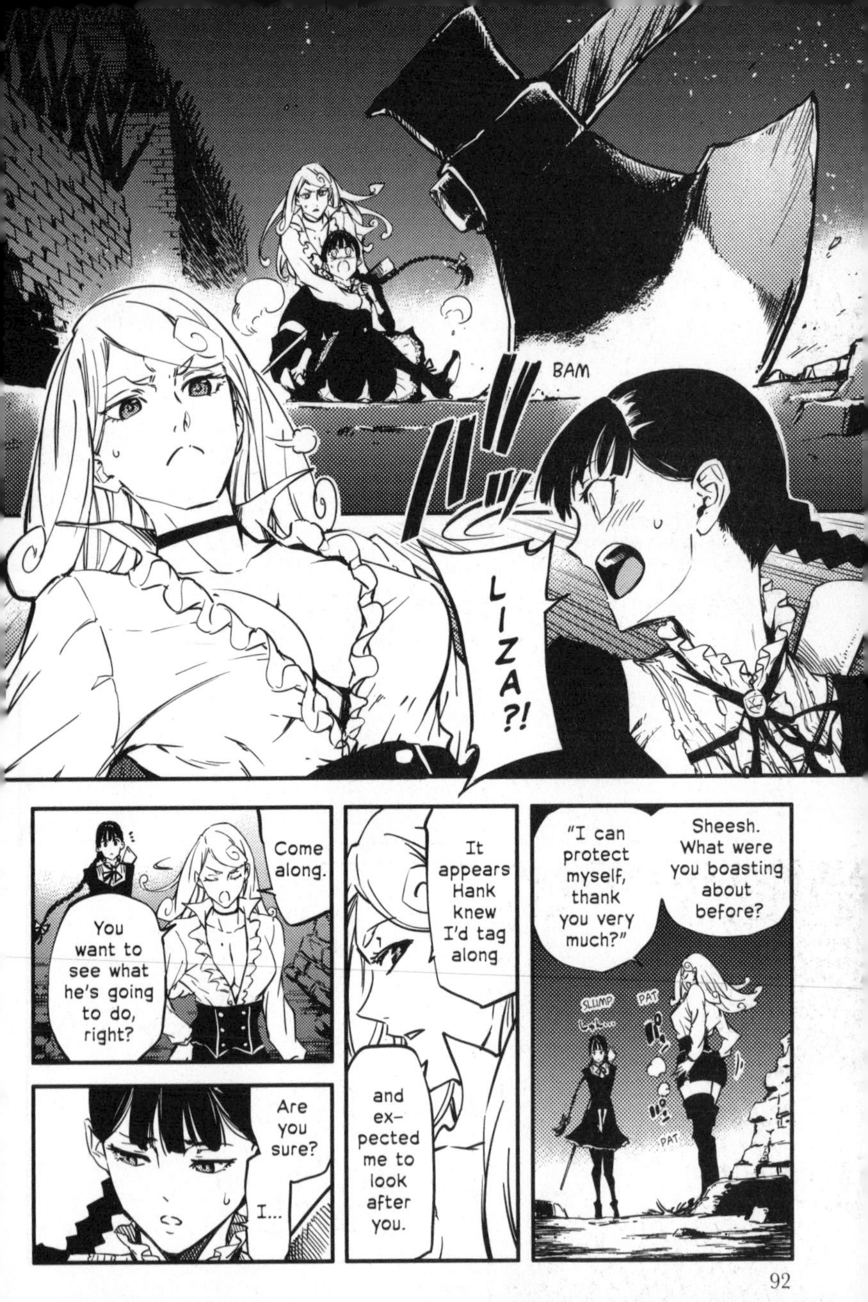
BAM
LIZA?!
Sheesh. What were you boasting about before?
"I can protect myself, thank you very much?"
SLUMP
PAT
PAT
It appears Hank knew I'd tag along
and ex-pected me to look after you.
Come along.
You want to see what he's going to do, right?
Are you sure?
I...

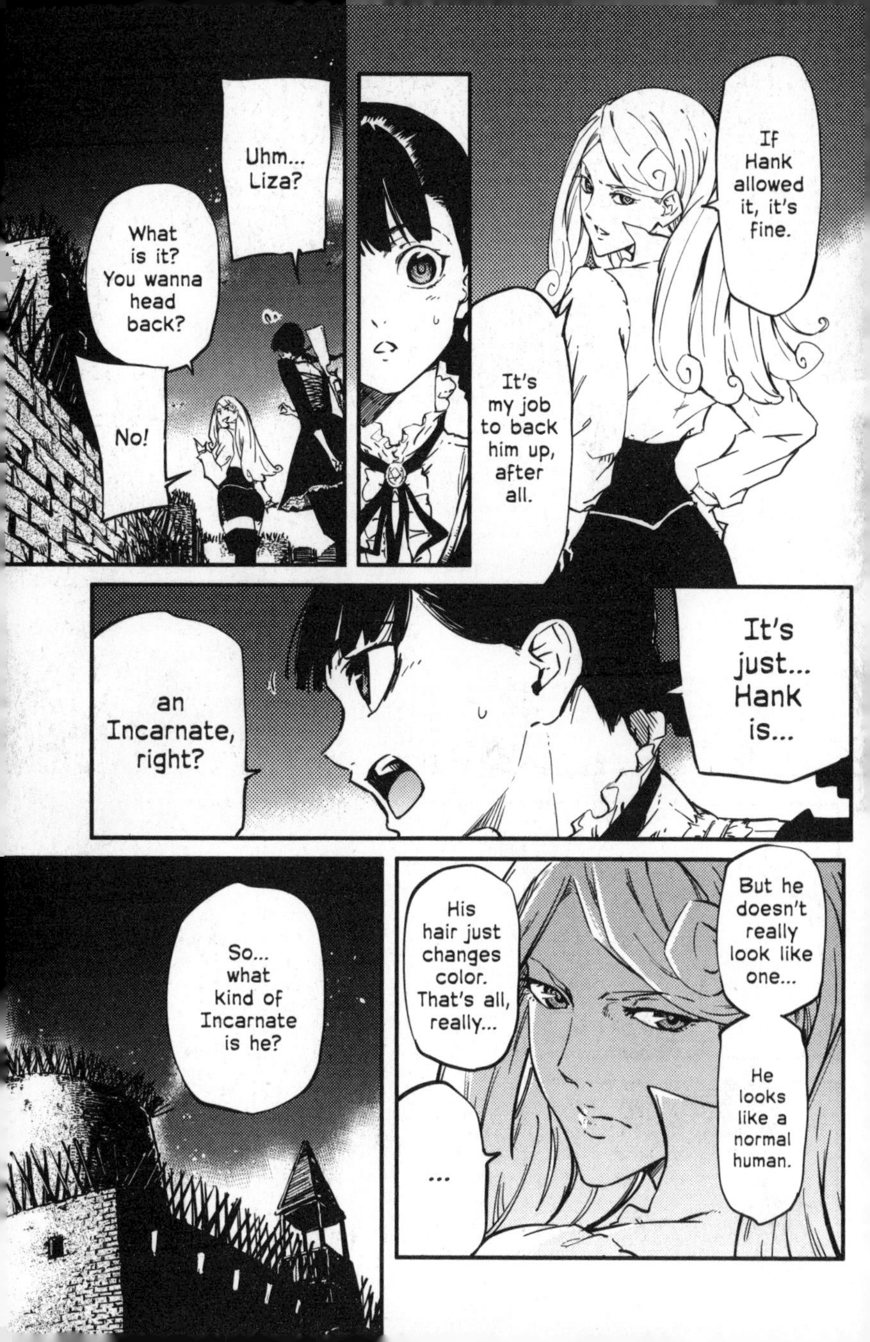
If Hank allowed it, it's fine.
It's my job to back him up, after all.
Uhm... Liza?
What is it? You wanna head back?
No!
It's just... Hank is...
an Incarnate, right?
But he doesn't really look like one...
He looks like a normal human.
His hair just changes color. That's all, really...
...
So... what kind of Incarnate is he?

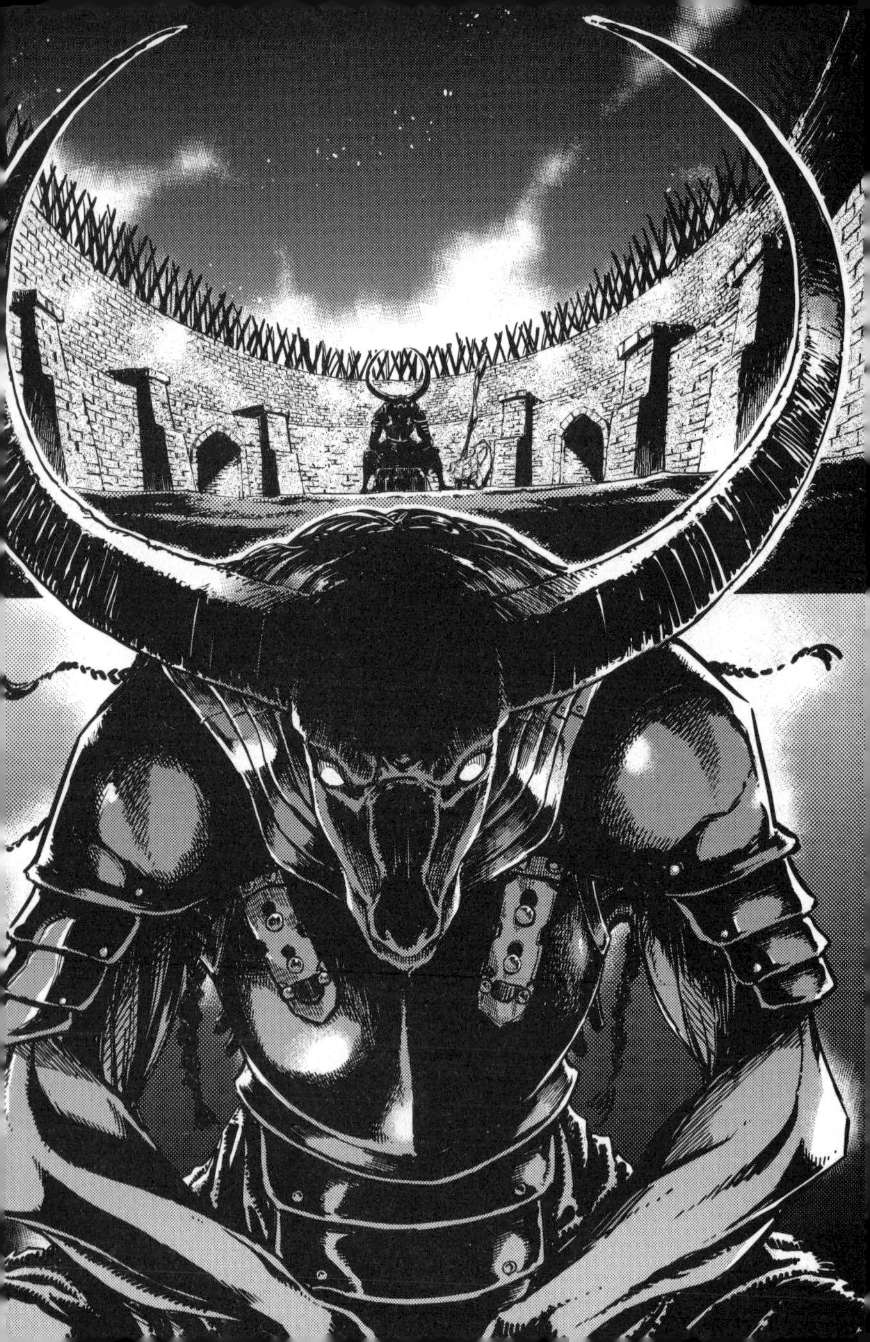

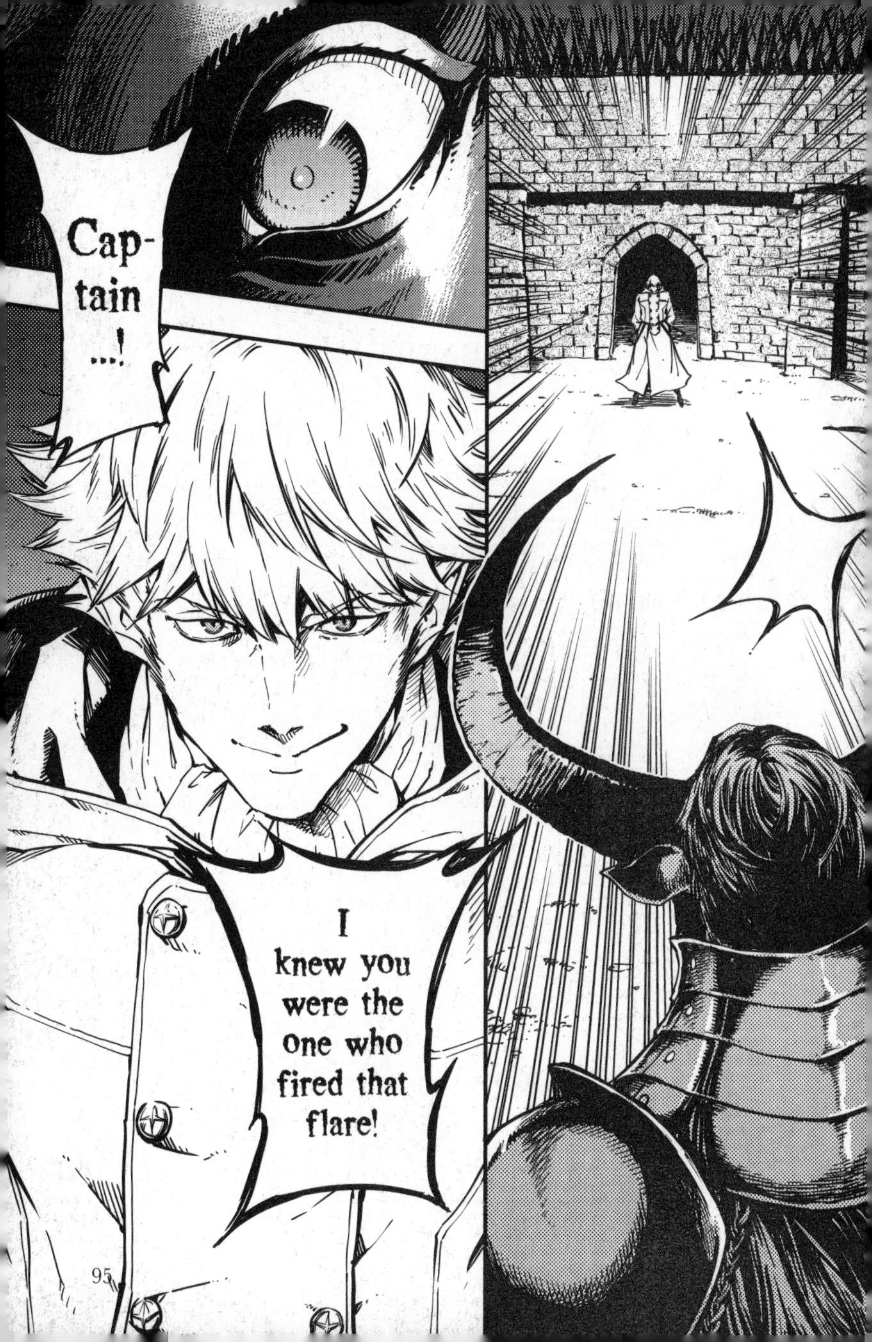
Cap-tain ...!
I knew you were the one who fired that flare!

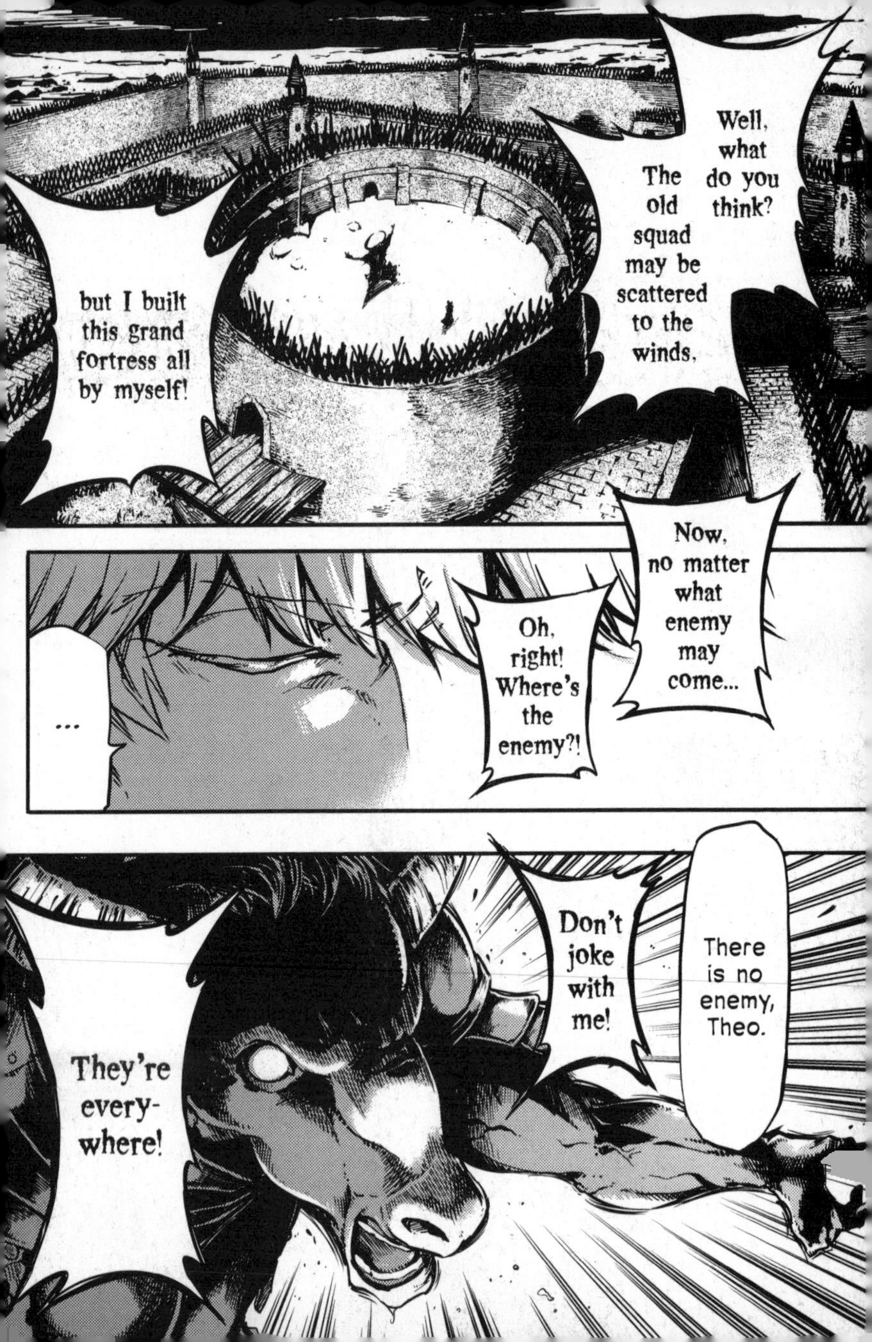
Well, what do you think?
The old squad may be scattered to the winds,
but I built this grand fortress all by myself!
Now, no matter what enemy may come...
Oh, right! Where's the enemy?!
...
There is no enemy, Theo.
Don't joke with me!
They're everywhere!

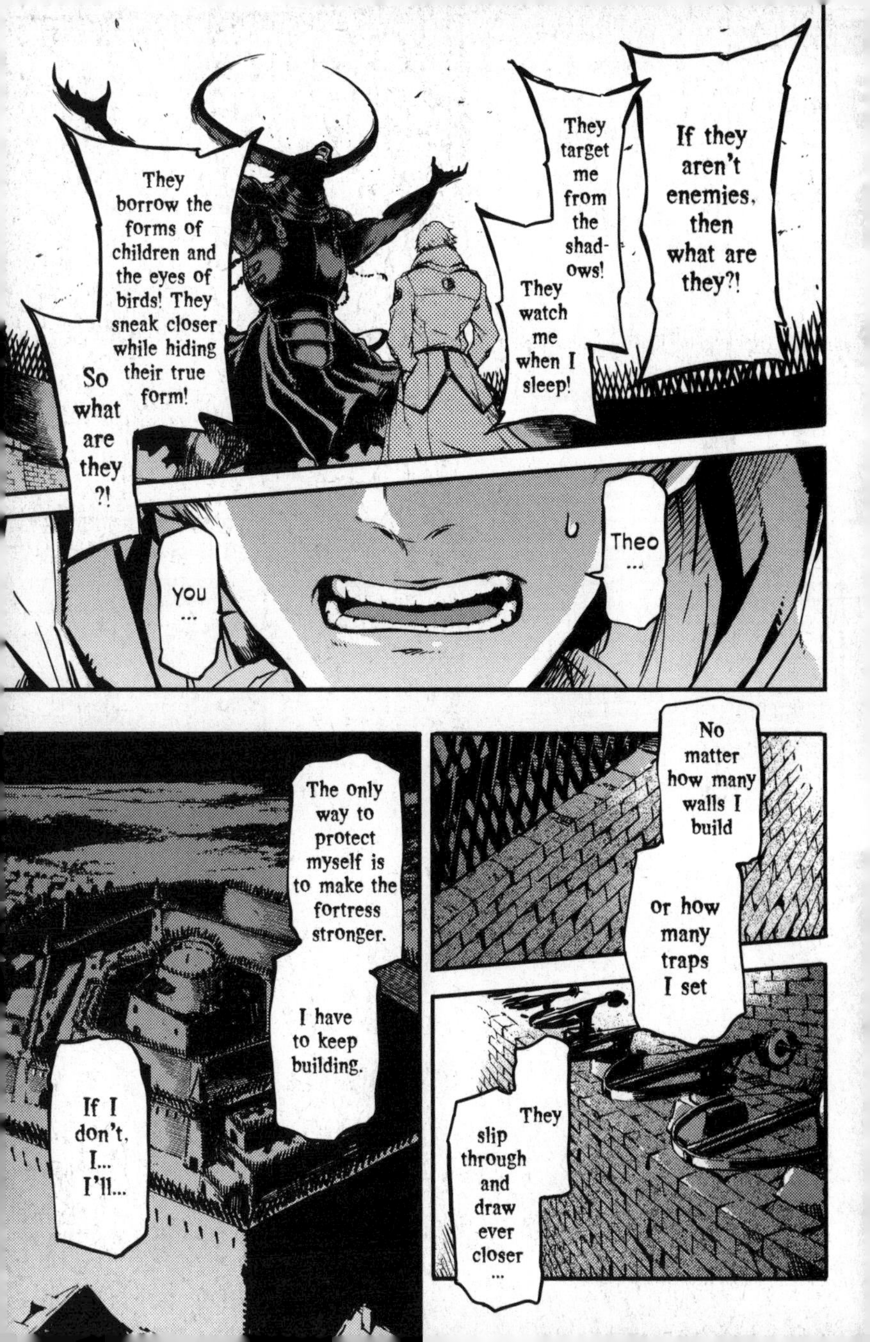
If they aren't enemies, then what are they?!
They target me from the shadows!
They watch me when I sleep!
They borrow the forms of children and the eyes of birds! They sneak closer while hiding their true form!
So what are they?!
Theo...
You...
No matter how many walls I build
or how many traps I set
They slip through and draw ever closer...
The only way to protect myself is to make the fortress stronger.
I have to keep building.
If I don't, I... I'll...

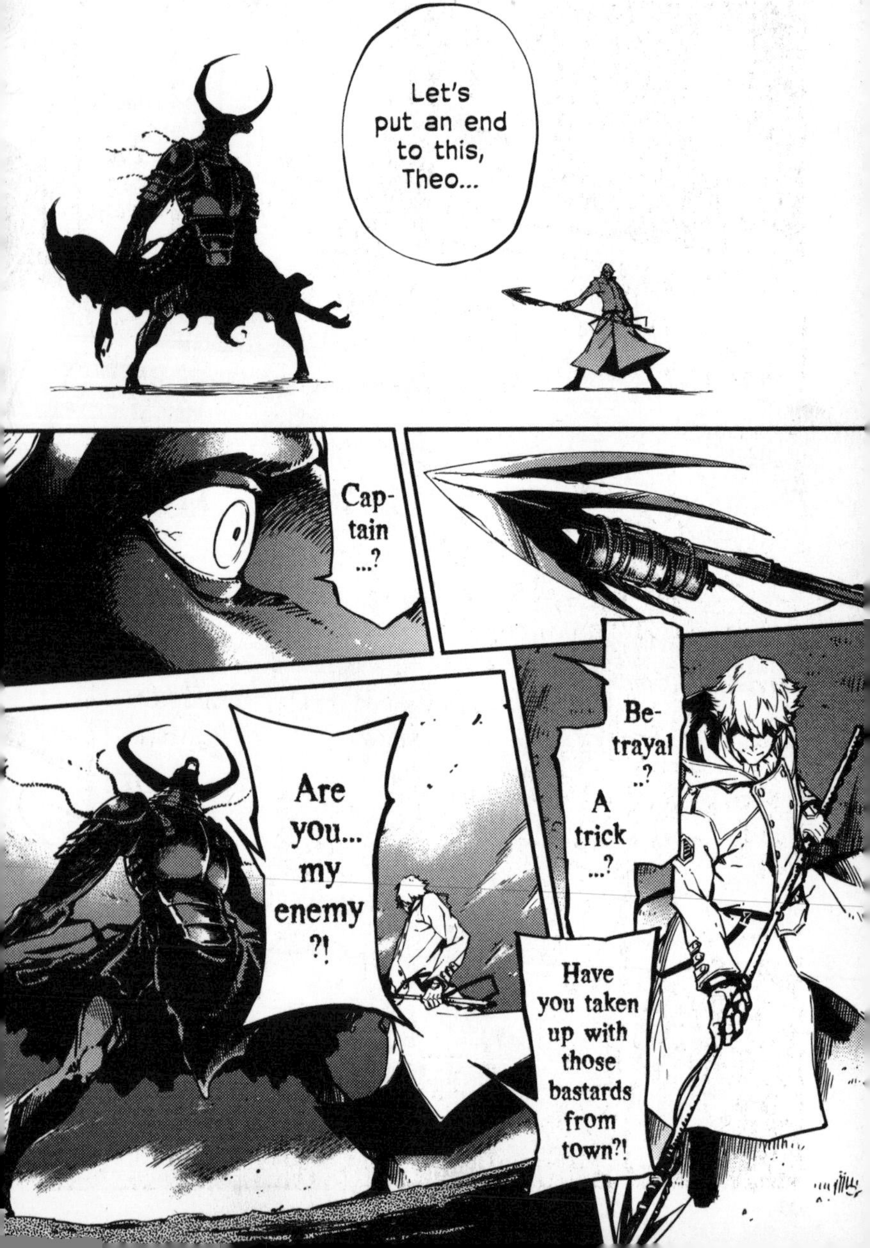
Let's put an end to this, Theo...
Cap-tain ...?
Be-trayal ..?
A trick ...?
Have you taken up with those bastards from town?!
Are you... my enemy ?!

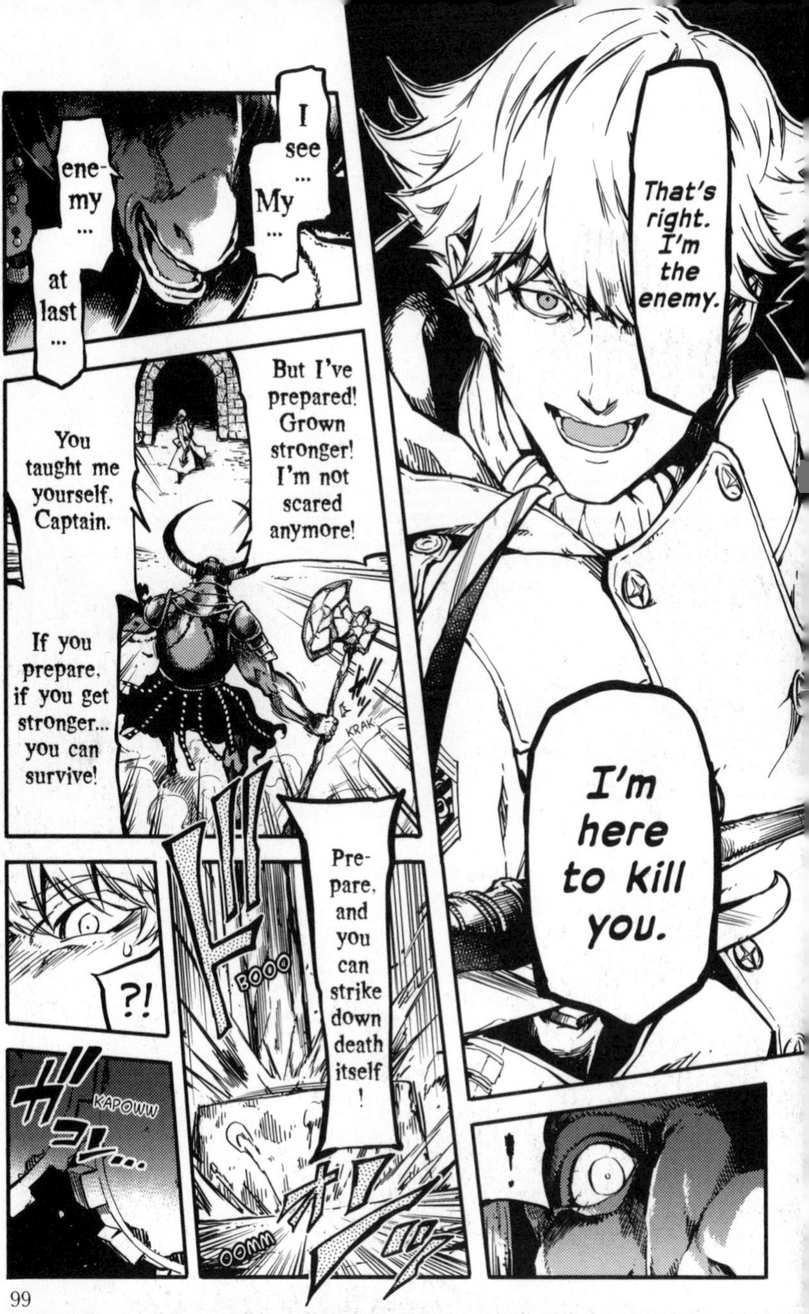

That's right. I'm the enemy.
I'm here to kill you.
!
I see... My...
enemy... at last...
But I've prepared! Grown stronger! I'm not scared anymore!
KRAK
You taught me yourself, Captain.
If you prepare, if you get stronger... you can survive!
Prepare, and you can strike down death itself!
BOOO
OOMM
?!
KAPOWW

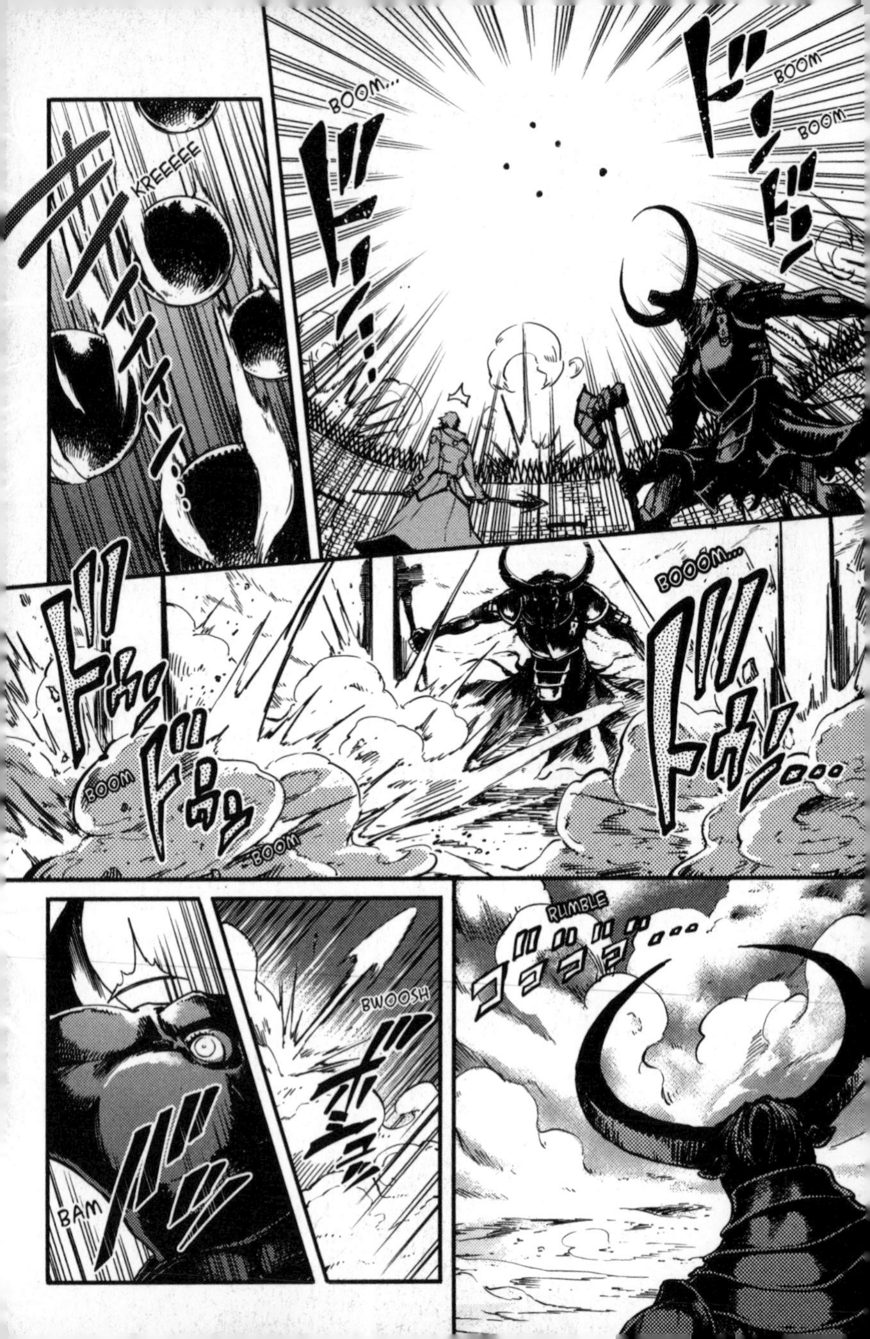
BOOM
BOOM
BOOM...
KREEEEE
BOOOM...
BOOM
BOOM
RUMBLE
BWOOSH
BAM

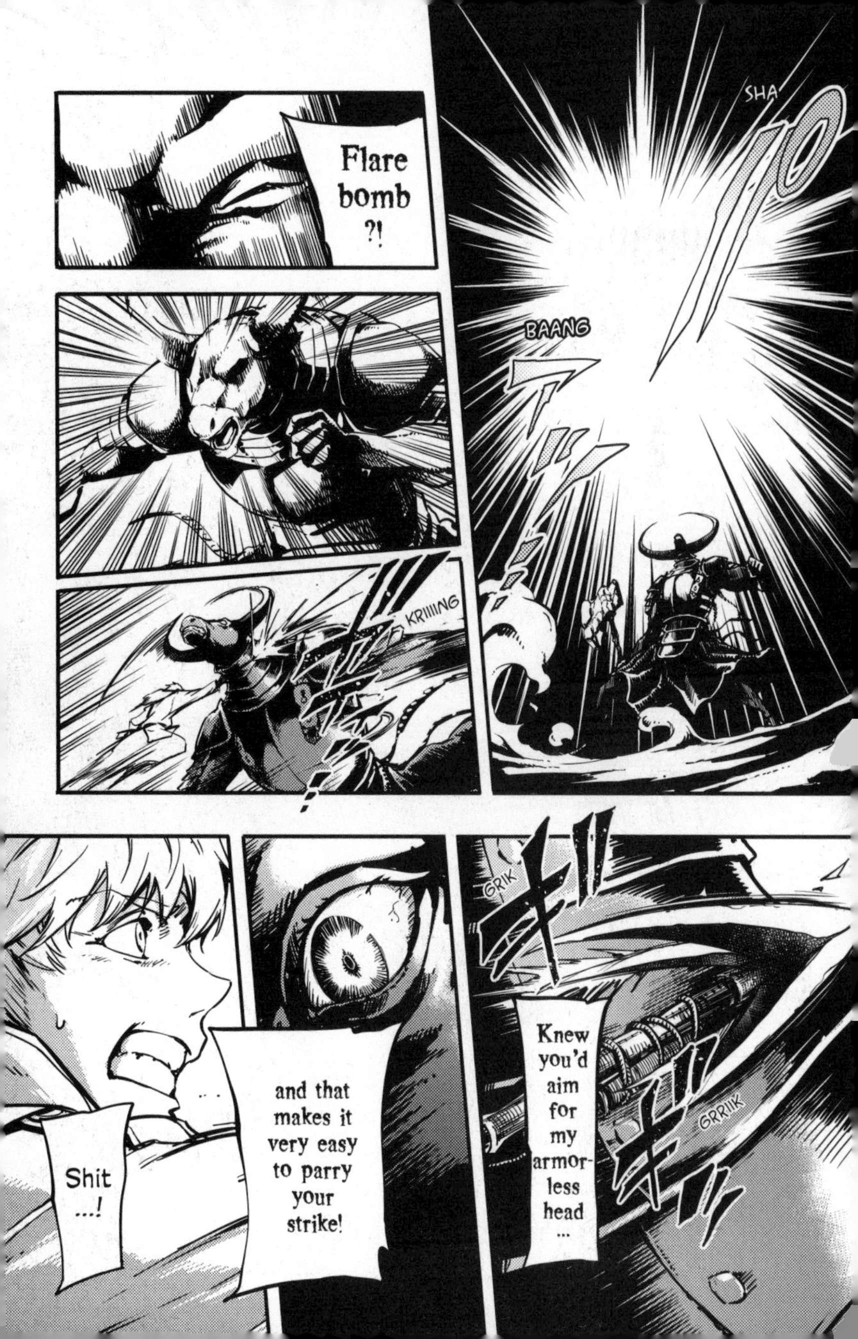
SHA
BAANG
Flare bomb ?!
KRIIING
GRIK
Knew you'd aim for my armor-less head ...
GRRIK
and that makes it very easy to parry your strike!
...
Shit ...!

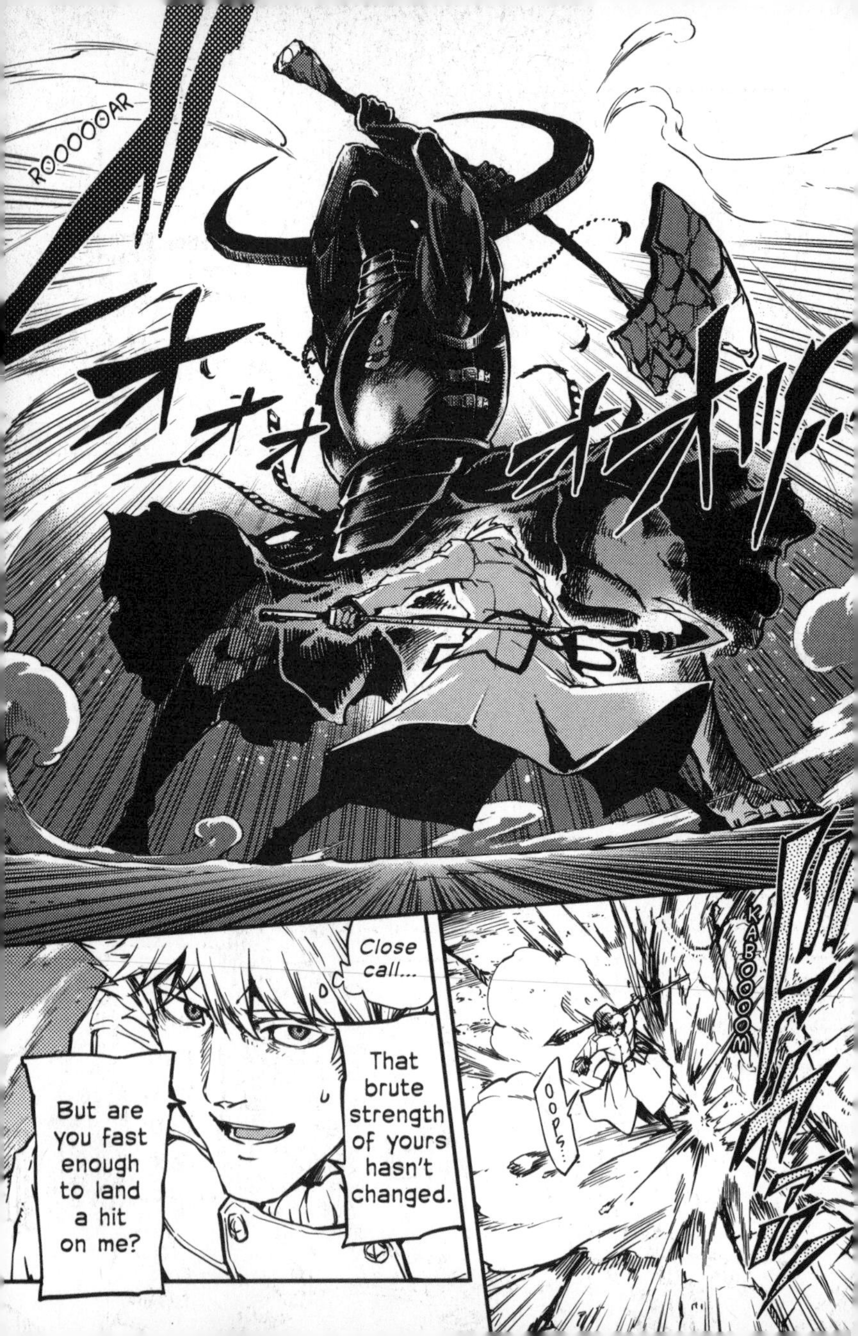
ROOOOOAR
KABOOOOM
Oops...
Close call...
That brute strength of yours hasn't changed.
But are you fast enough to land a hit on me?

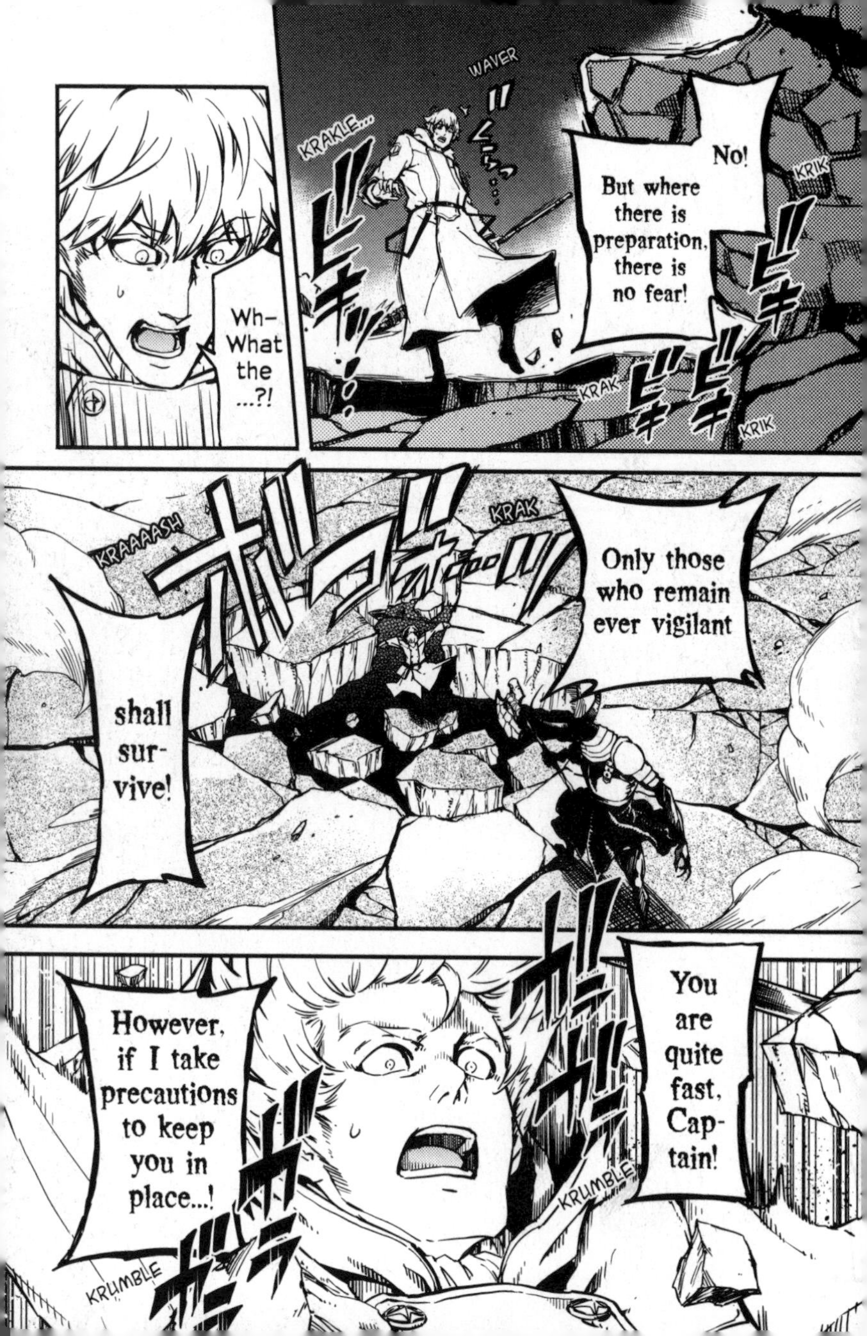
No! But where there is preparation, there is no fear!
KRIK
WAVER
KRAKLE...
KRAK
KRIK
Wh– What the ...?!
Only those who remain ever vigilant
KRAK
KRAAAASH
shall survive!
You are quite fast, Captain!
KRUMBLE
However, if I take precautions to keep you in place...!
KRUMBLE

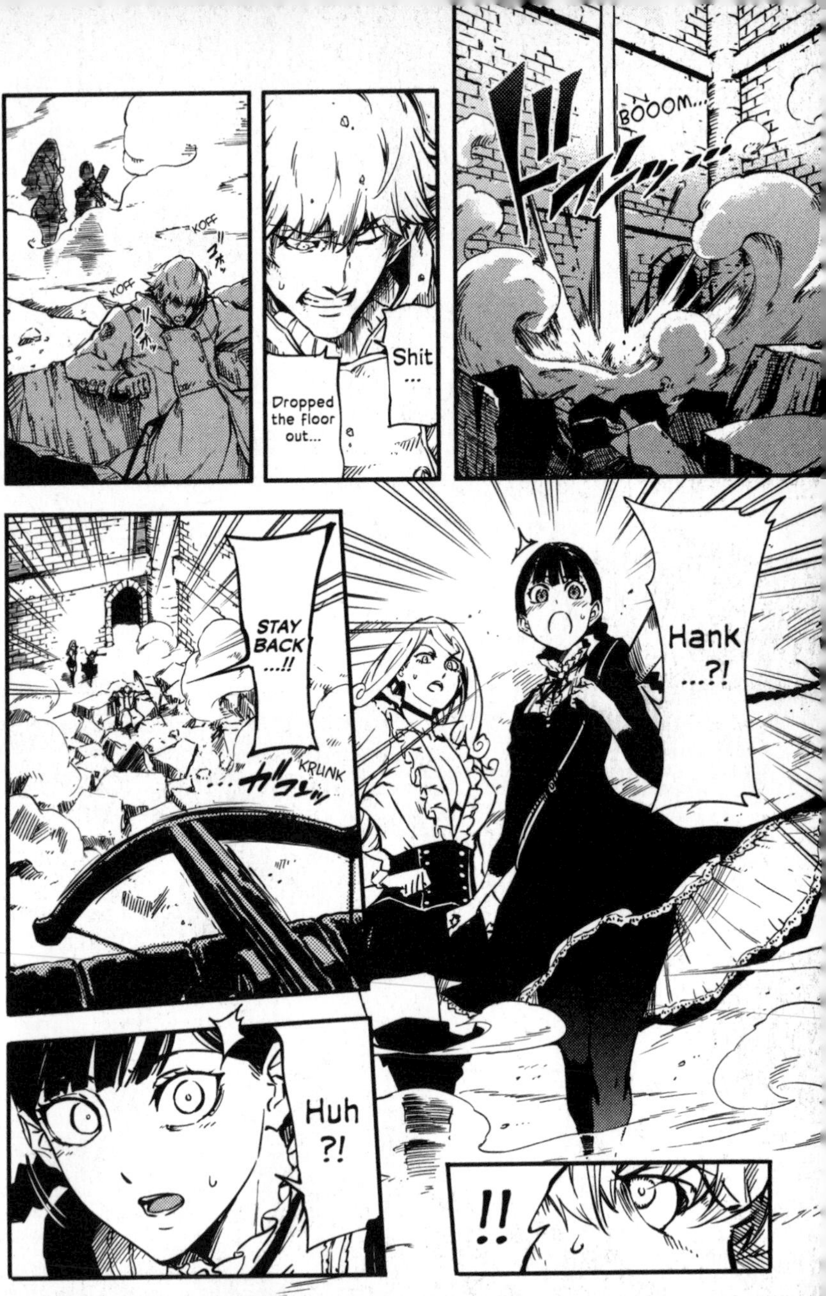
BOOOM...
Shit...
Dropped the floor out...
KOFF
KOFF
Hank...?!
STAY BACK...!!
KRUNK
!!
Huh ?!

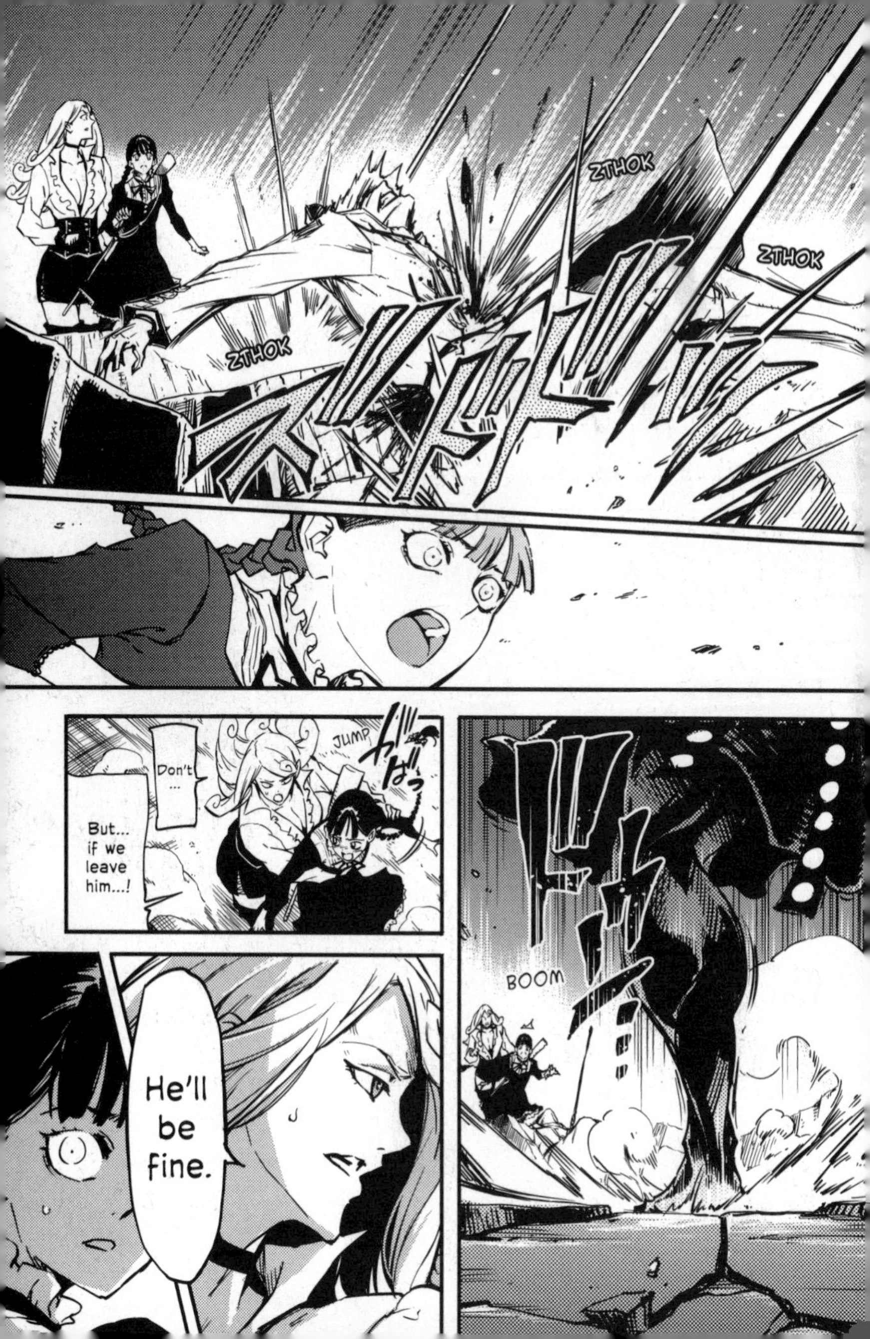
ZTHOK
ZTHOK
ZTHOK
BOOM
JUMP
Don't ...
But... if we leave him...!
He'll be fine.

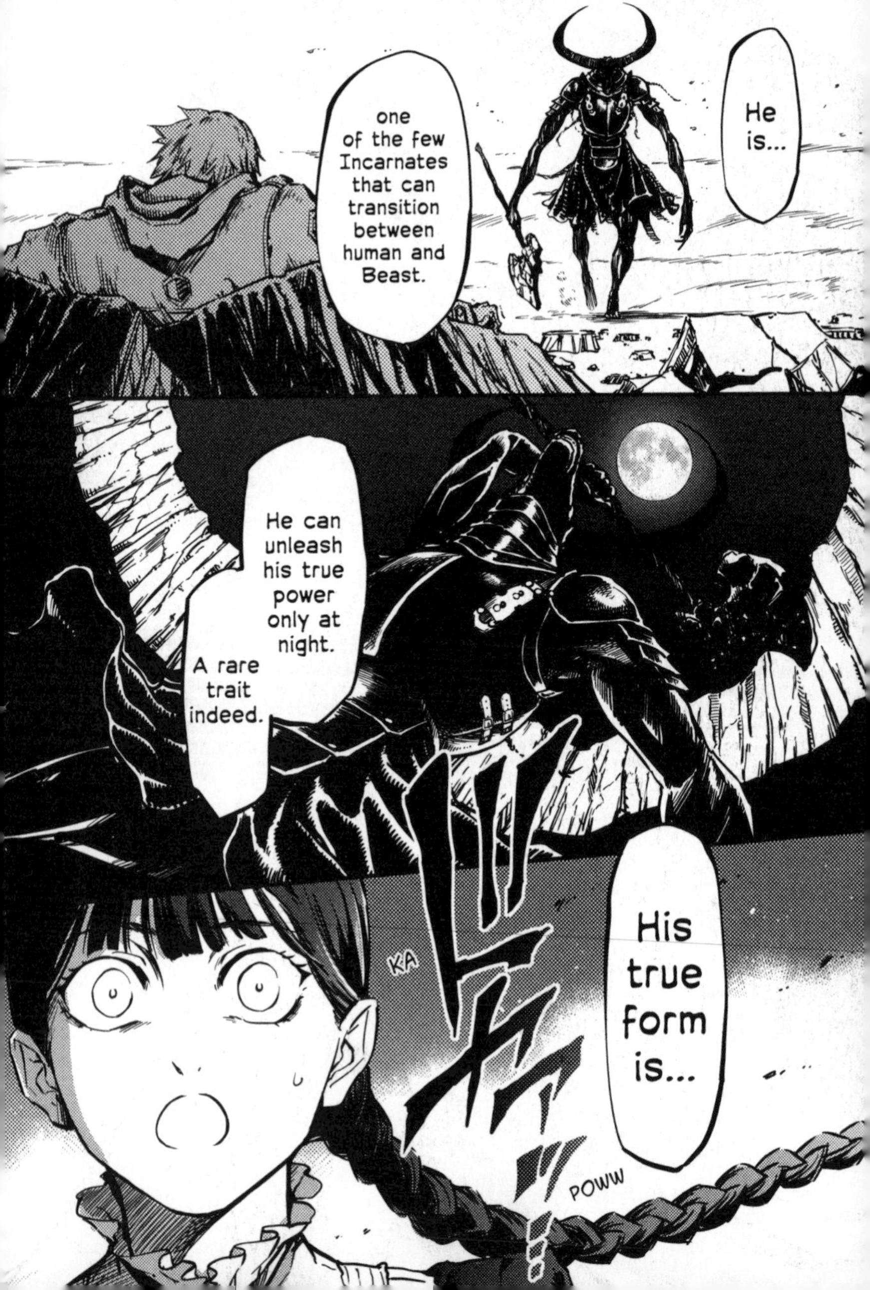
He is...
one of the few Incarnates that can transition between human and Beast.
He can unleash his true power only at night.
A rare trait indeed.
His true form is...
KA
POWW

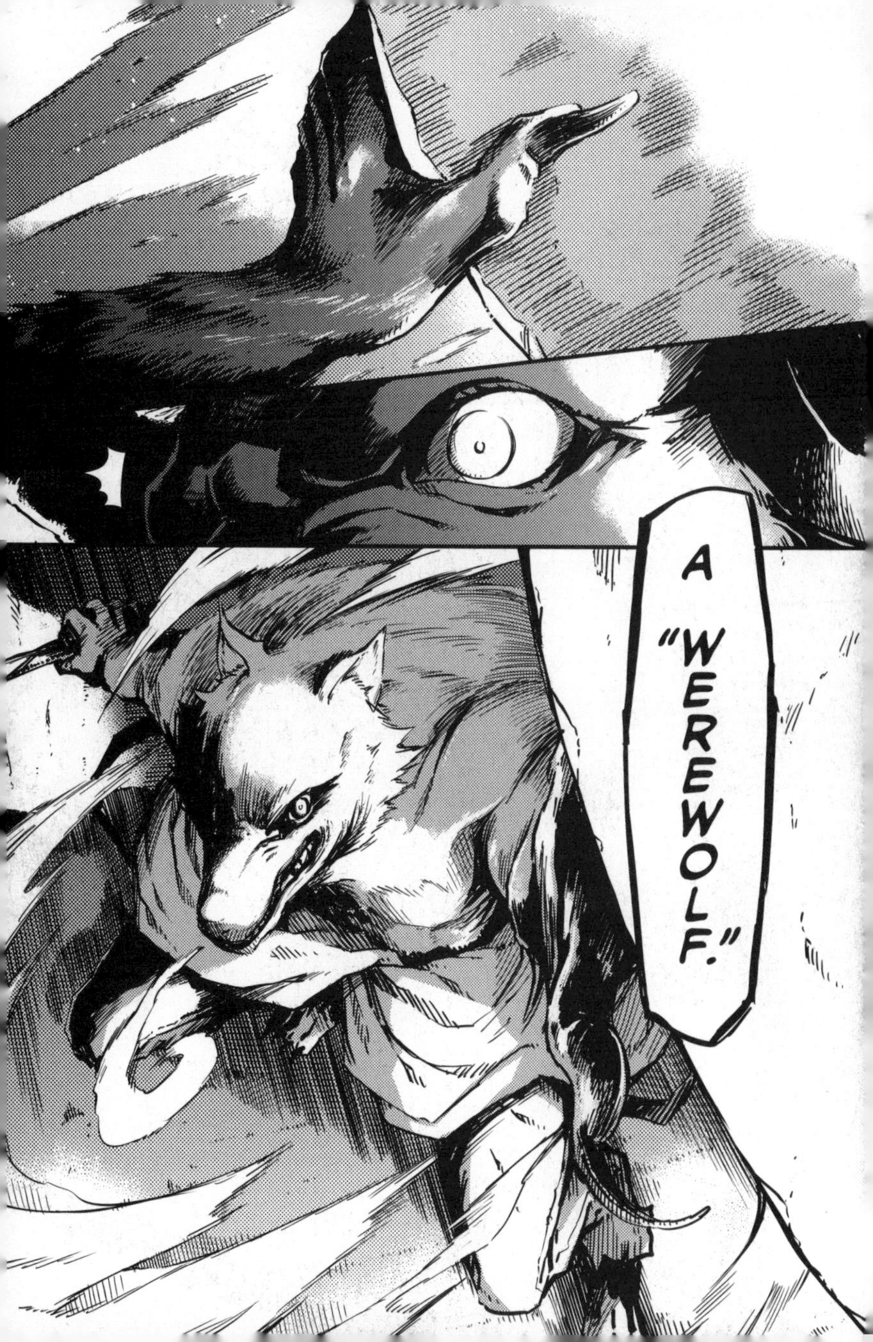
A "WEREWOLF."

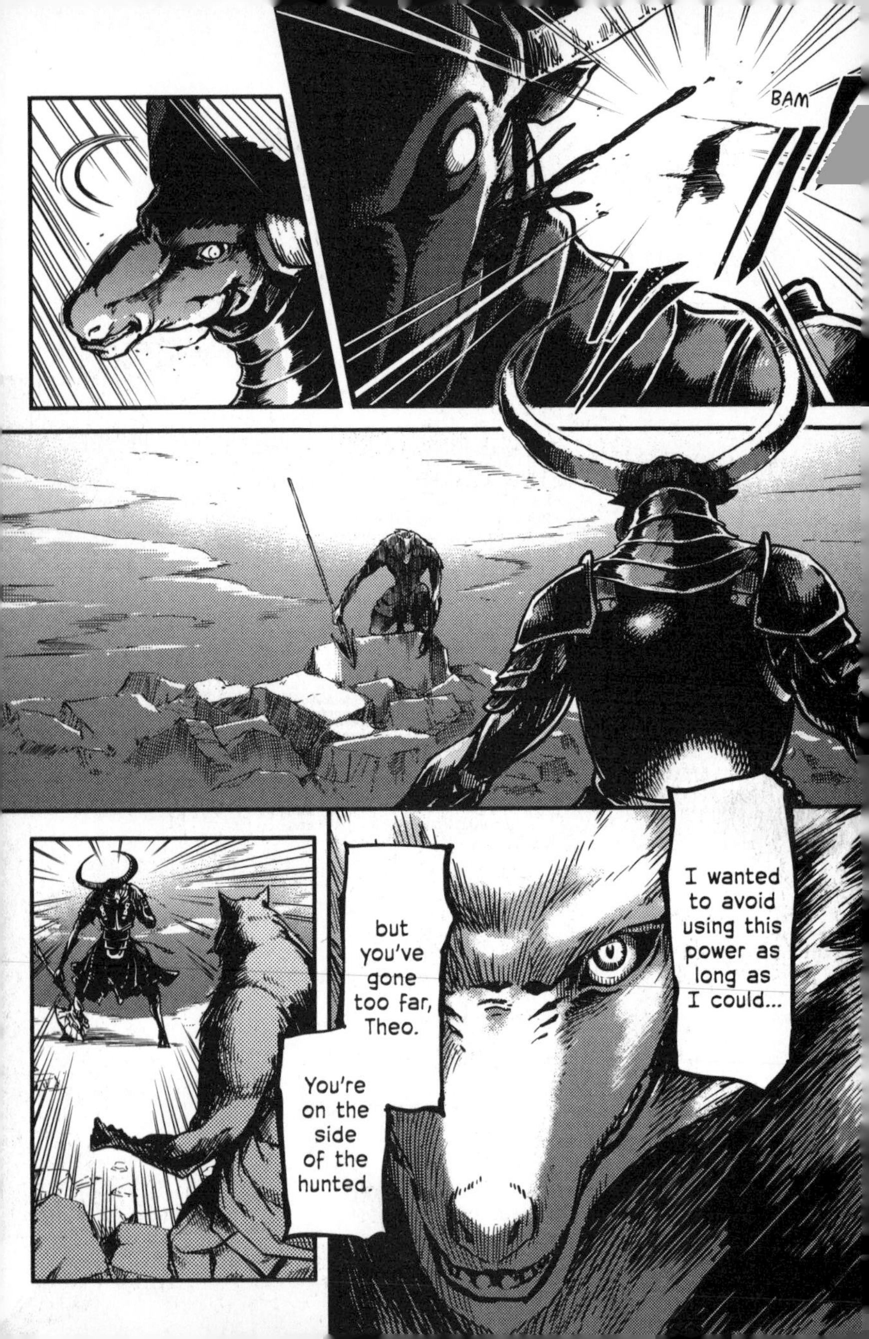
BAM
I wanted to avoid using this power as long as I could...
but you've gone too far, Theo.
You're on the side of the hunted.

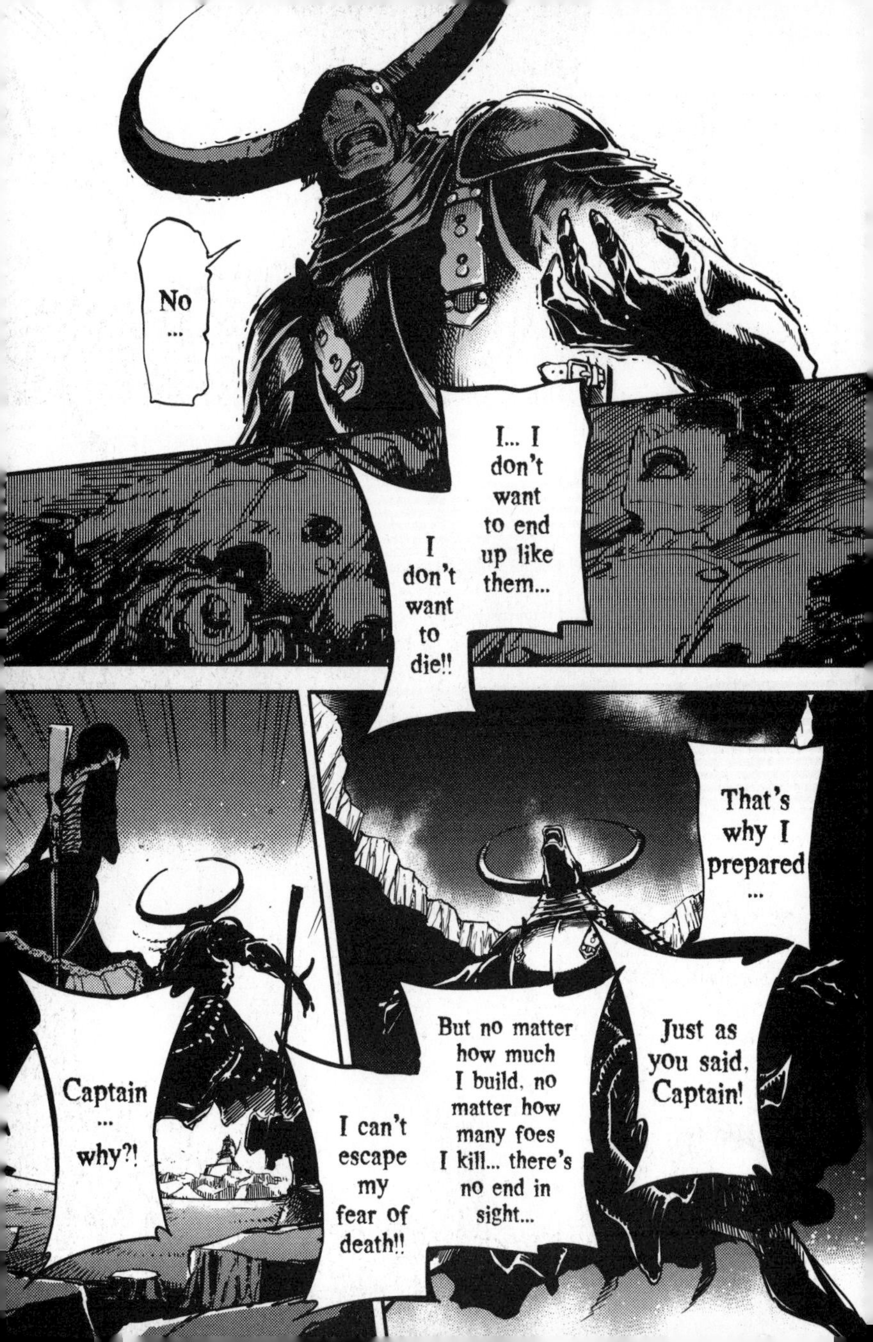
No ...
I... I don't want to end up like them...
I don't want to die!!
That's why I prepared ...
Just as you said, Captain!
But no matter how much I build, no matter how many foes I kill... there's no end in sight...
I can't escape my fear of death!!
Captain ... why?!

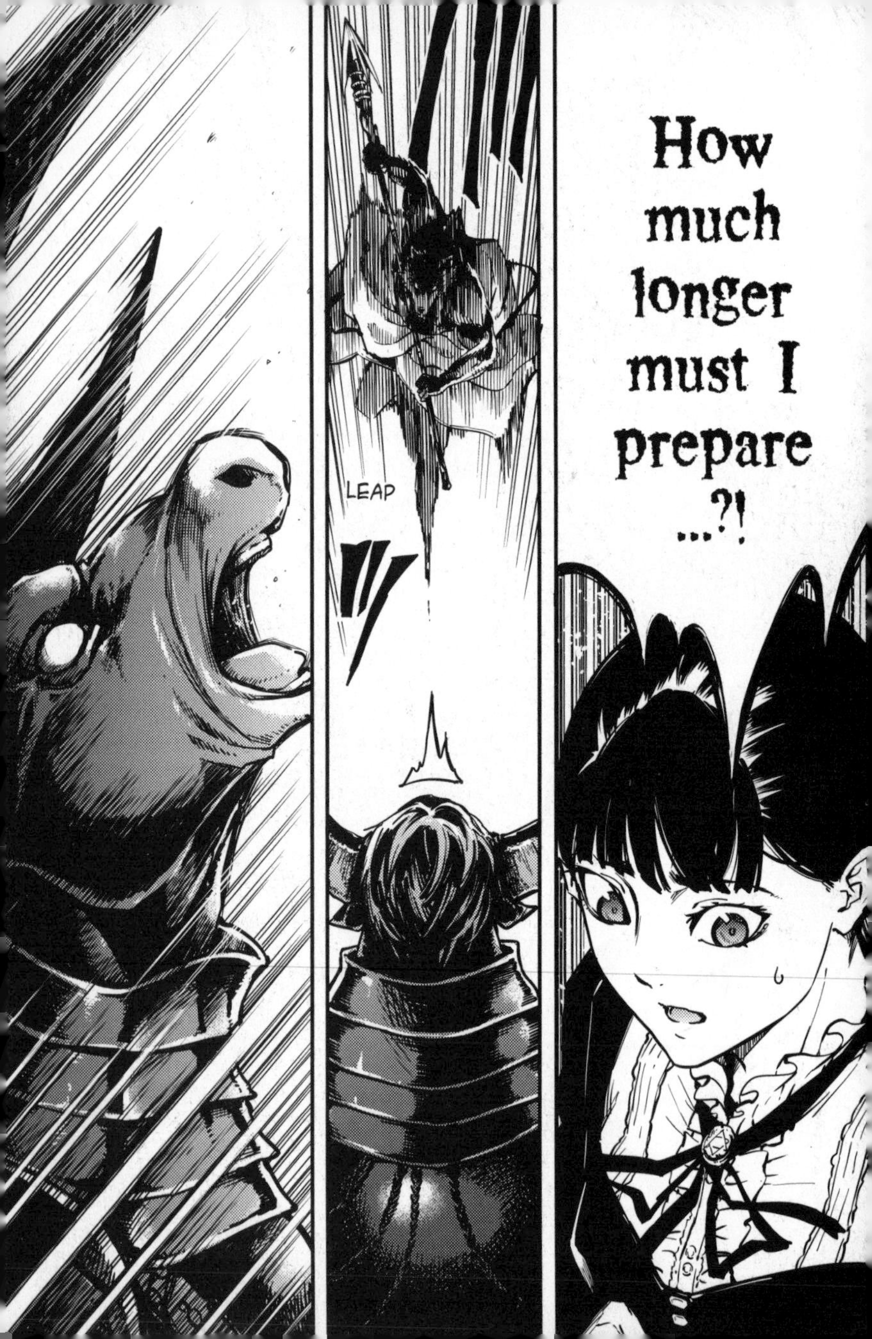
How much longer must I prepare ...?!
LEAP

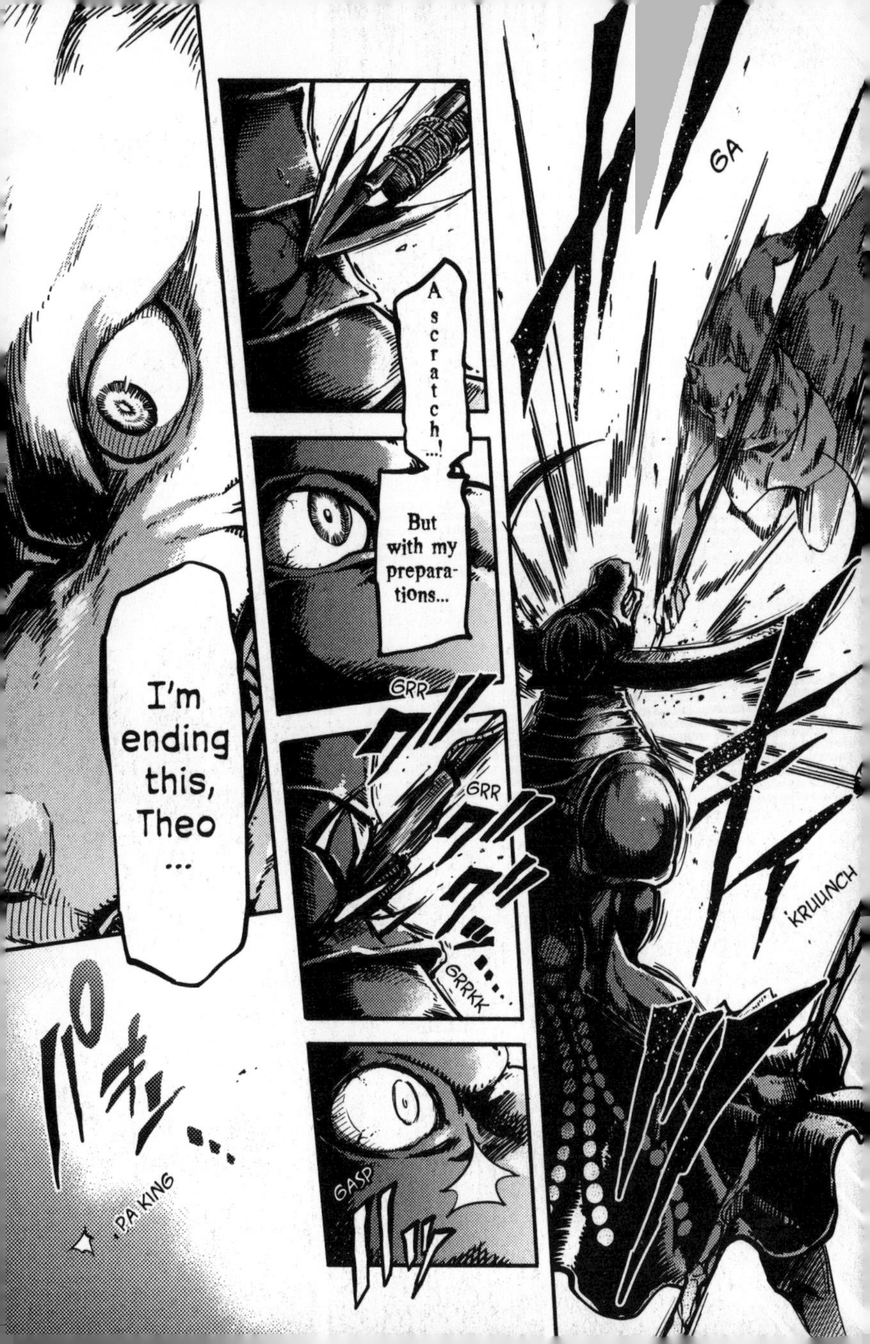

GA
KRUUNCH
A scratch!...
But with my prepara-tions...
GRR
GRR
GRRKK
GASP
I'm ending this, Theo ...
PA KING

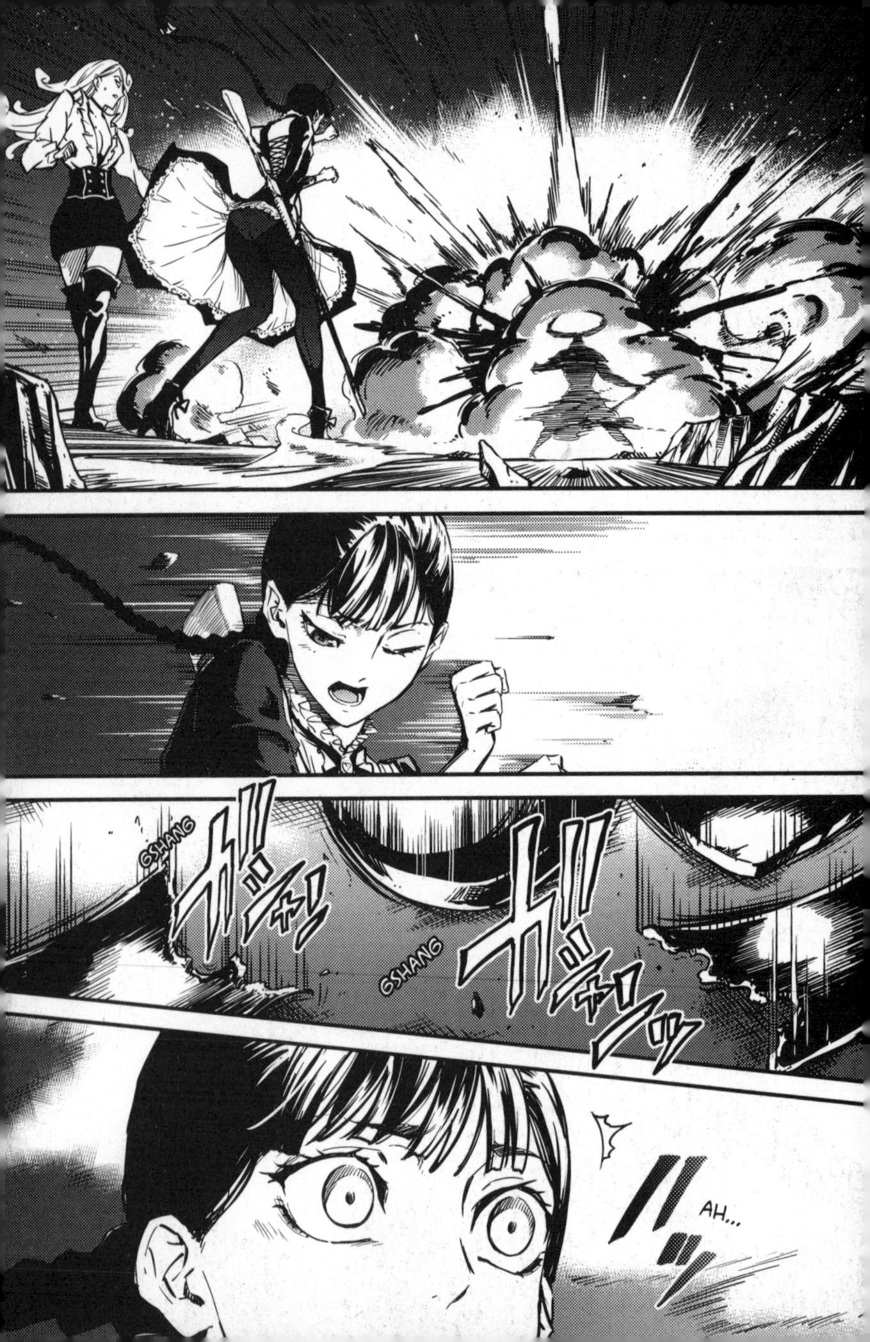
GSHANG
GSHANG
AH...

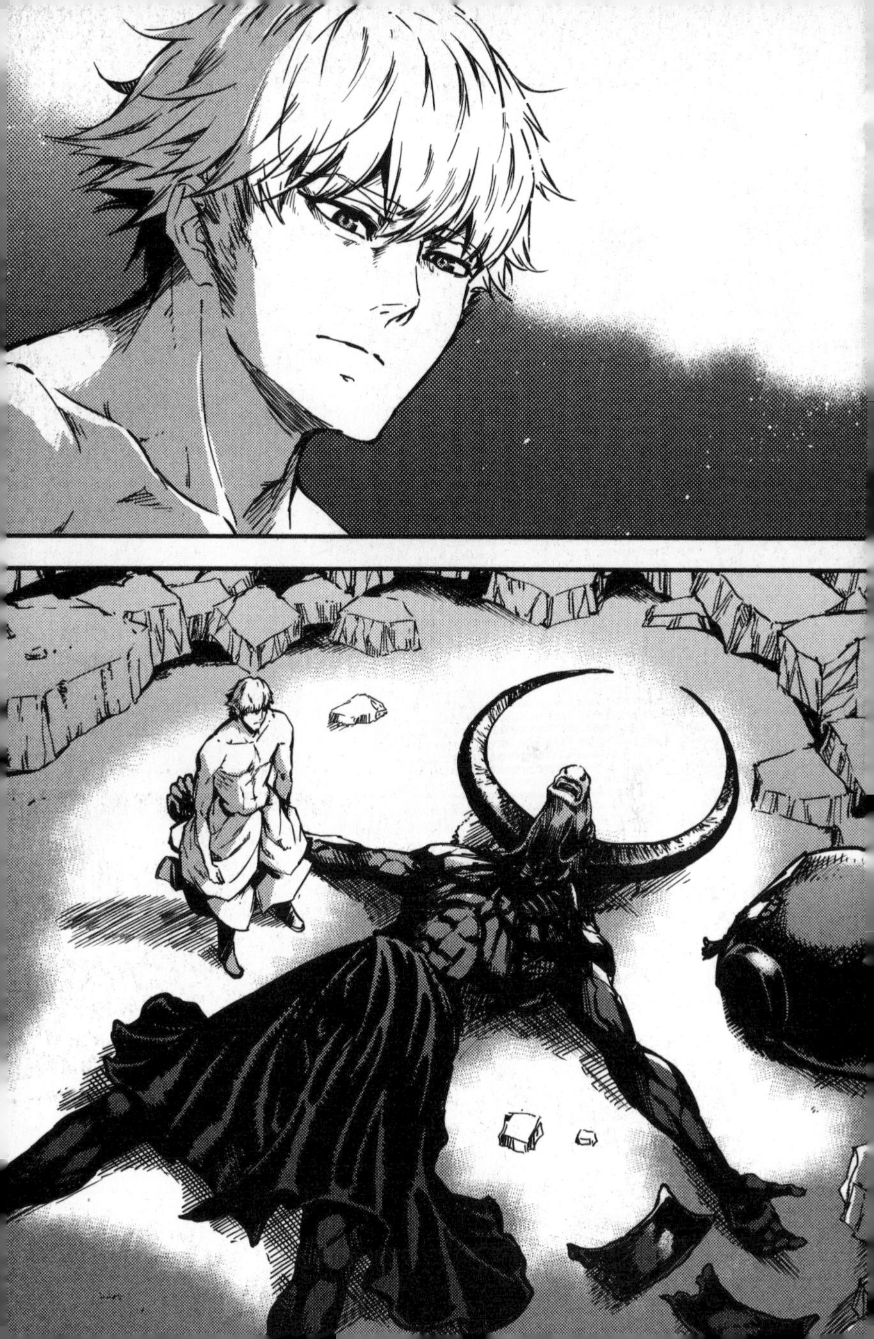

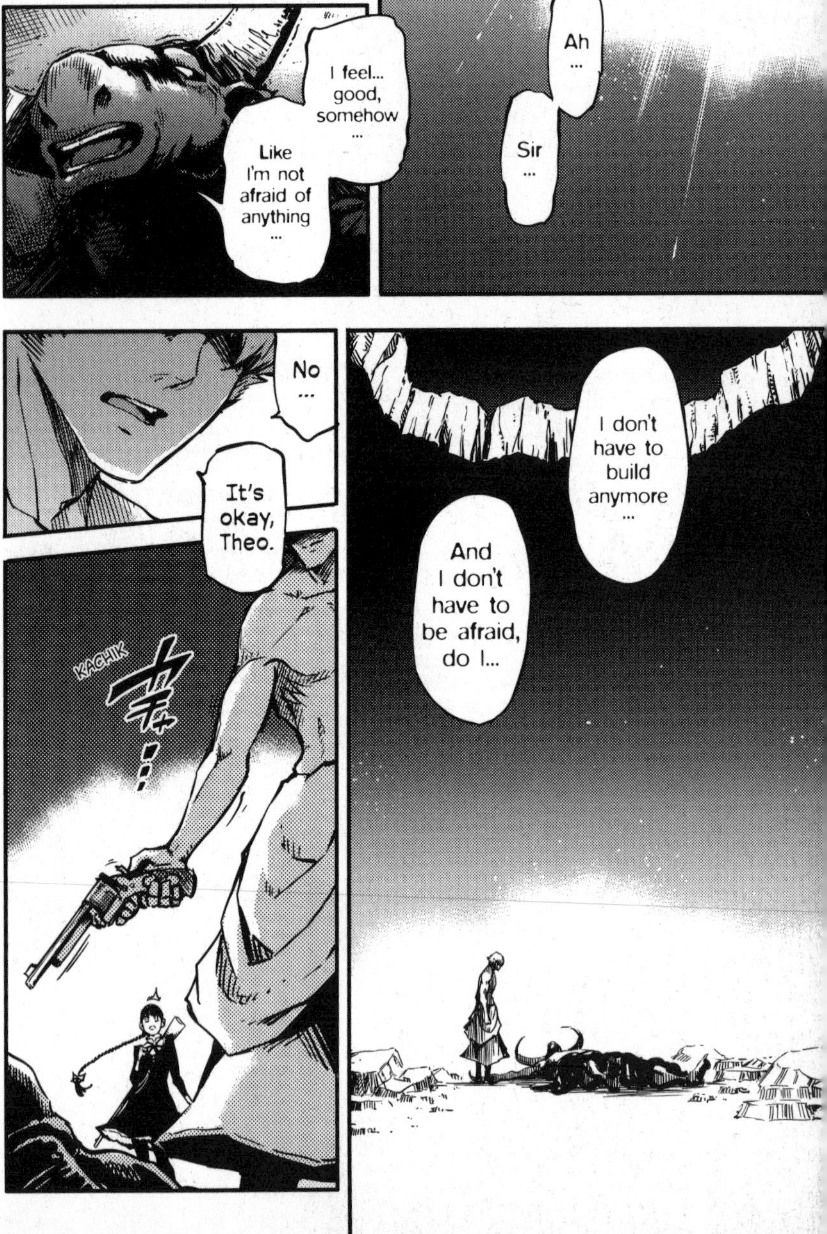
Ah …
Sir …
I feel… good, somehow …
Like I'm not afraid of anything …
I don't have to build anymore …
And I don't have to be afraid, do I…
No …
It's okay, Theo.
KACHIK

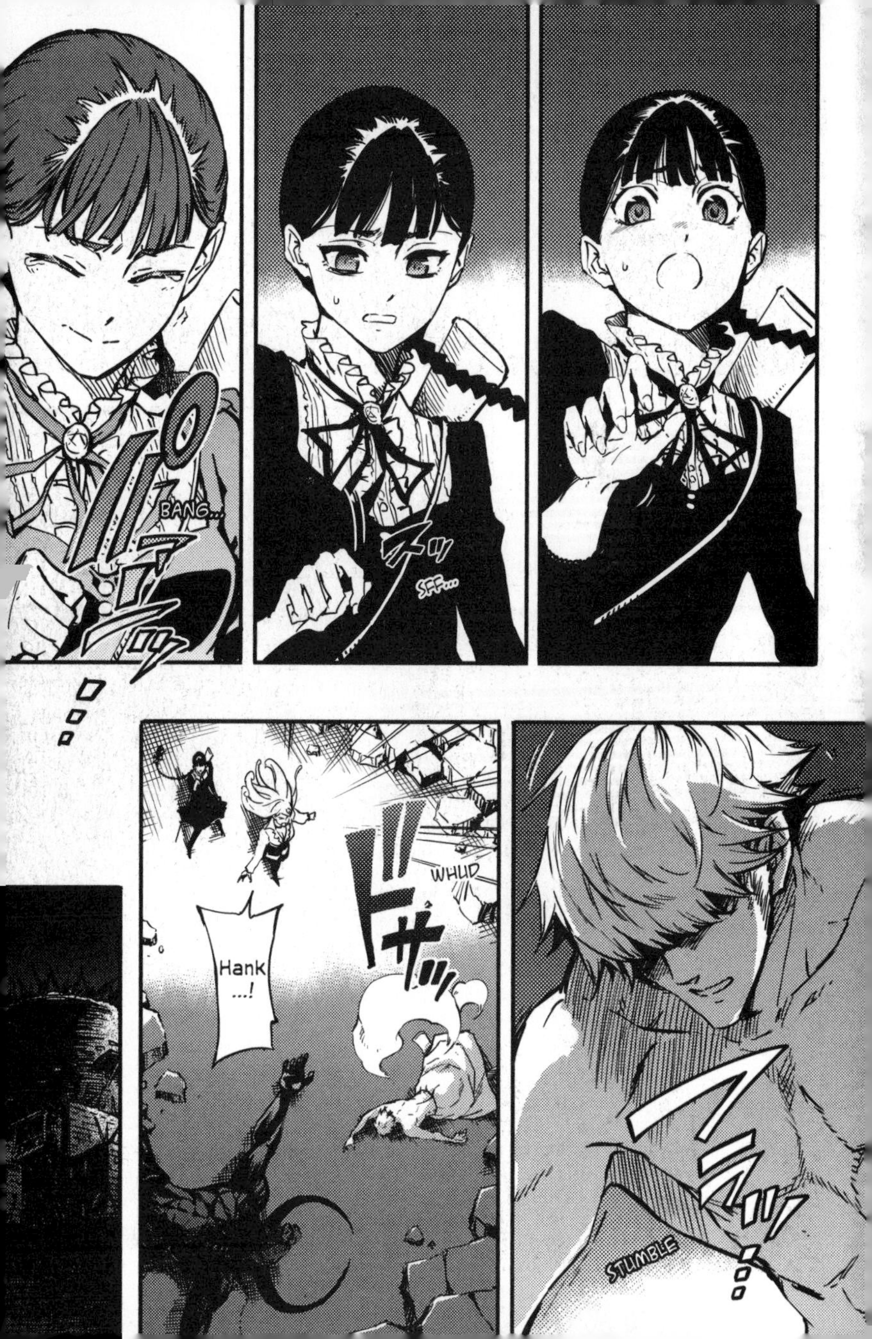
SFF...
BANG...
STUMBLE
WHUD
Hank ...!

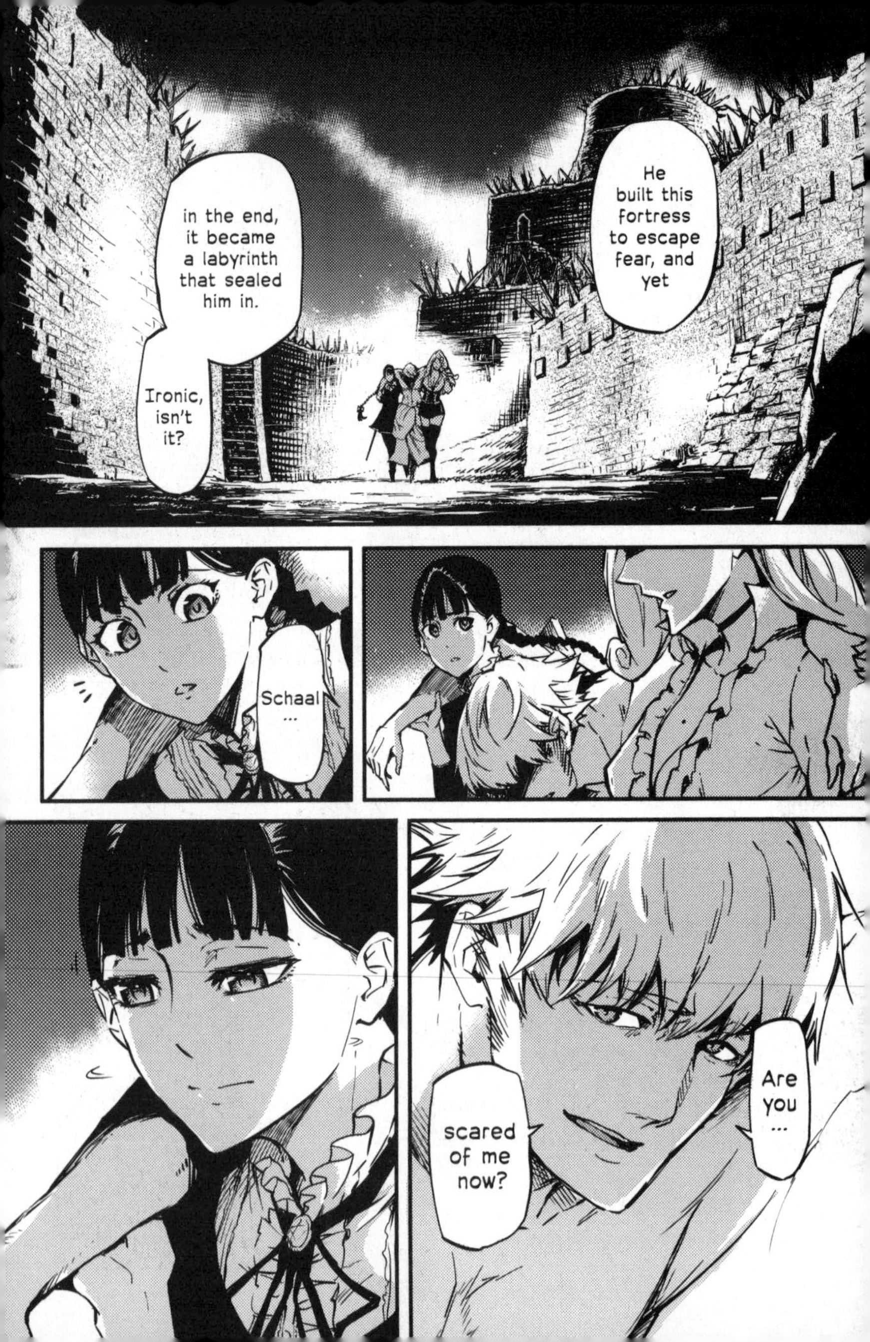
He built this fortress to escape fear, and yet
in the end, it became a labyrinth that sealed him in.
Ironic, isn't it?
Schaal ...
Are you ...
scared of me now?

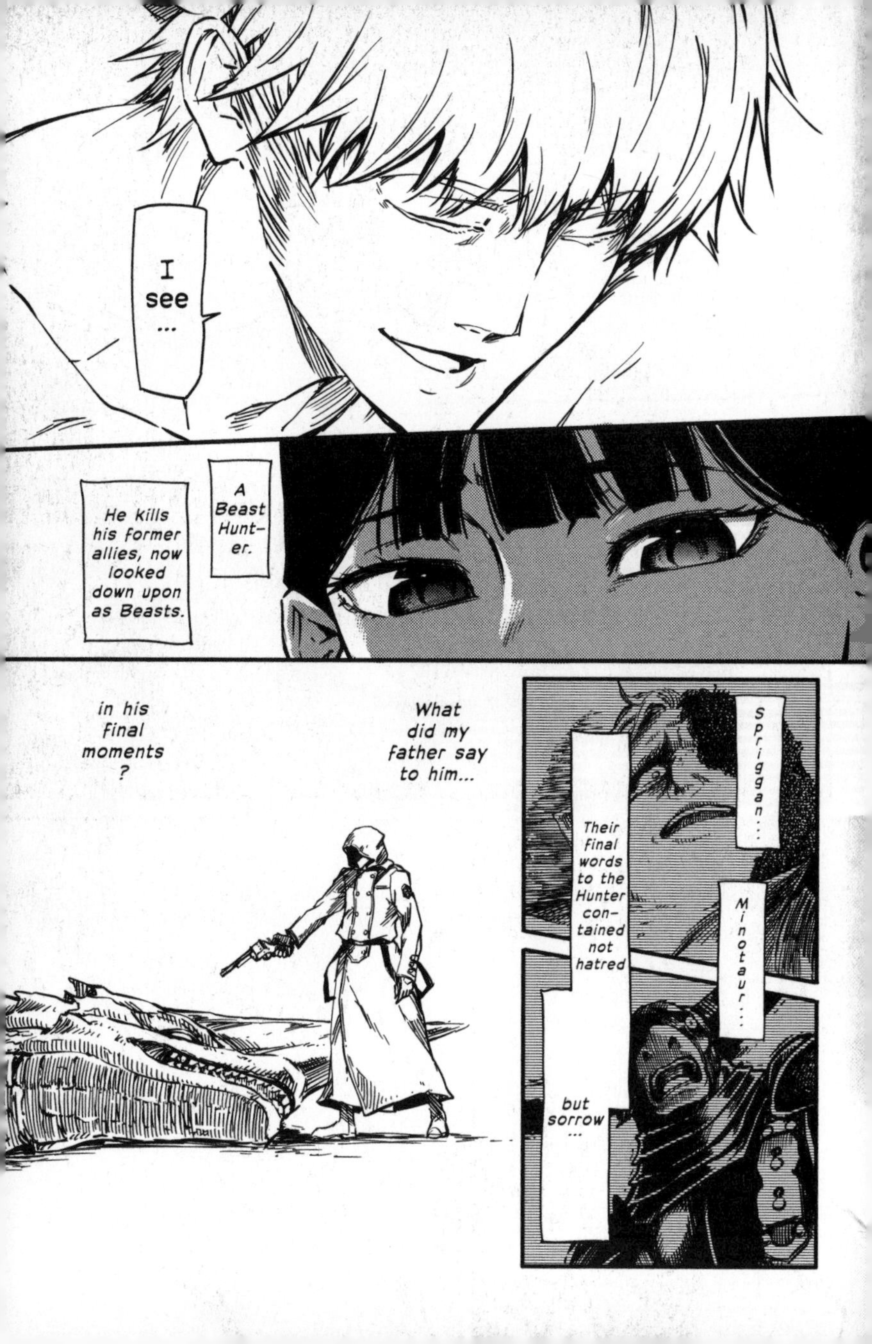
I see...
A Beast Hunter.
He kills his former allies, now looked down upon as Beasts.
Spriggan...
Their final words to the Hunter contained not hatred
Minotaur...
but sorrow...
What did my father say to him...
in his final moments?

To the Abandoned
Sacred Beasts

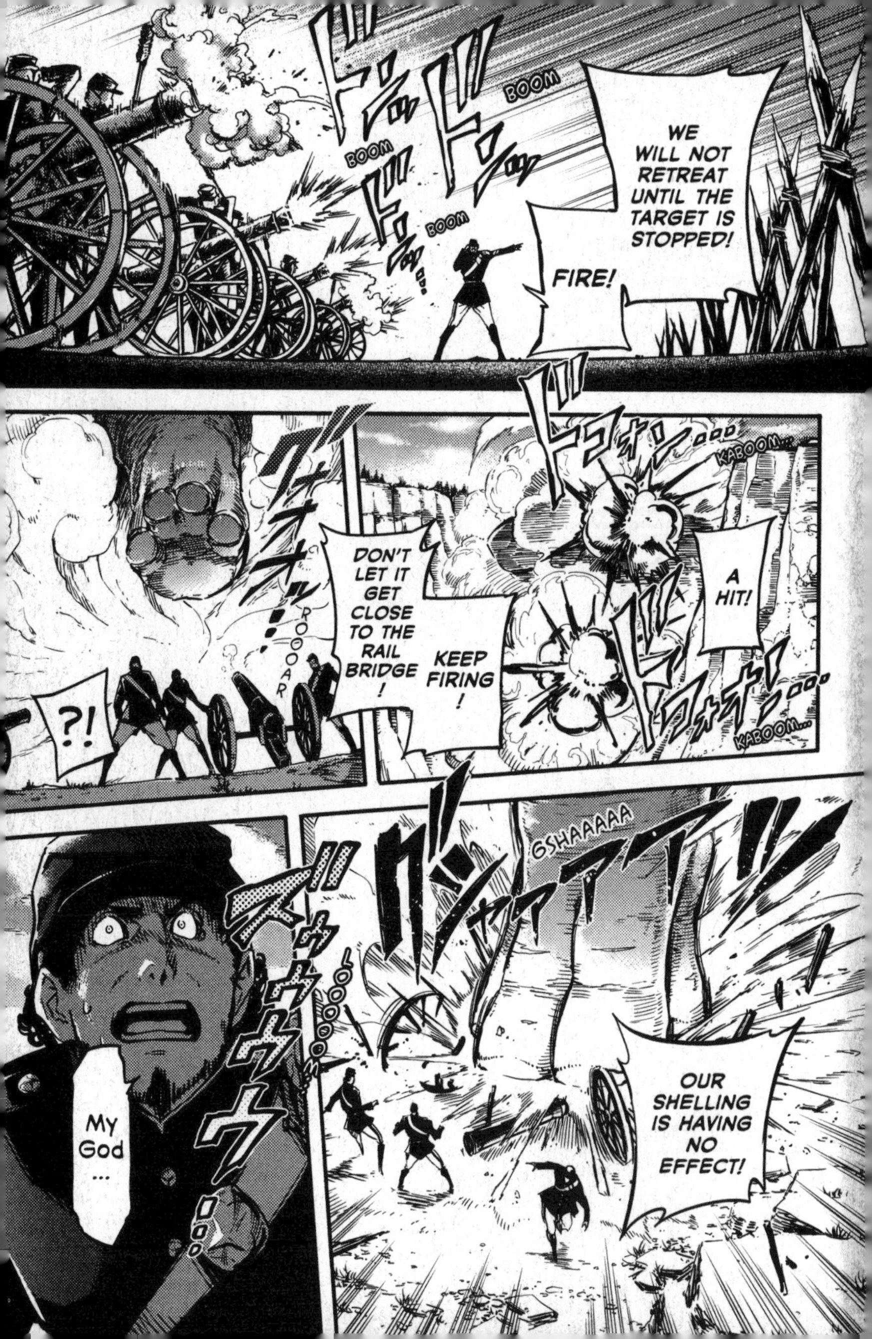
WE WILL NOT RETREAT UNTIL THE TARGET IS STOPPED!
FIRE!
BOOM
BOOM
BOOM
KABOOM...
A HIT!
KABOOM...
KEEP FIRING!
DON'T LET IT GET CLOSE TO THE RAIL BRIDGE!
ROOOAR
?!
GSHAAAAA
OUR SHELLING IS HAVING NO EFFECT!
LOOOOOO
My God...

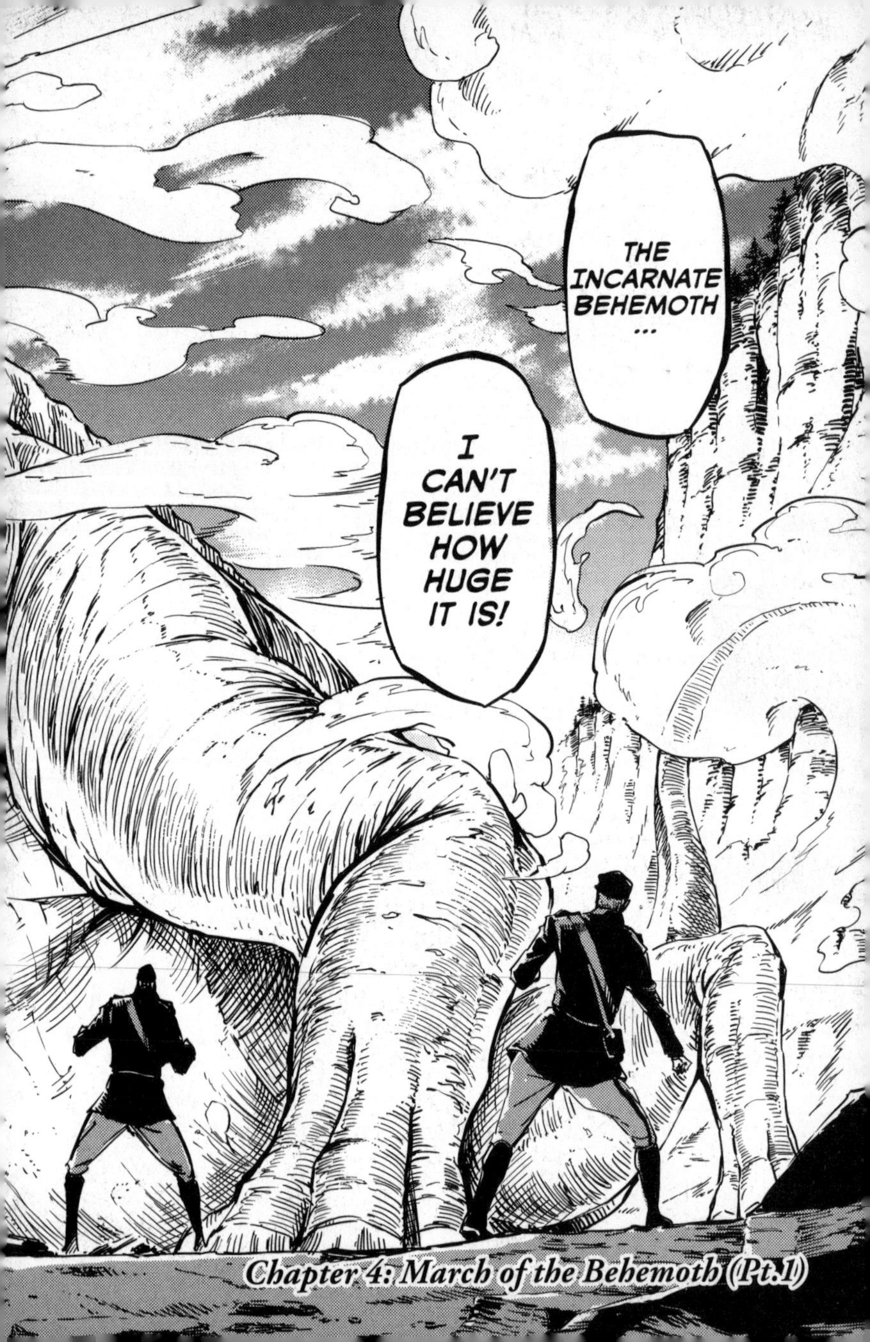
THE INCARNATE BEHEMOTH ...
I CAN'T BELIEVE HOW HUGE IT IS!

Chapter 4: March of the Behemoth (Pt.1)

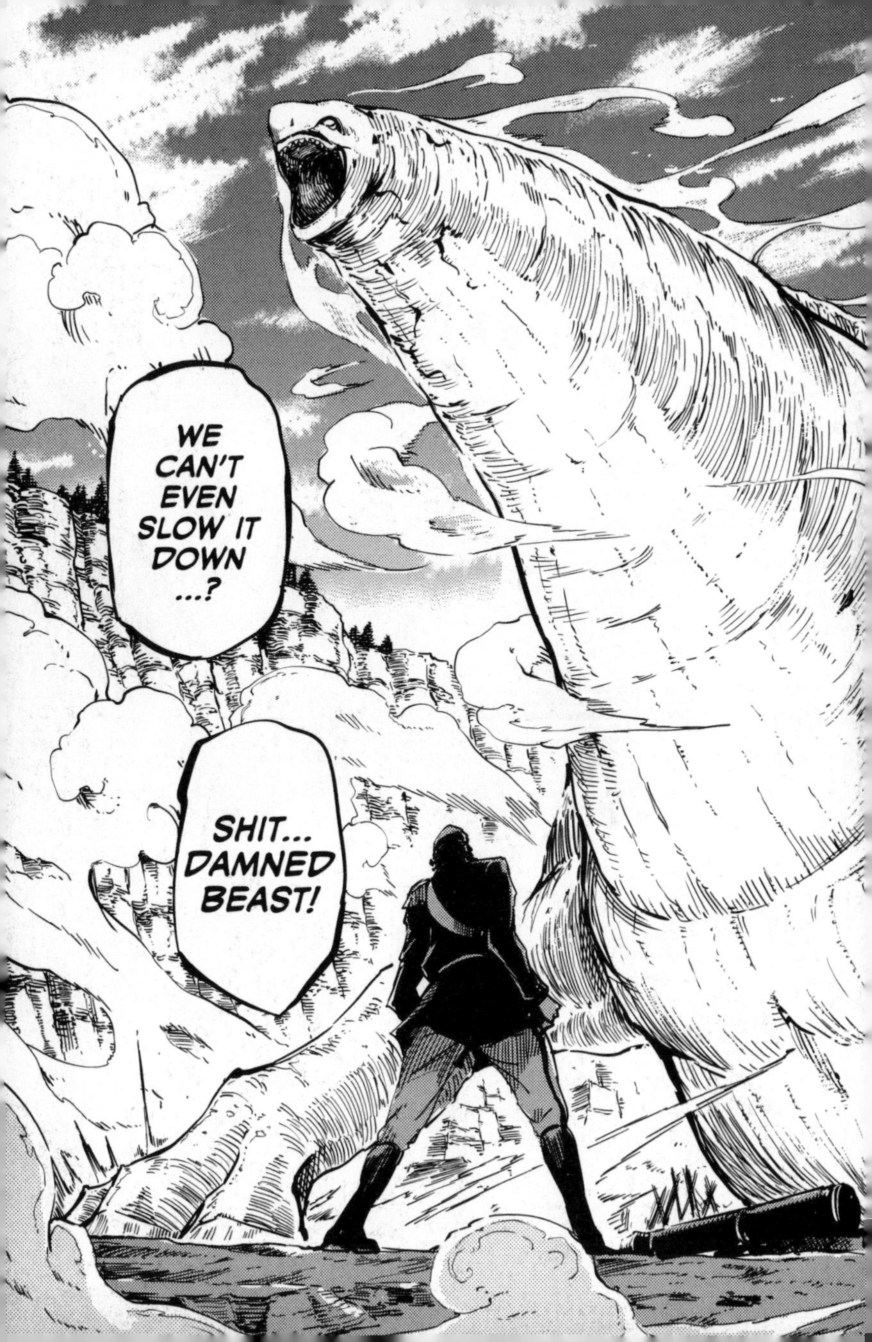
WE CAN'T EVEN SLOW IT DOWN ...?
SHIT... DAMNED BEAST!

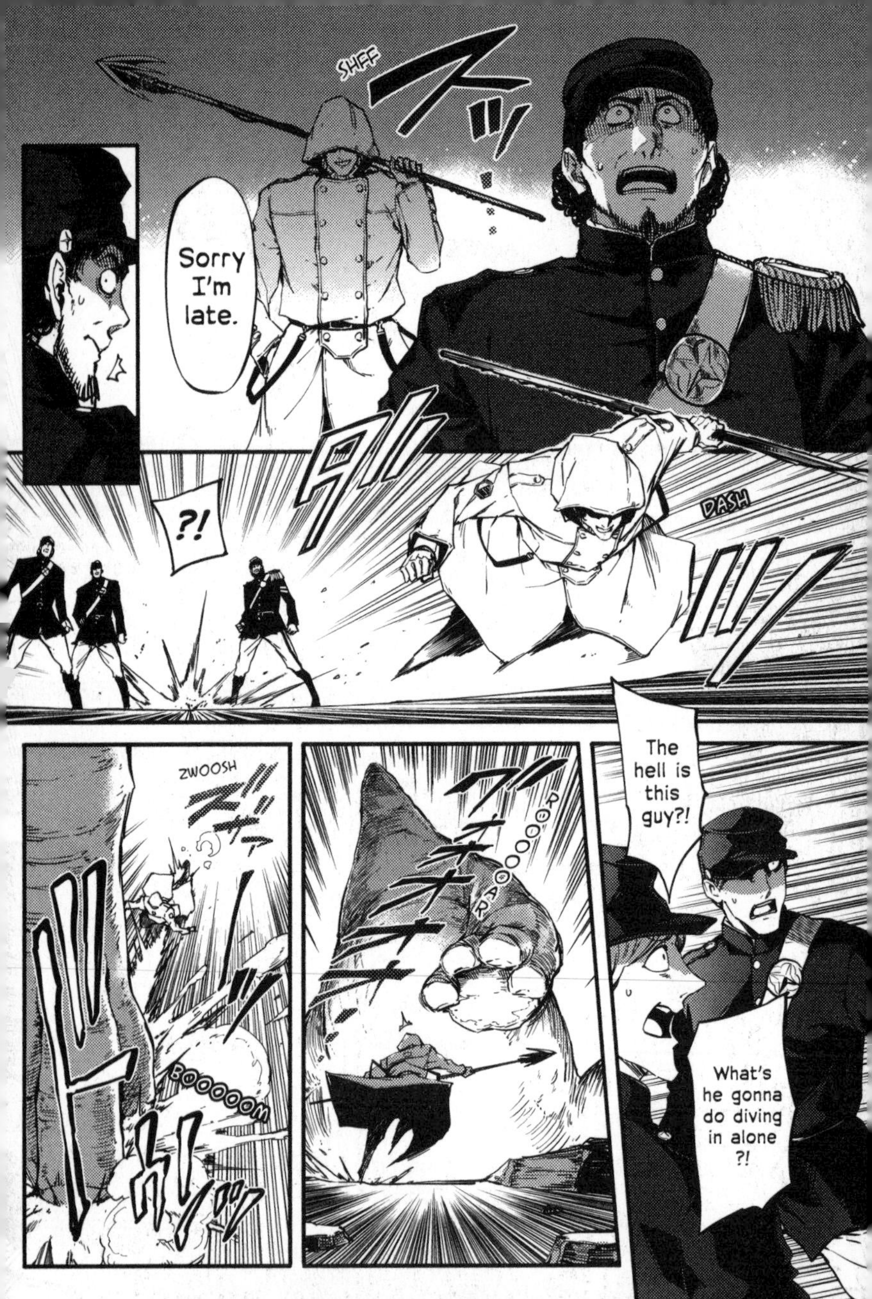
SHFF
Sorry I'm late.
DASH
?!
The hell is this guy?!
What's he gonna do diving in alone ?!
ROOOOOOAR
ZWOOSH
BOOOOOOM

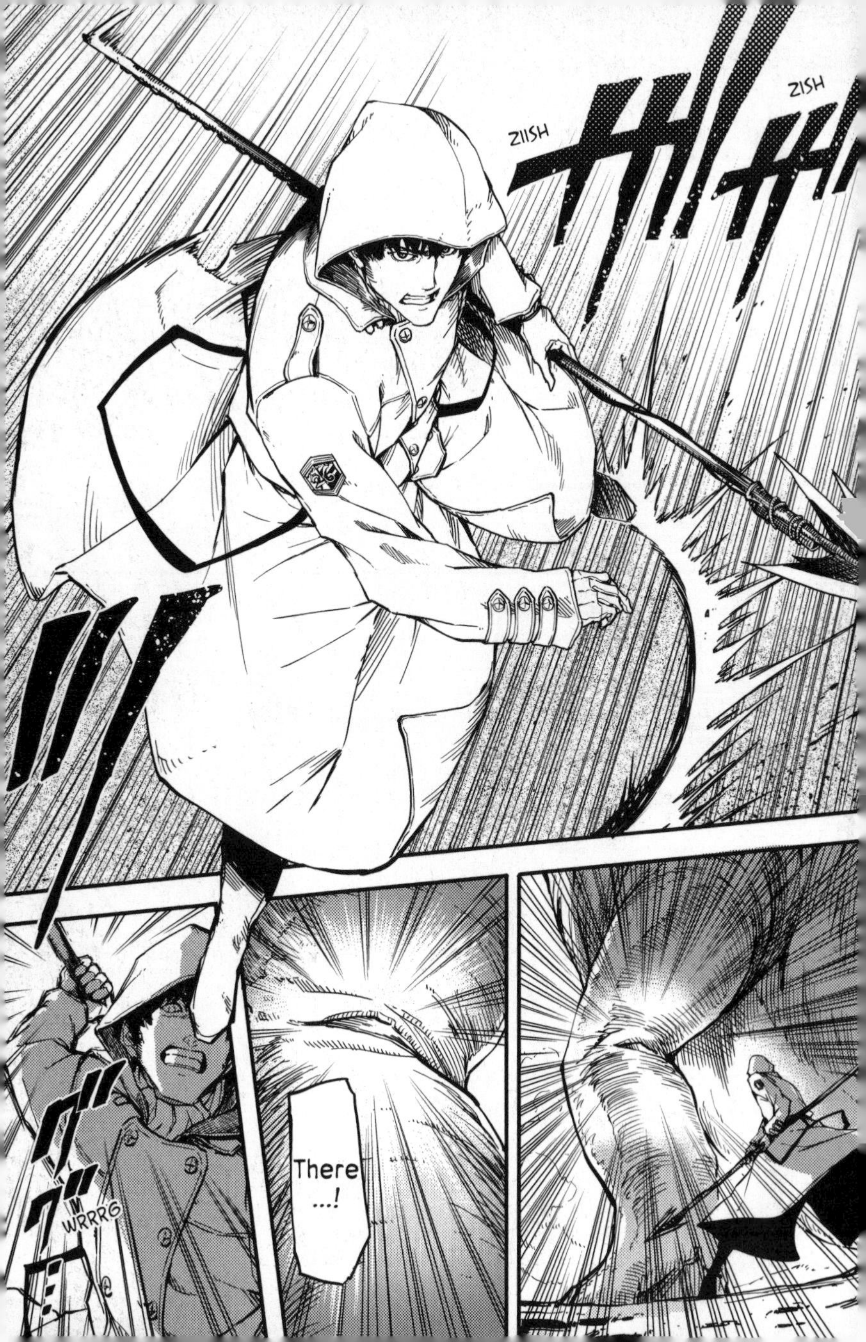
ZISH
ZIISH
There ...!
WRRRG

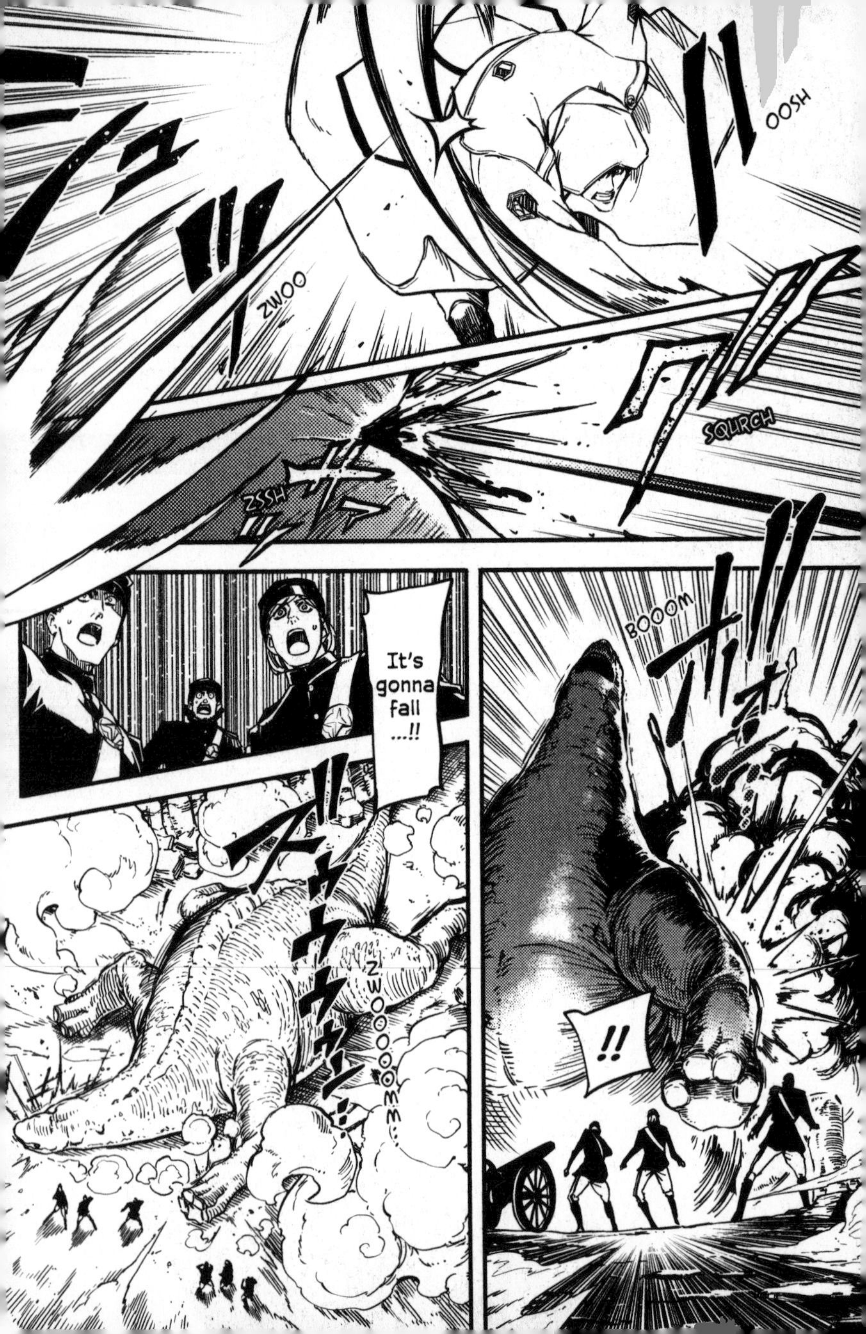
OOSH
ZWOO
SQURCH
HSSZ
BOOOM
!!
It's gonna fall ...!!
ZWOOOOOOMM

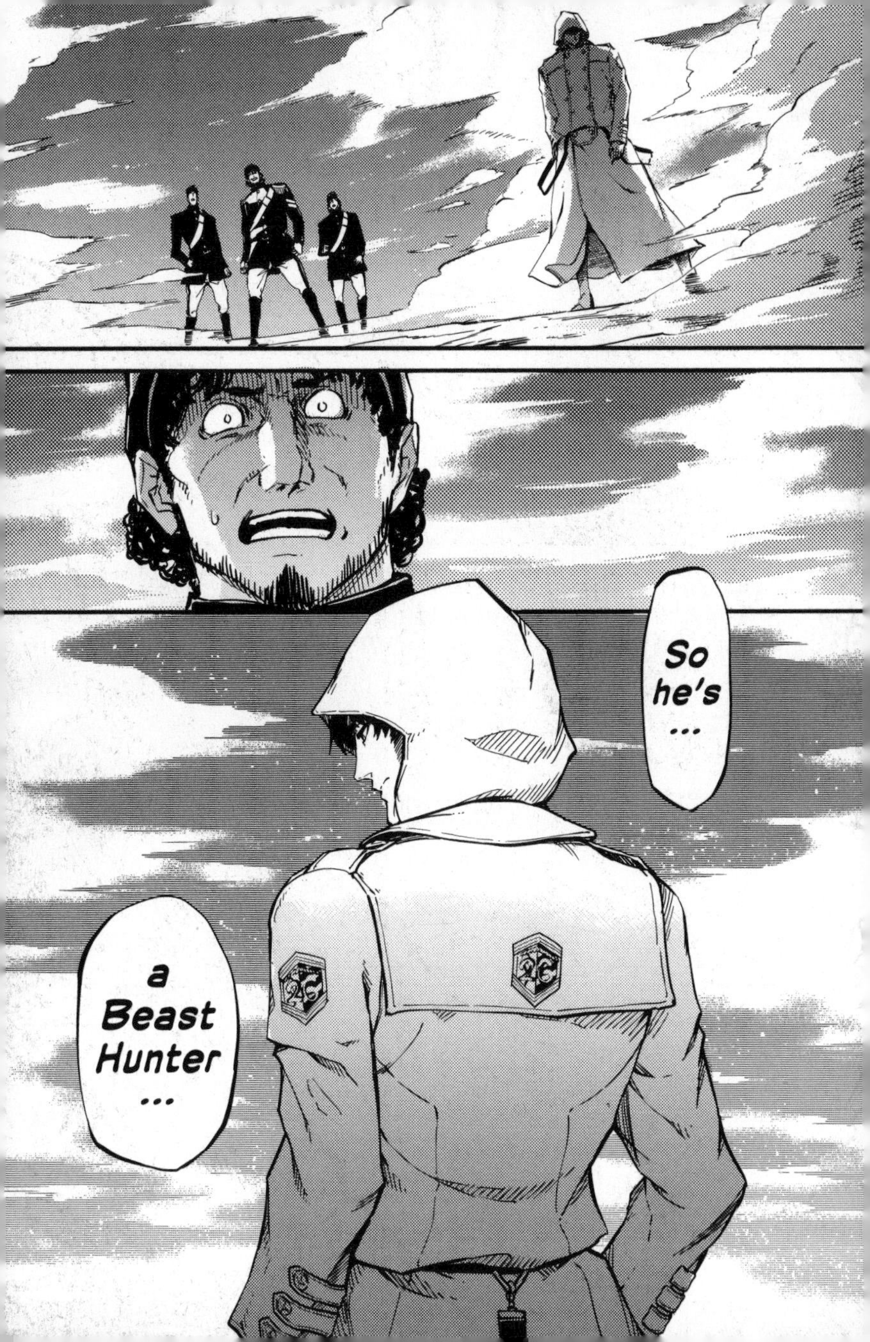
So he's ...
a Beast Hunter ...

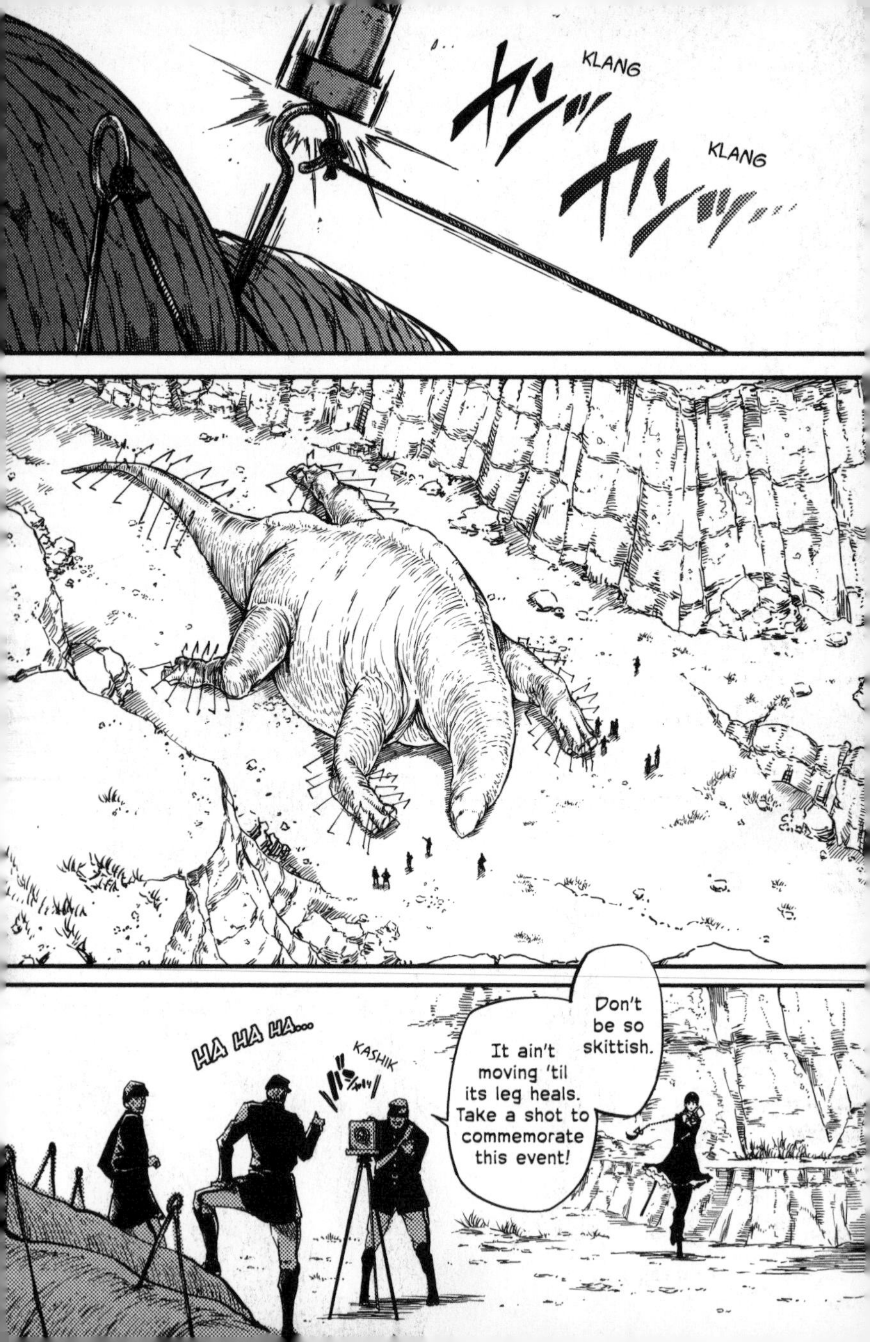
KLANG
KLANG
Don't be so skittish.
It ain't moving 'til its leg heals. Take a shot to commemorate this event!
KASHIK
HA HA HA...

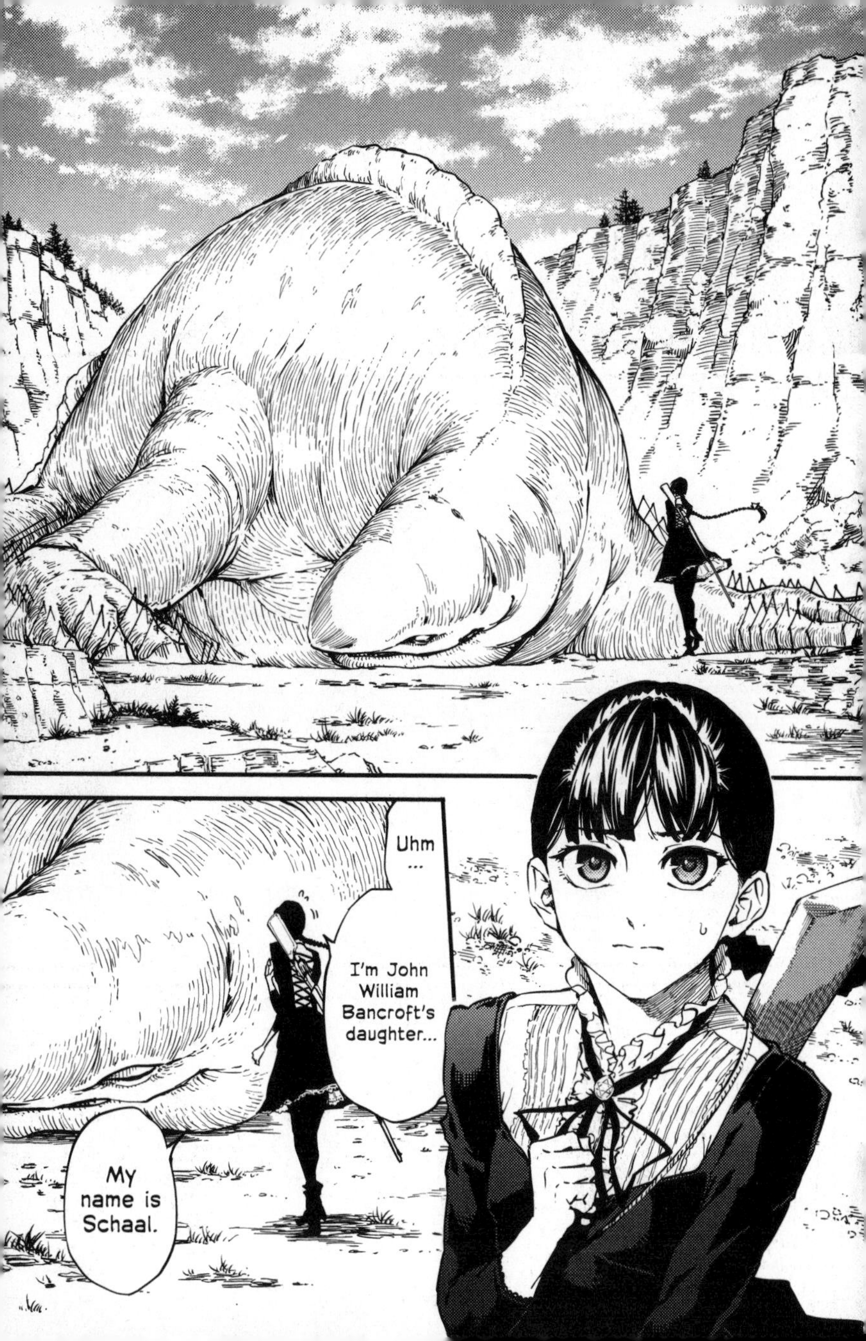
Uhm ...
I'm John William Bancroft's daughter...
My name is Schaal.

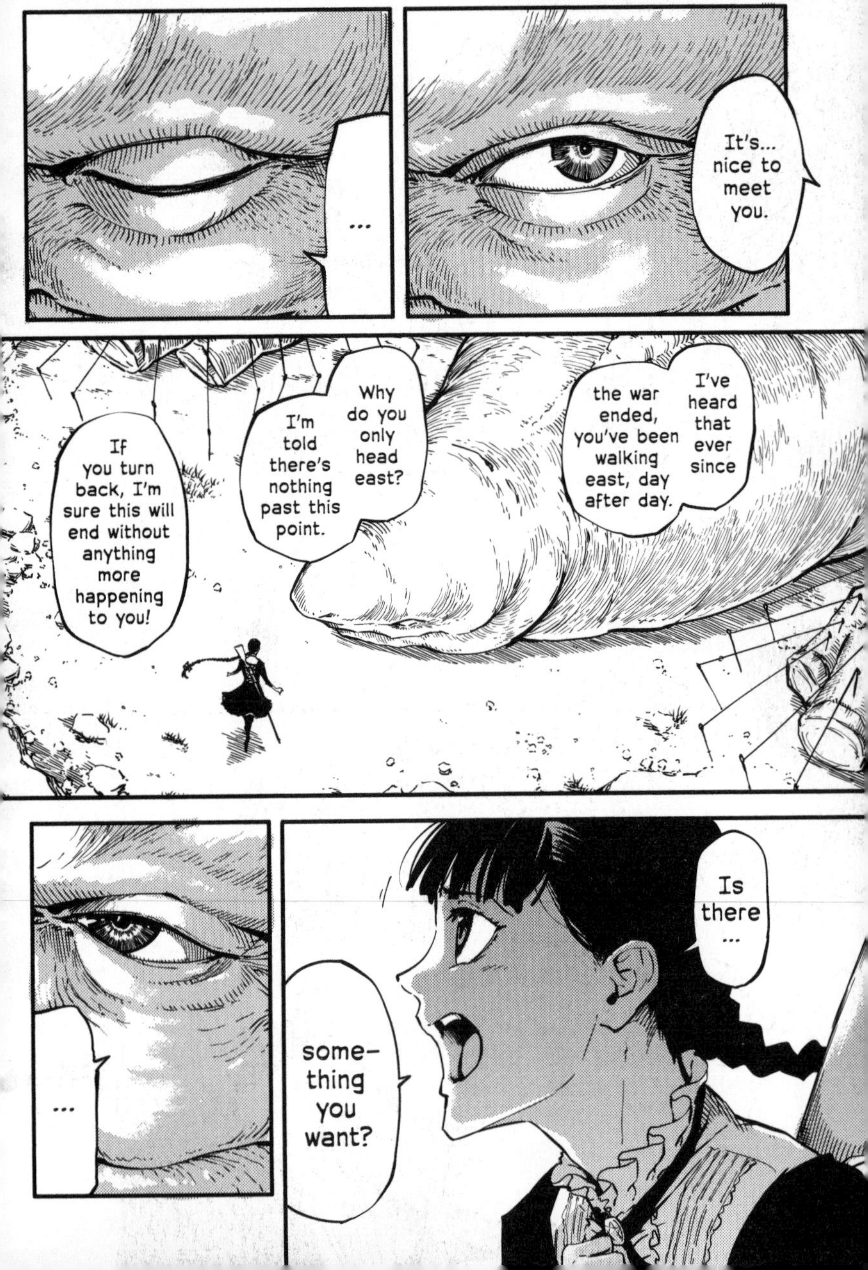
It's... nice to meet you.
...
I've heard that ever since the war ended, you've been walking east, day after day.
Why do you only head east?
I'm told there's nothing past this point.
If you turn back, I'm sure this will end without anything more happening to you!
Is there ...
some-thing you want?
...

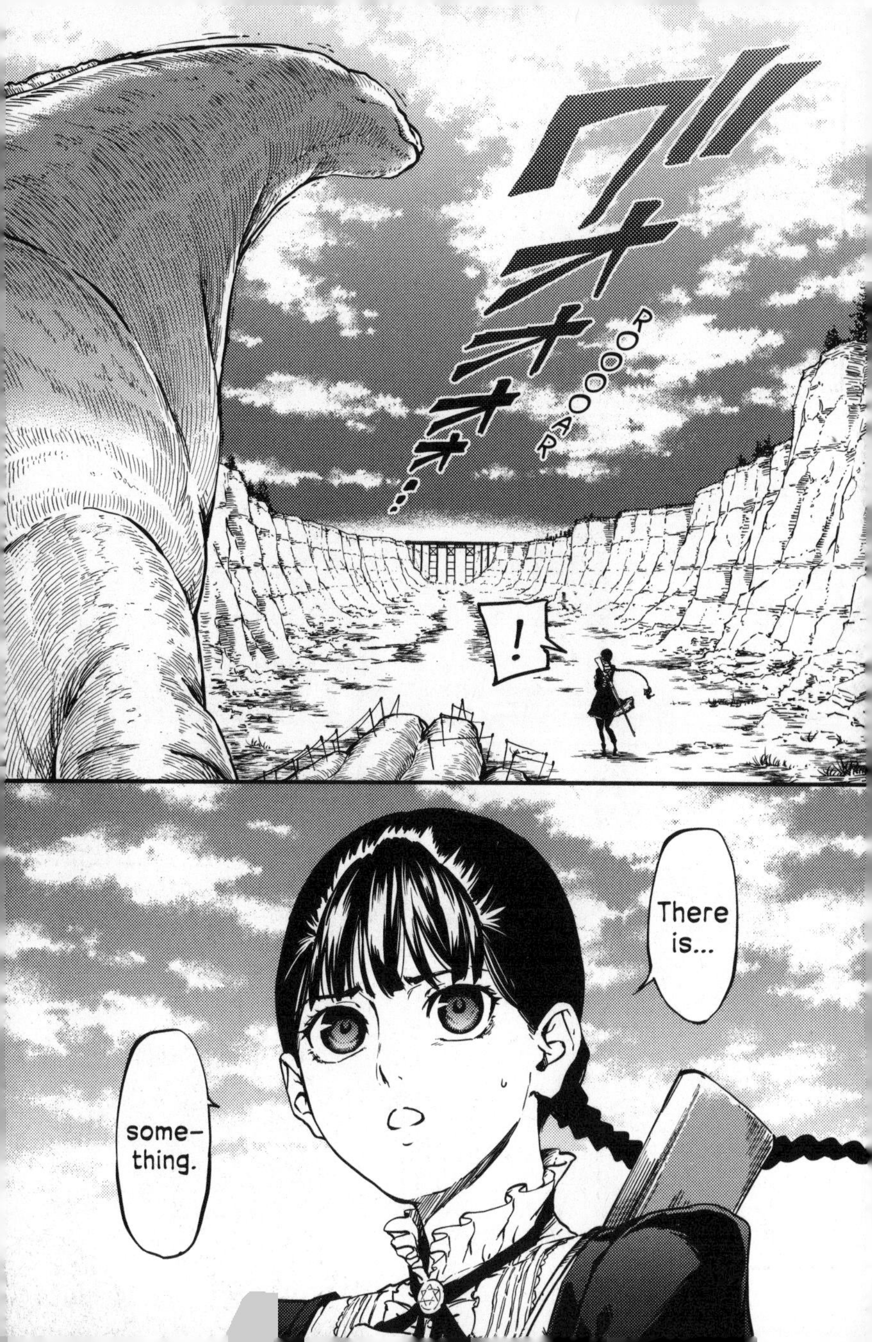
ROOOOAR
!
There is...
some-
thing.

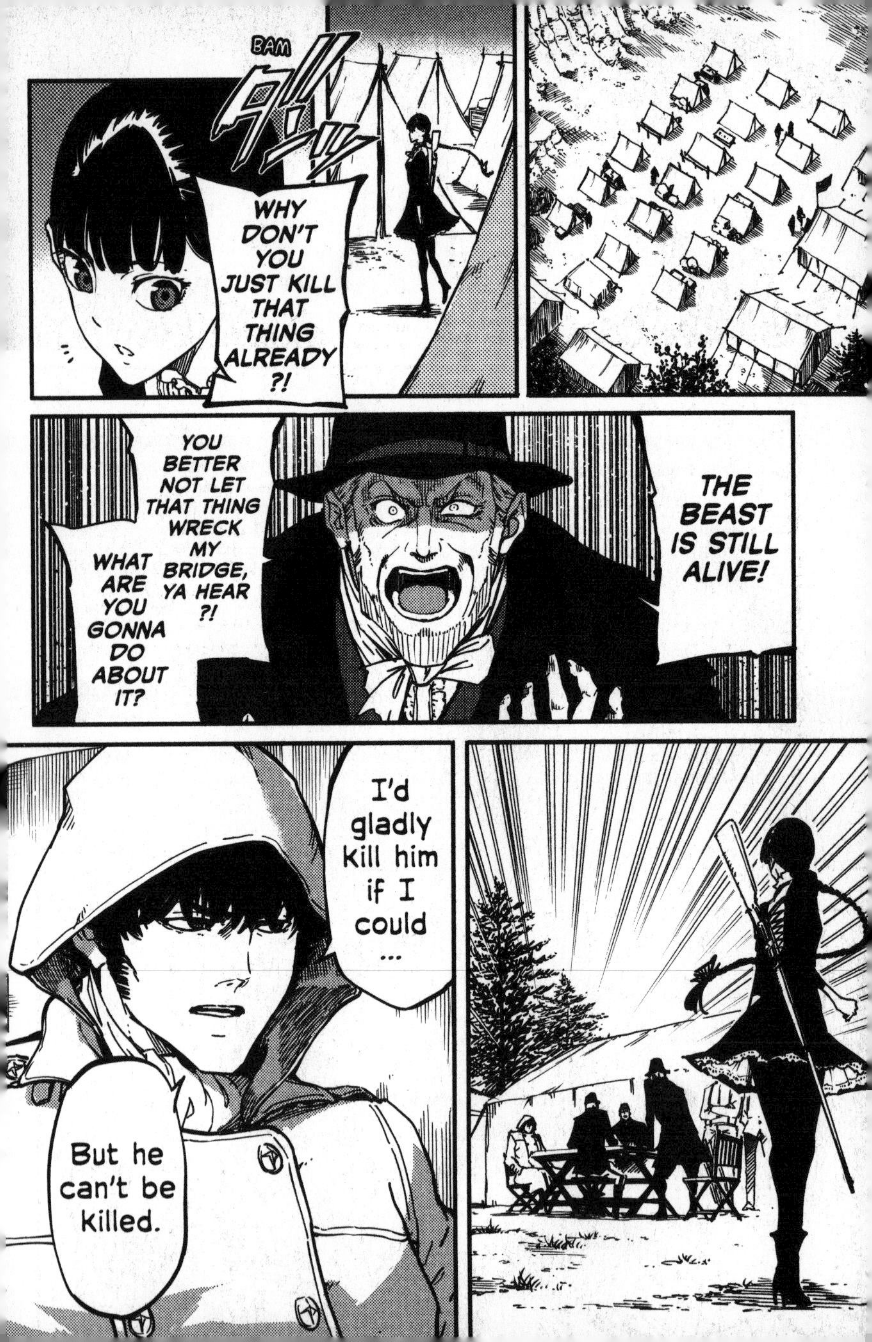
BAM
WHY DON'T YOU JUST KILL THAT THING ALREADY?!
THE BEAST IS STILL ALIVE!
YOU BETTER NOT LET THAT THING WRECK MY BRIDGE, YA HEAR?!
WHAT ARE YOU GONNA DO ABOUT IT?
I'd gladly kill him if I could...
But he can't be killed.

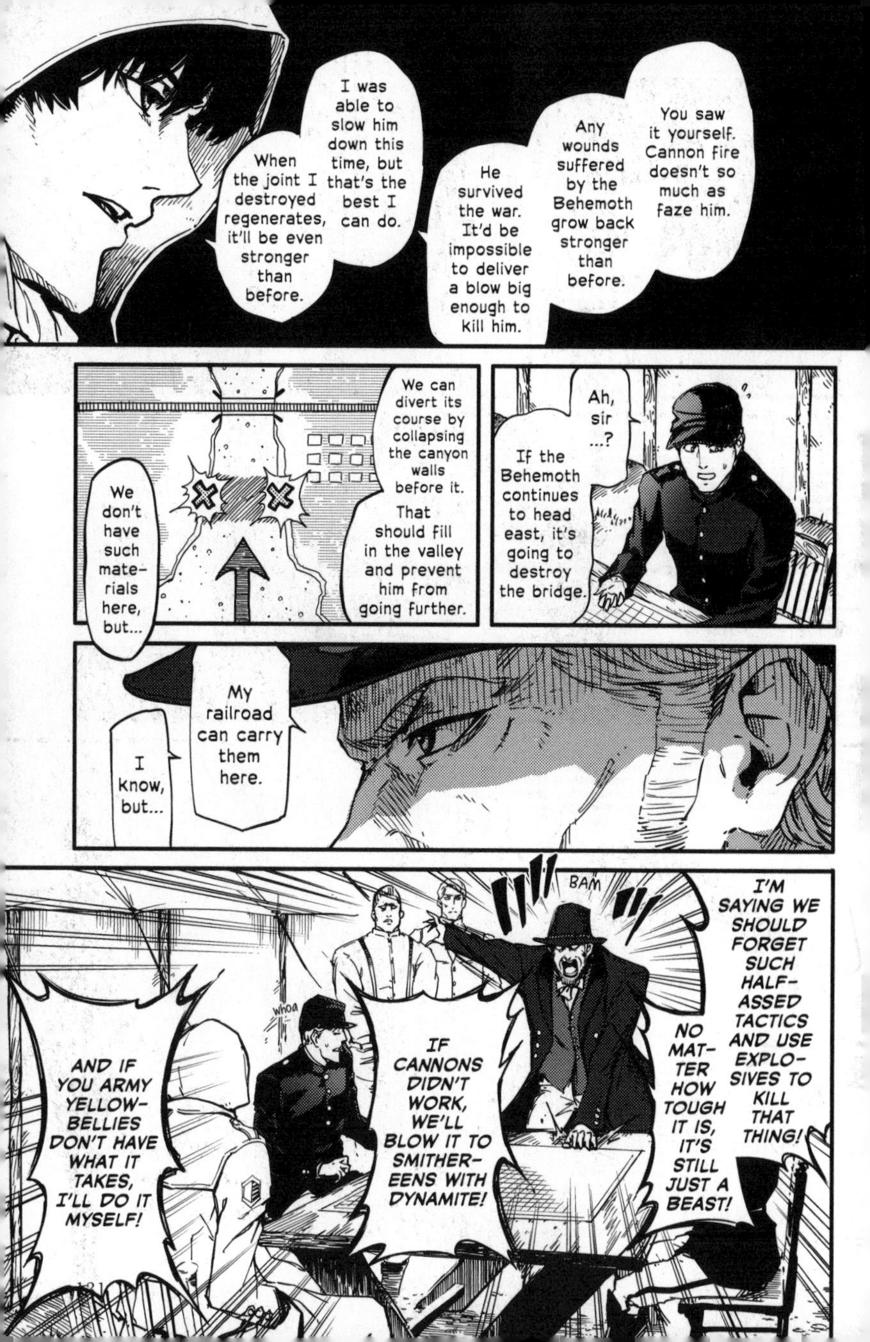
You saw it yourself. Cannon fire doesn't so much as faze him.
Any wounds suffered by the Behemoth grow back stronger than before.
He survived the war. It'd be impossible to deliver a blow big enough to kill him.
I was able to slow him down this time, but that's the best I can do.
When the joint I destroyed regenerates, it'll be even stronger than before.
Ah, sir ...?
If the Behemoth continues to head east, it's going to destroy the bridge.
We can divert its course by collapsing the canyon walls before it.
That should fill in the valley and prevent him from going further.
We don't have such materials here, but...
My railroad can carry them here.
I know, but...
BAM
I'M SAYING WE SHOULD FORGET SUCH HALF-ASSED TACTICS AND USE EXPLOSIVES TO KILL THAT THING!
NO MATTER HOW TOUGH IT IS, IT'S STILL JUST A BEAST!
IF CANNONS DIDN'T WORK, WE'LL BLOW IT TO SMITHEREENS WITH DYNAMITE!
whoa
AND IF YOU ARMY YELLOW-BELLIES DON'T HAVE WHAT IT TAKES, I'LL DO IT MYSELF!

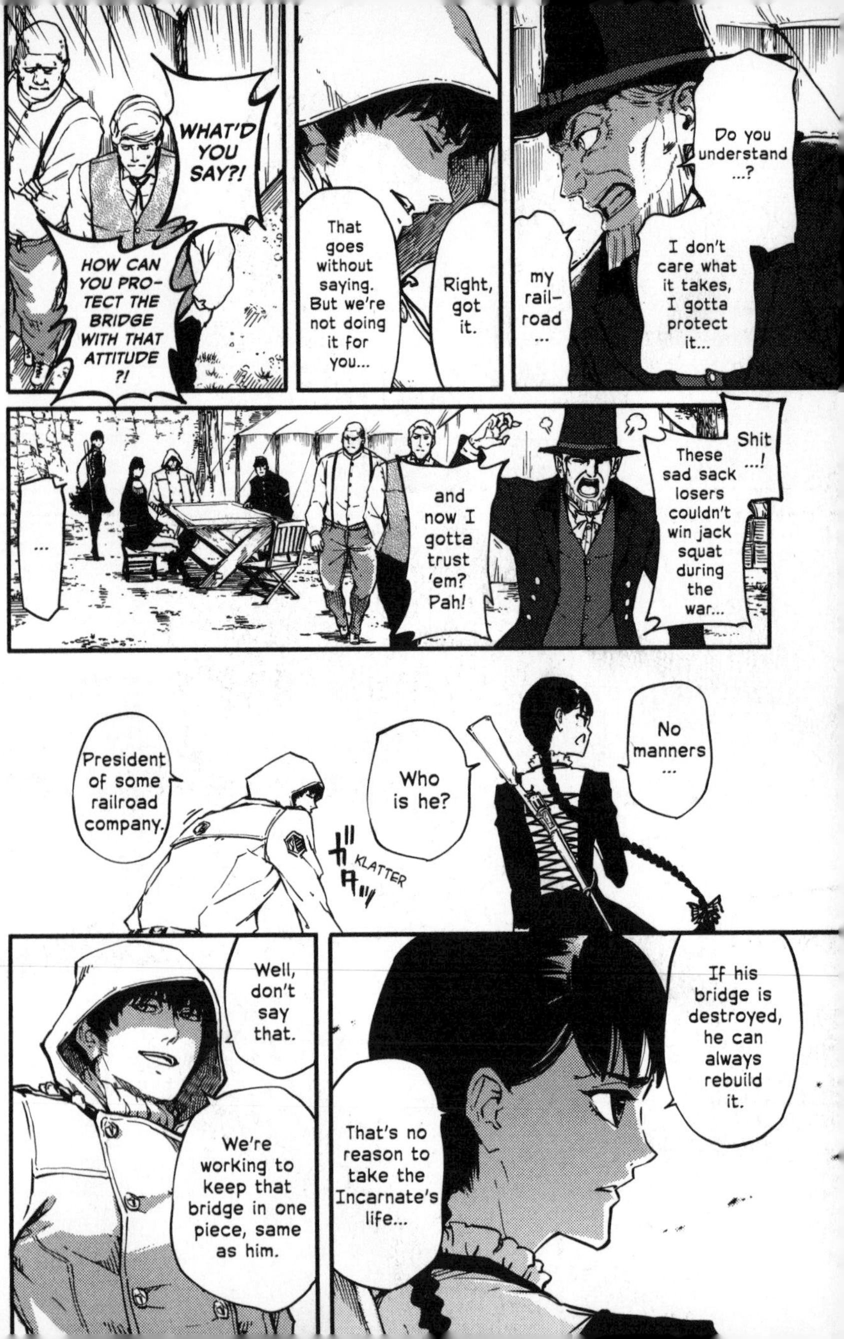
Do you understand ...?
I don't care what it takes, I gotta protect it...
my rail-road ...
Right, got it.
That goes without saying. But we're not doing it for you...
WHAT'D YOU SAY?!
HOW CAN YOU PROTECT THE BRIDGE WITH THAT ATTITUDE ?!
Shit ...!
These sad sack losers couldn't win jack squat during the war...
and now I gotta trust 'em? Pah!
...
No manners ...
Who is he?
KLATTER
President of some railroad company.
If his bridge is destroyed, he can always rebuild it.
That's no reason to take the Incarnate's life...
Well, don't say that.
We're working to keep that bridge in one piece, same as him.

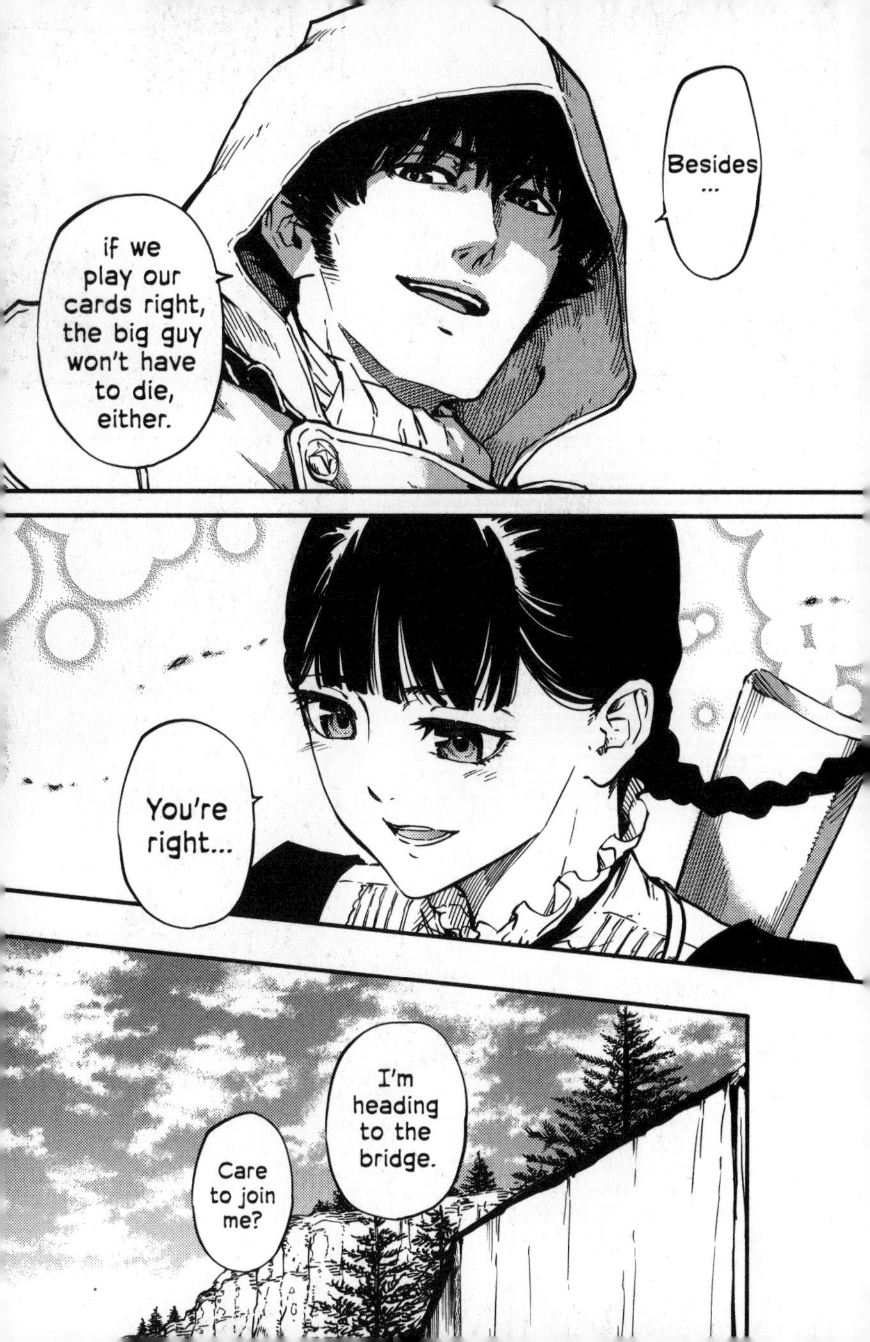
Besides ...
if we play our cards right, the big guy won't have to die, either.
You're right...
I'm heading to the bridge.
Care to join me?

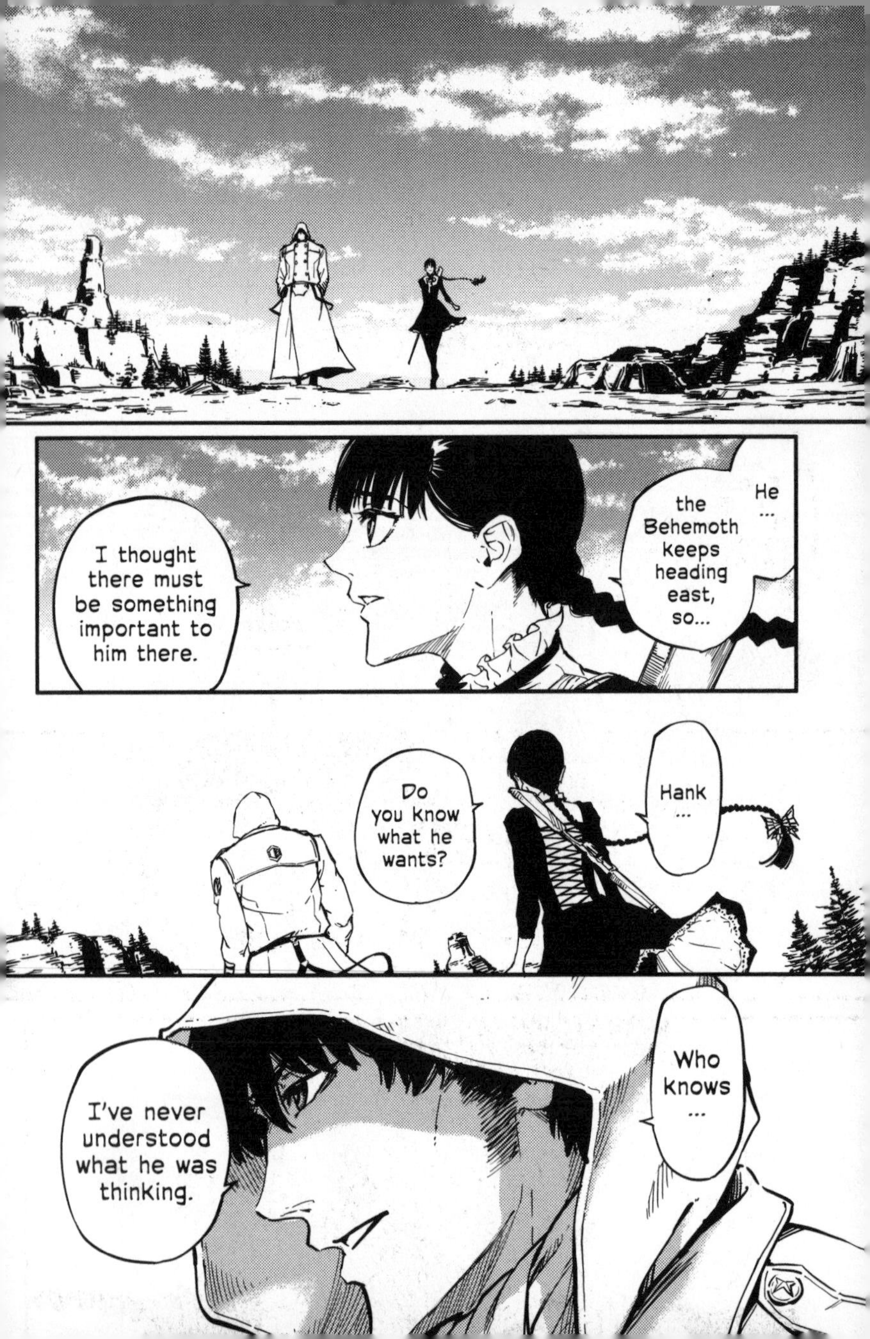
He ... the Behemoth keeps heading east, so...
I thought there must be something important to him there.
Hank ...
Do you know what he wants?
Who knows ...
I've never understood what he was thinking.

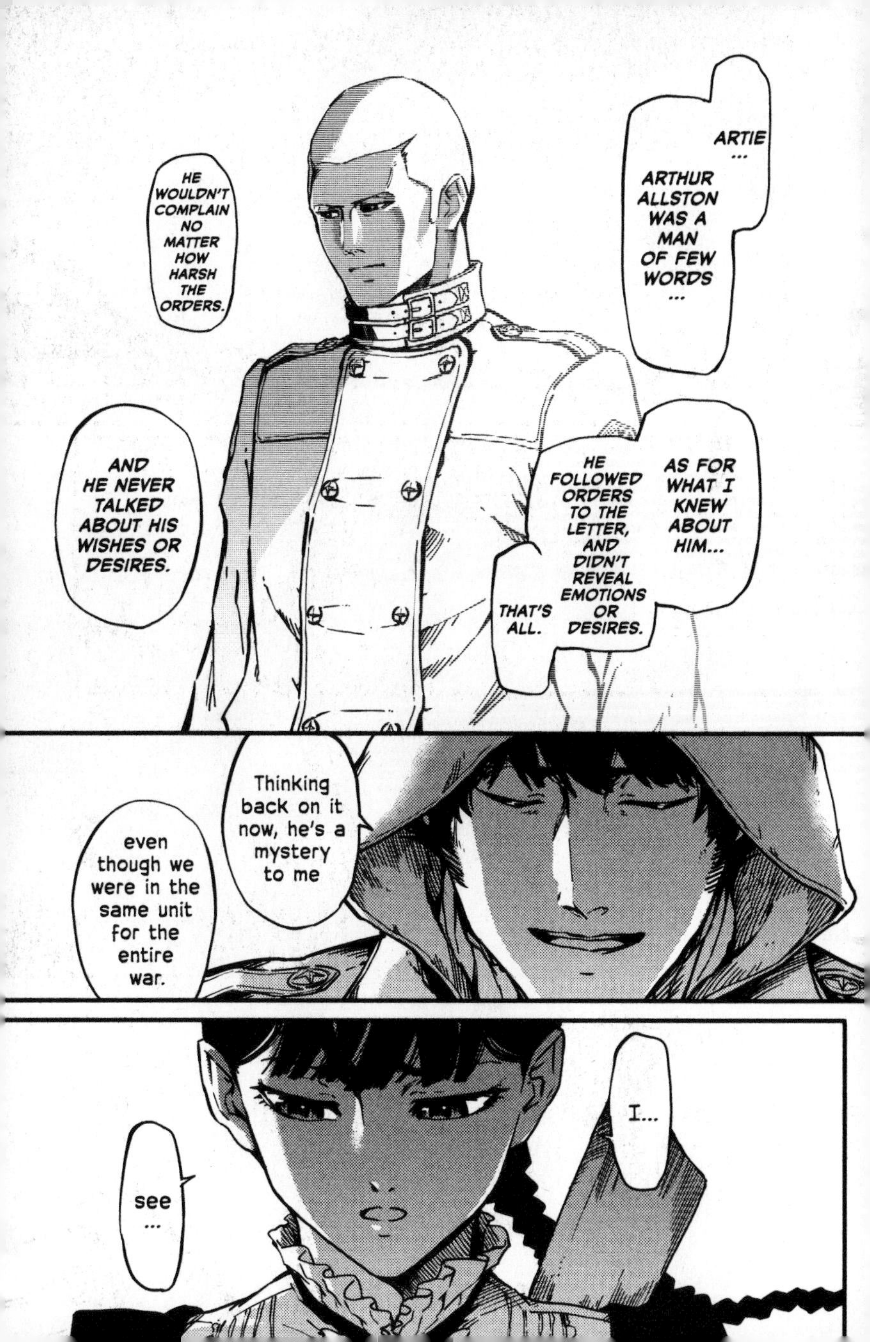
ARTIE ... ARTHUR ALLSTON WAS A MAN OF FEW WORDS ...
HE WOULDN'T COMPLAIN NO MATTER HOW HARSH THE ORDERS.
AS FOR WHAT I KNEW ABOUT HIM...
HE FOLLOWED ORDERS TO THE LETTER, AND DIDN'T REVEAL EMOTIONS OR DESIRES.
THAT'S ALL.
AND HE NEVER TALKED ABOUT HIS WISHES OR DESIRES.
Thinking back on it now, he's a mystery to me
even though we were in the same unit for the entire war.
I...
see ...

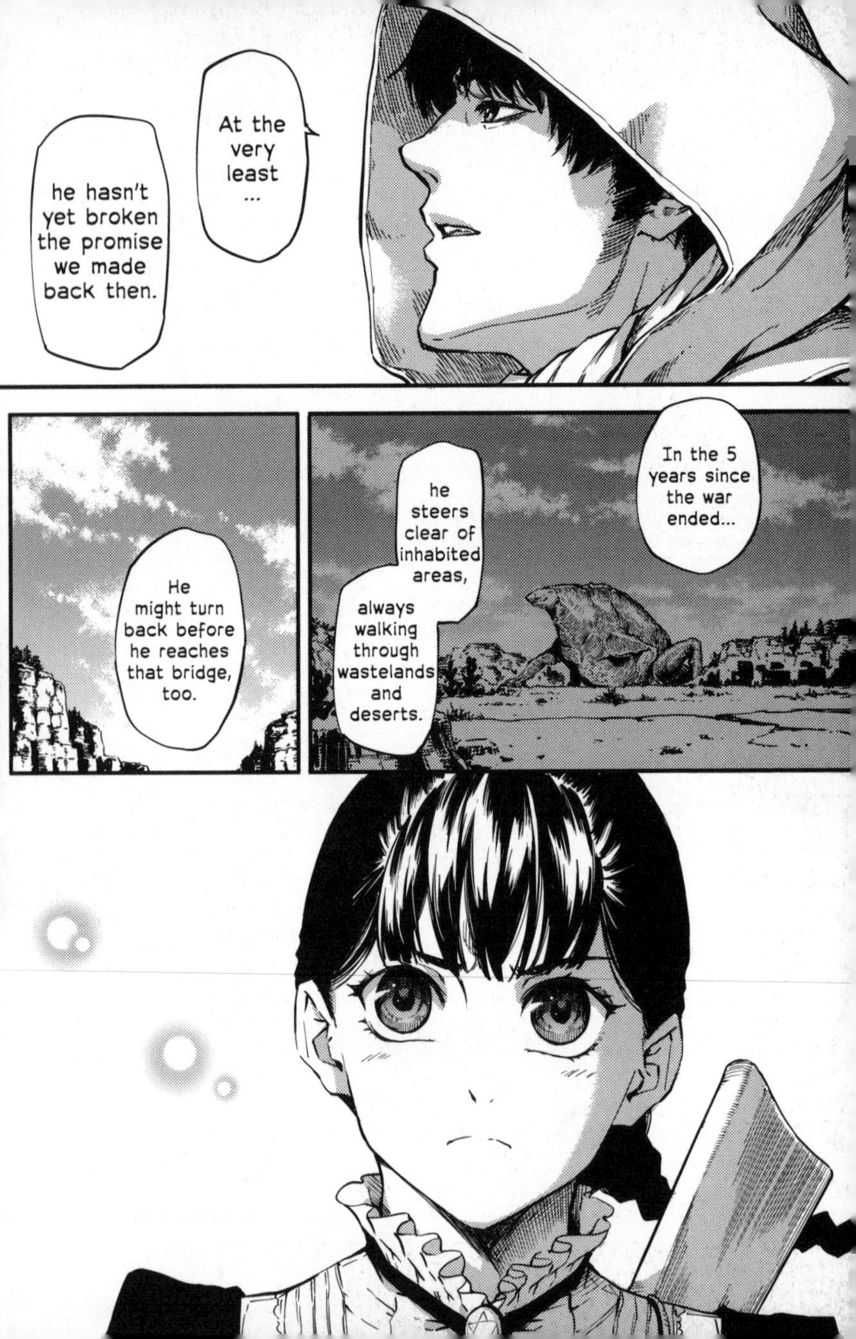
At the very least ...
he hasn't yet broken the promise we made back then.
In the 5 years since the war ended...
he steers clear of inhabited areas,
always walking through wastelands and deserts.
He might turn back before he reaches that bridge, too.

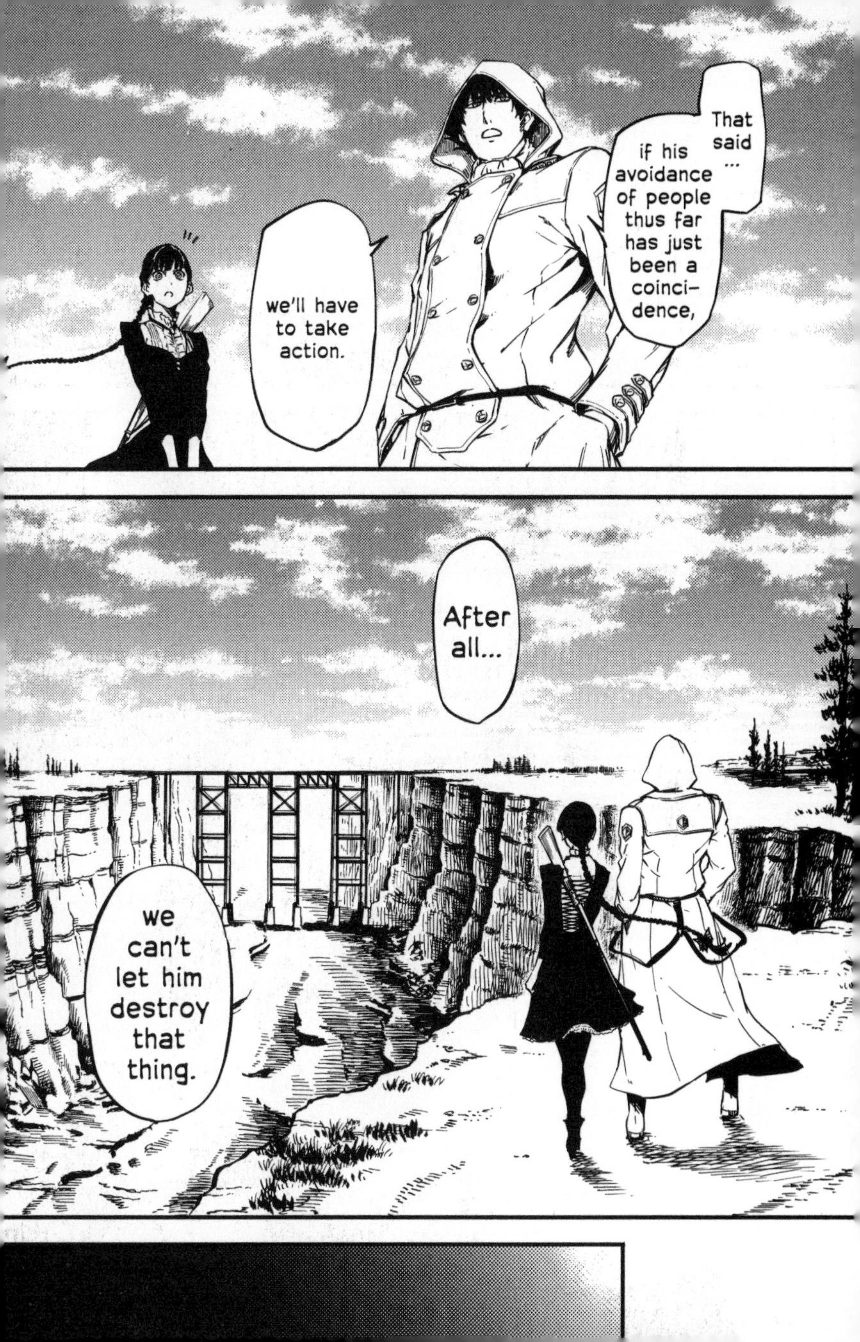
That said... if his avoidance of people thus far has just been a coinci-dence,
we'll have to take action.
After all...
we can't let him destroy that thing.

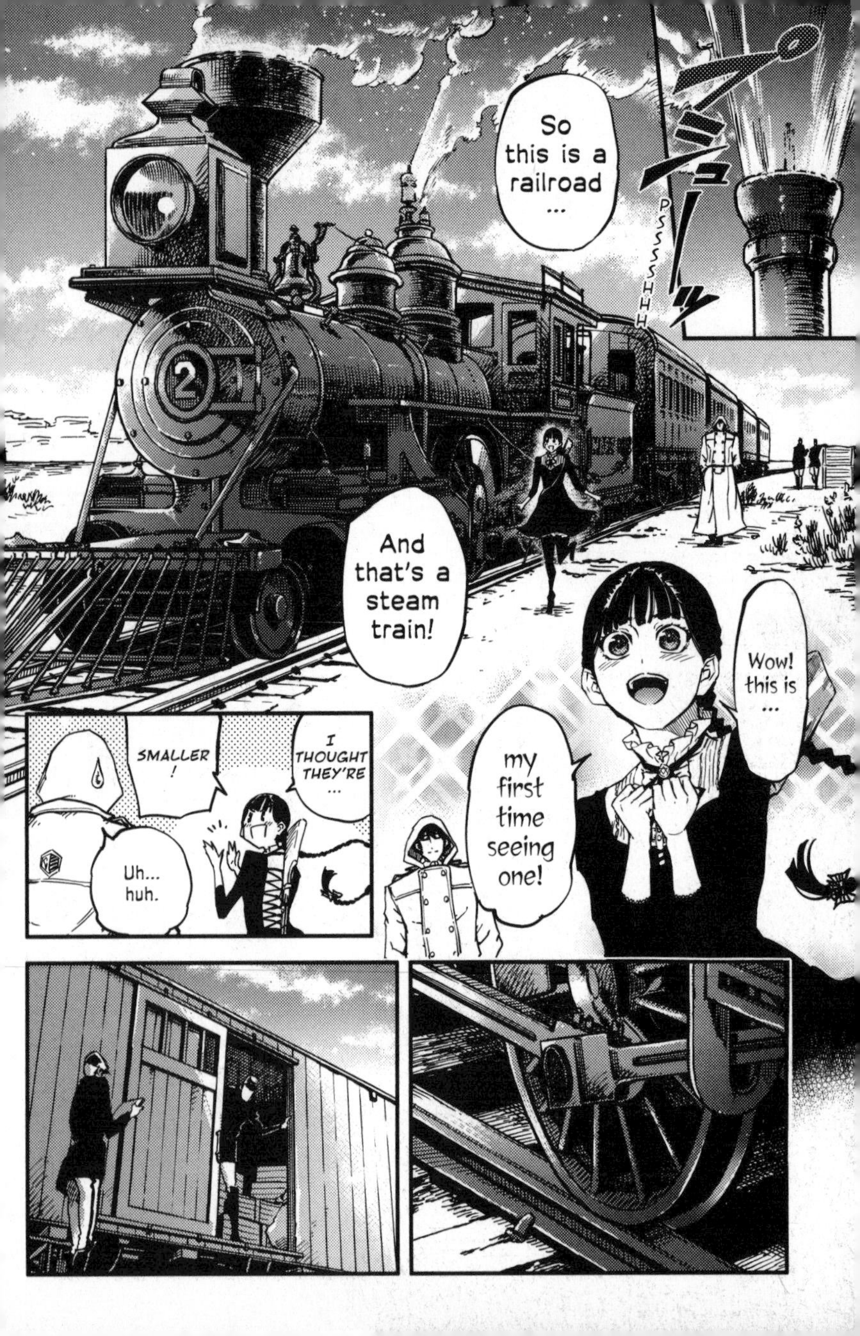
PSSSSHHH
So this is a railroad ...
And that's a steam train!
Wow! this is ...
my first time seeing one!
I THOUGHT THEY'RE ...
SMALLER!
Uh... huh.

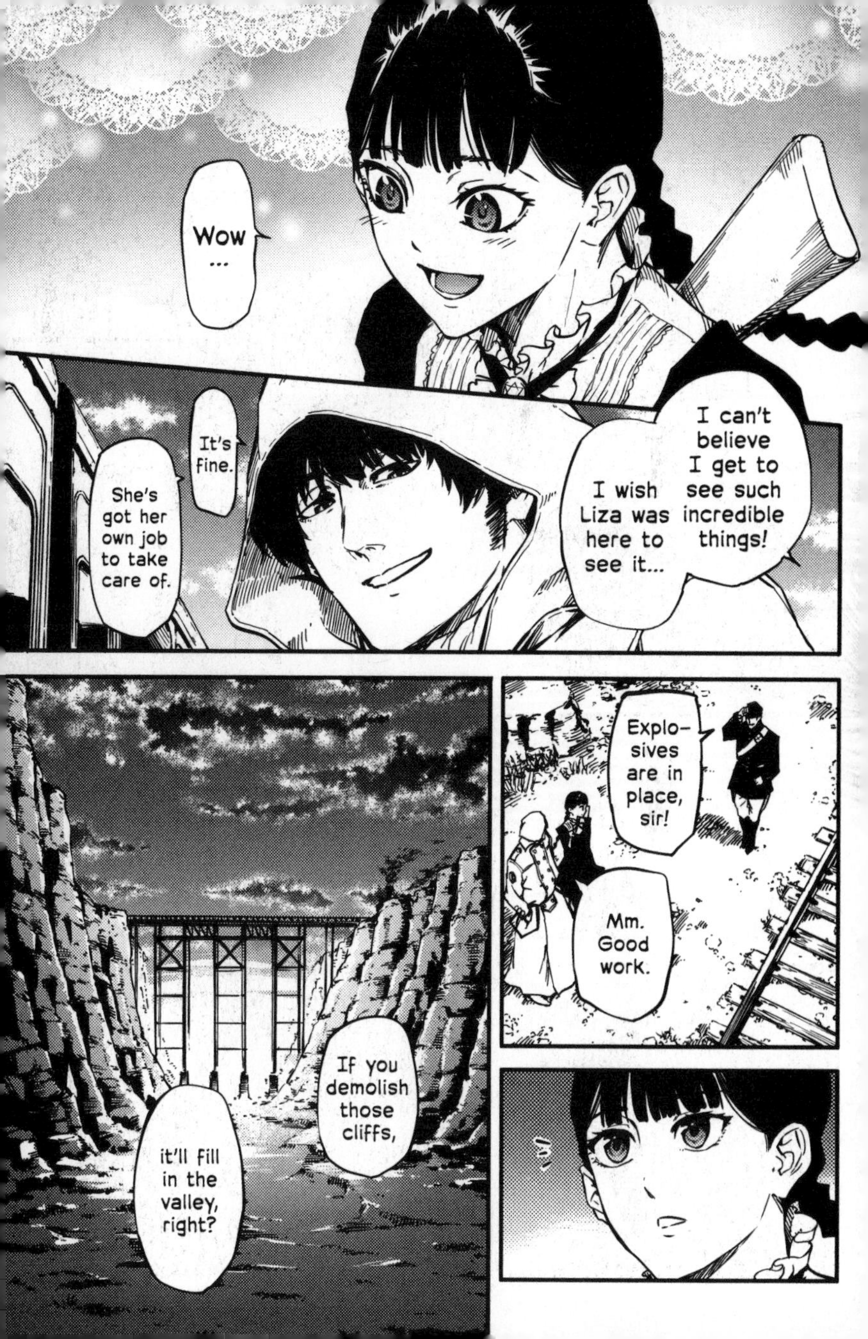
Wow ...
I can't believe I get to see such incredible things!
I wish Liza was here to see it...
It's fine.
She's got her own job to take care of.
Explosives are in place, sir!
Mm. Good work.
If you demolish those cliffs,
it'll fill in the valley, right?

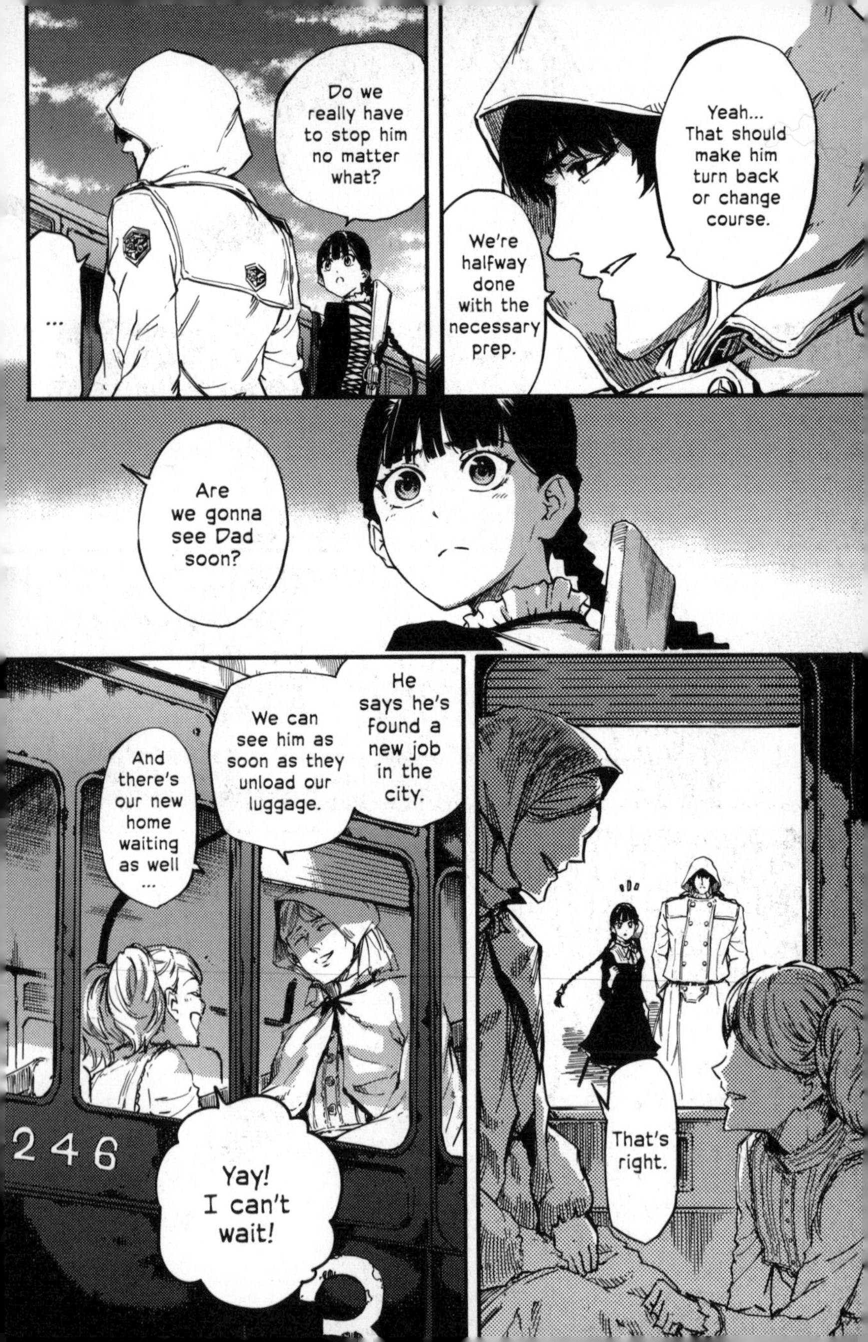
Yeah... That should make him turn back or change course.
We're halfway done with the necessary prep.
Do we really have to stop him no matter what?
...
Are we gonna see Dad soon?
That's right.
He says he's found a new job in the city.
We can see him as soon as they unload our luggage.
And there's our new home waiting as well ...
Yay! I can't wait!
246

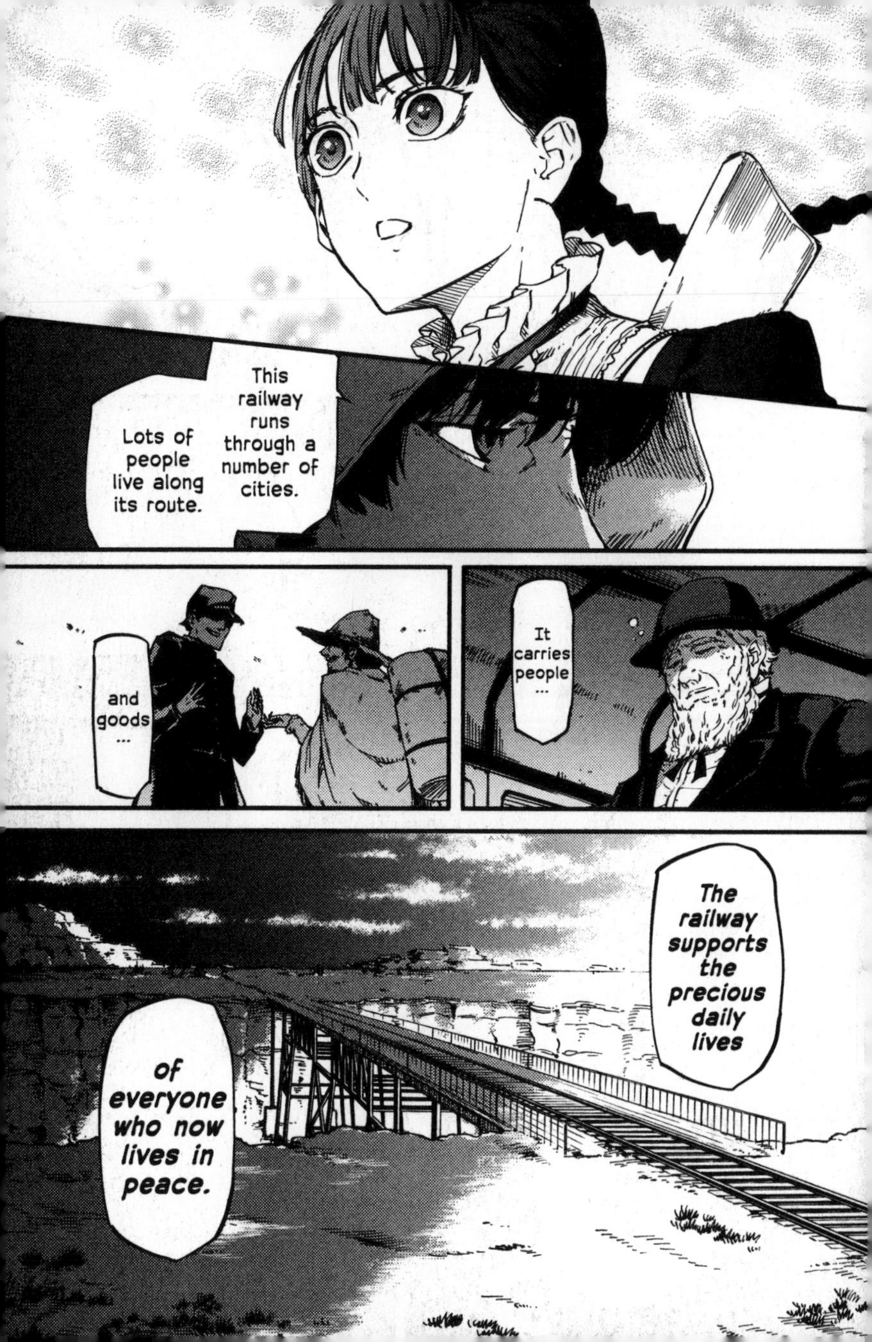
This railway runs through a number of cities.
Lots of people live along its route.
It carries people ...
and goods ...
The railway supports the precious daily lives
of everyone who now lives in peace.

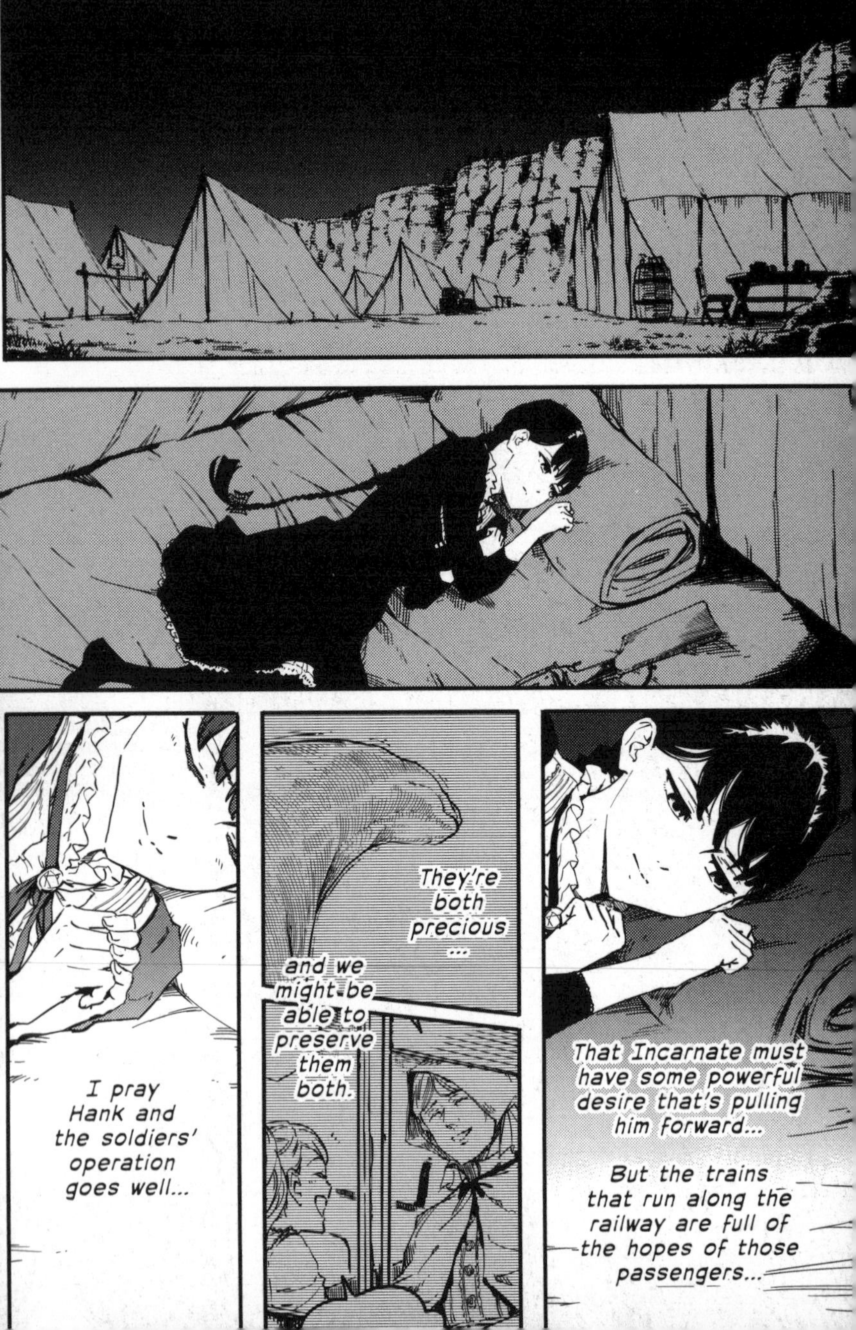
That Incarnate must have some powerful desire that's pulling him forward...
But the trains that run along the railway are full of the hopes of those passengers...
They're both precious...
and we might be able to preserve them both.
I pray Hank and the soldiers' operation goes well...

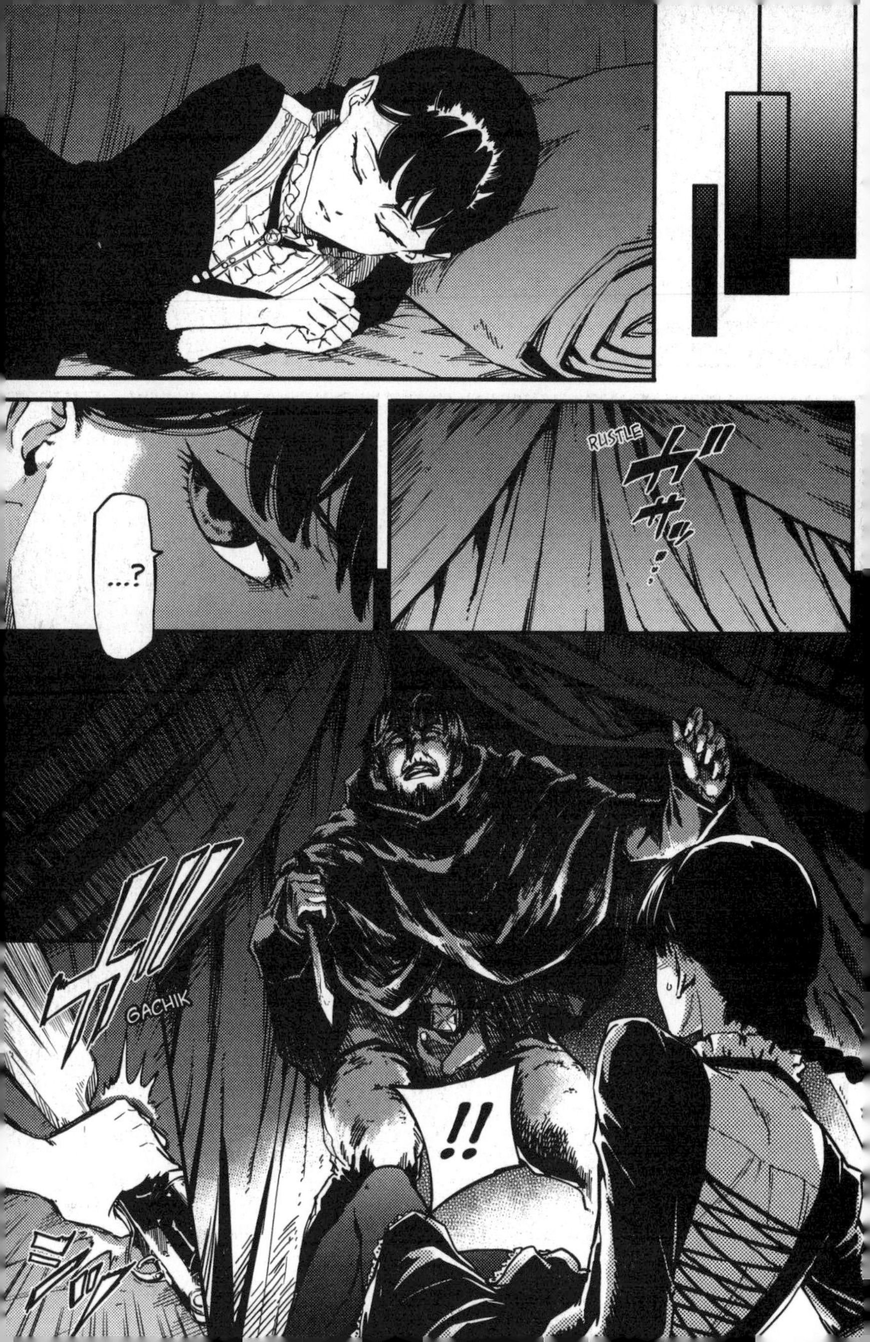
RUSTLE
...?
!!
GACHIK

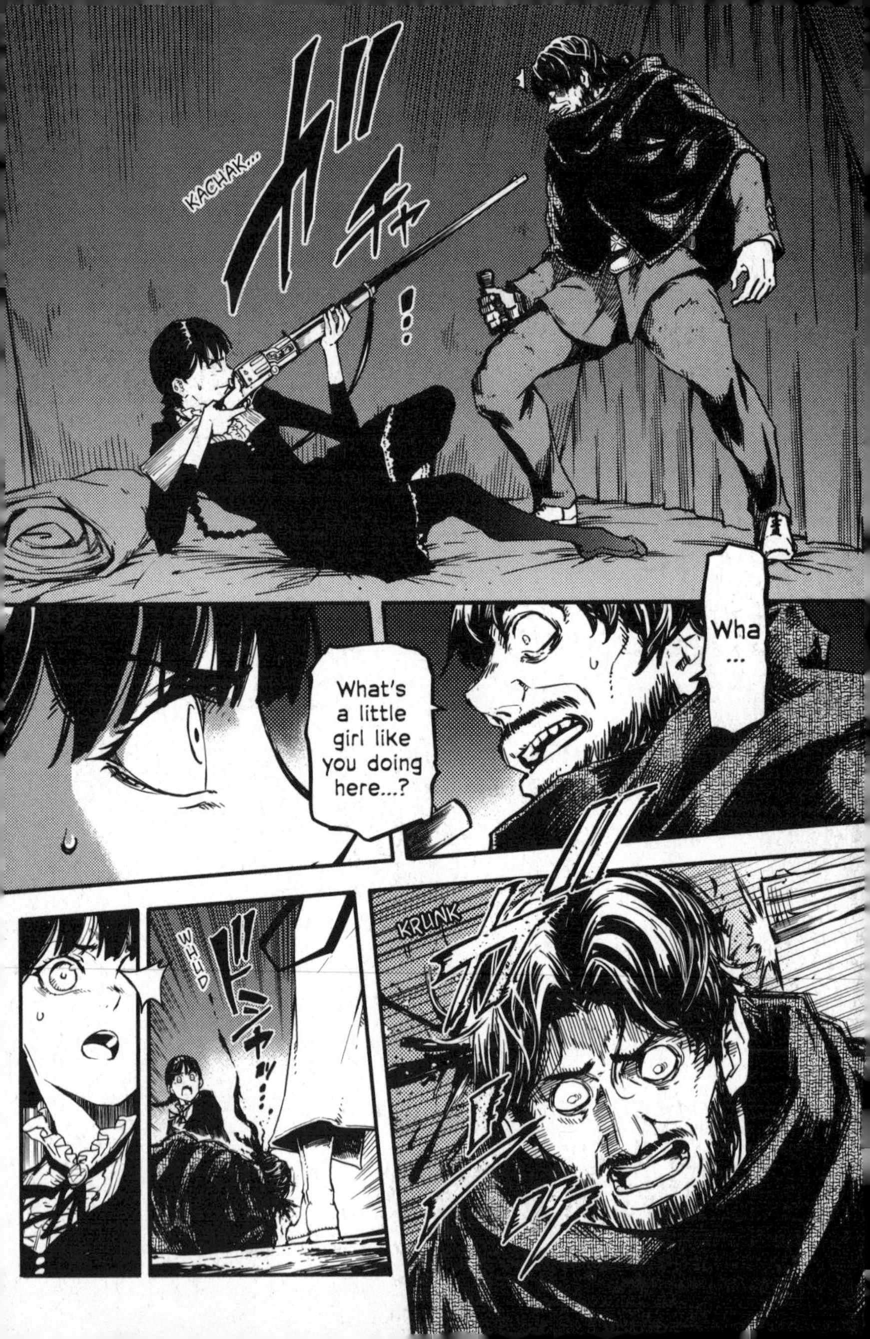
KACHAK...
Wha ...
What's a little girl like you doing here...?
KRUNK
WHUD

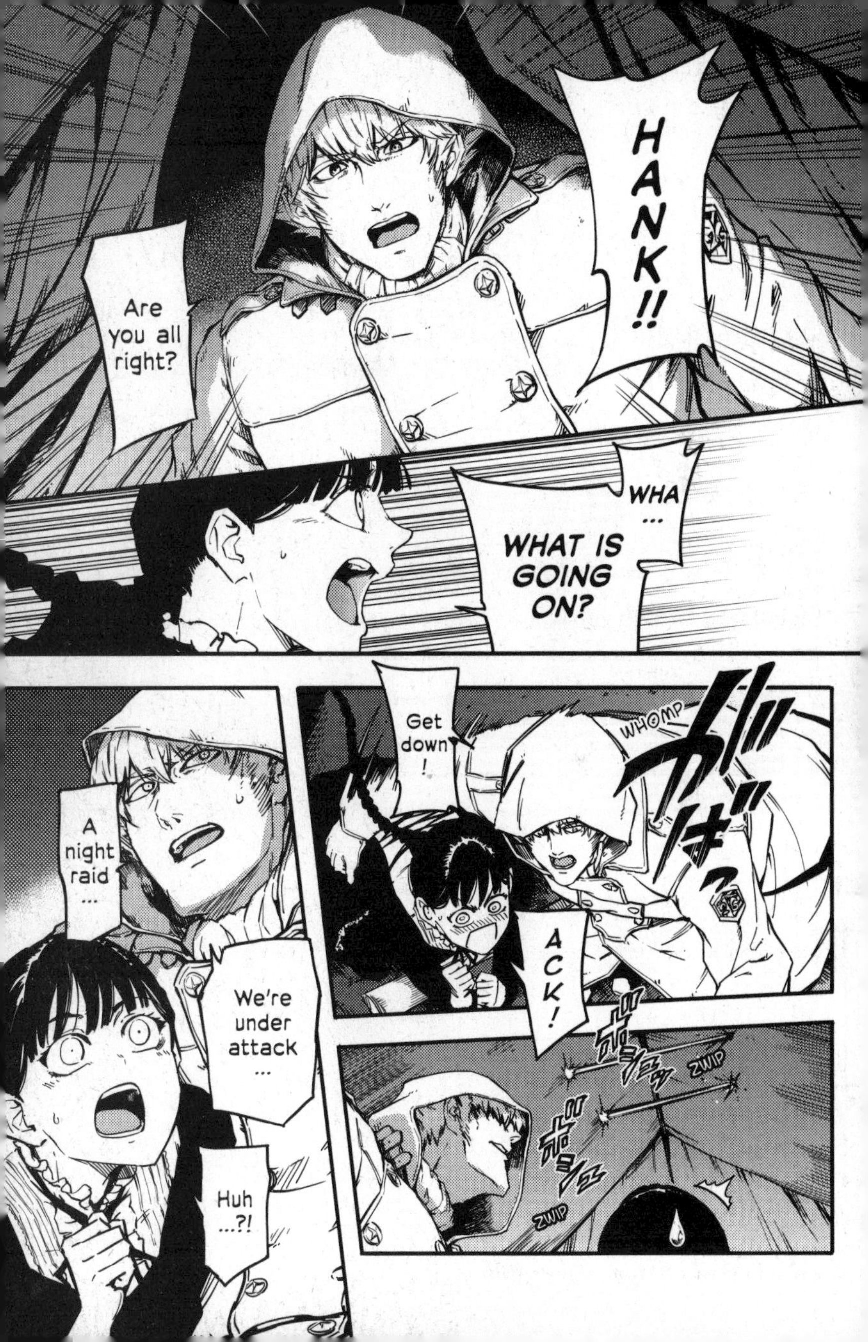
HANK!!
Are you all right?
WHA... WHAT IS GOING ON?
Get down!
WHOMP
ACK!
ZWIP
ZWIP
A night raid...
We're under attack...
Huh...?!

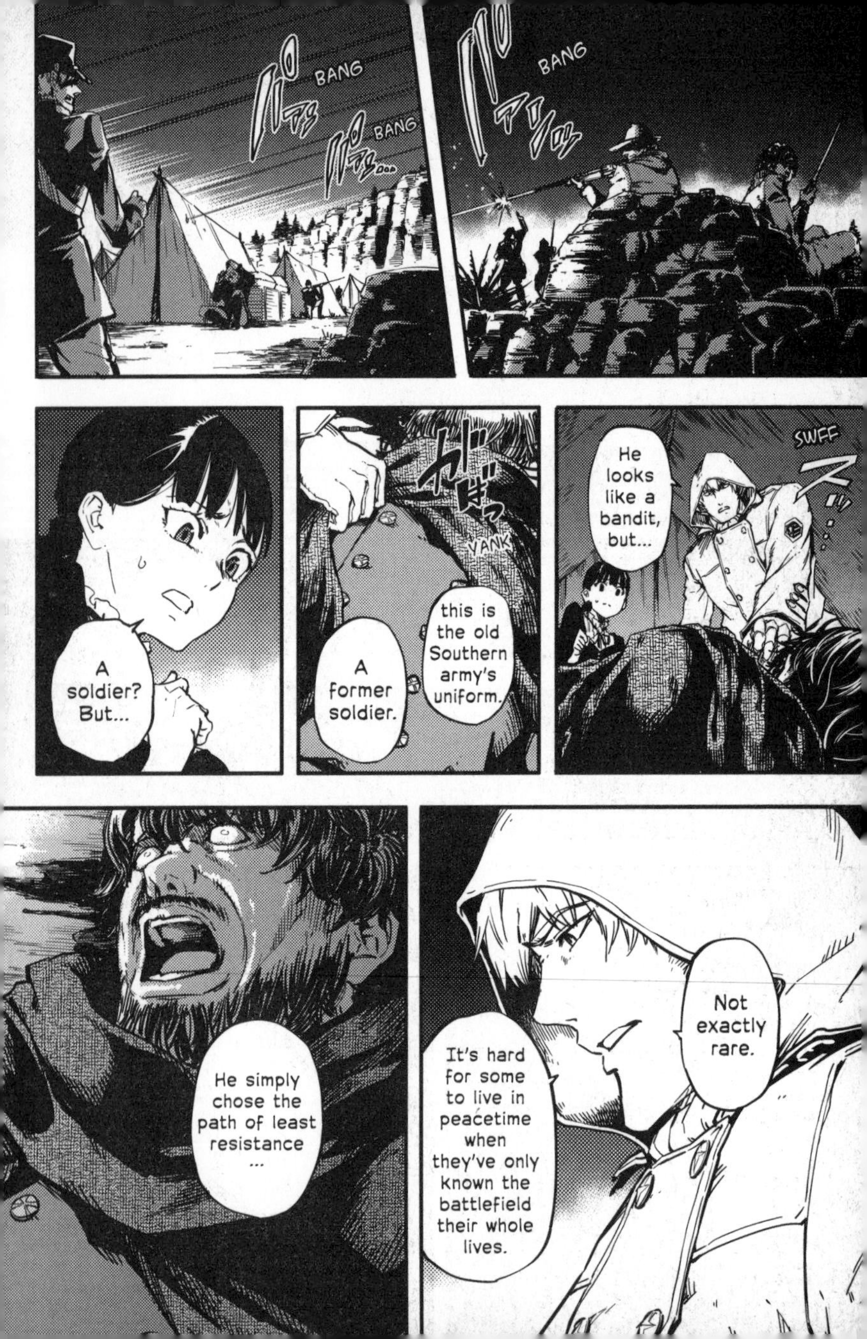
BANG
BANG
BANG
SWFF
He looks like a bandit, but...
YANK
this is the old Southern army's uniform.
A former soldier.
A soldier? But...
Not exactly rare.
It's hard for some to live in peacetime when they've only known the battlefield their whole lives.
He simply chose the path of least resistance ...

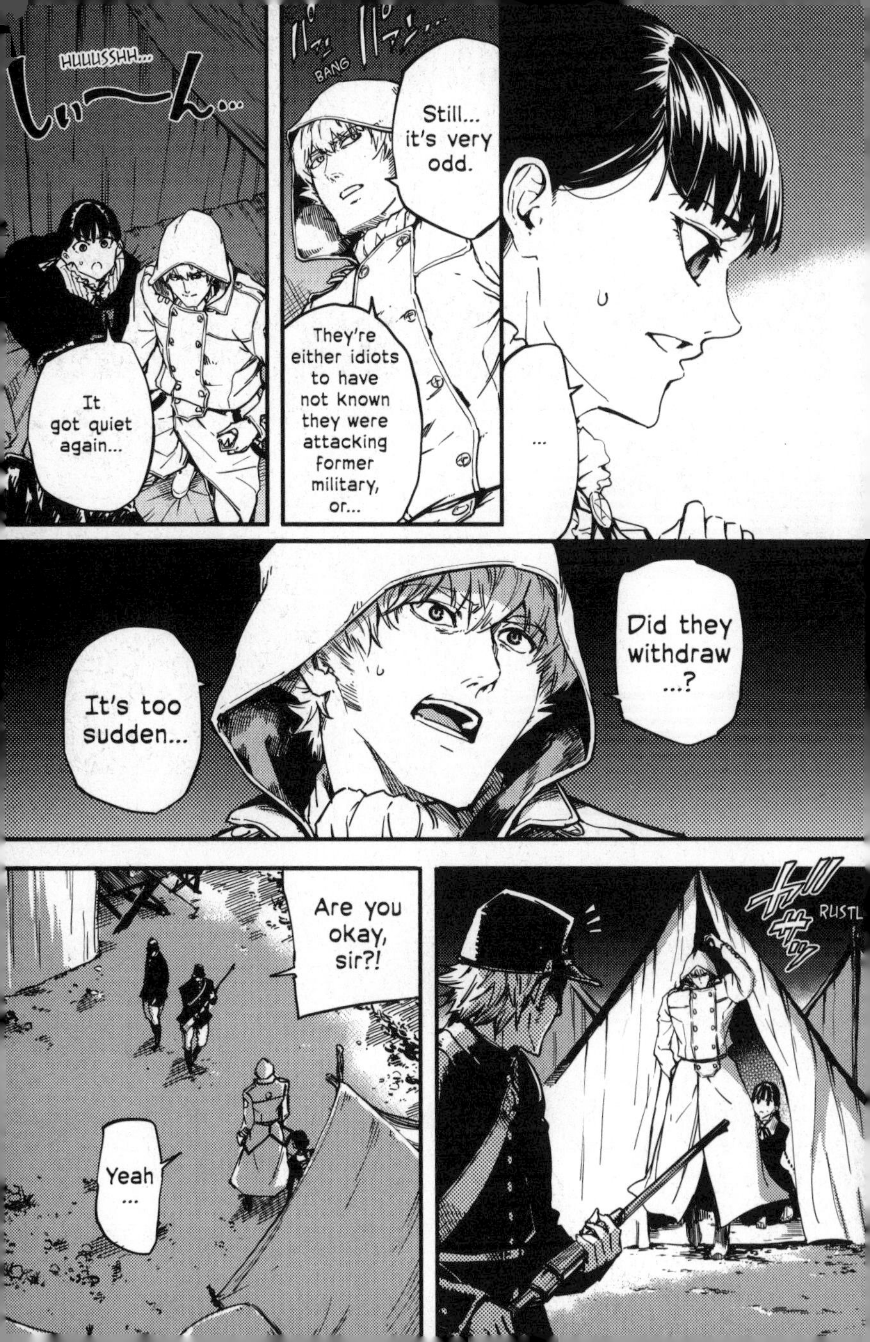
...
BANG
Still... it's very odd.
They're either idiots to have not known they were attacking former military, or...
HUUUSSHH...
しぃーん...
It got quiet again...
Did they withdraw ...?
It's too sudden...
RUSTL
Are you okay, sir?!
Yeah ...

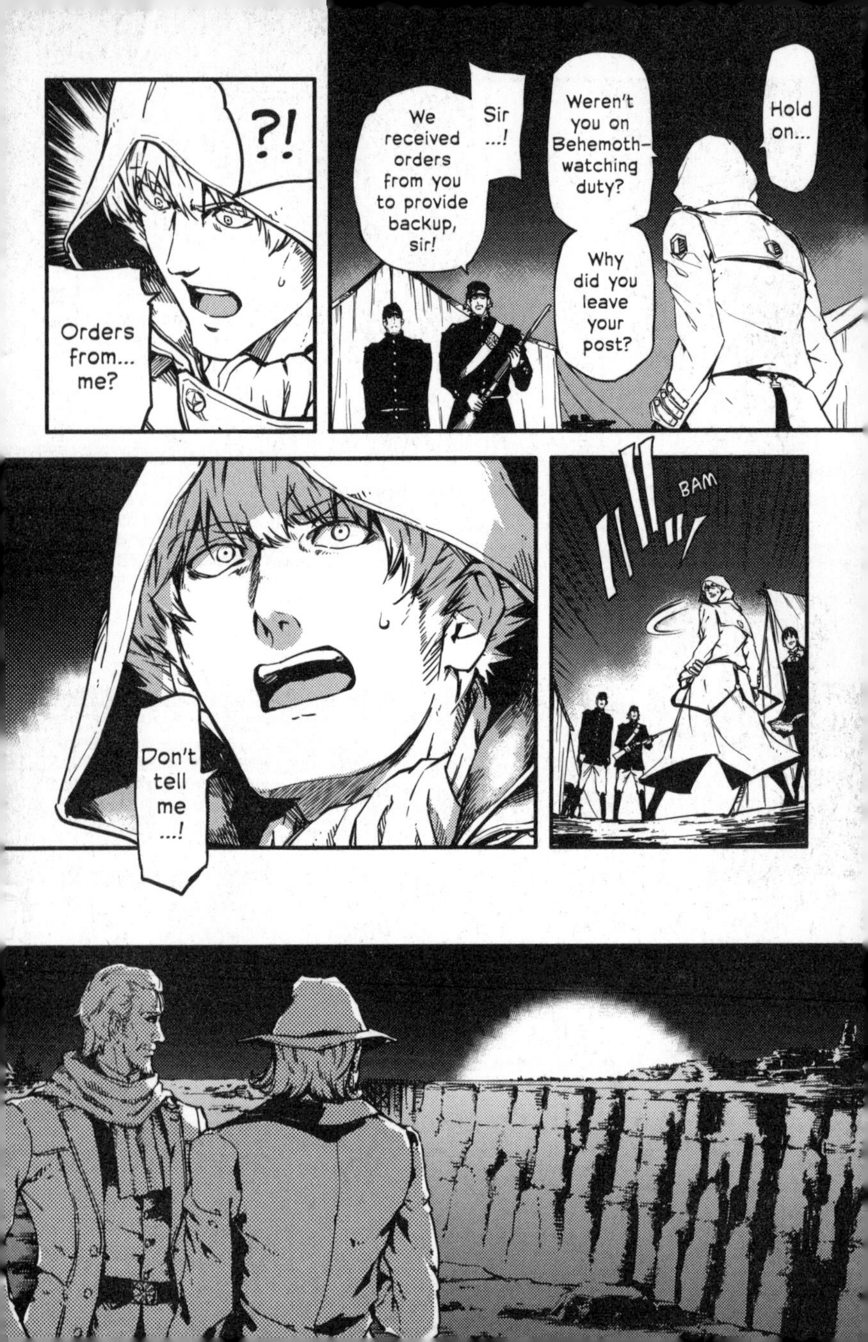
Hold on...
Weren't you on Behemoth-watching duty?
Why did you leave your post?
Sir ...!
We received orders from you to provide backup, sir!
?!
Orders from... me?
BAM
Don't tell me ...!

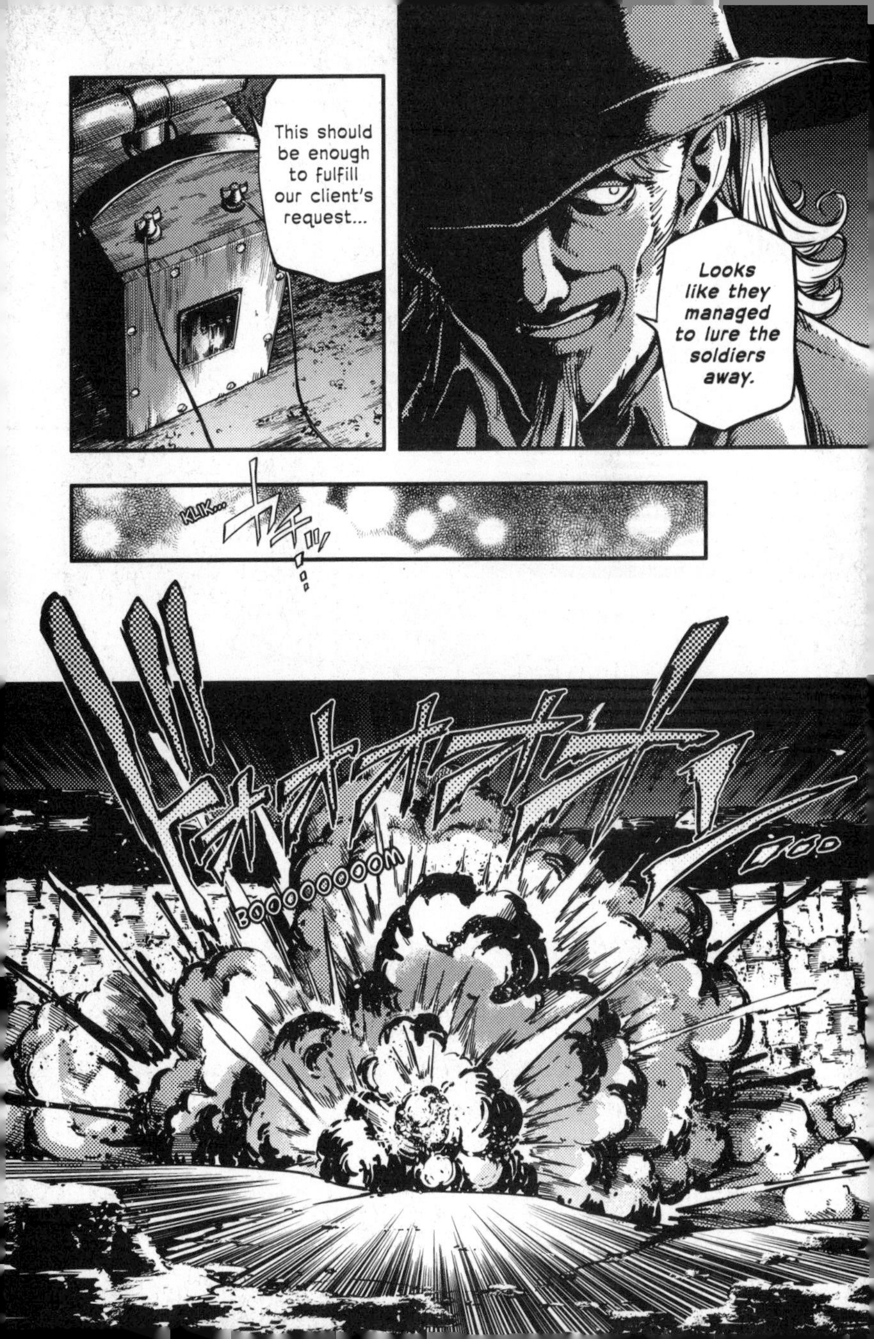
Looks like they managed to lure the soldiers away.
This should be enough to fulfill our client's request...
KLIK...
BOOOOOOOOM

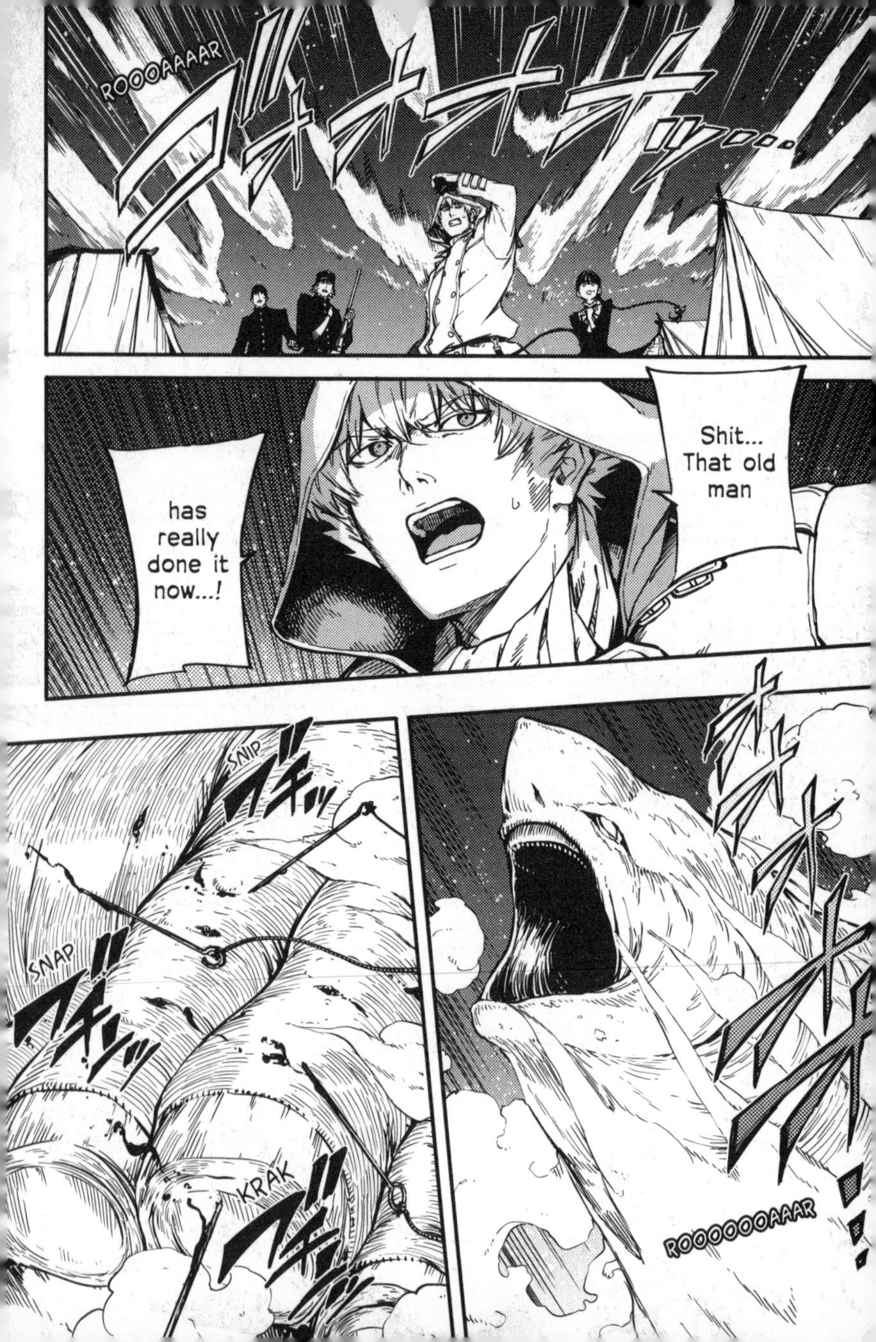
ROOOAAAAR
Shit... That old man
has really done it now...!
ROOOOOOAAAR
SNIP
SNAP
KRAK

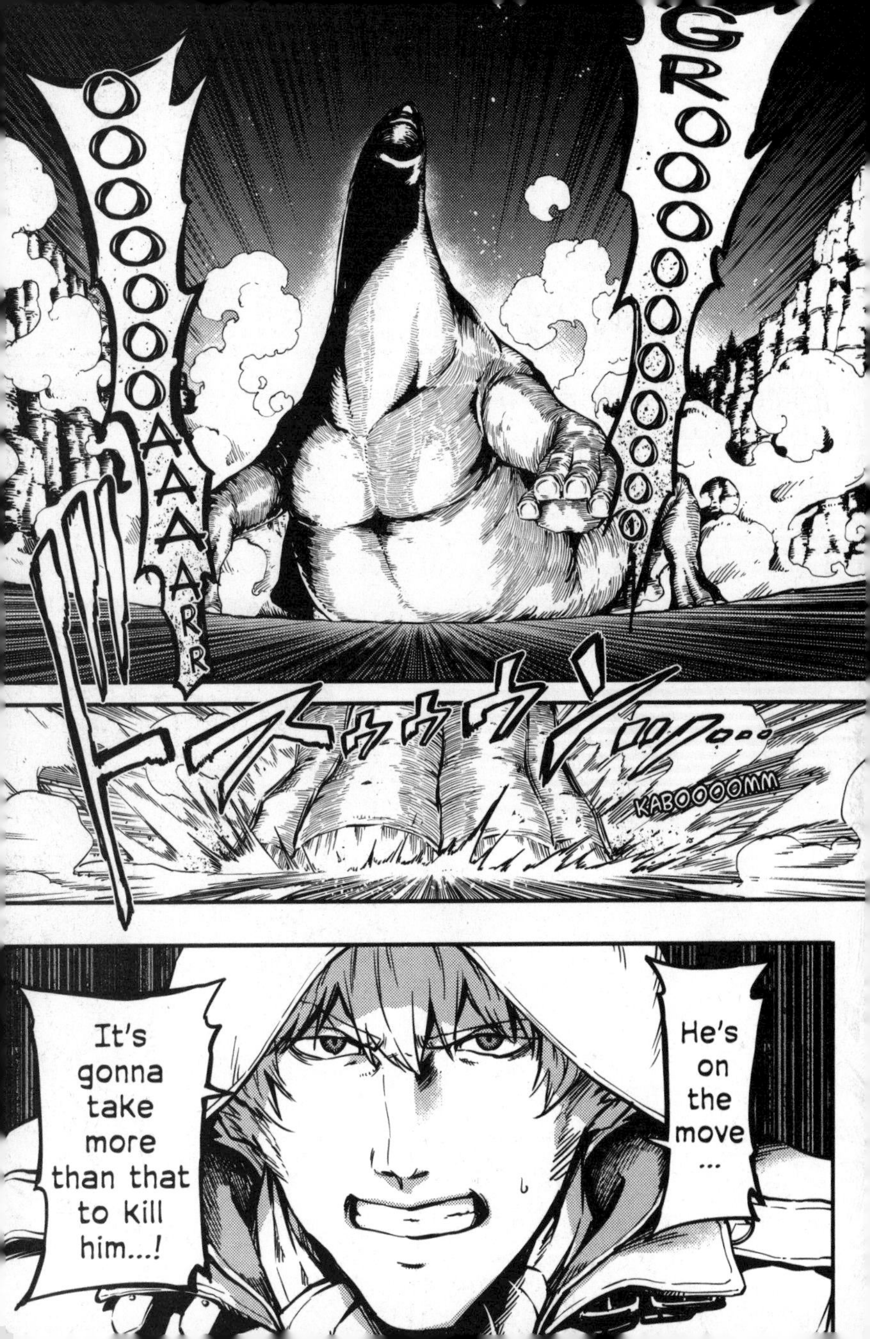
GROOOOOOOOOOO
OOOOOOOOAAAARR
KABOOOOMM
He's on the move ...
It's gonna take more than that to kill him...!

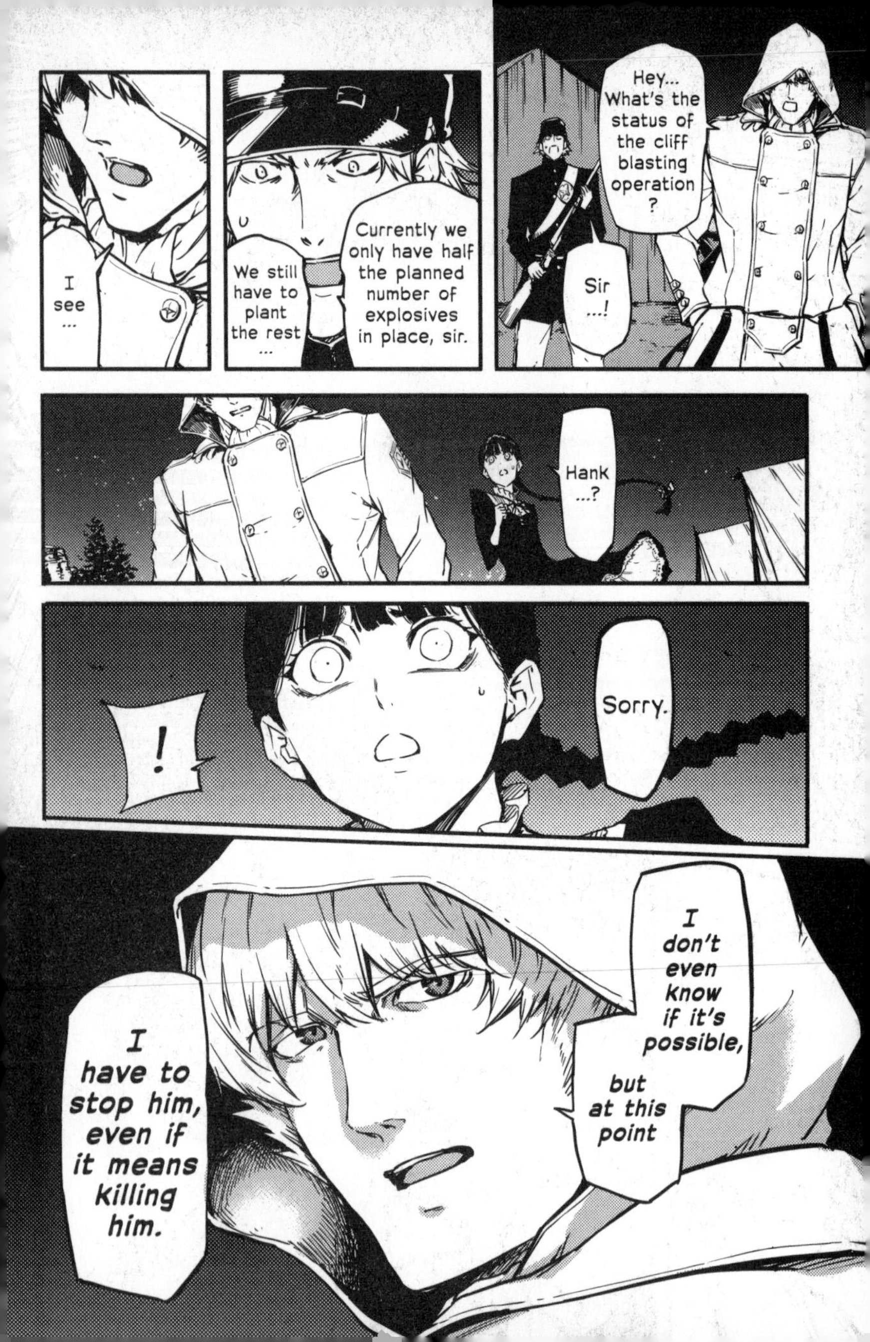
Hey... What's the status of the cliff blasting operation?
Sir ...!
Currently we only have half the planned number of explosives in place, sir.
We still have to plant the rest ...
I see ...
Hank ...?
Sorry.
!
I don't even know if it's possible,
but at this point
I have to stop him, even if it means killing him.

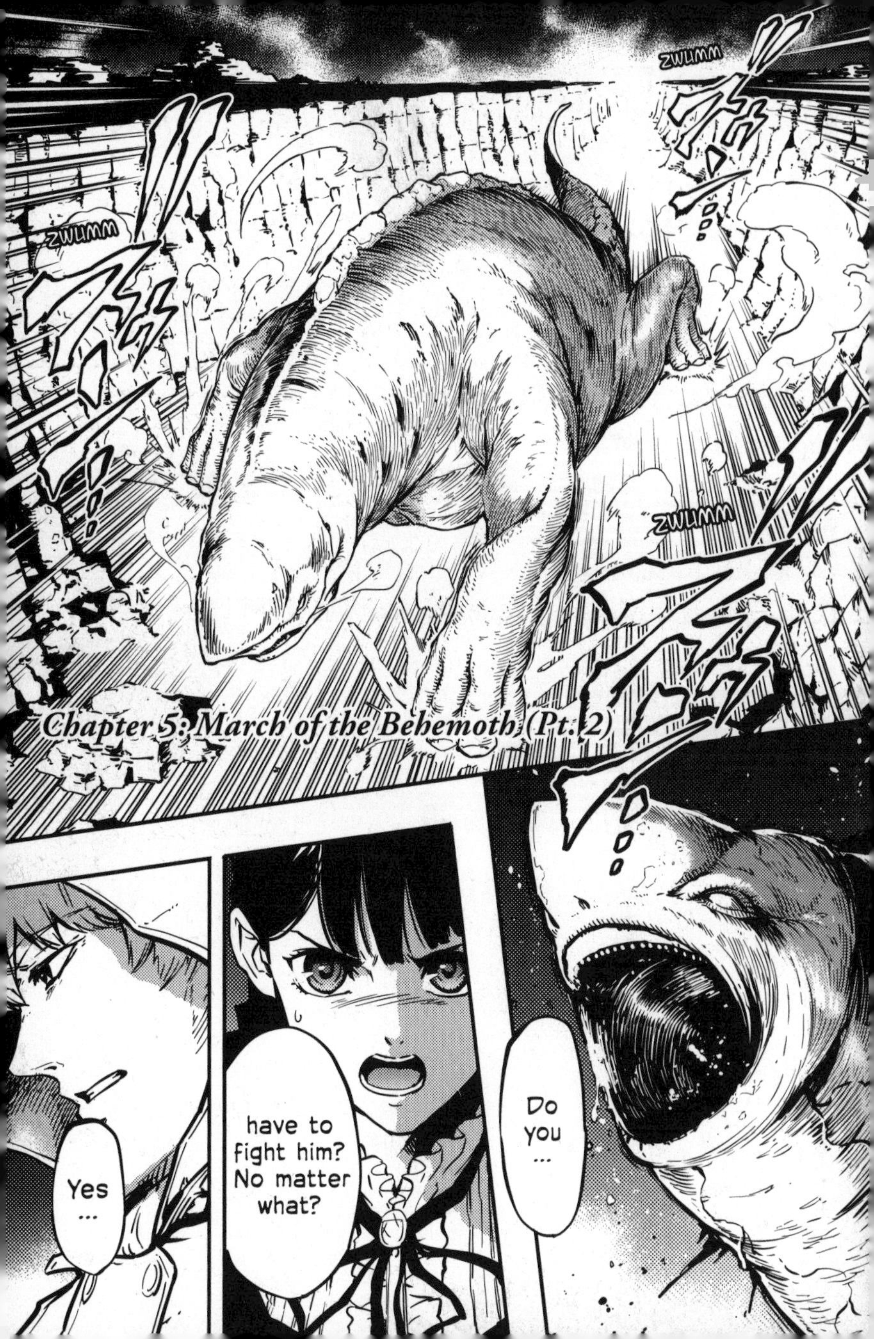
ZWUMM
ZWUMM
ZWUMM
Chapter 5: March of the Behemoth (Pt. 2)
Do you ...
have to fight him? No matter what?
Yes ...

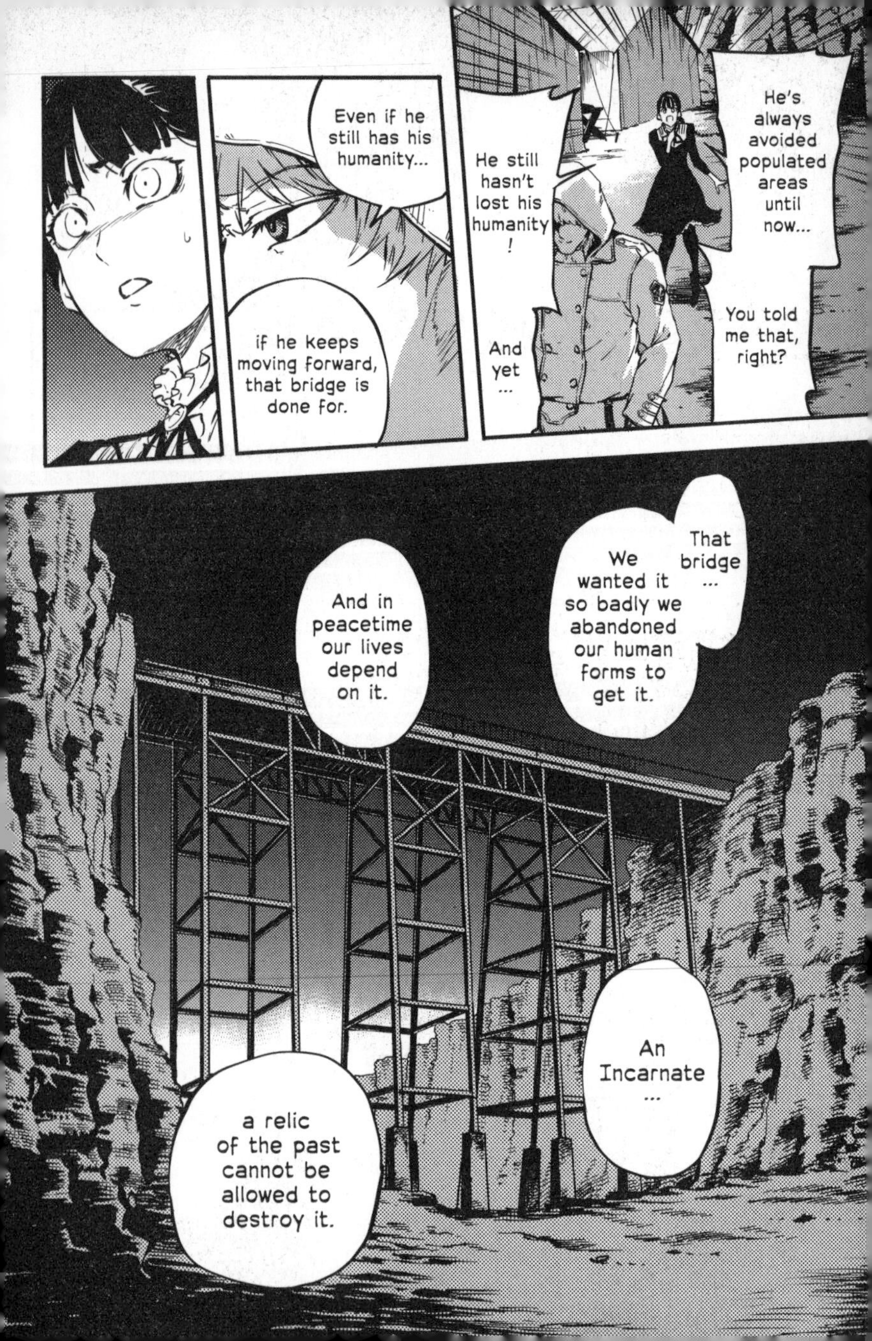
He's always avoided populated areas until now...
You told me that, right?
He still hasn't lost his humanity!
And yet...
Even if he still has his humanity...
if he keeps moving forward, that bridge is done for.
That bridge...
We wanted it so badly we abandoned our human forms to get it.
And in peacetime our lives depend on it.
An Incarnate...
a relic of the past cannot be allowed to destroy it.

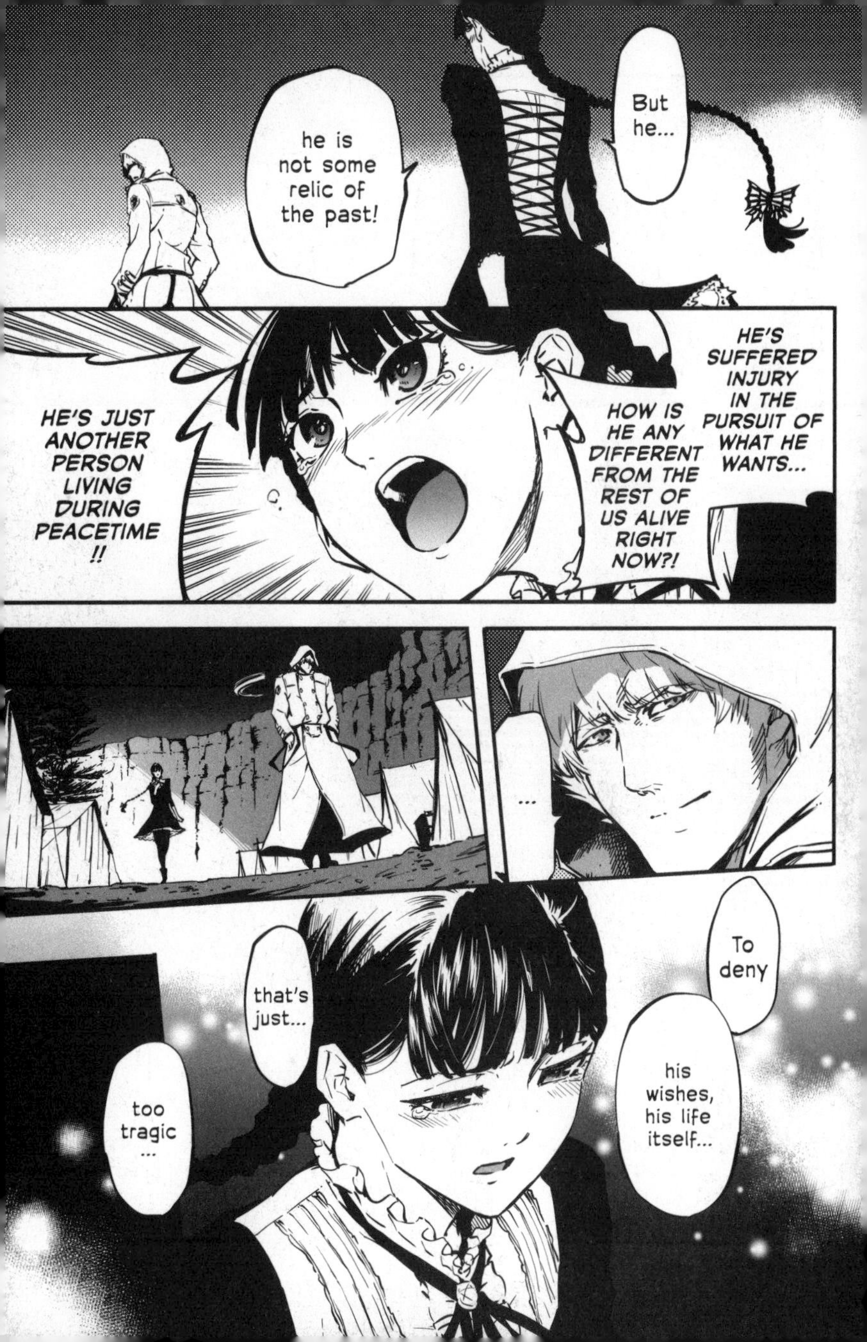
But he...
he is not some relic of the past!
HE'S SUFFERED INJURY IN THE PURSUIT OF WHAT HE WANTS...
HOW IS HE ANY DIFFERENT FROM THE REST OF US ALIVE RIGHT NOW?!
HE'S JUST ANOTHER PERSON LIVING DURING PEACETIME !!
...
To deny
his wishes, his life itself...
that's just...
too tragic ...

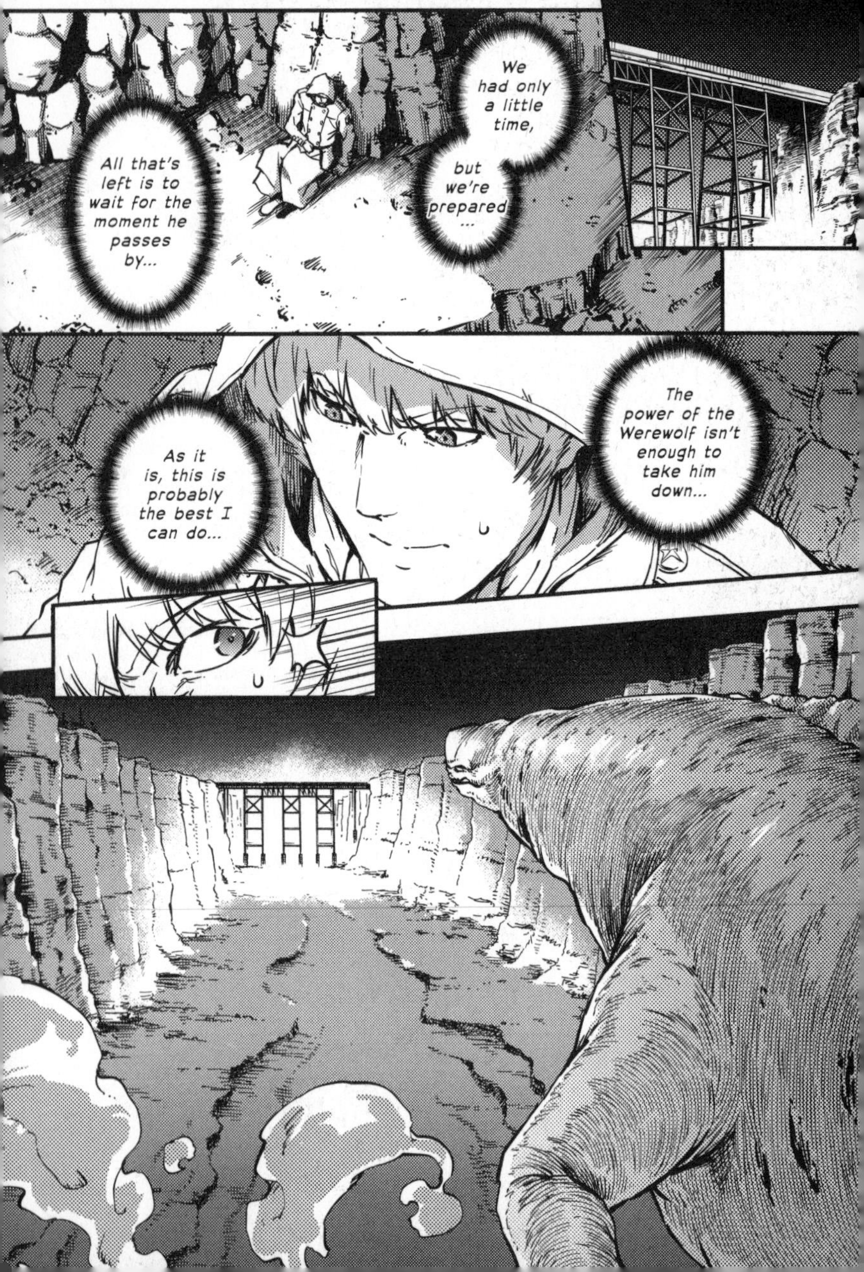
We had only a little time,
but we're prepared...
All that's left is to wait for the moment he passes by...
The power of the Werewolf isn't enough to take him down...
As it is, this is probably the best I can do...

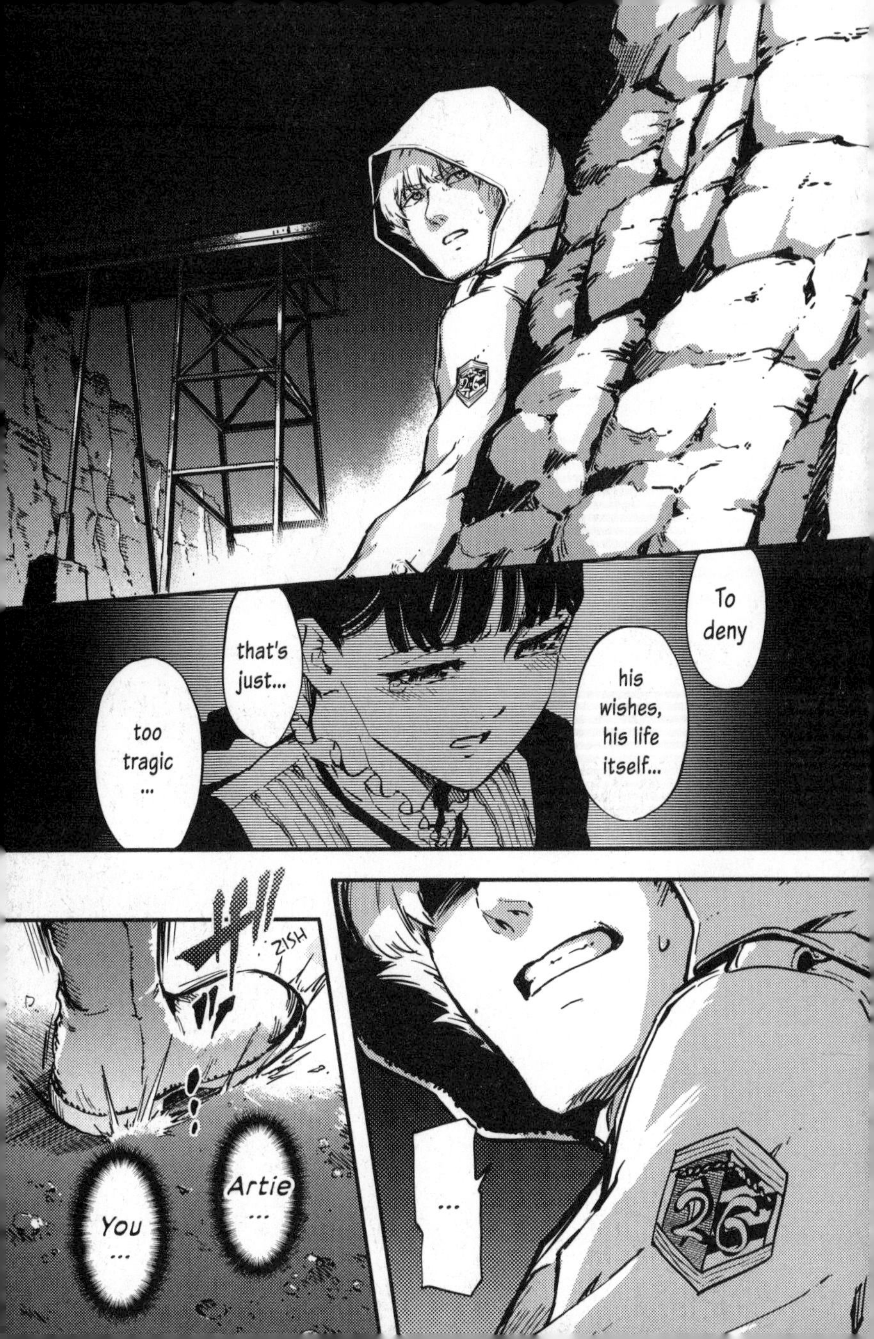

To deny
his wishes, his life itself...
that's just...
too tragic ...
...
ZISH
Artie ...
You ...

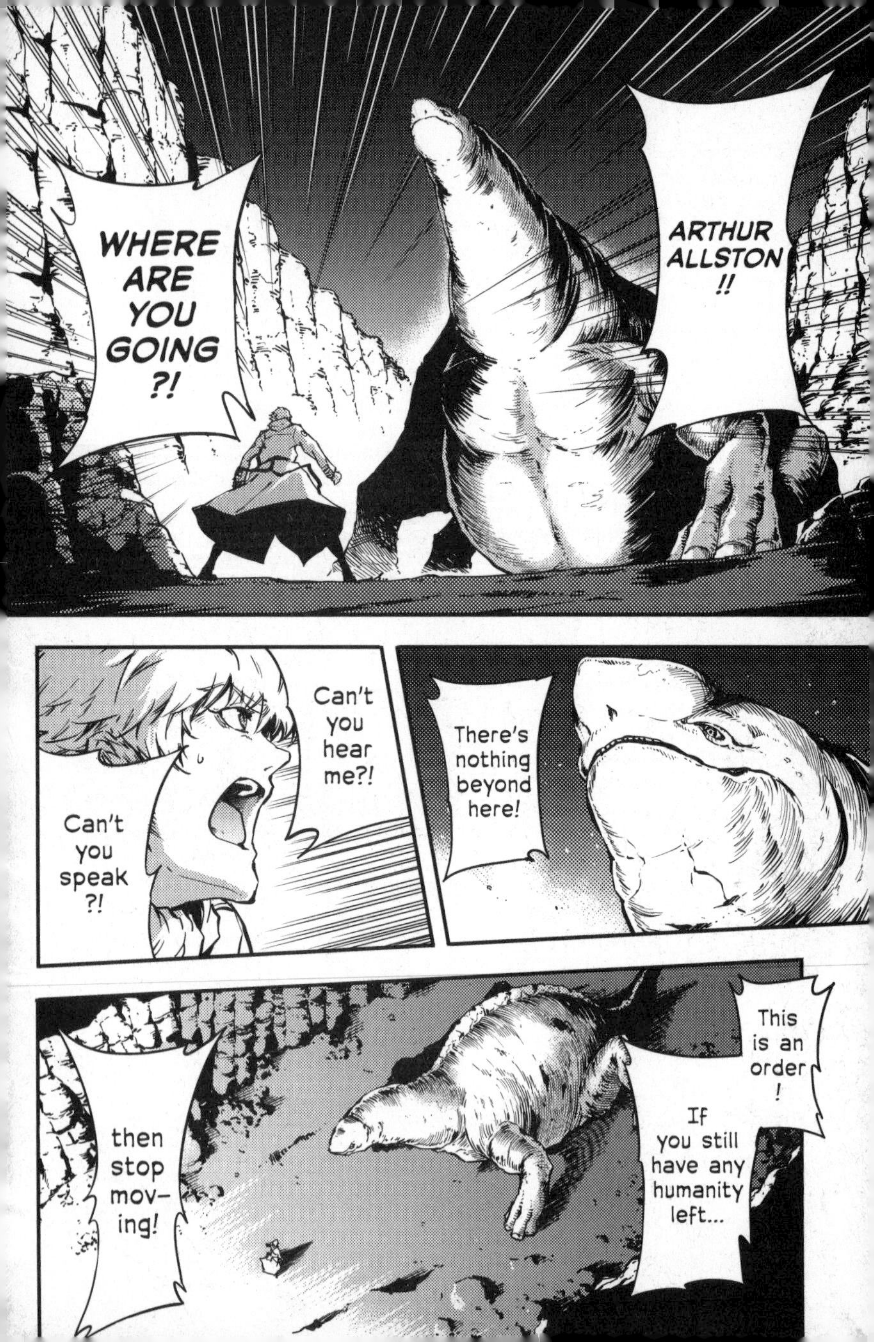
ARTHUR ALLSTON !!
WHERE ARE YOU GOING ?!
There's nothing beyond here!
Can't you hear me?!
Can't you speak ?!
This is an order !
If you still have any humanity left...
then stop mov-ing!

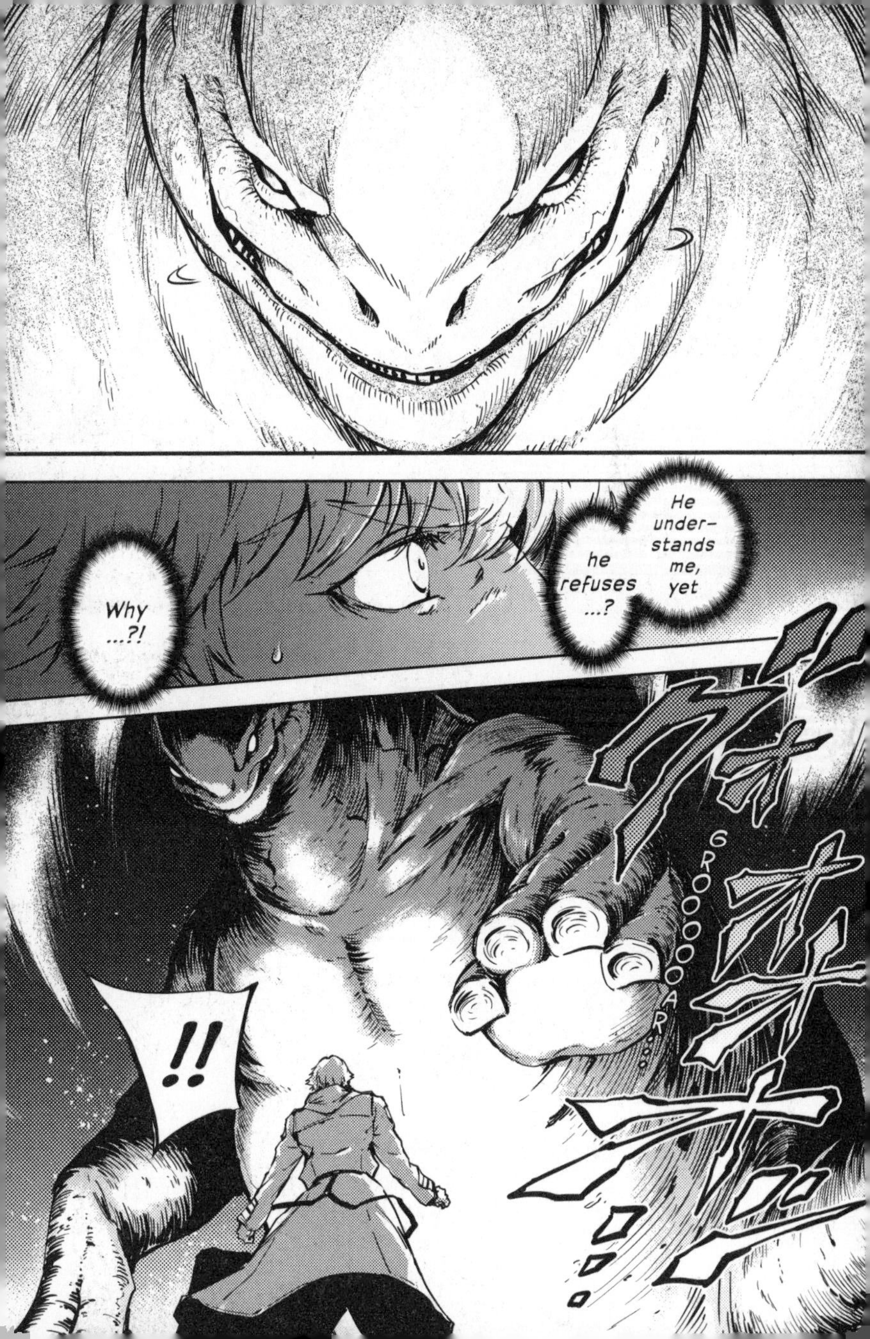
He understands me, yet he refuses ...?
Why ...?!
GROOOOOOAR...
!!

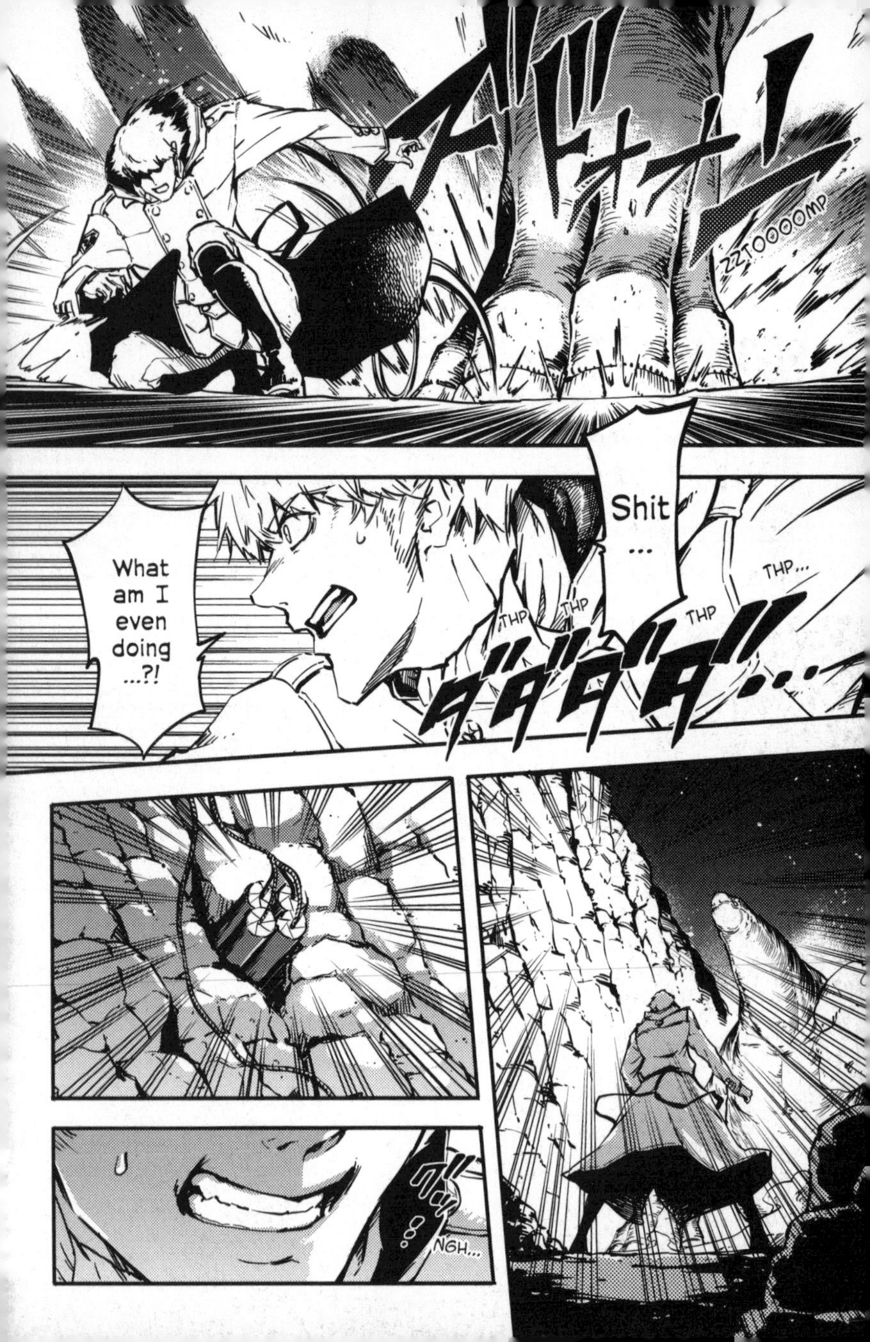
ZZTOOOOOMP
Shit ...
THP...
THP
THP
THP
What am I even doing ...?!
NGH...

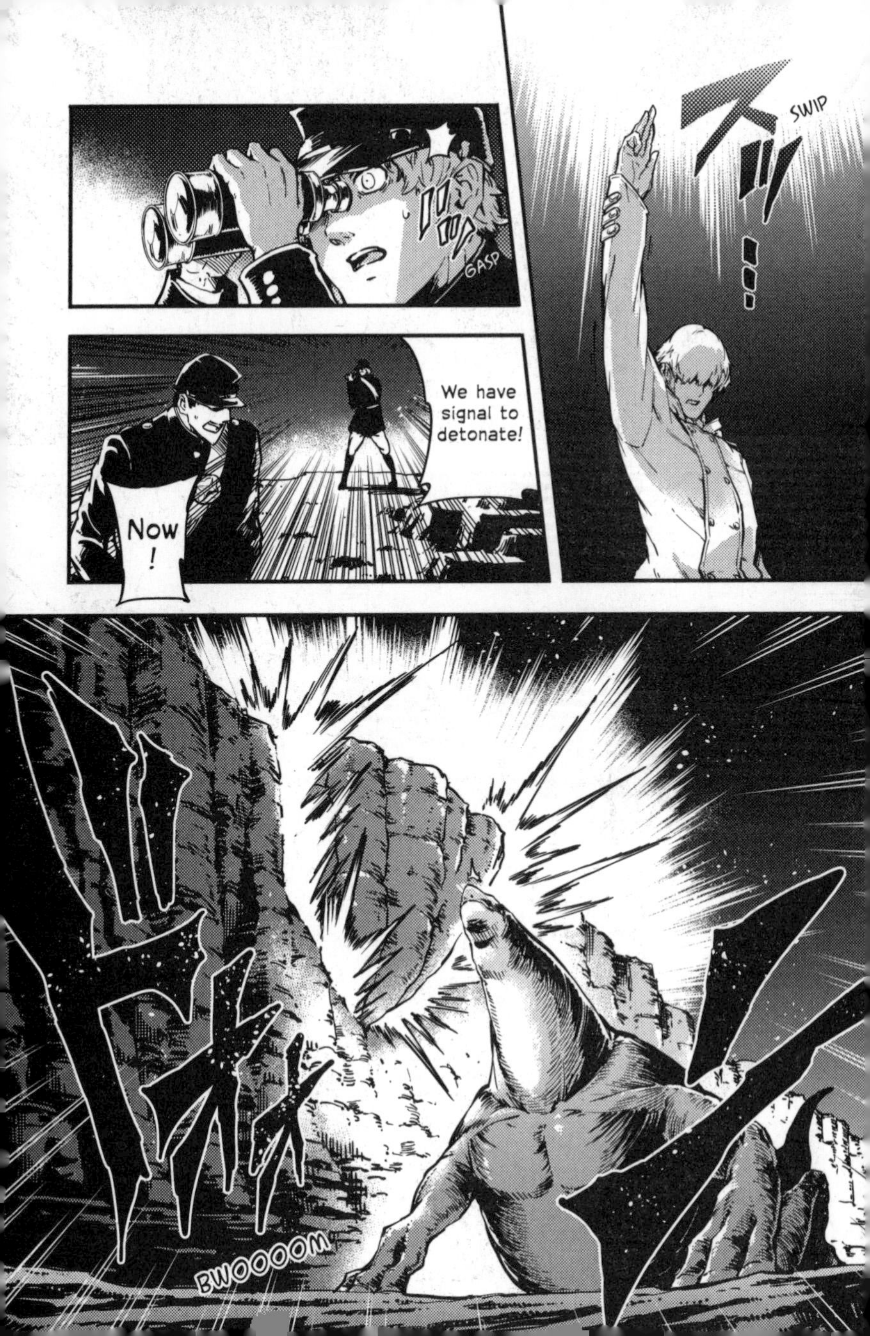
SWIP
GASP
We have signal to detonate!
Now!
BWOOOOM

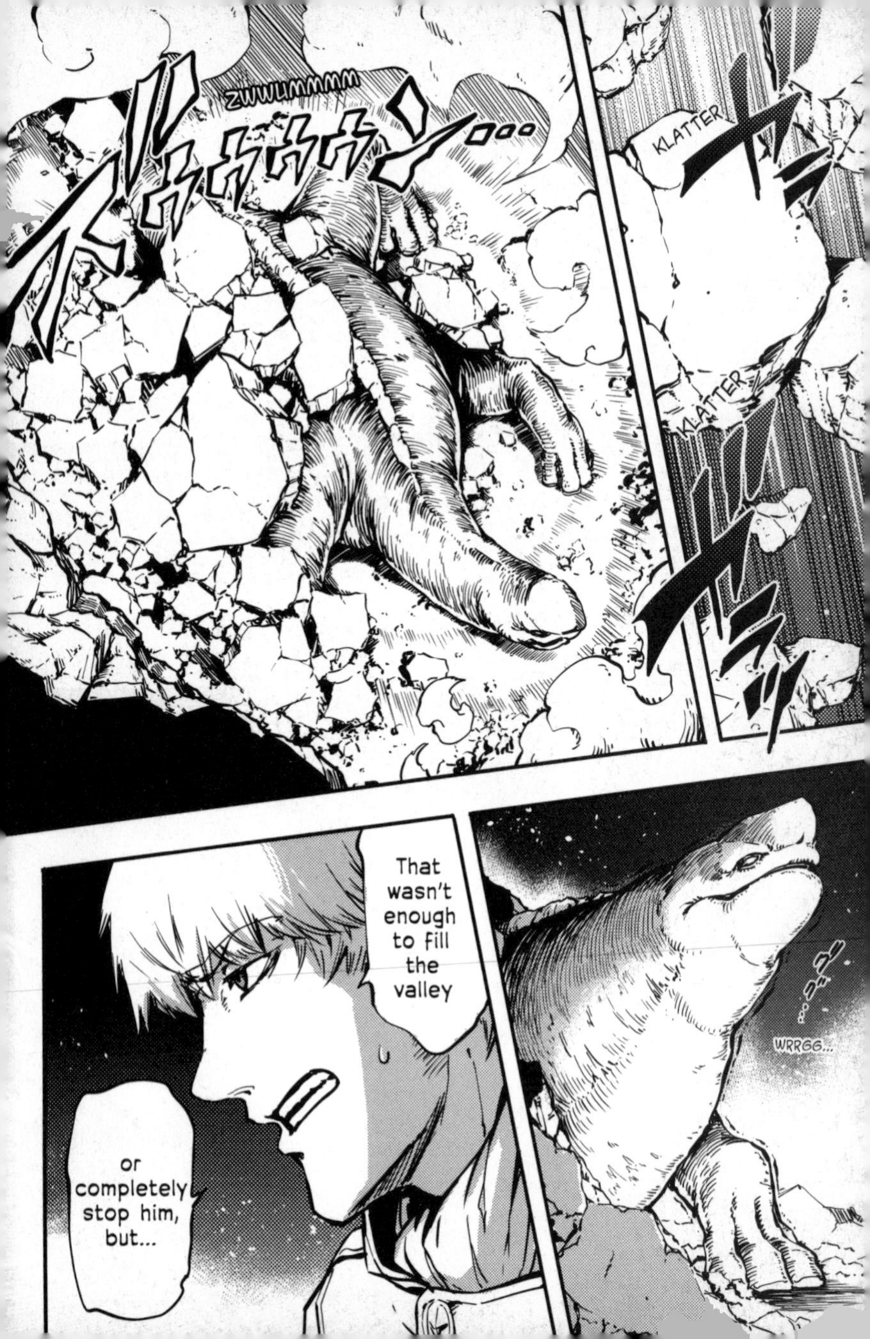
KLATTER
KLATTER
ZWWUMMMM
WRRGG...
That wasn't enough to fill the valley
or completely stop him, but...

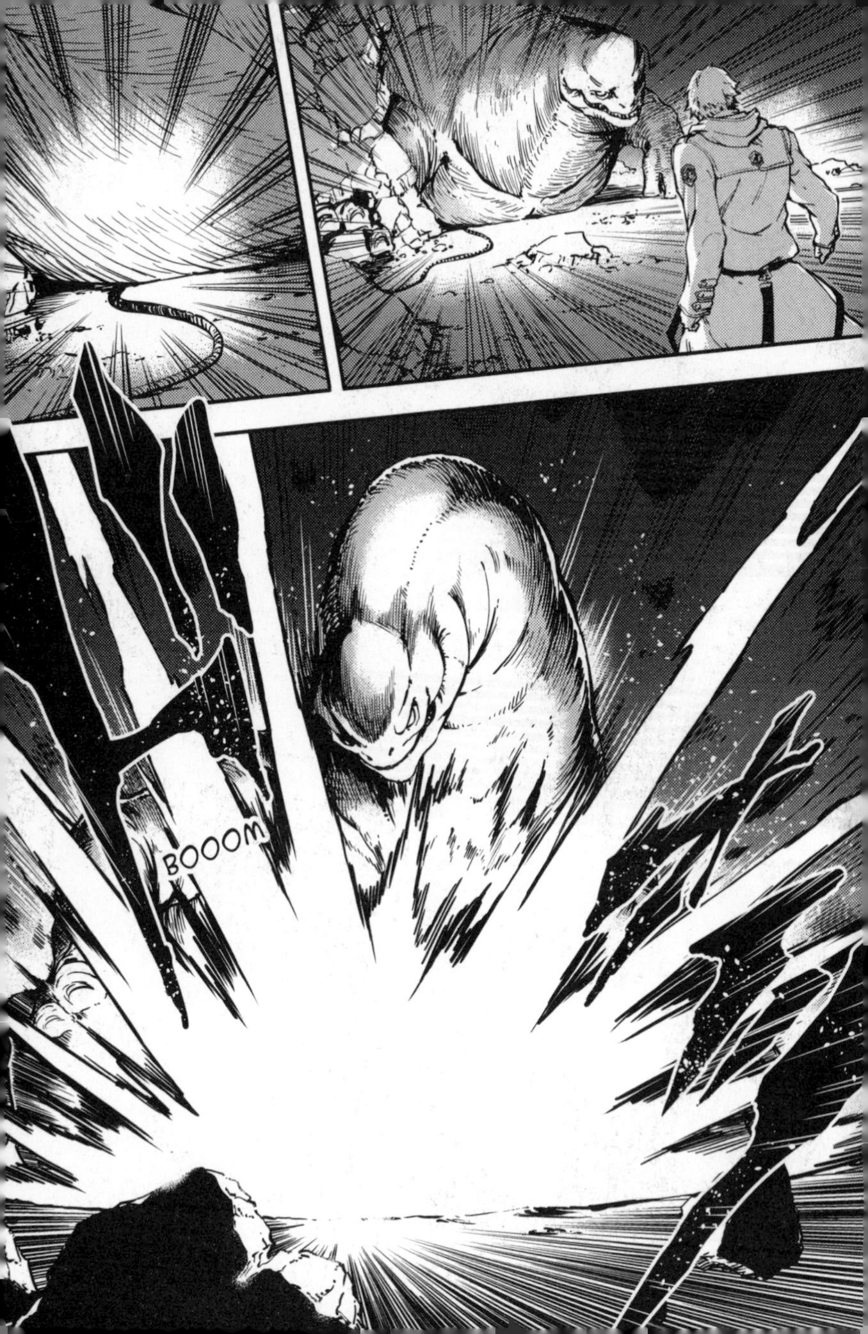
BOOOM

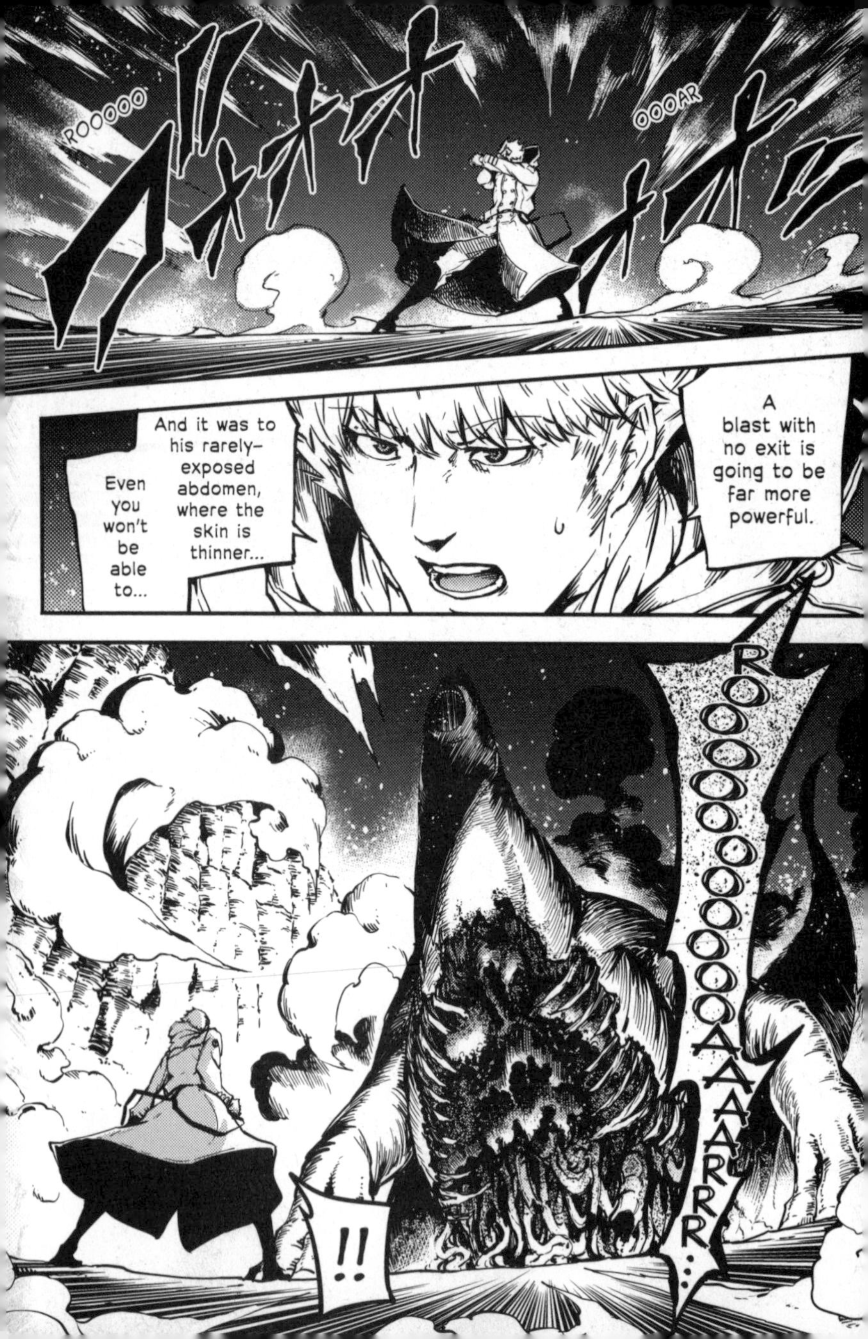
ROOOOO
OOOAR
A blast with no exit is going to be far more powerful.
And it was to his rarely-exposed abdomen, where the skin is thinner...
Even you won't be able to...
ROOOOOOOOOOOOOOAAAARRR...
!!

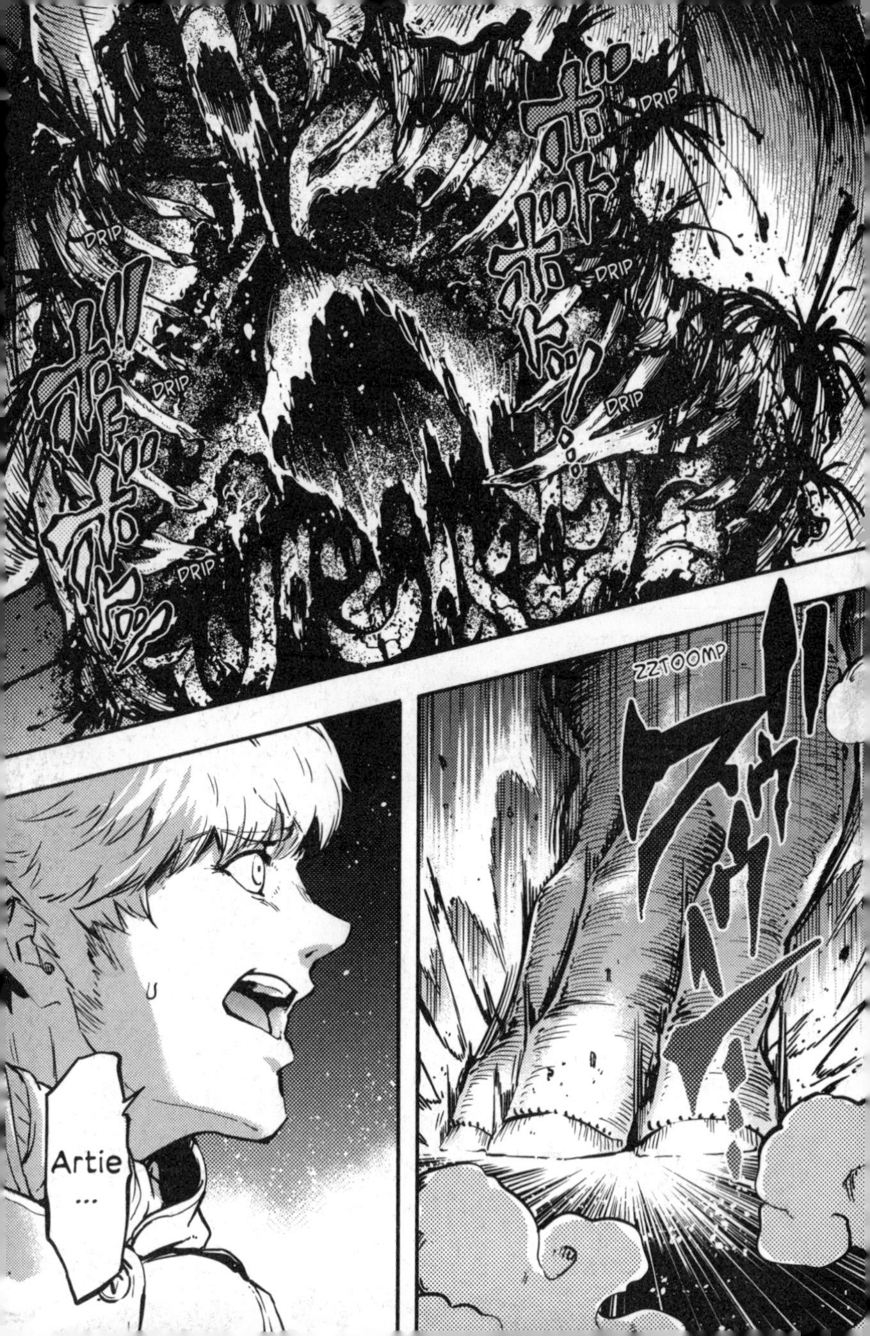
DRIP
DRIP
DRIP
DRIP
DRIP
DRIP
ZZTOOMP
Artie
...

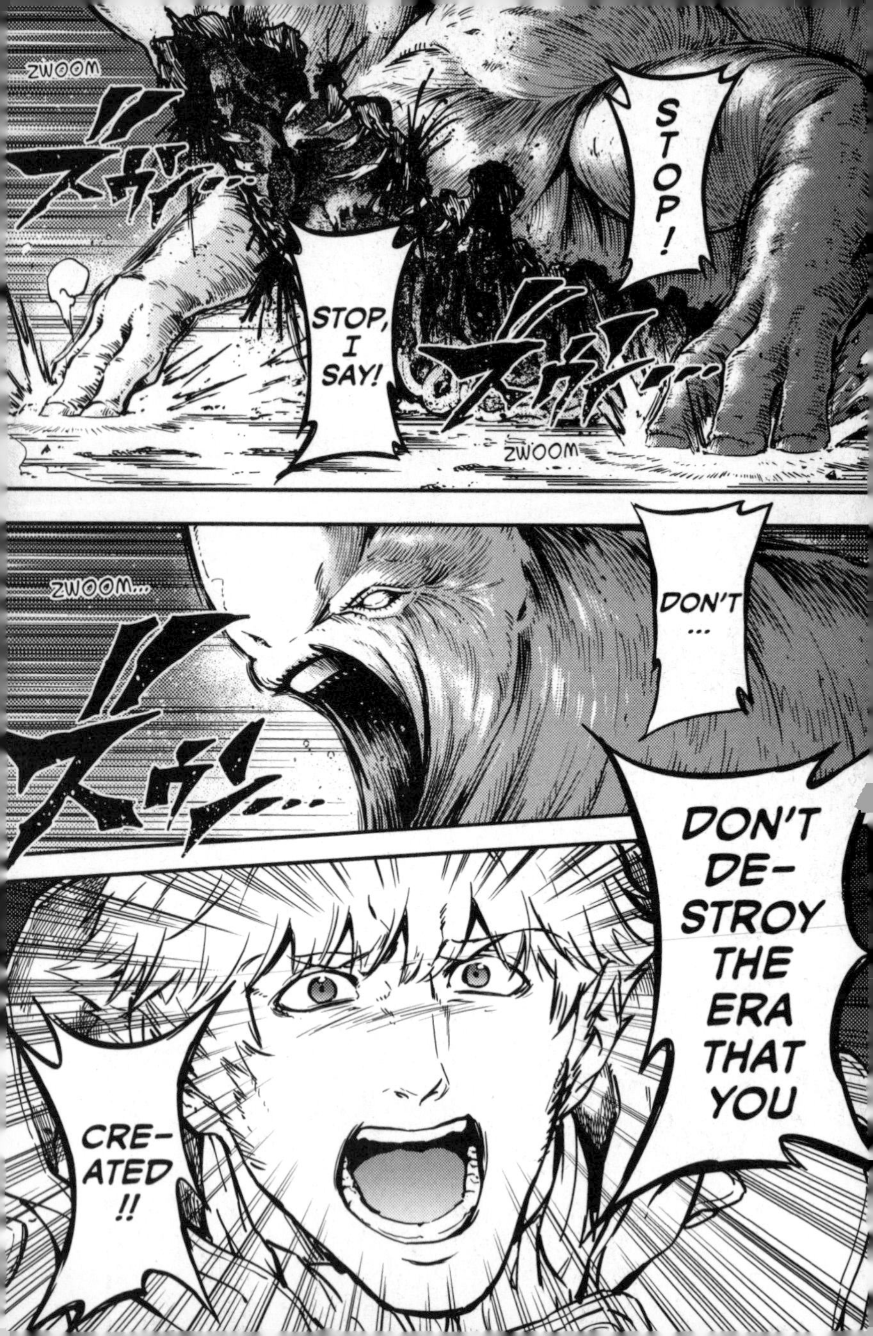
STOP!
ZWOOM
STOP, I SAY!
ZWOOM
DON'T ...
ZWOOM...
DON'T DE-STROY THE ERA THAT YOU
CRE-ATED !!

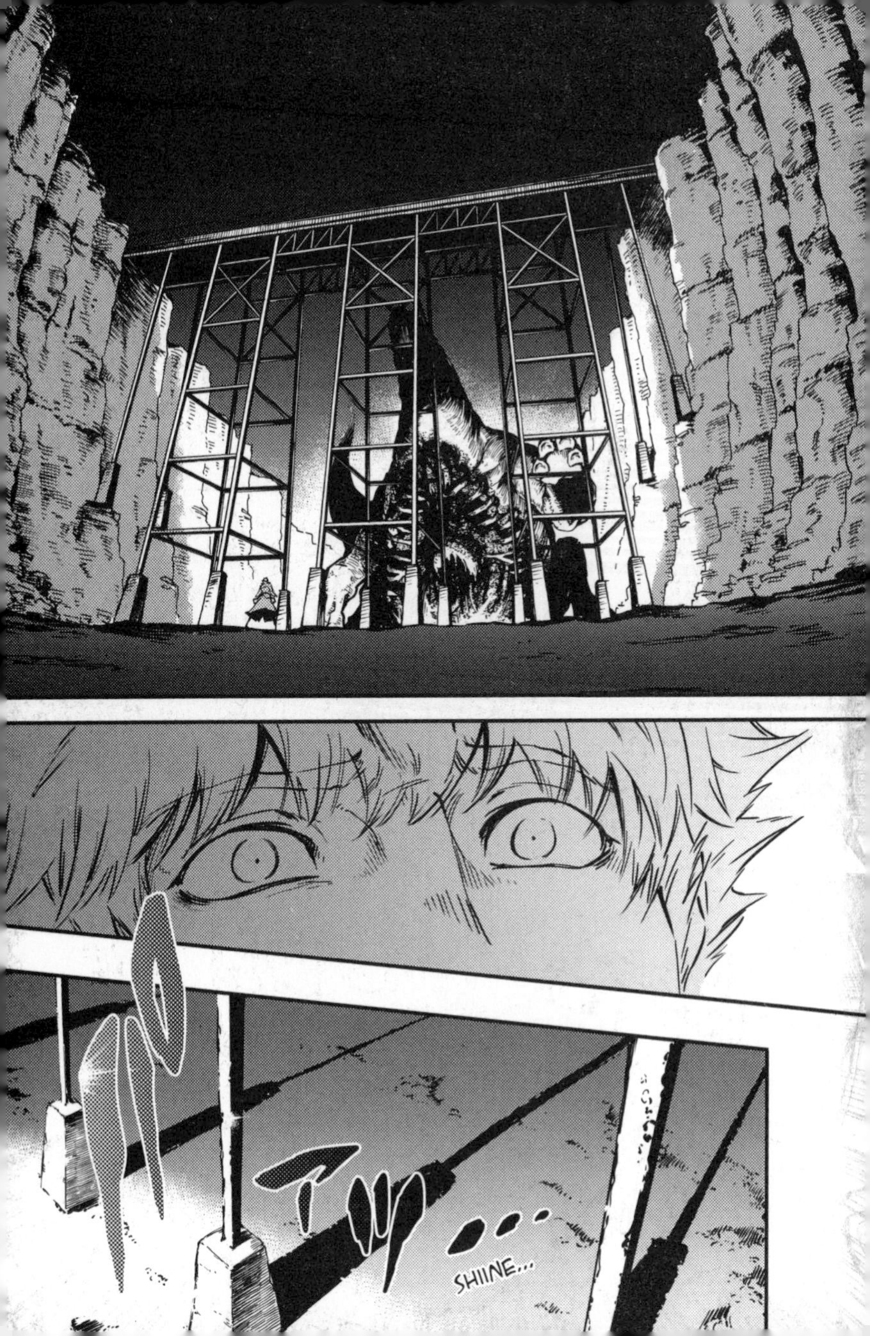
SHIINE...

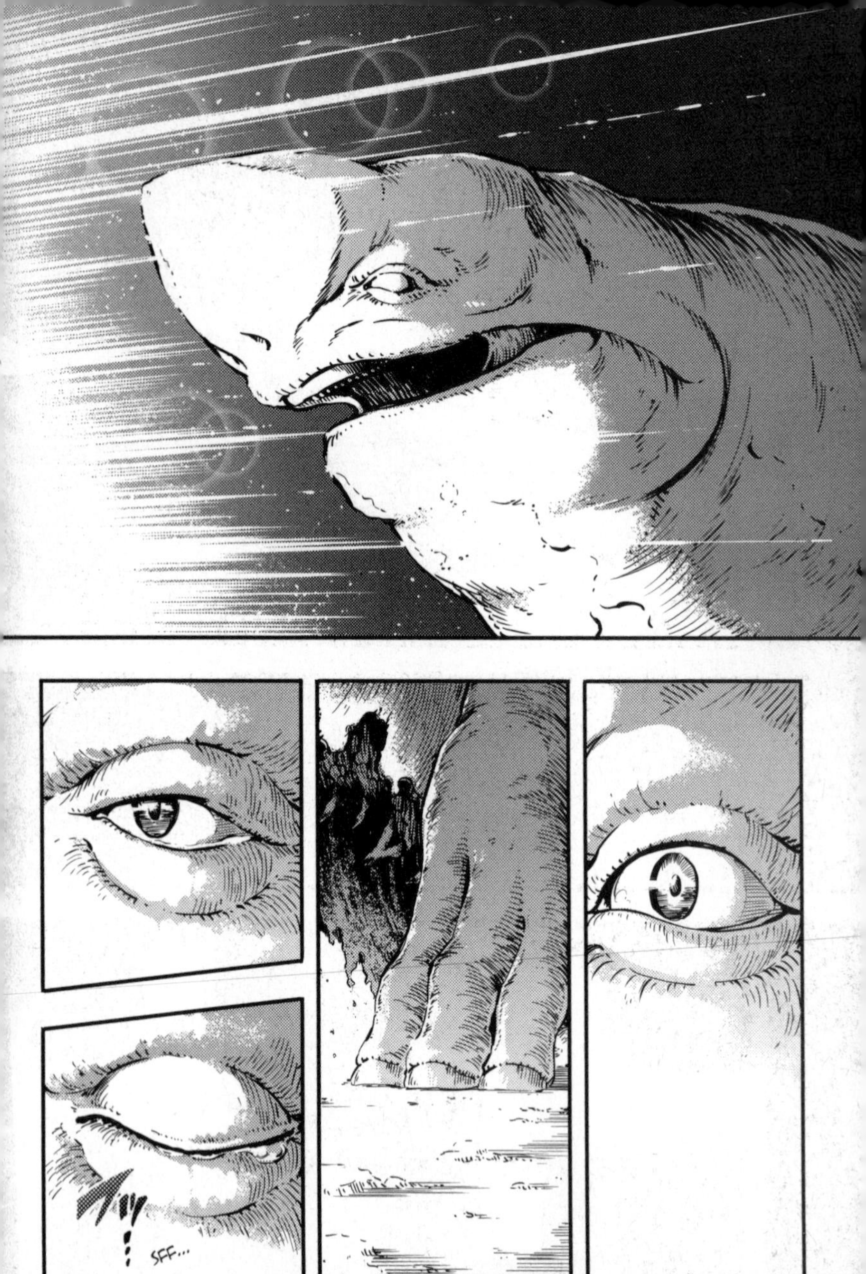
SFF...

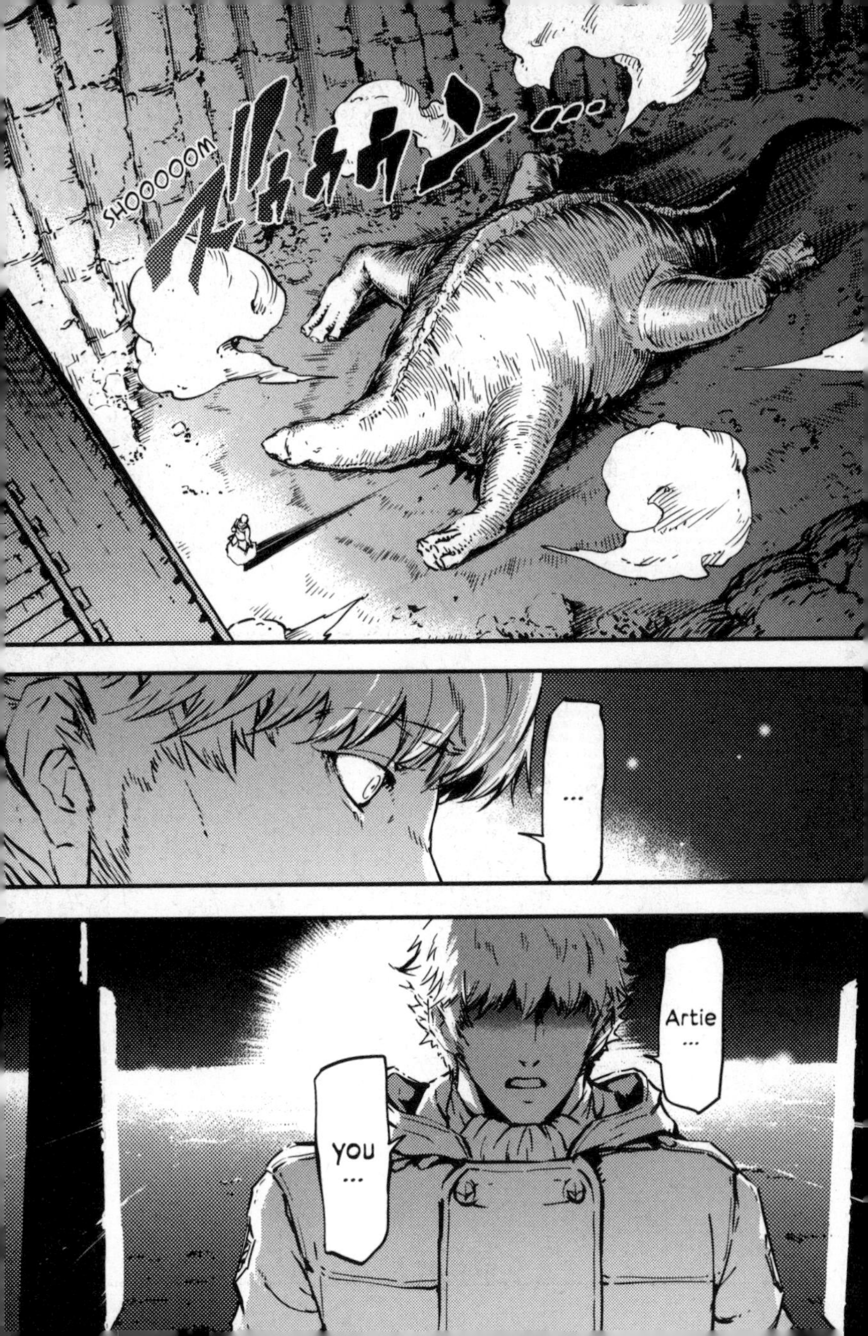
SHOOOOOM
...
Artie ...
You ...

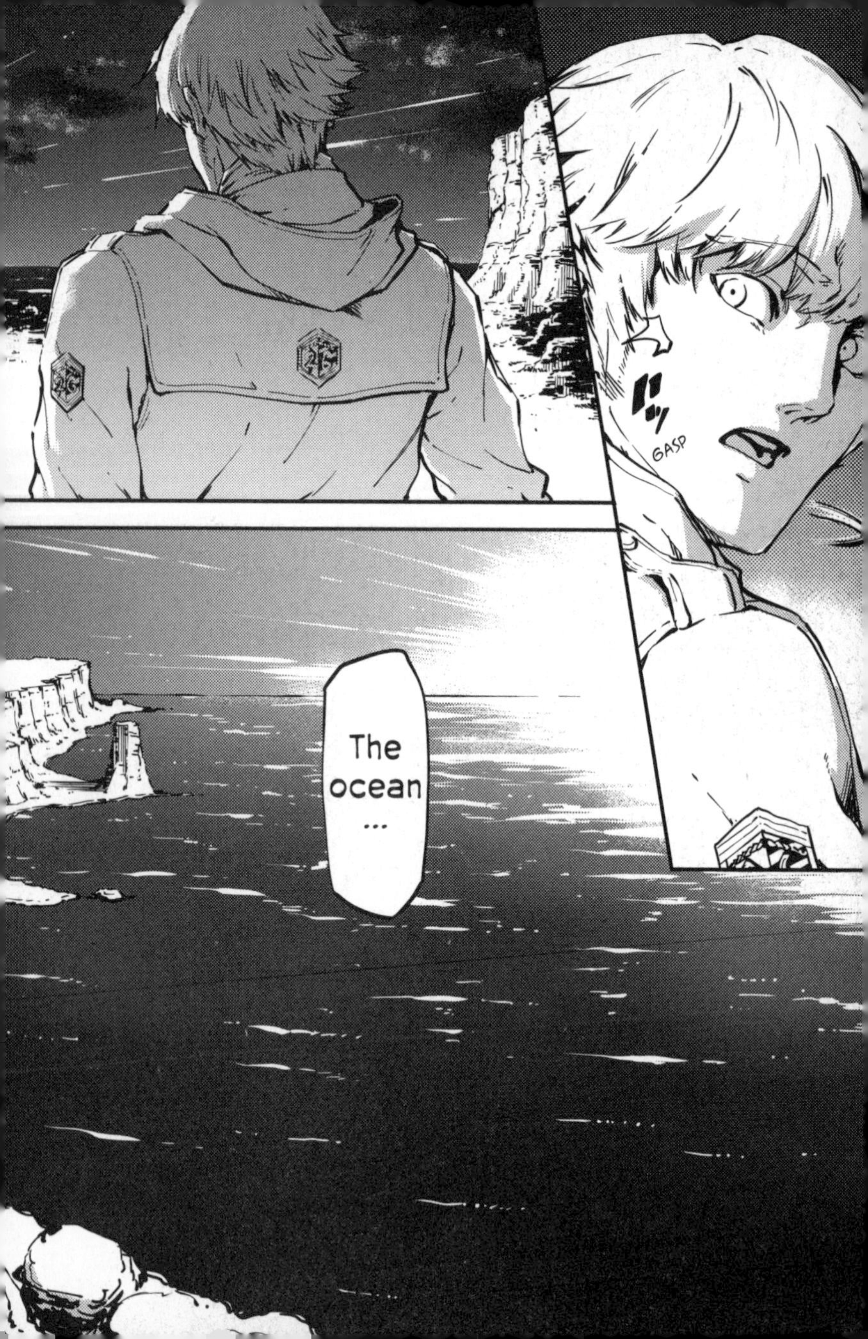
GASP
The ocean ...

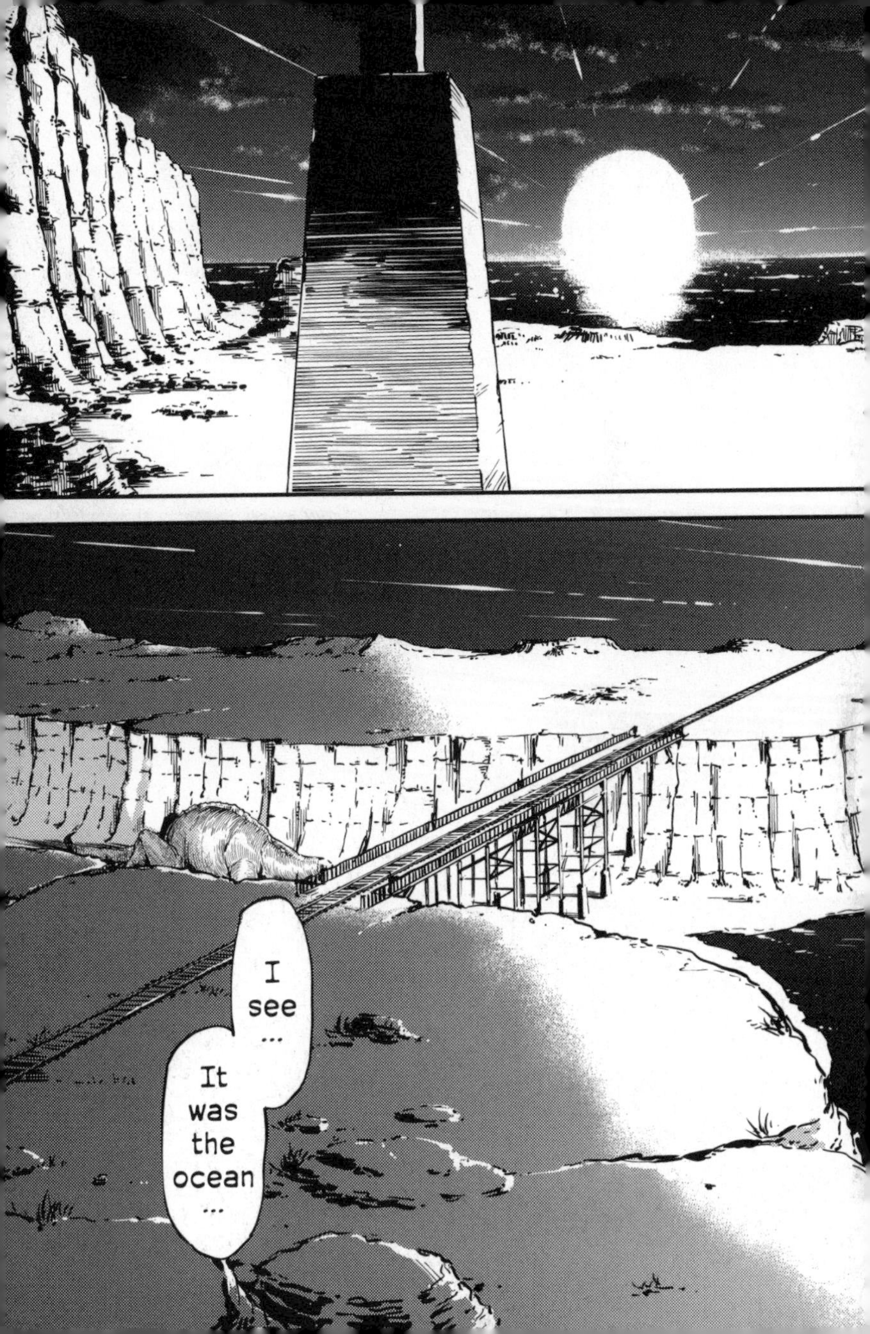
I see ... It was the ocean ...

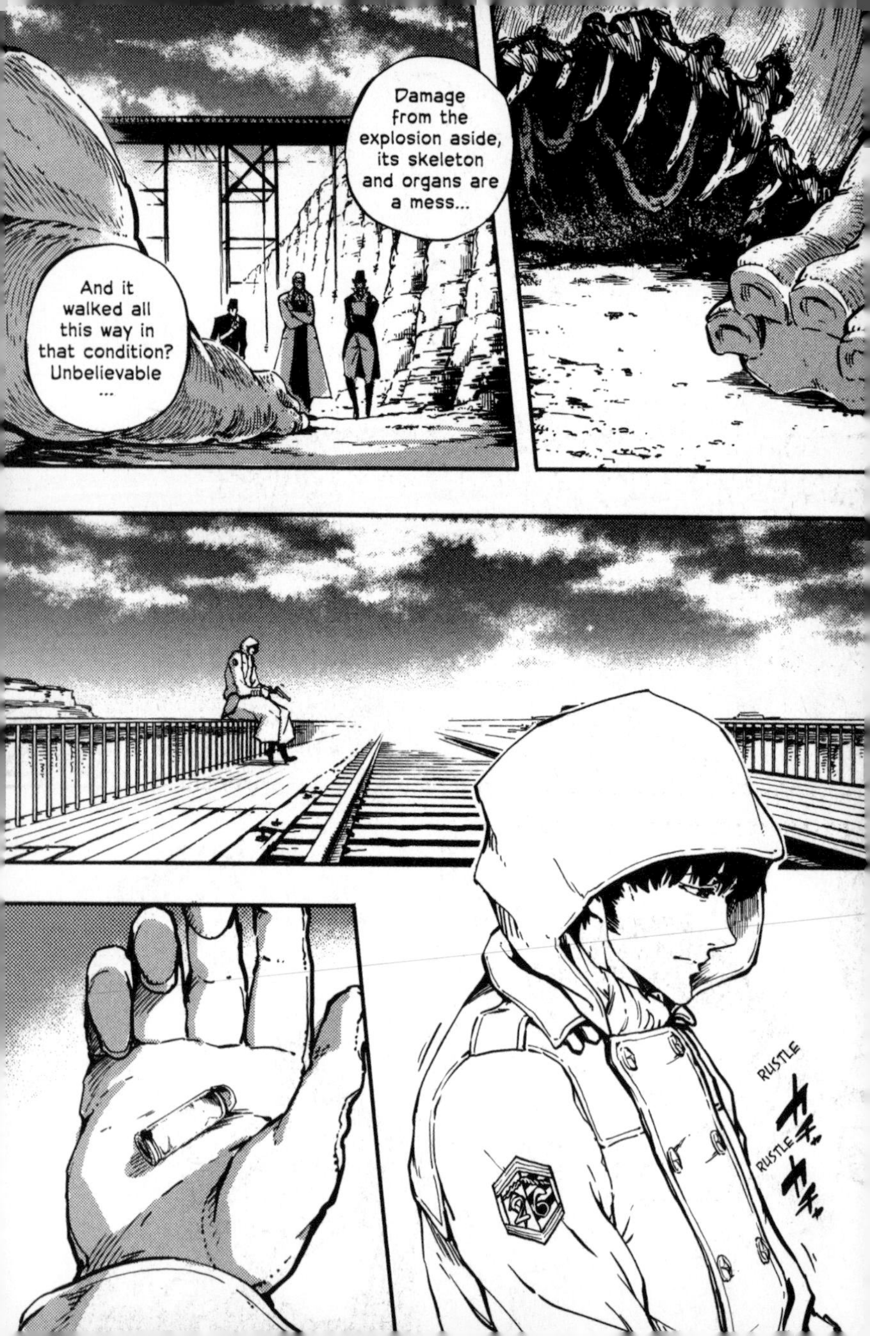
Damage from the explosion aside, its skeleton and organs are a mess...
And it walked all this way in that condition? Unbelievable ...
RUSTLE
RUSTLE

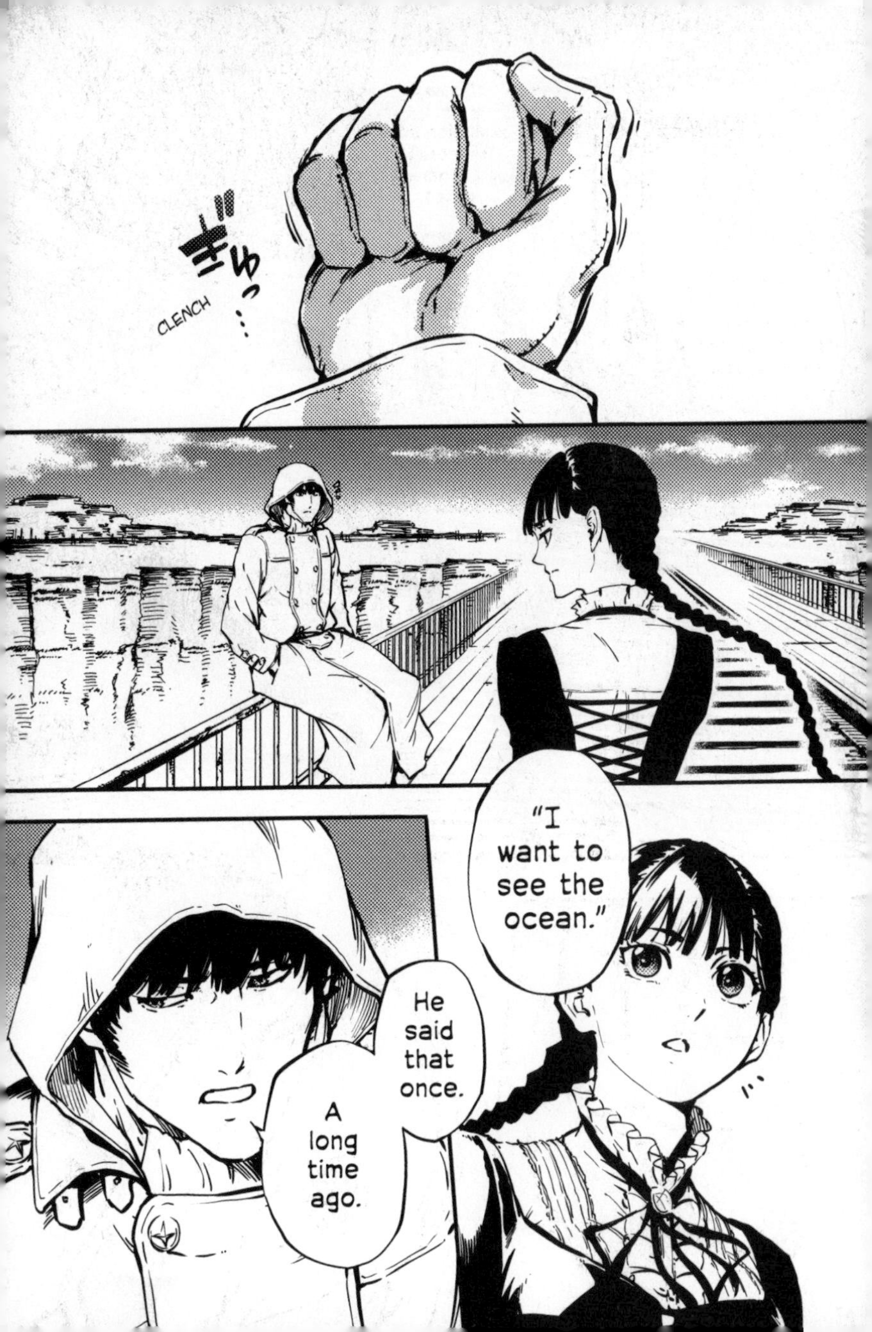
ぎゅっ
CLENCH
"I want to see the ocean."
He said that once.
A long time ago.

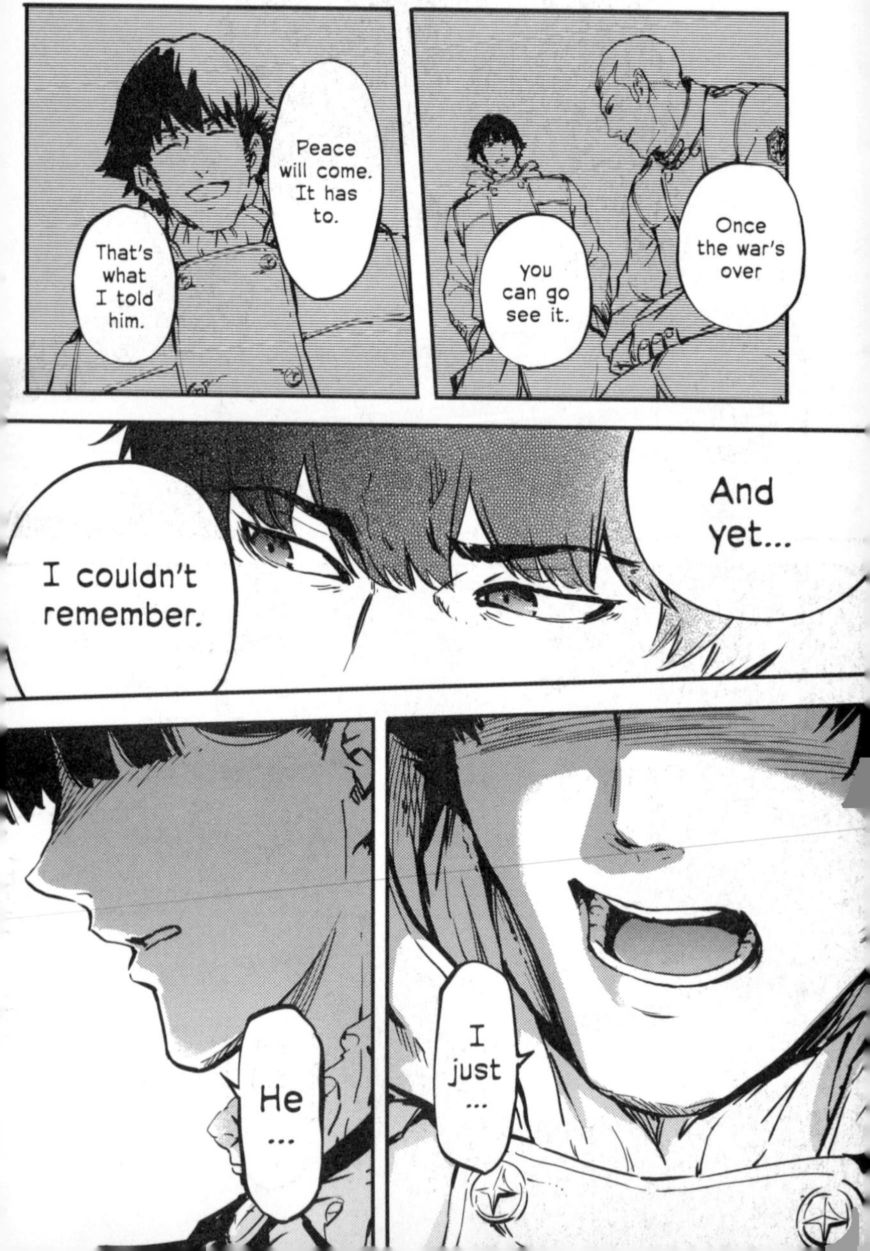
Once the war's over
you can go see it.
Peace will come. It has to.
That's what I told him.
And yet...
I couldn't remember.
I just ...
He ...

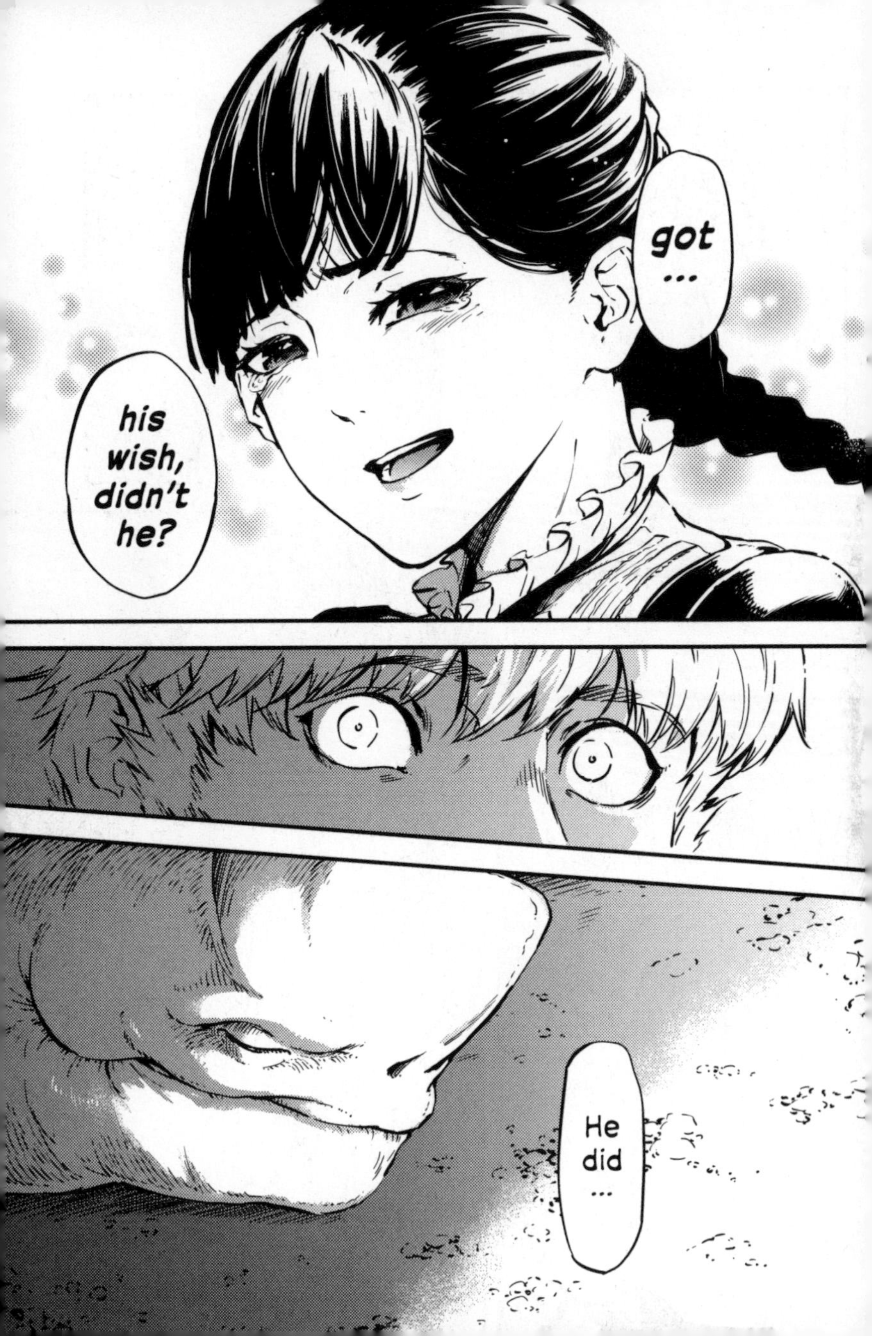
got ...
his wish, didn't he?
He did ...

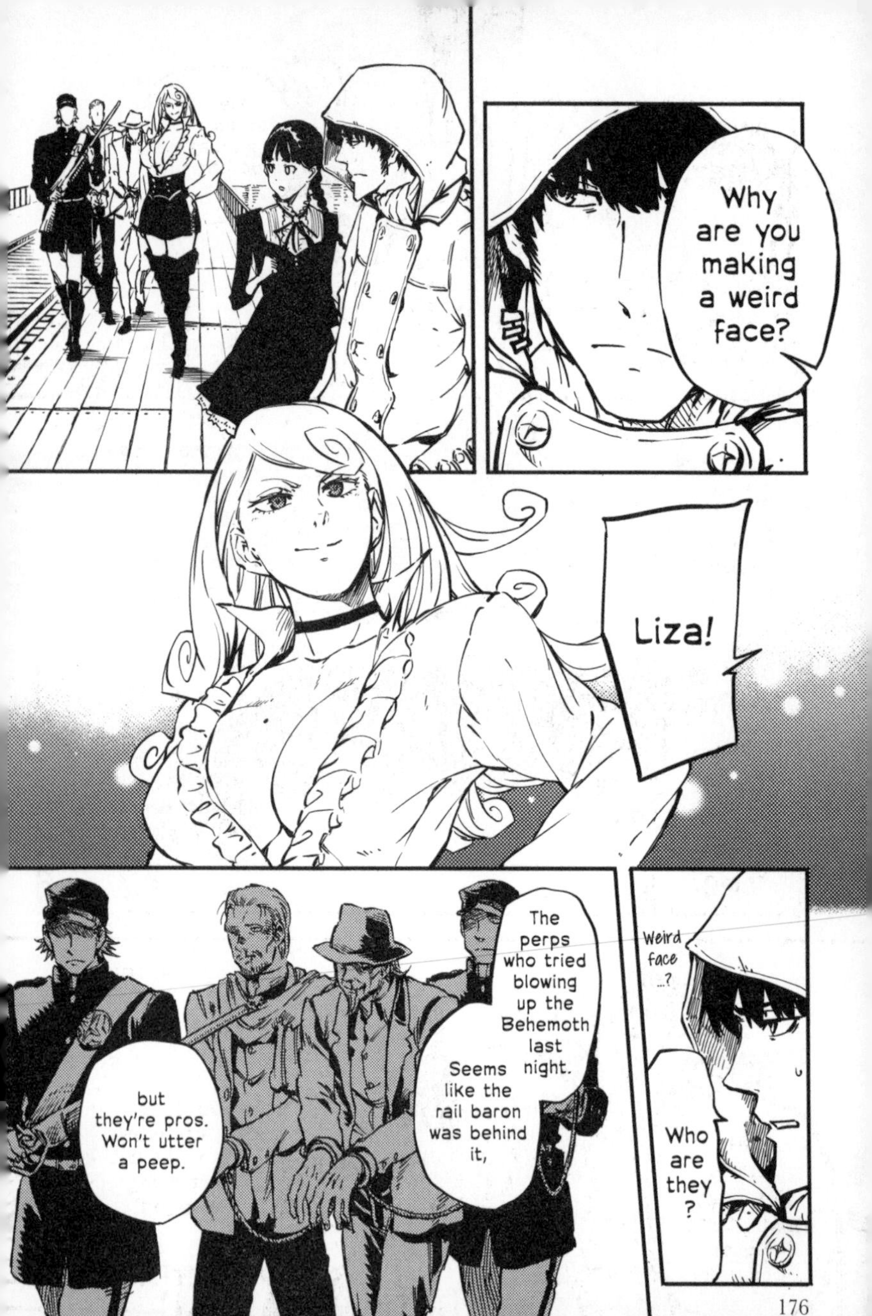
Why are you making a weird face?
Liza!
Weird face ...?
Who are they?
The perps who tried blowing up the Behemoth last night.
Seems like the rail baron was behind it,
but they're pros. Won't utter a peep.

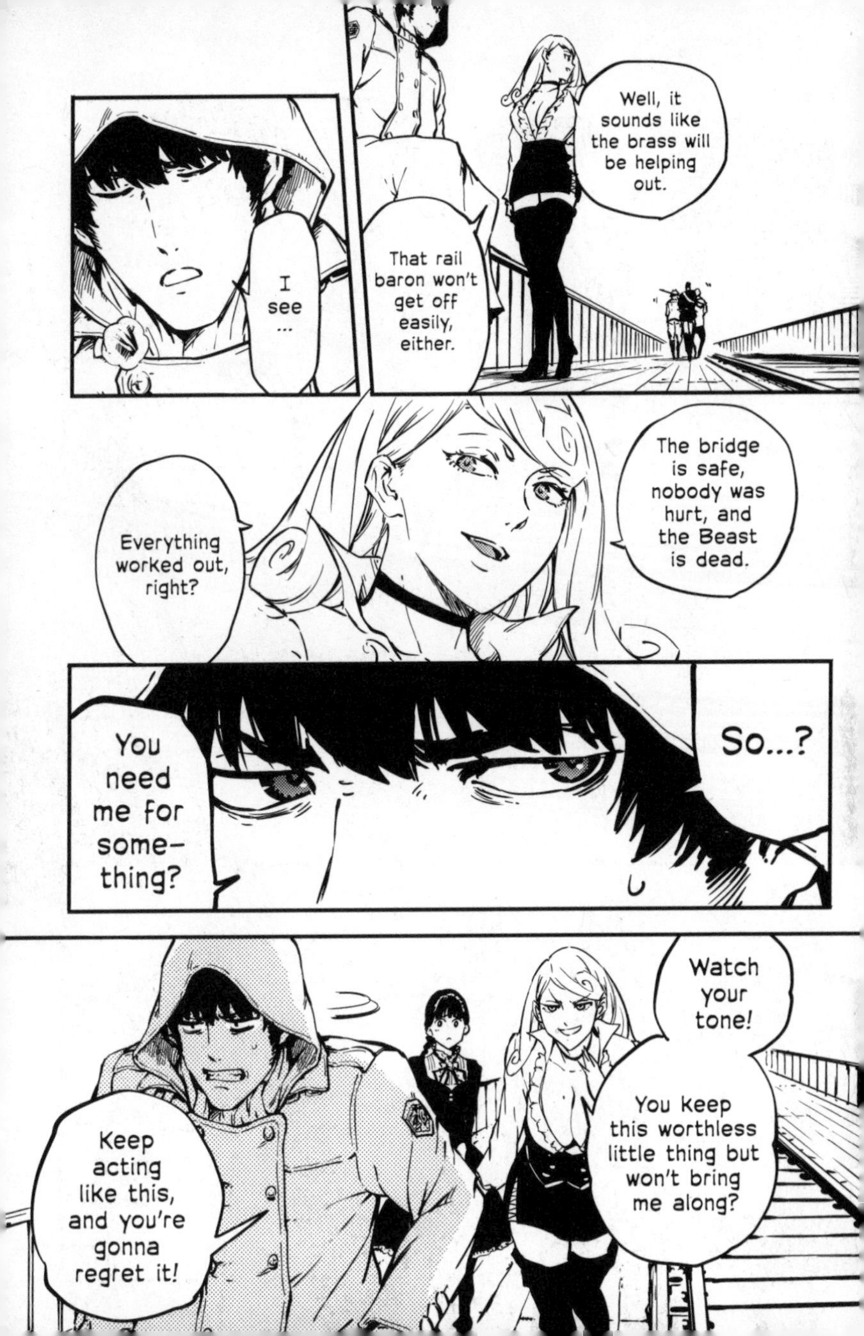
Well, it sounds like the brass will be helping out.
That rail baron won't get off easily, either.
I see ...
The bridge is safe, nobody was hurt, and the Beast is dead.
Everything worked out, right?
So...?
You need me for some-thing?
Watch your tone!
You keep this worthless little thing but won't bring me along?
Keep acting like this, and you're gonna regret it!

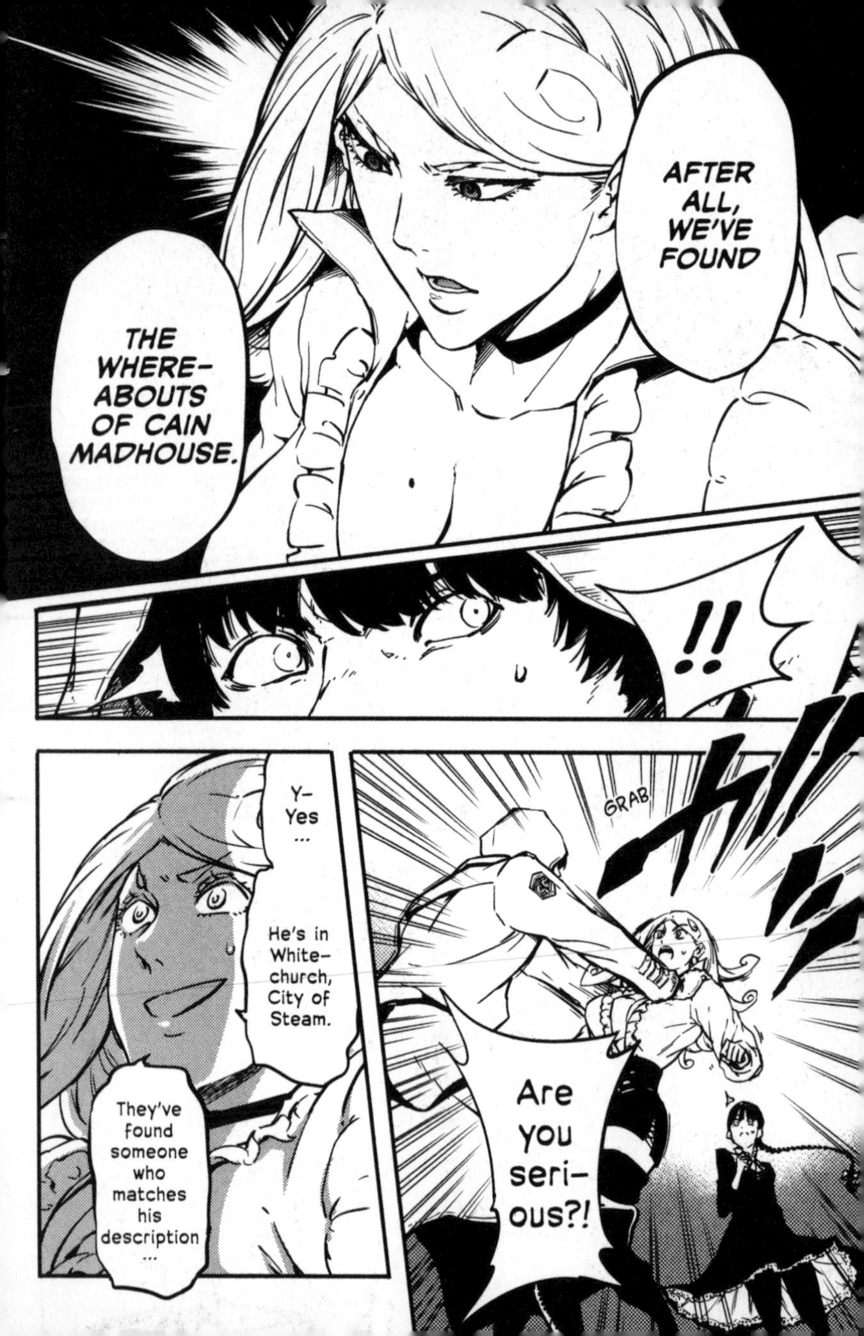
AFTER ALL, WE'VE FOUND
THE WHERE-ABOUTS OF CAIN MADHOUSE.
!!
GRAB
Are you seri-ous?!
Y-Yes ...
He's in White-church, City of Steam.
They've found someone who matches his description ...

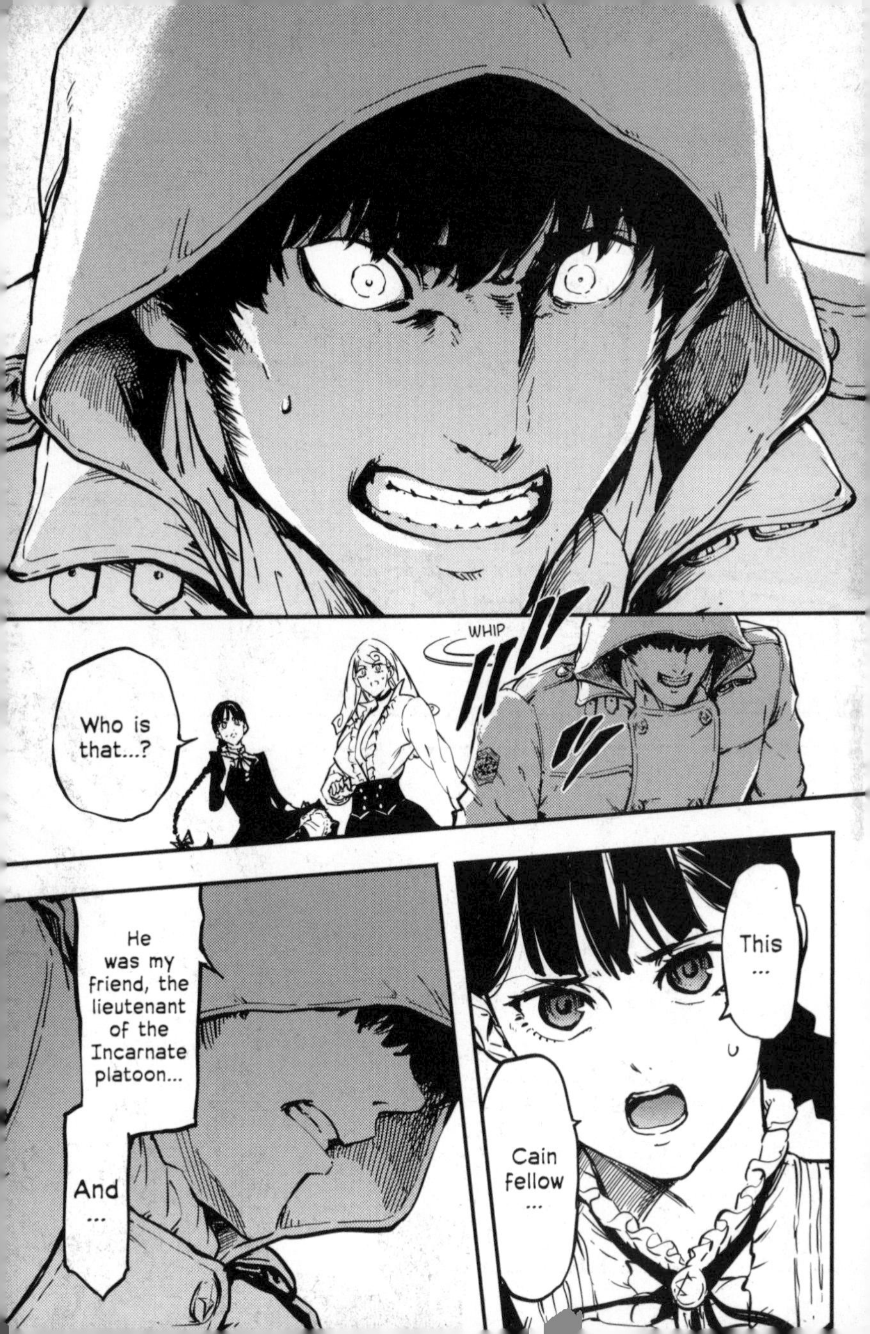
WHIP
Who is that...?
This ...
Cain Fellow ...
He was my friend, the lieutenant of the Incarnate platoon...
And ...

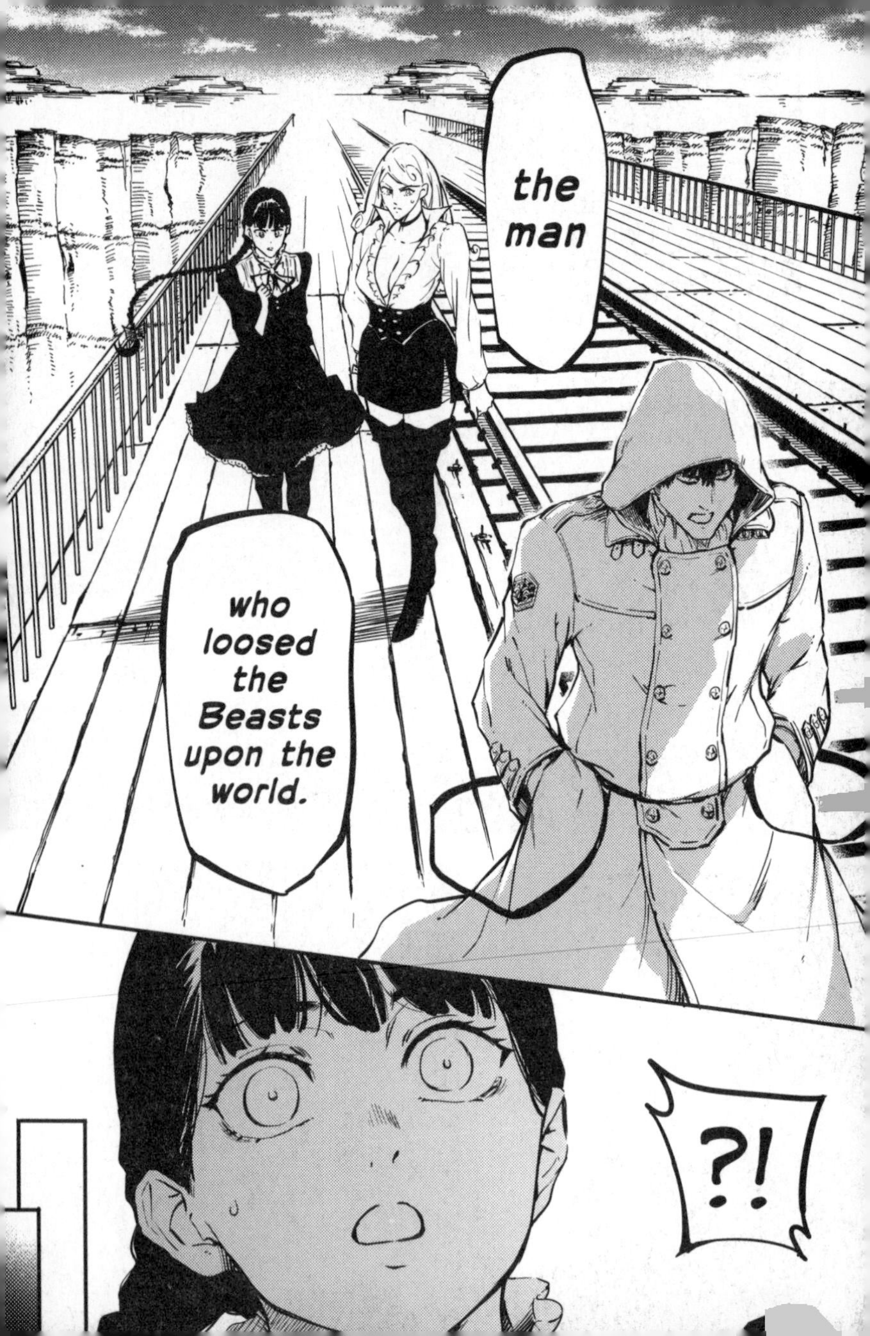
the man
who loosed the Beasts upon the world.
?!

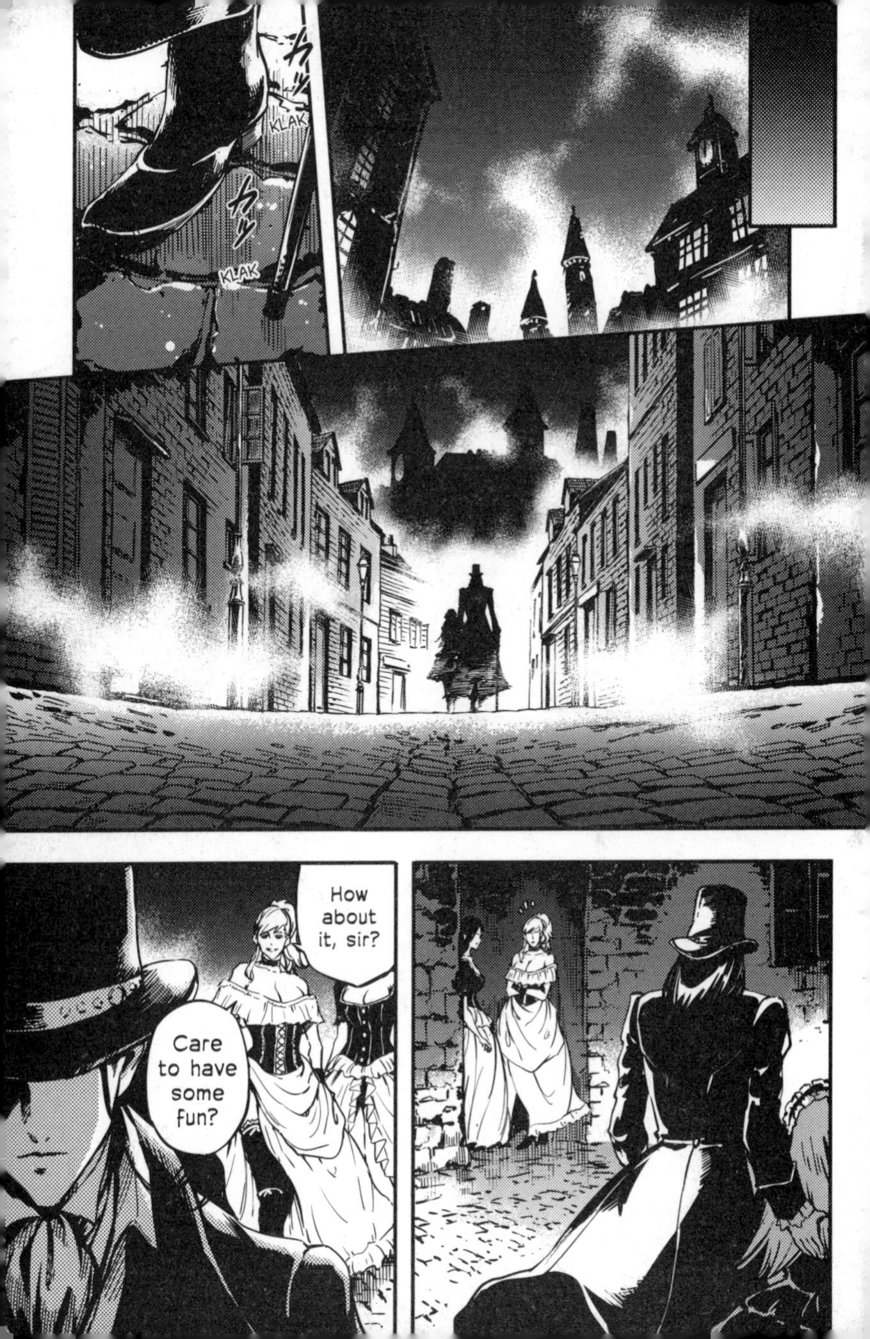
KLAK
KLAK
How about it, sir?
Care to have some fun?

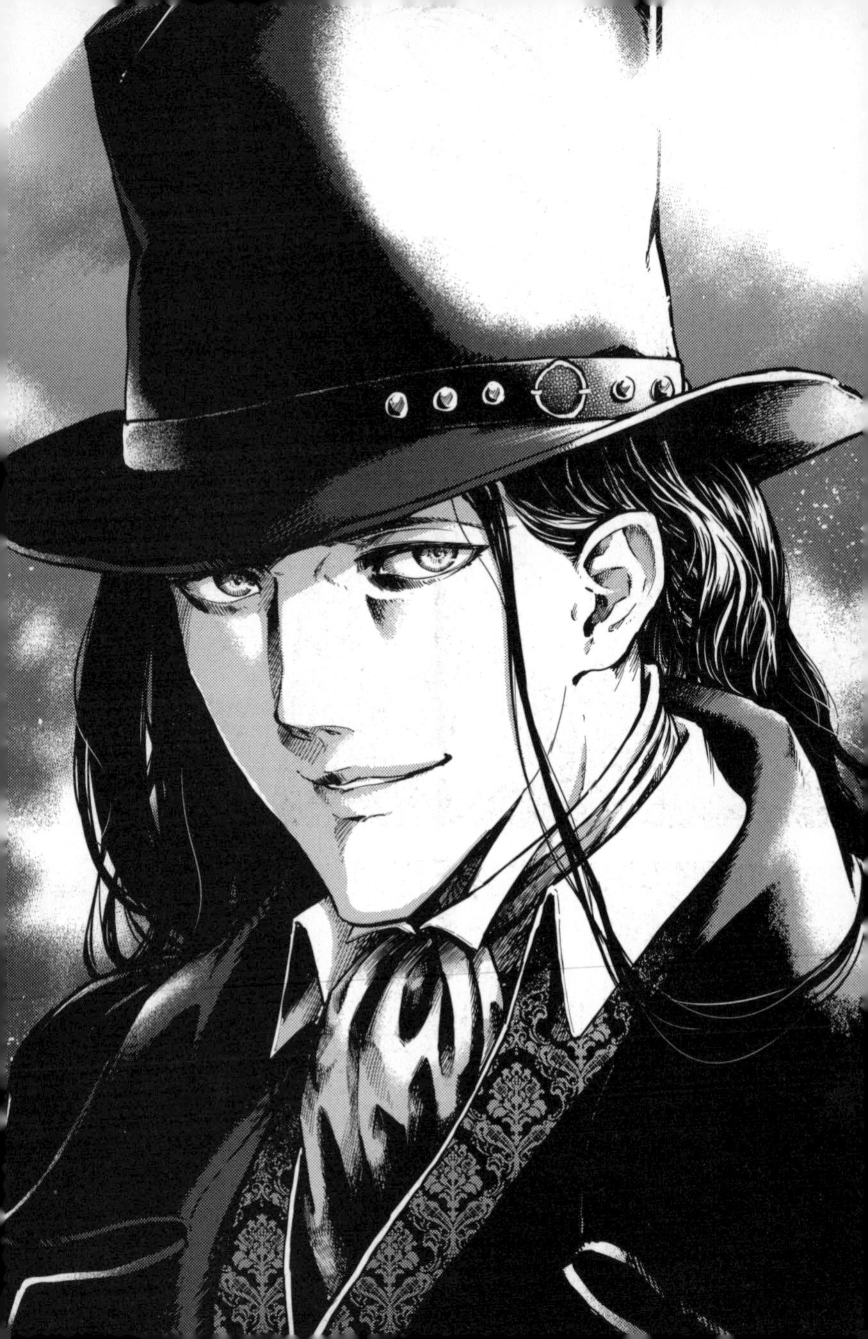

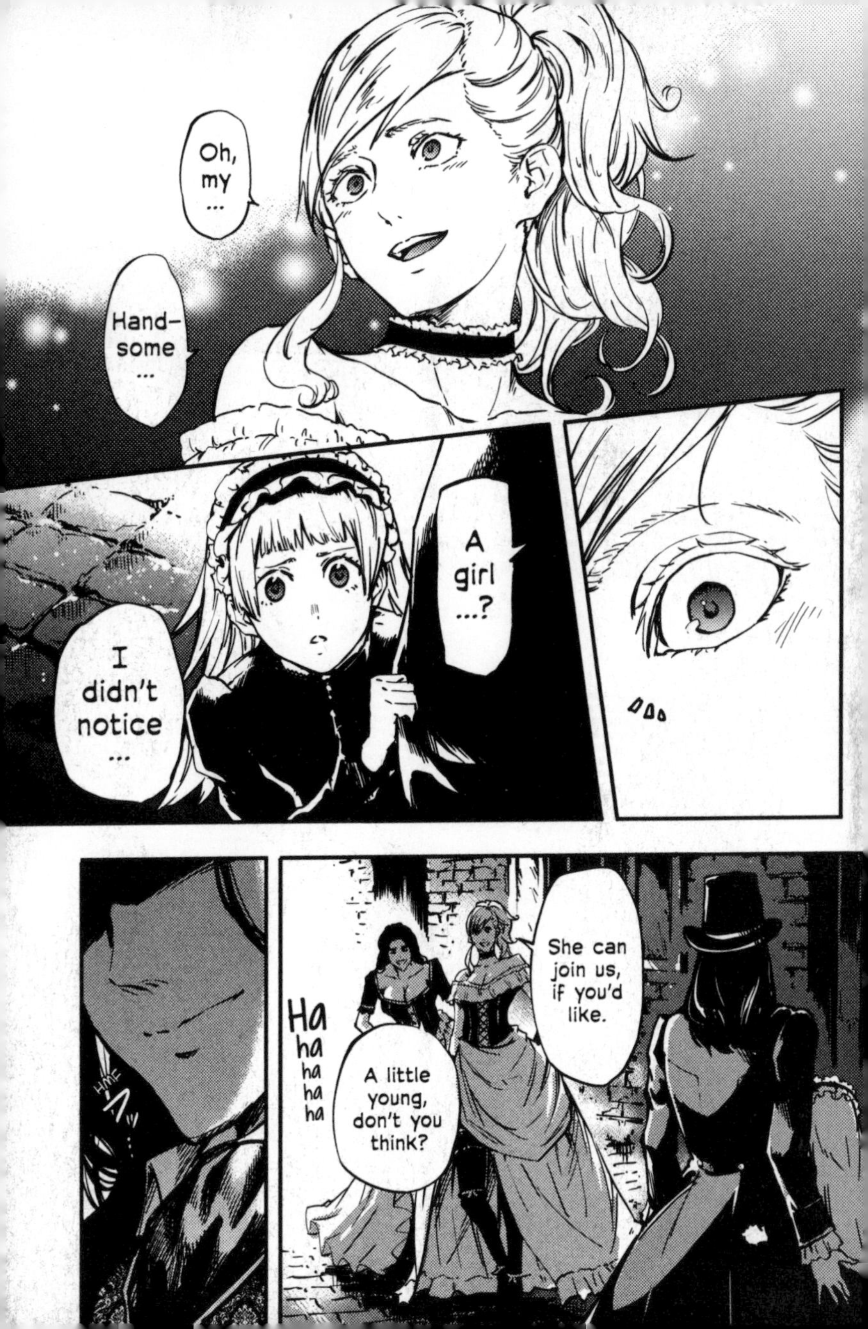
Oh, my ...
Hand-some ...
A girl ...?
I didn't notice ...
She can join us, if you'd like.
Ha ha ha ha ha
A little young, don't you think?

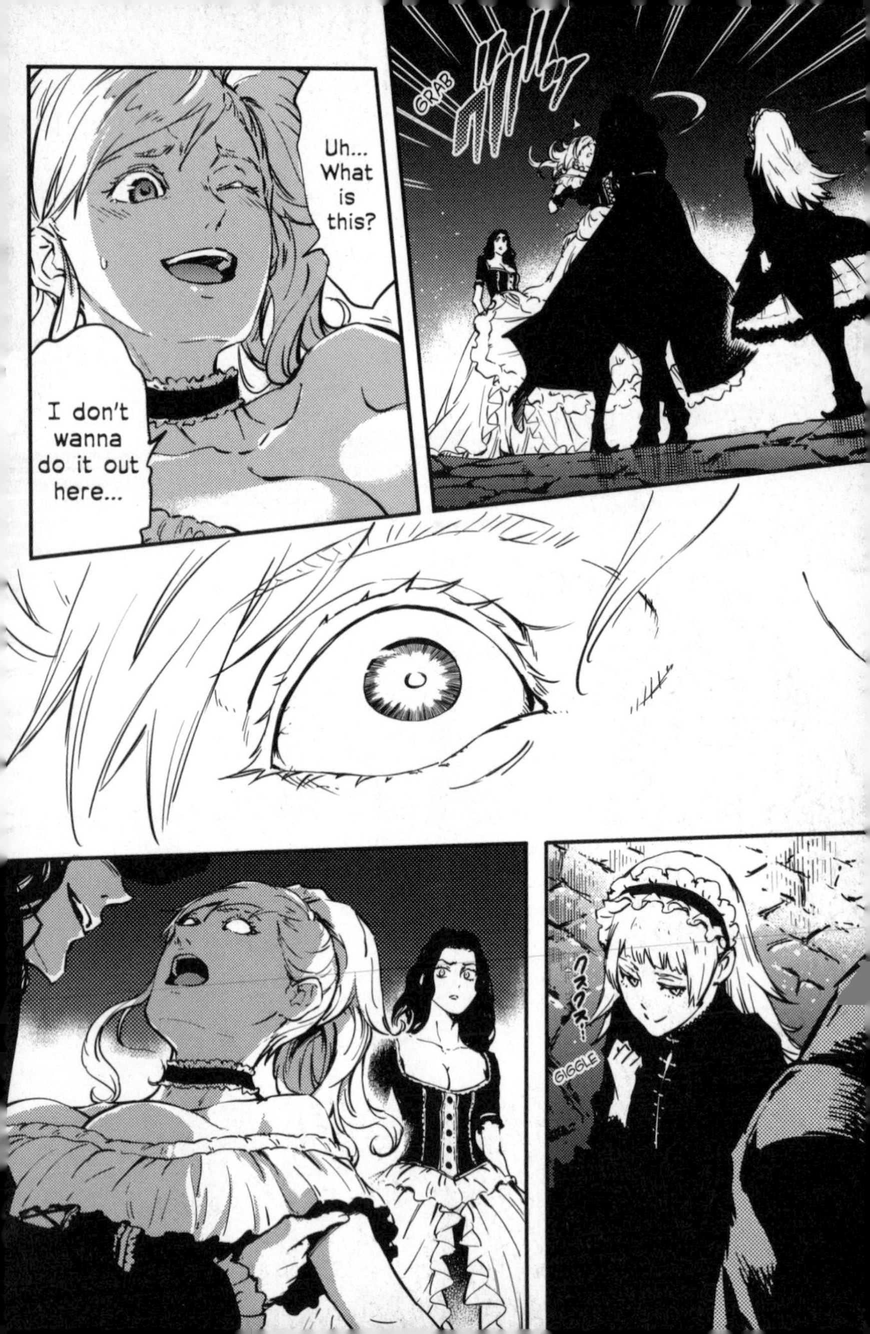
GRAB
Uh... What is this?
I don't wanna do it out here...
クスクス
GIGGLE

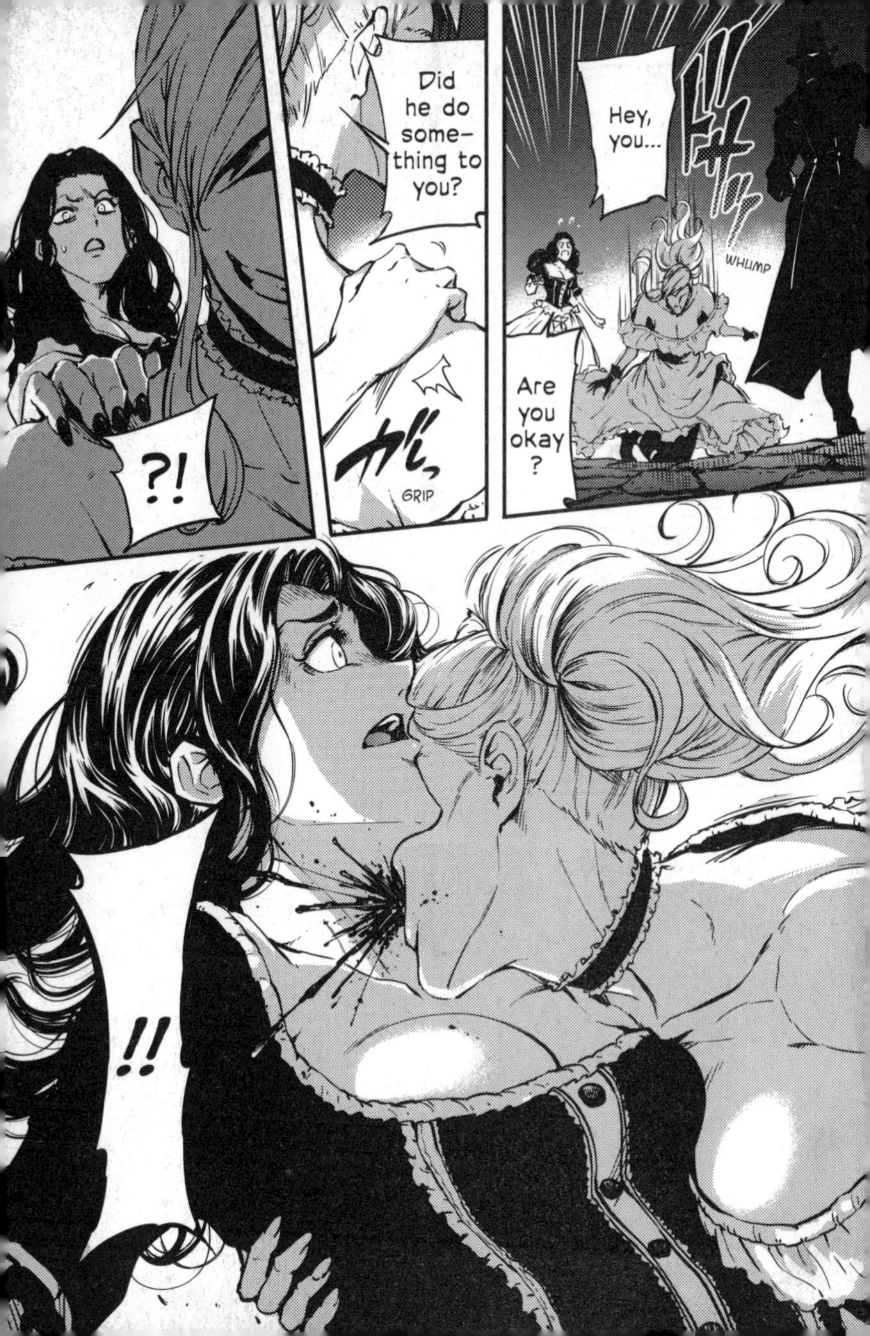
Hey, you...
Are you okay ?
WHUMP
Did he do something to you?
GRIP
?!
!!

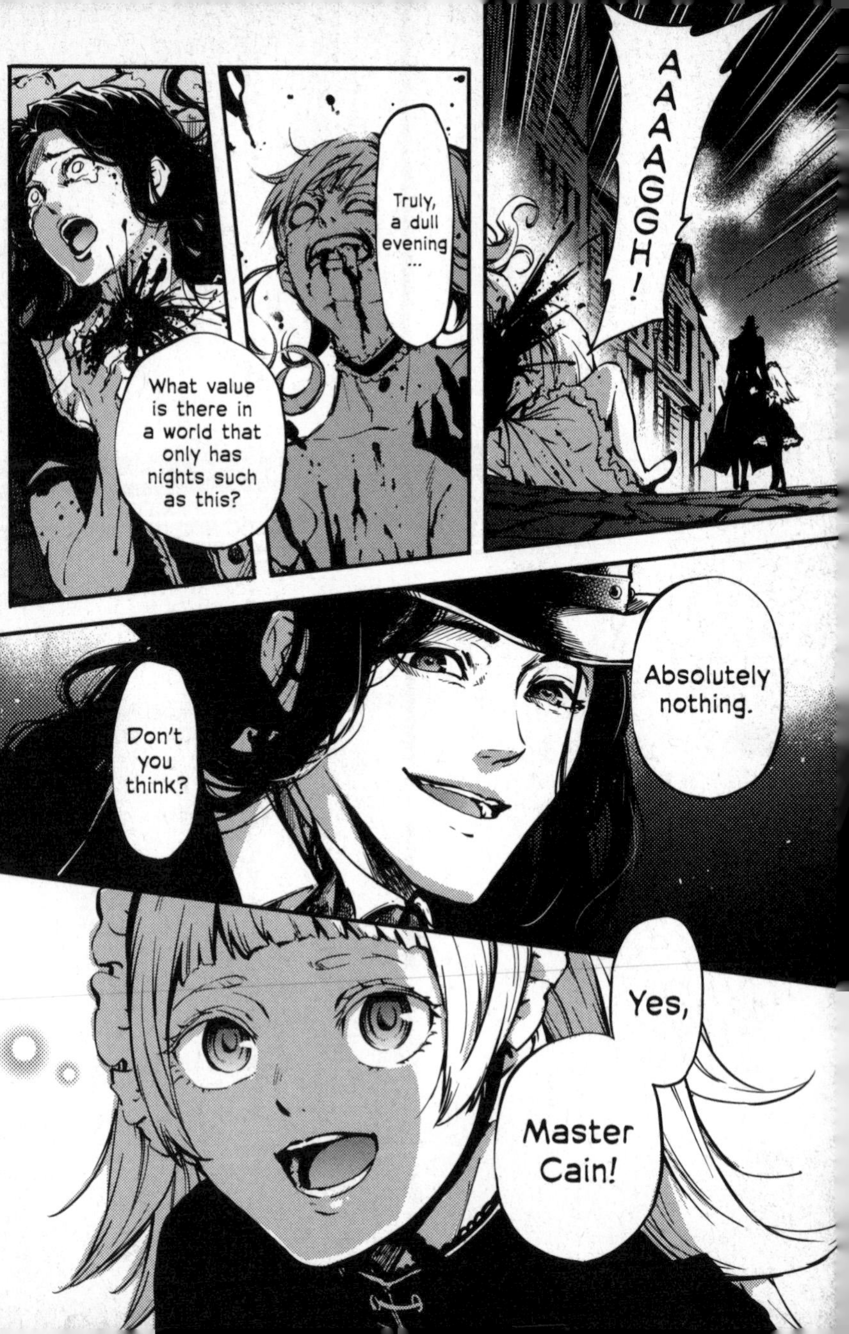
AAAAGGH!
Truly, a dull evening ...
What value is there in a world that only has nights such as this?
Absolutely nothing.
Don't you think?
Yes, Master Cain!

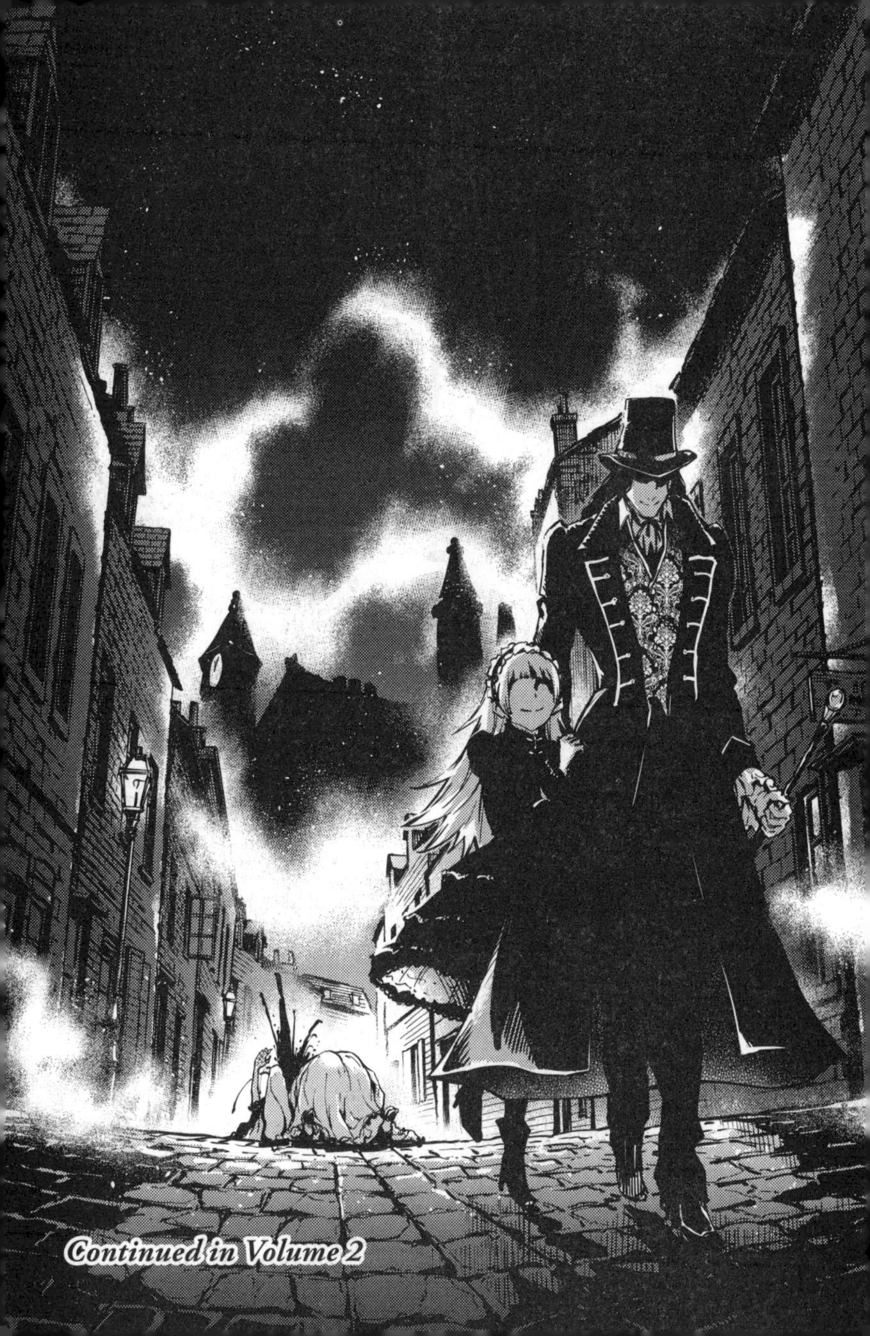
Continued in Volume 2

Encyclopedia Entries

file no. 1 | *Incarnate Spriggan*

Height: 10 to 26 ft.

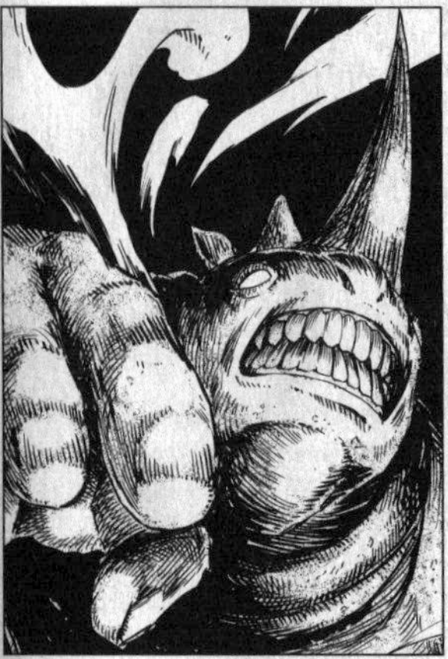

A protector of treasure in ruins and fortresses capable of enlarging to enormous size in order to throw off enemies.

An Incarnate capable of enlarging its body, the Spriggan possesses a flexible frame covered in a unique fatty tissue. The highly-concentrated nutrients in the fatty tissue are consumed during the growth process, fueling cell multiplication and skeletal transformation, thus enabling it to nearly triple its stature. A horn composed of hardened dermis and keratin makes its attacks in this form even more powerful.

By adjusting its size, the Spriggan can thrive in both long battles (by remaining smaller and consuming less energy) and shorter skirmishes in its larger incarnation with its attendant explosive power.

file no. 2 | *Incarnate Minotaur*

Height: 16 ft.

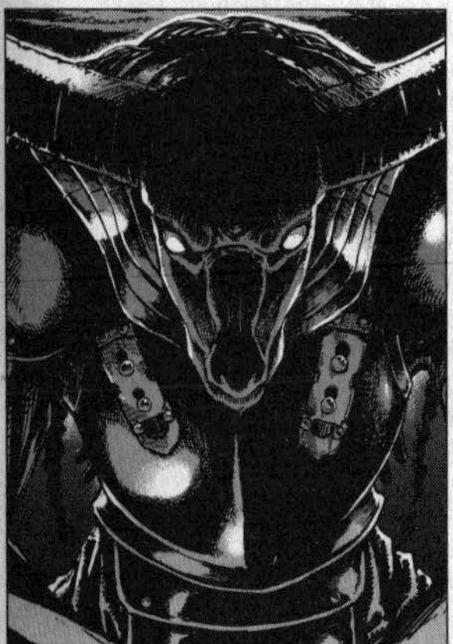

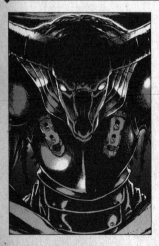

Sealed in an underground labyrinth, this fearsome creature has the head of a bull.

Boasts agility and superhuman strength. Many Incarnates are incapable of precision work due to their non-humanoid appendages, but the Minotaur retained a high level of dexterity even as it became an Incarnate.

Its massive frame bestows inhuman power, making it particularly useful for constructing field fortifications, and its nimble fingers allow it to handle small components and a wide variety of weaponry. While its large size makes quick, rapid movements difficult, by using a specialized long axe and old-fashioned yet sturdy armor and helmet, the Minotaur exhibits its unique defensive capabilities.

The Minotaur's expert knowledge of infrastructure and traps can be seen in the fortresses it constructed, many of which survived the end of the war.

Sacred Beasts

file no. 3 | *Incarnate Behemoth*

Total Length: 164 ft.

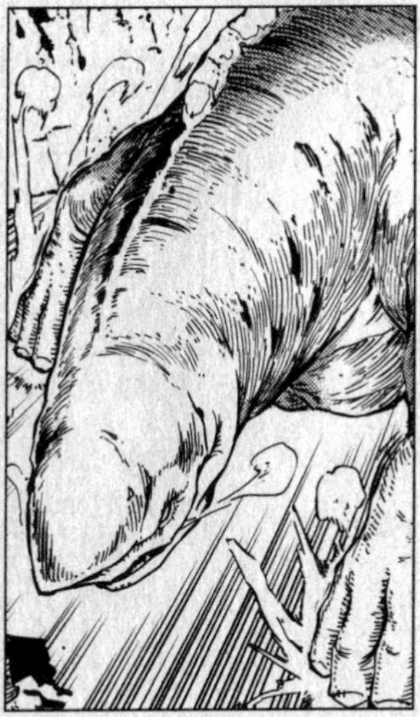

Created by God as the largest living creature and ordained to become sustenance for man in the end-times.

This massive Incarnate possesses regenerative abilities.

The Behemoth can regenerate damaged parts of its body to be even stronger than before in a matter of hours. The thick skin covering its enormous body can withstand gun and cannon fire alike, and only grows stronger with sustained damage, allowing the Behemoth to become nigh-invulnerable within a short timeframe.

However, its sheer weight places incredible strain on its joints and skeleton, and excessive movement can mean death. As a result, the Behemoth is forced to move at a snail's pace; even keeping pace with its fellow Incarnates is a challenge, let alone charging the enemy head-on.

The psychological damage inflicted on the enemy by the sight of the massive creature drawing unflinchingly towards them more than made up for the creature's other deficiencies, however.

file no. 4 | *Bomb-lance*

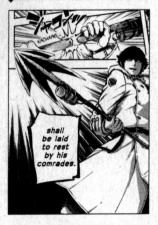

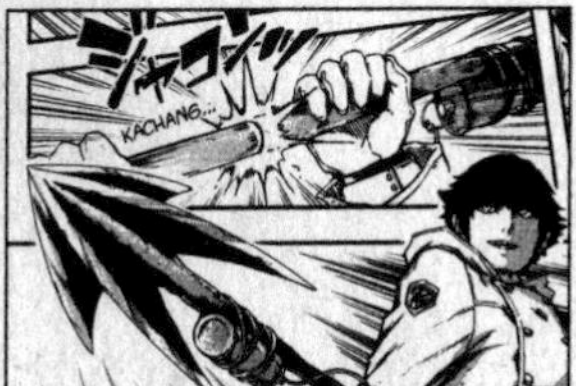
KACHANG...
shall be laid to rest by his comrades.

Used by a Beast Hunter to fight Incarnates, the Bomb-lance is a lance with an explosive spearhead. The spearhead, which strongly resembles a whaling harpoon, is connected to a collapsible rod. While simple in design, the Bomb-lance's extreme heaviness and uneven weight distribution makes it almost impossible for average humans to wield.

By leveraging its weight, a Beast Hunter can drive the lance beneath the skin of the target, detonating the explosive from a distance by pulling on the wired detonator. The resulting explosion is capable of blowing through an Incarnate's skin and muscle tissue, enabling the Beast Hunter to bore the lance even deeper into its prey.

Incarnates possess superhuman life force that makes them impossible to kill without striking deep within their bodies, and the Bomb-lance is the Beast Hunter's ace in the hole, specifically designed for such a purpose. Despite its ramshackle appearance, the weapon consists of made-to-order parts that can only be used once, making it quite an extravagant weapon.

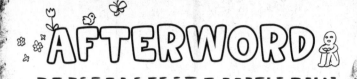

AFTERWORD

Hello, MAYBE here! Despite looking like a single person's name, we are actually a two-person writer/artist team.

Believe it or not, we were contacted to create a manga series for *Bessatsu Shonen Magazine* (the current home of this manga) before it even started publication. We wondered what kind of story we were going to create, but things just kept happening (one of our other works was made into an anime, for example), pushing our start date back. By the time we finally decided, "Okay, let's get this started," we pretty much ended up throwing all the ideas we'd had until then into making "To the Abandoned Sacred Beasts."

It's quite a different creation from what we've made in the past, and while we're anxious, we hope you enjoy reading it.

With such a long title, we've come to calling it "Sacred Beasts" for short, but it doesn't seem to have caught on, so call it whatever you like.

Now, then. Here's hoping we get volume 2 out safe and sound!

—MAYBE

memo
December: Releasing volumes of "Sacred Beasts" and "Wedding Rings"
God, I'm tired.
Work, old man!

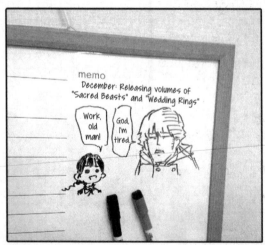

• The studio whiteboard

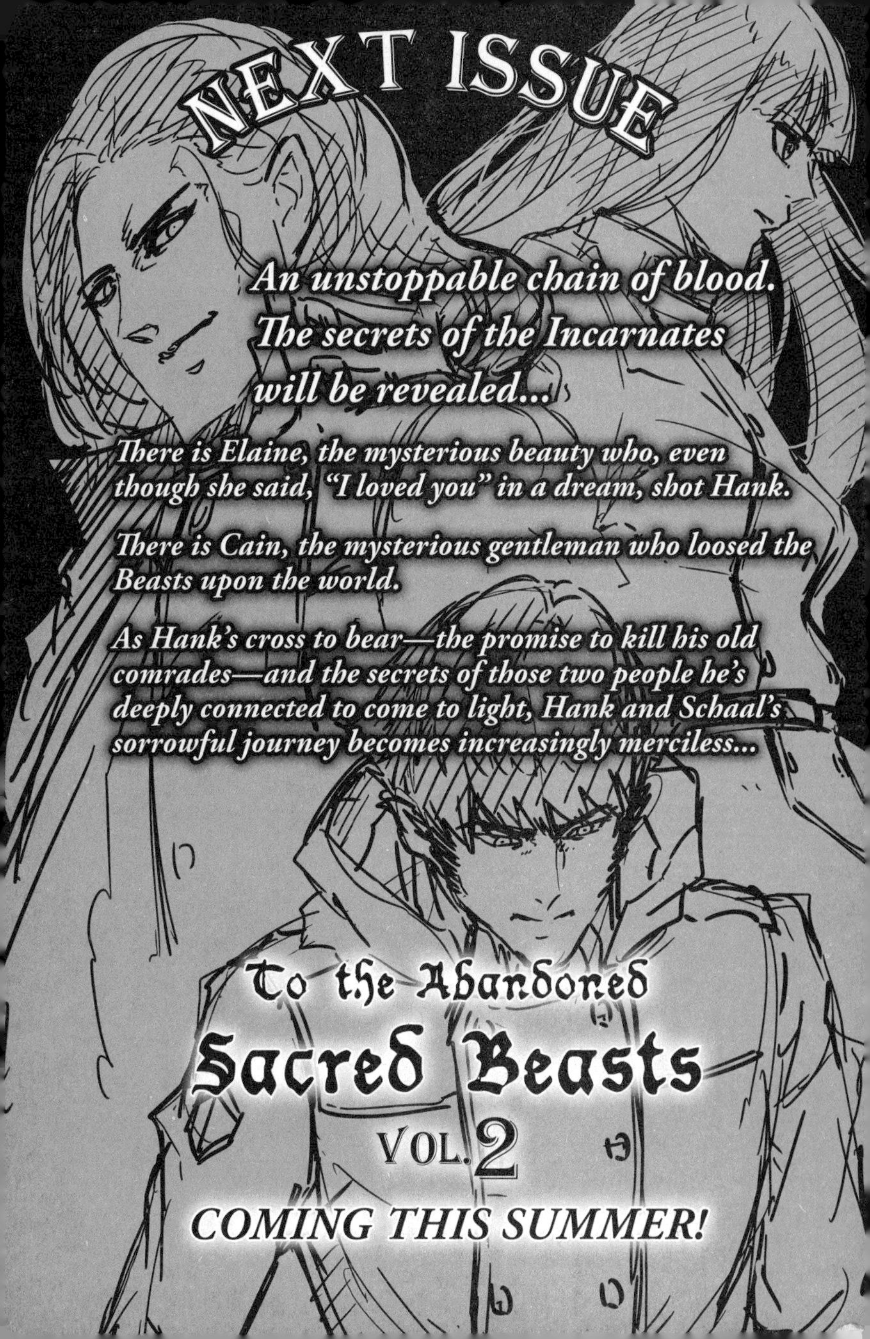
NEXT ISSUE
An unstoppable chain of blood.
The secrets of the Incarnates
will be revealed...
There is Elaine, the mysterious beauty who, even though she said, "I loved you" in a dream, shot Hank.
There is Cain, the mysterious gentleman who loosed the Beasts upon the world.
As Hank's cross to bear—the promise to kill his old comrades—and the secrets of those two people he's deeply connected to come to light, Hank and Schaal's sorrowful journey becomes increasingly merciless...
To the Abandoned
Sacred Beasts
VOL. 2
COMING THIS SUMMER!

To the Abandoned Sacred Beasts
Volume 1

Translation: Jason Moses
Production: Grace Lu
Anthony Quintessenza

Copyright © 2016 MAYBE. All rights reserved.
First published in Japan in 2014 by Kodansha, Ltd., Tokyo
Publication rights for this English edition arranged through Kodansha, Ltd., Tokyo
English language version produced by Vertical, Inc.

Translation provided by Vertical Comics, 2016
Published by Vertical Comics, an imprint of Vertical, Inc., New York

Originally published in Japanese as *Katsute Kami Datta Kemono-tachi e 1* by Kodansha, Ltd.
Katsute Kami Datta Kemono-tachi e first serialized in *Bessatsu Shonen Magazine*,
Kodansha, Ltd., 2014-

This is a work of fiction.

ISBN: 978-1-942993-41-4

Manufactured in Canada

First Edition

Vertical, Inc.
451 Park Avenue South
7th Floor
New York, NY 10016
www.vertical-comics.com

Vertical books are distributed through Penguin-Random House Publisher Services.